From the West Comes the Wind

The first in the Earth and Gods Series

M.E. Hosking

Dedicated to my younger self, for whom this book was written.

MAP

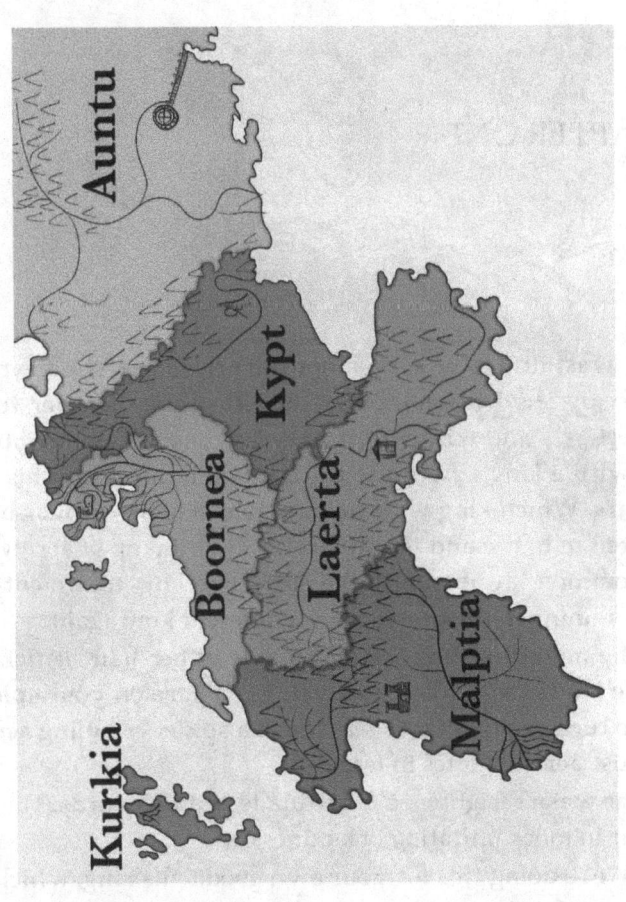

CHAPTER ONE

Nicke

There was little to be said about the grievances she'd experienced, or the joy she'd beheld, other than that they led her to her fate rudderlessly and without pretence. It was always going to end like this: with a king's sword to the back of her neck and his curses in her ears. Which king was the question. Whether it was her father, defeated in battle and finally broken by a snapped arrow shaft, or her common-law brother, the scars from his treatment over the years shining in the firelight. Or a different king again.

The metal touched the shorn side of her hair. It tickled in an obtuse kind of way. The way you feel a gaze on your spine telling you to turn around. Or the feeling of a spider crawling across your skin just before it bites in fear.

She wasn't frightened of the blade, but the words. They bit into her ear in mock imitation of kindness.

"We're doing this for your own good," the king, whichever one it was, said. "There's too much of your mother in you."

Something her brother used to say before he slapped her. Something her father used to say, shaking his head in a nostalgic fog.

She didn't hear anything else before the blade cut through.

* * *

It was a fortunate thing that Nicke's screams in sleep never translated to screams in life. The idea of the household running to her aid was one she didn't relish, even if their concern might have been genuine. There were too many reporters among them; too many of her brother's whispers ready for scraps in exchange for the excuse that meant the next beating. Not that she blamed them: if the situation was reversed, she might have named their transgressions.

She tilted her head towards the east and gauged the sun through the high slit in the mudbricks. Its beams travelled the length of the room and gave warmth to the various woollen and silken colours spread across the floor. Blues, reds and yellows swallowed the light greedily, shining each in their own way. She adored the rug for its brightness and as the last vestige of her mother at the height of her power. It was the only evidence she had of a home denied. Her mother's prayers wove the fabric just as surely as her hands tied the knots. Some nights, the remembrance of her fingers in the cloth was the only thing separating life from oblivion.

Shivering, Nicke left the woollen blankets of the bed and let her feet into the fibres of the floor. Helen was her mother's name, the beauty who was born of Malptia and was lost because of it. It wasn't a coincidence. Helen the mother was named for Helen of the songs in the hope that her extensive grooming would bear fruit.

It bore fruit in one hand, and shrivelled it in the other.

The morning wasn't necessarily cold. Spring wind wound through the valley and the storm that had buffeted the windows the night before had turned to merely a breeze. Gooseflesh erupted anyway as Nicke flitted across the bedroom and towards the blinds. Deep blue, the colour of the sea off the coast of her birthplace and the sky at its darkest, adorned the only view of the outside world. Light was another forbidden thing; another boundary to push. Iron nails lined the thick cloth and pulled the fabric taut. She could only skim her fingers across the wood of the windowsill, exposing the tips to the garden.

Knocking sounded from the hall.

"Good morning, Nicke," Demetria said as she ducked her head into the room.

"Good morning," Nicke mumbled in reply, throat not working since being cut in the dream.

Her woman's maid stalked the space, flicking bed covers, opening trunks and kicking up dust from the floor.

"How did you sleep?" When she didn't answer, Demetria turned her stark green eyes to her and grimaced. "Well?" she demanded as she picked a deep blue peplos from a chest in the farthest corner of the room.

"Well." Nicke cleared her throat.

The maid's lips thinned in a harsh line and she strode towards her, clothing and jewellery in hand. "Bad dreams?" she asked gently.

Nicke didn't want to elaborate. Silence descended until Nicke's dark, heavily curled hair was tamed and her jewellery and dress were fitted. It was easier that way. These were the rituals they performed every morning, even though Demetria belonged to Nicke's brother's wife and was roundly known for her intricate cooking style. She was wasted as a maid, truth be told. As Demetria clipped the red cloak of the Rex to the gold about her shoulders, Nicke became lost in thought.

The woman wasn't an obvious choice for a spy. Her ruddy-brown hair was held close to her scalp by leather ties that ruthlessly bound it away from her wide mouth and sharp chin. Alix demanded it, even as her own black locks reigned free. Or perhaps because of it. Demetria was tethered to her, but even the queen resented the marks her husband left on his charge's skin: Nicke doubted she would seek to place some there herself by enlisting Demetria as one of Lyon's own.

The maid was the age of a matron, but without the husband or children to prove it. It was a rare thing for a person to be owned directly by another rather than by the city. Demetria was a gift from Boornea, her brews famous even at fourteen. Nicke let out a small breath, remembering the price of a husband and how much wives were willing to pay for one.

As Demetria finished the hair and let it free over the edges of the cloak, her voice sounded quietly.

"You're to stay in the house today. No errands have been called and there have been no letters for you."

It was a statement of fact said in a kind way, but the words still burned. Nicke's fingers tingled where the sun had hit their edges, just beyond the garden. The craving to feel the sun on her face intensified.

"But," Demetria continued, voice still low but more buoyant than before, "we have a few slaves arriving from Kypt that I need to administer. Will you help?"

"Yes, I can help."

She nodded her head and left Nicke to her room.

* * *

It wasn't quite true that there were no letters. It would be an unusual day to have nothing to respond to from the Credo or the War Rooms. Nicke took her leisure in the morning by plying a troublesome wool that had shed far too much in its short life. Without further intervention, it may have disintegrated completely and left her with the honour of being forever wasteful. Rather than submit to such a fate, the undyed silk sourced from Kypt, their ally in the north, would be plied and then strengthen the wool. It was a little unsatisfactory to have the silk remain undyed but leaving her sanctuary to seek an acid bath may rouse her brother.

Once plied, the natural shine of the silk hid behind the fraying wool, creating a halo of red. It was a striking combination, but not one that would end up on the loom. The state colours were red and blood and all members of the Rex must wear them. Red was the marker, the reminder.

Nicke tried to keep it to her cloak, where it hid the scars of multiple canings and whippings. The jokes told by their enemies were that they had red backs to better hide the wounds they received. It made them more fearsome in battle. They never lost on land.

Today's scroll from the War Rooms proved it wrong. The Kyptian slaves were the answer to an unasked question and the guarantee that Laerta's northern neighbours refused to be forgotten. Though they were not at war and had not engaged in Kurkia in order for Kypt to win back the territory, the slaves were gifts regardless. Laerta had sent three ships, and there was a reason they were lauded as hoarding victories on land: Laerta was useless at sea.

The scroll requested presence for the next war meeting: today, as the sun arrived at its zenith. Nicke had no inkling of the sun since her room was bathed in a semi-darkness, but the missive would have needed urgency. More than once, the king had interfered with a summons when it had arrived too early. Sophos would have ensured this one came at a time enough to give her notice, but not time enough for Lyon to keep her here. So, the zenith would be soon.

She collected her sandals and wrapped the leather around her ankle with an austerity befitting a princess. The colour of wet sand, they blended with her skin and complimented the blue of her peplos. The red on her back finished the look and ensured no one, other than those permitted, would speak to her. The red wasn't only Rex and wasn't only to hide Nicke's wounds and their scars; it was to mark her as property of the crown. At his Majesty's pleasure.

Hair in her eyes and ringing in her ears, she took careful steps into the corridor and listened like a hummingbird under the shadow of a hawk. Nicke heard a shuffling down the corridor, close to the receiving room, and paused. She waited, stock still, for the sound to cease. It was the same stillness that affected her heart when she used her knife; the same statuesque fleetingness that halted her breathing when she dived into the river; the same silence that descended into her mind when faced with a map and impossible odds.

The echo quieted, then stopped, and she began to move again. Slowly, surely, towards the kitchen at the back of the house where the king never ventured. Demetria would be there, but she would have been the one to take the message and place it under Nicke's door, so would be expecting her.

"I'm to go to the War Rooms," Nicke said evenly as she walked past the tubs inset to the wall. Demetria was washing plates from the breakfast Nicke had been denied.

"Oh," the maid said, looking up sharply with bright green eyes. Nicke paused at the bewildered look on her face. "The new slaves are here!" she almost yelped.

"Yes, but Sophos has summoned me."

"Yes, yes of course," she replied, looking back down to her work. "I just thought I wouldn't have to sort the new ones by myself."

"Is there something—" Nicke started.

"No, no!" Demetria finished. Though her hands were covered in water and dirt, she flapped them about in denial of her agitation, spreading drops around the kitchen.

"Sophos can wait," Nicke demanded. "Tell me what's wrong."

Demetria looked back down at the tub and then back up at Nicke. She made a decision between the actions: a responsibility feared and then halved.

"There are three that I don't know how to place, that's all. One is much bigger than the rest, but his eyes are too quick for the mines and I worry he would scarper. Another is the opposite: small but with a dull wit." She sighed quietly, perhaps waiting for Nicke to prompt her.

"And the other?" she said.

"What other?" Demetria said.

"The third," Nicke cocked her brow. "You said three."

Demetria's breath quickened again and she met Nicke's eyes with something just short of decisiveness.

"I think I'll place him in the fields here. Old Smit can deal with him. Or..."

"Or...?"

She picked up a towel and began drying her hands. She was delaying which could only mean good news.

"Or we could place him with Lysander."

"Lysander? Why?"

"Because the slave is smart and strong: a dangerous combination in this house. He'd have a better chance being under the hand of one of the soldiers."

The quiet between them stretched until it broke with a quiet twang. Demetria likely thought she'd overstepped and that Nicke's silence belied her fury, but it wasn't that at all. Because Lysander wasn't just any man and this slave must be similarly unique.

"Can I meet him?" Nicke asked in favour of the thousand other questions in her mind.

"The War Rooms..."

Nicke flicked her wrist, knowing those men would wait for her. You don't start war talks without your brightest mind, and she was the strongest light in that room.

Demetria nodded then led her to the yard behind the house, between the two outbuildings that flanked the garden. They were made of sand coloured mudbrick and framed by cedar wood beams. Notches were cut into the wood on the eastern side of the garden to mark how tall each king grew during their childhood. The king before last stood tallest when he came of age, and the current king stood at least a foot below that. The eldest and heir, a teenager, stood below him while the youngest and spare barely made it to Nicke's elbow. They were no doubt about to spurt to new heights.

Nicke glanced briefly at her covered window and saw the wind battering it. That air could be entering her room and circulating to help her breathe at night. Not for the first time, she awoke the deep resentment of her birth. But more than that, it brought forth resentment of her blooded sister and their defeated father.

Three slaves were on their knees in the grass just beneath the jacaranda tree. It was close to early summer and the blooms were about to fall and cover the ground in a lavender carpet, but not yet. One slave was large, with honeyed skin bought from days under the sun and black hair curling around his ears. Another slave was smaller, wiry, with slumped shoulders from the way the chains drew his weak arms down to his thighs. The third slave wasn't as large as the first. He didn't have any distinguishing marks or scars that spoke of his previous masters having a difficult time with him. But there was an air; an acknowledgement that this man's shoulders were too broad with combat to have ever tilled a field. His hair was an auburn that fell to his neck in generous waves, and his skin was red with too much sun. The gifted slaves had walked the way from Kypt, and the spring sun was harsh in the mountains. Nicke's study of him came to an end when he lifted his head: the chin dominant on his face and surpassed only by the brilliant green of his eyes. A colour she'd only seen once or twice in her short life. She stared at him unashamedly. He was merely a slave after all.

"What's your name?" she asked once she knew exactly how many golden threads wove through his iris.

He waited, refusing to acknowledge the question.

"Does he speak?" she asked Demetria who was standing to her right shoulder. She was peeking from behind, almost afraid. Her silence was more deafening than his.

"Yes," he said with the tilt of a Kurdan accent. It told Nicke enough of him: likely caught in the conflict she was expected to mop up once she attended the War Rooms. "He speaks."

"*He* is obviously not used to being a slave."

His laugh filled the air and Nicke found the hair on her neck rising. Following deeply held instincts, she glanced around the yard in search of the king or queen, hoping against hope they hadn't heard this man's baritone. He noticed, of course. Nicke would expect the sea of his eyes to swallow all they touched.

"Your name." Her tone brokered the command for what it was.

Eyes still glinting with laughter, he answered.

"Zephyros."

* * *

The walk to the War Rooms was a venture into unknown jungle and a climb up a hillock behind the house. Hidden from the city major, the small compound was minutely defensible with a ditch dug around the edges and venomous traps hidden just beyond the tree line. Not just the snakes, spiders and scorpions that held the greenery in their grasp, but pits lined with poisoned spears and snares waiting. It had been this way since before Laerta had conquered Boornea for its fertile ground and would likely be this way until every one of their names had turned to dust. One small path led in and out, and it was guarded heavily all along its length by Laertans in the trees and soldiers in the shrubs.

Nicke picked her way along it carefully, her red cloak the marker that she was friend rather than foe. Were she wearing any other colour, she'd be snatched immediately from this path and not even questioned before meeting her end. It was a secret way, only walked by the generals and the king. But with this blood red to hide the scars, they let her through.

The compound itself was ordinary by most standards; mistakable as anything other than where battle decisions were made. The same mudbrick used in the city, but painted with green and dark brown to hide its presence in the woods. Three buildings flanked a yard where soldiers sat and ate and sparred. These krypteia, the fiends charged with protecting the Rex, weren't a part of the forces that moved through the world and agitated for dominance. Rather, they stayed in the polis and its surrounds to be the last line of royal defence. Nicke's eyes glanced over them, taking in the faces she knew to be spies for the king, those she knew to be spies for the queen, and those that belonged to her as their general. Nicke's power was smaller than the Majesty, but here, in these War Rooms, it was felt the most. She spotted a blond head among the dark.

"Lysander," she called, gesturing to him with a single finger. He came quickly with a spring in his step.

"Nicke," he said as they walked to the outer edge of the jungle, where they could be neither seen nor heard.

Nicke's hands reached for her peplos to smooth it down, in vain it turned out. She could barely look into his dark blue eyes as they no doubt studied the movement.

With his large shoulders squared and his feet placed together, his stance was that of a librarian speaking quietly with a student rather than a man trained on the harshest battlefield, ill-suited though he may be. A long scar moved when he smiled, and he was smiling. She momentarily lost her train of thought.

"What did you need, Nicke?" he purred.

Taking a breath, she looked down at her satchel and pulled a sheet of paper from its depths.

"A slave," she said, passing it to him. "We have a Kurdan slave that Demetria thought to place in your household."

His eyes scanned the stewardship papers. Slaves in Laerta belonged to the state, the city, but their care was the responsibility of the homes in which they worked. Demetria was right about this slave: he'd be dead in the king's household before daybreak tomorrow. He needed a hand that wouldn't simply dispose of him.

"Kurdan you say?" Lysander said.

"Yes, one of the Kyptian shipment."

Lysander thinned his mouth. "That's why you're here. When will you tire of cleaning up messes that you don't create?"

She didn't have an answer for him. He pressed for one anyway in his agitation. He'd always been the one to question the ethics of their assignments in the Credo: how and why elected tactics would affect common people. Collateral damage was his forte, and he eagerly sought solutions to military problems with politics. It was one of the reasons he had been recommended to Tertiary in the first place. He was ranting now, about Kypt's newfound need to reclaim their ceded colony, about Laerta's response and how Auntu would answer it. She trailed his jaw with her eyes and snatched glimpses of his lips as they decried militarism.

"Are you quite done?" she asked pointedly. "Or should I simply keep Zephyros?"

"It's a shame really," he said, putting the paper into his front pocket. "If he's likely to be such a pain in the arse for the king, he's also exactly the kind of slave you should have around."

Nicke shook her head. "Lyon would just hurt him for sport."

"Like he does you?"

It was a quick quip nestled comfortably within their banter, but from Lysander's mouth it sounded like a promise of retribution.

Gently, so gently that the wind could wisp away the gesture, he reached for a strand of hair dangling in front of her ear. He paused before he gained it, eyeing her for permission to touch. Such boons were not hers to grant, and despite desperately craving his warmth, she shook her head in stark denial.

Lysander smiled sadly and dropped his hand.

"I'll take your slave if you deliver him yourself," he declared.

She laughed outright at him and his smile widened. She left him smiling and retreated to the southern building.

* * *

The War Rooms were unexpected. The vaulted ceiling, graced with the ever watchful eyes of Laertan men under their red cloaks and with bloody spears in their hands, felt oppressive under the pressure and expectations of the other generals and lieutenants in the room. Nicke stood close to the head of the table, just to the right of the king. It wasn't only the expectations that iced her veins. Every time the king gestured, she flinched.

"Kypt's gifts pose a problem," Sophos began, rolling out a map of the region in front of them. "They aren't a gift-giving state, no matter what they profess. They only barter and trade."

"A hundred slaves is hardly a war bargain," Jonn, the other general, said. The three of them, the generals who had passed the stringent tests set by the ephors and Senate on graduation from the Credo, stood as a triangle around the circular table. Lyon, the king, stood between Nicke and Sophos with Jonn standing directly in front of him. Their respective lieutenants, specifically chosen from the Secondary, were dotted between them and around the room. David, Nicke's second, was standing in the corner with hooded eyes, watching the map. She'd already consulted with him on this point, but implored him to keep quiet.

Nicke's own rise had occurred when she was only twenty: the youngest ever to complete the tests. Having been honed for it by Laerta's finest, she stood here as the city's sharpest blade even if she never held the weapons herself.

"We did send them ships willingly," Nicke said. "This may simply be a reward for fulfilling their request."

"Would you pay more or less for it?" Sophos asked her as he steepled his fingers in front of his mouth. His grey hair made his beard shine. That he had reached an age to grow grey was testament to his prowess on the field.

She didn't even pause to answer. "I'd pay less. They didn't send mere slaves, but people with skills and trades."

"So, the question is what do they want in exchange for their gift?" Lyon said. He sat while the rest of them stood. Nicke didn't mind. It meant that she could react quicker if he was to strike.

"I know what they want," Jonn said. "They want war. We're still recovering from the war with Malptia, let alone the maintenance of Boornea. Kurkia is not our concern."

She shook her head. "It is." She gestured to the island to the north of Malptia. Originally a Kyptian colony, Kurkia asserted itself ten years ago in a bloody conflict that remained ongoing. Kypt was a long-term ally of Laerta and assisted them with warring against Malptia. Laerta providing aid to Kypt was considered a given, until the extent of Laerta's troubles could be exposed. Not enough troops and too little training for the ones they did have prevented the city's full assistance.

If Laerta didn't engage, and lose, then they could still claim to be unbeatable on land.

"It is our concern," Nicke continued.

"Why?" Lyon asked, lounging in his chair with his wrist suspended on a bent knee. She didn't glance at him, but knew his middle-aged face would have a droll look on it.

"Kurkia requested aid from Auntu," she said simply. "Laerta maintains the presumption that if Auntu is involved, we must retaliate?"

"Of course," Lyon growled, curling his fist.

"And how ill-prepared we are for war wouldn't change that?" she challenged.

He growled again and Nicke had her answer.

"There you have it. Kurkia has called for aid from Auntu, so Laerta, being faced with the irresistible prospect of war with her sworn enemy, must be involved."

Nicke didn't hear the knife exit its sheath, just the burn of the king's blade as it entered the skin of her arm. The instinct driving her caused her to struggle against his rooted hand and the resulting slice ran from her shoulder to her wrist. Bleeding, always the colour of the Rex, her blue peplos turned black as the flay deepened in hue.

Nicke bit her lip to stop her screams. Lyon again raised his arm and gestured for the men around them to step away.

"Say it again, Nicke," Lyon purred.

Her limbs shook. She knew better than to wipe at the blood or to speak. Both would lead to further wounds and difficult healing.

"Say it," he barked.

It was always the same.

"I'm sorry, my king," she whispered. The oppression of the room began to sing in her bones. Each eye flowed between her and the man in front of her.

"For what?" he prompted as if he was speaking to a child.

"For my callousness."

"And...?"

"For my..."

He waited as she swallowed.

"For my cowardly Malptian blood."

"There," Lyon said soothingly. He sheathed his knife as Nicke watched only the floor. The blood still flowed, dripping, but at least no other wounds would amount. "Isn't that the truth?" He turned to the rest of the men of the room, seeking each of their eyes in turn.

"Yes, Rex," Sophos intoned dispassionately even as his beads sang their disapproval. The rest of the men echoed him.

"You're dismissed," Lyon said.

Nicke turned to leave with the others when the king grasped her injured arm. "This wound is unlikely to scar," he whispered in her ear. His breath was like smoke and she fought the impulse to step away. "More's the pity. Scars mark you when you forget yourself, as you did here."

"I'm sorry, king."

"I told you when you were a child to call me brother, Nicke."

"Yes, brother," she repeated. Her voice wasn't her own and it was as if the sun had disappeared behind the clouds. Cold crept and she shivered.

"You were the perfect gift from your broken father," he continued. "And I make it my mission to break you, too."

With an inhale that caught strands of her hair, he drew his blade again and cut further into her wound. She screamed then, pushing from him to release herself, but he moved his free hand to her throat and held so, so tightly that she almost lost herself to the frenzy of loosening his grip. He held for however long it took him to plunge his blade into and through her wrist. The knife skewered between her bones into the hard wood of the maps. She knew her scream would be heard throughout the jungle; be heard by every man hidden there. He twisted and withdrew the knife, pushing her to the table and onto the floor. Nicke gazed at the blood as it flowed freely through her fingers. Red, like the cloak.

And like the cloak, the red of the Rex would cover the scar.

"Whether you believe it or not, sister, I don't like hurting you. Doing so hurts me and my queen, and Alix frets so." He tutted his mouth and knelt in front of her. "No more such words, yes, sister?"

She nodded, mumbling agreement. He smiled, stroked the right side of her face, and left her to the War Rooms. She gazed up once her soul had returned to her body and met the eyes of every figure in the frieze. Each one had a furrowed brow, a strong chin, and eyes that promised death to their opponents. And she was simply a cog in their machine. Nothing more. Nothing less.

* * *

Her arm dripped until she made it back to the city. By then the blood was brown and dried to the skin. The trail left behind was like horrible breadcrumbs, leading the king home. Demetria was waiting at the gate when Nicke arrived. The maid looked at her with pity and her thin mouth underlined her fury.

"Let's get you cleaned up," she said.

It was always the same. The king would expect his work tidied before he or the queen had to set eyes on it. Dust from the road made Nicke look like a spectre; like a scythed goddess roaming the country looking for lambs. Once she may have been, but Lyon had been working hard to destroy that part of her.

Demetria set to work using cold woollen cloths knitted to provide enough rough edges to scrape away the blood. Her red hair had loosened from its hold and was draped in front of her ears as she concentrated on her work. Nicke looked at her face and felt an unanswered echo of recognition. It disappeared when Demetria next spoke.

"You have to be more careful. Next time he might go for your other hand and leave you unable to write."

"I always stand on his left," Nicke said dispassionately.

It was always the same. The king brutalised her. Demetria cleaned it up. And then they continued as if it hadn't happened. Each time Nicke hoped it would be different; that someone, somewhere would hear her screams and come running. But as long as the Rex kept it an un-hidden secret, Nicke was powerless.

Demetria hummed a Laertan lullaby as she worked.

After a while, she knotted the cloth to keep it in place and began clearing the rags she had used. Most would end up buried in the garden, the wool unable to be washed of the blood. She stood and surveyed Nicke through hooded eyes.

"You have to stop challenging him. If he doesn't receive a

challenge, he won't lash out."

"I know. But usually the War Room exempts me: it's presumed that there's an amnesty in order to provide our true opinions."

Demetria thinned her mouth again. Nicke dropped her head.

"I'll try harder," she mumbled, smoothing down her skirts. She felt the single tip of Demetria's finger lift her chin to look up into the trees.

"You are, and always will be, a Malptian princess, Nicke. You don't look at the floor." Her eyes blazed like the comet that graced the skies on the day of Nicke's birth. Red, flaring. Nicke nodded and Demetria removed her finger.

Nicke stood, her arm searing at the action. She grimaced, but ignored it.

"I presume Zephyros is ready to go?" she said as Demetria continued clearing the area.

"Yes." Demetria's voice was husky, almost reluctant. "It's a shame really. We could use his skills around here."

"His skills?"

"Yes. Turns out other than speaking out of turn and generally making mischief, he can also carve wood and speak three languages."

Nicke looked at her wordlessly. She herself could only speak two, the language of her birth and Laertan.

"Jury's out on whether he can write or read, though," Demetria continued. She paused, the tub of soiled water on her hip and the sun on her face. "Lysander should be able to teach him if he can't."

Nicke turned away at the mention of him. She didn't enjoy his fury at her injuries when it placed him so close to death itself. He would have heard her scream today; he would have heard her pain as the knife entered her wrist. He could do nothing except watch, as he had for years.

Demetria knew, of course. The only respite Nicke received was when she and Lysander were together.

"He asked me to deliver him," Nicke said carefully, the undertone of need lacing through her words. Perhaps there was a letter, a document, a map, even a bowl of porridge that could be used as an excuse other than the slave.

Demetria was not much older than Nicke, but had perfected the concerned elderly matron look. She used it now, surveying her charge closely.

"I think there was an item of clothing he asked me to mend. Wait here, I'll go and fetch it."

Nicke didn't smile. The eyes and ears of the walls piqued whenever her happiness became apparent. She would smile once she was safe within his walls.

It was an easy thing when they were younger. Her acceleration into the Tertiary stream of the Credo at twelve years old honed her strategy skills. War and battle was her directive: solve the approach to cliffs, to sea, to river, and ensure Laerta won. Her strategy was what broke the Boornean rebellion five years before, decimating the half-a-thousand strong force the natives had achieved. Laerta lost a tenth of the hoplites Boornea had. It was in the moments after, when Nicke's shining light blinded her keepers, that he'd first touched her. Other than the princes, the queen, and Demetria, it was the first kind touch she'd had since she'd left her homeland at three. A simple hand squeeze of congratulations turned into a palm to her lower back when entering a room which turned into fingers making circles into the inside of her elbow. He didn't flaunt it, didn't presume.

Nicke heard the rustling of feet on stone and turned to meet it. Zephyros walked towards her carrying a grey cloak with green embroidery along the hem.

"Demetria told me to find you," he said, still walking. Nicke cringed at his loud words and how comfortably he spoke them. The king would cut out his tongue for only this.

"Yes," Nicke replied more quietly. "I'm to take you to

Lysander's."

"Lysander," he said, feeling the name rolling around his mouth. "Sounds like a poet's name."

She stared at him. He didn't seem fussed by the attention and squared his shoulders at her. Shoulders that she would bet had neither borne a litter nor heaved a rake. They were muscular, strong, but articulated in such a way that suggested more agility and less brute strength.

"You have a lot of opinions." She started walking down the path, expecting him to follow. When he didn't, she turned and cocked an eyebrow. He waited, folding the cloak more closely to his body. She watched as his hands fluidly traced the green thread then met his eyes in question. While she surveyed his face, she saw it turn from smooth and unworried to furrowed and fierce.

"Who did that to you?" he demanded, pointing at her arm. She instinctively covered it in her cloak, the red hiding it too late. He walked to her then and reached for her. She reacted how she usually did when someone imposed on her person: she hissed and leapt back, all while eyeing her surroundings for spies.

"You aren't to touch me," she shrilled, wrapping her red around her. "It would mean death for you."

"I'm sorry," he said with his hands up deferentially. "It looks painful."

Not for the first time, she experienced the feeling that she was negating her own needs to keep all else safe. She needed touch, needed the comfort it brought. But bringing death onto others, those she liked, those she hated, was too much to bear.

He took a step back and bowed his head. "I'm sorry, Nicke," he said. He was genuine, and it felt like a spring wind on her face. He put his hand out, gesturing for her to lead on.

CHAPTER TWO

Zephyros

Zephyros had never been in a place that managed to be both cold and humid at the same time. He was still unsure of Laerta: of whether he'd stay or whether he'd make for the hills as soon as his masters were dreaming. It depended on the master, as it usually did. Depended on the food, too.

So far the house slave had kept him on a tight leash. Not physically, but mentally. He could feel her eyes as he walked south, towards the river, even though the king's house was far behind them.

The creature walking next to him may prove enough of a reason to stay. Her eyes were like sparks from a flint on a cold winter's night. Not only did they brighten the world, but the hazel reminded him of the forests of home. Tall, but not taller than him, she stood ramrod straight as she walked the path to Laerta's farms in a way that was otherworldly. Like she didn't belong here, and knew it. Nicke didn't have a husband, he didn't think, and if she did then he was a right bastard to allow the brutal treatment she received. It was treatment he hadn't expected in this city, what with its flagrant insistence of equality between all genders. He would have expected such a thing of Kypt, but not Laerta.

Zeph watched, candidly at times, as her mahogany hair swayed in the wind and he caught her scent. Vanilla and something else, something common but unusual in a perfume. He breathed it in heartily. It was a shame he wasn't staying in her household. He'd like to taste her eventually.

"Lysander is a good man," she said, eyes determinedly ahead of her. "He's a part of the krypteia, a soldier that protects the city."

Zeph knew the type. Likely tall. Armoured. Well read. Liked lamb and the comforts a plentiful farm could bring.

She glanced sidelong at him, likely checking if he was listening. He hummed an acknowledgement that seemed to satisfy her.

"He doesn't care for many slaves," she continued. "He usually sponsors them to the Credo and they become citizens in due course. He calls them his brothers and sisters. He has three so far." She stopped on the road and glanced about them, searching as if for phantoms. He followed her line of sight and saw nothing of interest: just the trees as they shadowed and the river as it ran.

"What are you looking for?" he asked.

She turned back to him. "Ensuring I slipped my guards." His eyes shifted to the bandaged arm still hiding under her cloak and the urge to lift the fabric and take a look overwhelmed him. He needed to see the damage, to assess how angry he should be about it.

"Who did that to your arm?" he asked again, interrupting her.

Her lips thinned and he watched the vein in her neck tick.

"My brother," she finally replied. He'd heard the tone before from other women. His instinct to reach again for her injury intensified.

"Sounds like a shit brother," he said, letting the obvious air in the afternoon sun. She didn't laugh. He longed to hear her laugh. He knew it would be sweet like honey.

"He isn't —" she began before stopping herself. Her breath left her in a huff, swirling the dust kicked up from the road. "He isn't really my brother."

She began walking again and he hurried to keep up.

"Then who is he?"

"My sister's husband. He likes me calling him brother."

Zeph stopped walking. His own understanding of the world erupted in his mind's eye, calculating. He'd been taught politics well from childhood, as well as how to hold a blade and how to slice with one. His slavery was recent, and regrettable, though he knew he had friends enough in Kypt, Kurkia and Boornea to carry him home should he need it. The states that occupied this part of the world were only a small section of those he learnt. Forced into the tutelage of his uncle, dead now, with a charcoal in one hand and a knife in the other.

Nicke was too far up the road to ask the question, so his strides lengthened until he was at her side.

"You're Malptia's Rose!" he cried.

She responded by punching him in the face.

He stumbled back, tripping on a stone and ending up in the dirt. He wound his jaw, checking for a crack, and found none. She was breathing hard and he couldn't help but survey her from top to toe, taking in her furious form.

"You could get me killed for that," she whispered fiercely.

"You should get angry more often," he breathed in reply, unable to keep the words in. "Your fire is glorious."

He meant it too. Her eyes were glowing; her skin glistened in the afternoon sun. Her hands clenched and unclenched in time with her breathing. He'd never seen anything like it.

Yes, he thought he'd like to stay for at least a while. See what this Lysander character was like, meet the locals. If he was to enter the Credo it would add to his quest to get home, too. Back to Kurkia and to the life he'd been stolen from. It had been a year since he'd seen the island's peak from the ships, its cool blue waves, the markets so full to bursting with life that he could barely tear his eyes away. Foolish and foolhardy had combined to make his life there forfeit in exchange for what? For Kypt to not be pushed back as easily as their generals had sworn.

Zephyros was still furious about how easily he'd been captured, taken, massed in the hull of a Kypt ship bound for that city. He'd looked behind him only once: when the sea was leached of sunshine and instead driven with blood. The blood of his men, destroyed because Kurkia had underestimated the winds.

Zeph bit his lip and got to his feet. He'd never been punched by a woman wearing gold before and it undid him in certain ways, and he shook the thoughts of home.

"I'm sorry," he said, for what felt like the fifth time.

She hesitated before saying, "I'm sorry too."

"For what?"

A small smirk tilted her lips to the right and he found his breath caught.

"For you."

"For me?"

"For you, because you'll have to explain to Lysander why you have a bloody nose, and he won't be particularly impressed."

He returned her smirk, assurance measuring itself along his shoulders as he slackened one ankle to stand off kilter. He opened his mouth slightly and was rewarded by her glance towards it.

"I think I can handle a soldier."

She looked him up and down, the derision in her eyes clear. Then she turned and walked away from him, and he followed.

* * *

The walk from the main part of the city, with its high Temple walls, intricate fountains, paved roads and chattering populace, ended with a dirt road going over a river. The stream snaked its way from the west to the east, tracking down the mountains that lay under the sun as it set. Crystal clear water held fish abundant, and nothing told this more than how the slaves of the households sat companionably with each other as they cast a line. Dressed neither poorly nor richly, many of them even had shoes on. Zeph momentarily looked down at his own form: the dirty chiton, the cloth booties, the rope tied about his waist. It was one of the reasons he felt the need to exude physical presence: it would distract from his station.

He wasn't born to slavery, or even poverty. His uncle kept them clean and fresh building ocean vessels. It meant he was good with his hands, and Zeph had more than one scar borne of his rough treatment.

As they walked, the cleared country around the city turned into golden scrub. The sun wafted through the trees and Zeph could smell the distinctive aromas of rose and chamomile. He didn't focus much on the beauty around them, instead marking the landscape. He was recently of his city's navy after all, and the lay of Laerta was difficult to discern from maps alone.

Nicke directed him onto a very small path through two tall cypress trees. It was the kind of direction where if you'd have blinked, it would have disappeared. Nicke's feet were sure as she moved over rocks and into hollows. She'd treaded this path many times, Zeph was sure of it.

"So who is Lysander other than a krypteia?" Zeph asked, pushing a stray branch away from his head.

She didn't hesitate before extolling the man's virtues, which told Zeph more than she probably intended to.

"He went through the first two years of the Tertiary stream of the Credo before choosing to become a krypteia. He was smart enough to continue but decided against it when his father died. He's one of the leaders, but likes to keep to the shade. We're almost at his estate."

"Old mate has a whole estate, does he? He's doing well for a soldier then," Zeph laughed. She rolled her eyes at him.

"His father was like you," she continued. "A slave brought here as a war prize from Auntu. It's easier for slaves brought in to rise in Laerta. The slaves born here have a harder time. The Sun King saw Lysos's potential and sponsored him. He ended up a lieutenant before he died in the Boornean rebellion."

Zeph opened his mouth intending to say one thing but instead said another.

"Does Lysander beat you too?"

Nicke stilled, but didn't stop walking. This was obviously dangerous territory for her.

"No," she whispered as the trees parted and they walked onto the back boundary of a farm fronting the river. "He's the only reason I'm still alive."

The two-storey stone house sat before them. It was light in colour and reflected the sun blindingly. A pen of pigs and goats surrounded the back and a verandah of sorts snaked to the front door. It was surrounded by open ground that turned to orchard further down towards the river. Nicke avoided the pigs, but not the goats, as she scaled the fence to the yard and dropped down inside it. She headed straight for the back door and knocked before she realised that she'd left Zeph behind. He eyed his cloth shoes and looked at the mud. He felt Nicke roll her eyes at him.

"Just wait there oh princely one," she called across the yard. "I shall attend the house and fetch you a litter!"

He grinned. "Be sure to make it silk!" he called.

She shook her head and disappeared through the door, closing it behind her.

He didn't waste time before circling the house. He checked the windows, the lines of sight, how many hounds his new master owned. Whatever he needed to steal away when the time was right. Zeph knew now that there was definitely something going on between Nicke and Lysander.

He had his arms crossed and was looking towards the small creek to the south of the property when the front door opened and a man stood at its threshold. Blond, with a large scar trailing across his cheeks and through the bridge of his nose, Zeph knew this must be Lysander. He was dressed modestly, his wealth apparent from the tricky dye techniques used in his clothing. A few beads clung to his hair, winking in the sunlight. Many of the men here wore beads, Zeph realised, and he wondered at them.

He said something but Zeph was too far away to hear him, so he trudged toward the door. Lysander moved to the side and let Nicke's head poke through the doorway, and she nodded gently.

"See what I mean," she said as he approached.

Lysander considered him, his eyes curious. "Maybe I should leash him?" he asked her.

Zeph stopped short.

Nicke chuckled quietly. "He'd hate it: you definitely should."

Lysander looked down at her and his face softened, a smile teasing his mouth.

"Come in, Zephyros," he said as he turned. "And stop planning your escape, I'm not going to chain you."

Zeph followed them, grumbling, into the house. It was sparsely furnished, rugs here and there, linen curtains to keep out the afternoon sun and a bench with a tub on top for washing. A large dining table dominated the space. He presumed there would be an outdoor kitchen somewhere, and likely bedrooms upstairs. He hadn't seen any slaves' quarters as he'd done his inspection of the property, but as far as he knew they could be kept to the trees.

"I'm Lysander," the man said as he gestured to a floor cushion. "Please sit."

Zeph sat, but hesitantly. Slaves didn't usually sit while their masters stood.

"I've agreed to take you off the king's hands. Now, tell me what I'm working with."

It was Zeph's turn to look curious. Baffled, truly.

Lysander took pity on him. "I can only admit you to the Credo if you have some sort of inherent talent or skill. Otherwise they'd admit anyone and we'd have no slaves left." Lysander reached into his pocket and retrieved a scribed piece of paper with a red seal. He passed it to Zeph and Zeph looked it over. It was his details: his name, his build, his origin of Kurkia. How he'd come to his last master and how they'd despaired of him. He looked up and found Lysander's open face.

"So you can read, then," he said. "That's a start."

"Damn it," Zeph cursed, drawing laughter out of Lysander. It was a rich sound that bounced off the walls.

"He can also carve and speak three languages," Nicke explained, ticking them off her fingers as she spoke.

"Four," Zeph corrected. "Four languages."

Maybe he should diminish himself: be smaller and quieter and survive until they underestimated him and he could walk out of this city. He'd already betrayed his ability to read, probably to write too, but he couldn't bring himself to deny his prowess with language. It was like he was born knowing all human tongues.

"Which ones?" Nicke asked eagerly.

"Laertan," Zeph said. "Kyptian. Kurdan."

"Yes, yes, those I'd guessed," Nicke replied in frustration.

He paused pointedly, looking directly into her eyes as he revealed the fourth. The culmination of his uncle's teaching and his own interest. Why that country, what had drawn him to the limping city which had been on its knees for the better part of a generation, was unknown to him. Something about the weather, or the stories of their flower festivals, may have been it.

"Malptian," he answered easily, like it was no big thing. Like it wasn't the language he knew was forbidden to her: her home, her people. The ones she was forced to betray again and again.

She swallowed quietly, and that was the end of the moment of knowledge between them.

"Do you spar?" Lysander asked.

"Not my masters I don't," Zeph replied.

Lysander laughed. "Oh you will. Language and carving will only get you so far. We're a warring country. War sustains us. War sets us free."

It was Zeph's turn to laugh and Lysander's mirth was echoed in the lines around his eyes.

"Yes, I can spar," Zeph admitted finally.

"Good. There is a trunk out on the verandah. Go and find something suitable. I'll be out in a minute."

Zeph did as he was told and found the trunk full of weapons and armour: both old and pitted and new and shining. He selected a kopis and a spear and sat on a bench, waiting.

His eyes wandered back to the house, and he spied Lysander's hand gracing Nicke's cheek. He shouldn't watch, but if her reaction to him today was any indication, the touch Lysander was gifting her was both rare and dangerous. Zeph looked as Lysander's mouth lightly touched Nicke's forehead, and then her injured wrist in a fashion so gentle it made Zeph's heart squeeze. He turned his head as she exited the house and made her way immediately behind and into the trees, likely finding her way home.

Lysander watched her go, and then turned to his new charge.

"Okay," he said. "Ground rules. Firstly, call me Lysander and nothing else. Two, curfew for slaves is sundown unless you have written permission from me. Krypteia hunt after dark, so make sure you always have some kind of paperwork on you. Three, you're no longer Kurdan or Kyptian or whatever you used to consider yourself. You're Laertan. What this city wants from you, it gets. Fourthly, you will graduate from the Credo and you will do me proud as your brother. Understood?"

Zeph nodded, then raised his hand to ask a question. Lysander huffed at him.

"Are you always like this?"

"Yes," Zeph replied as he lowered his hand. Lysander gestured at him to ask his question. Zeph stood before asking, and looked up to the tip of the spear he had chosen. It glistened in the sun and winked at him, like it was in on the joke.

"What's a Credo?"

"What?" Lysander yapped.

"I've heard it mentioned a few times. What is it?"

"Ahh," Lysander uttered, unsure if Zeph was joking. "It's a school."

"Oh, like for kids."

"And it's where we learn strategy and war."

"Oh," Zeph repeated in the same tone. "Like a barracks."

Lysander made a pained noise. "Yes and no. It honestly doesn't matter. All you need to do is be admitted, and the rest will follow."

He took a spear from the trunk and readied it in front of him, tip forward. Zeph eyed it carefully. Lysander's shoulder relaxed and dipped below his forearm, and Zeph readied his own arm to deflect the strike.

It came quickly, accurately and with strength, but Zeph deflected it. It came again and Zeph simply batted it away like a cat. Lysander grimaced at him.

Then Lysander didn't jab, but rather swung his kopis with his left arm. Surprised by the appearance of the blade, Zeph was slow to deflect but managed it with a step back. He didn't have the hands to utilise both the kopis and the spear effectively because he'd never been taught how, and it was obvious that Lysander knew this. His new master battered him until he was losing ground and unable to gain an opening. Then, quicker than the eye could track, Zeph lost his kopis. It just flew out of his hands like it had taken flight.

Then he heard the clang: the distinctive sound of metal on dirt that meant he'd been disarmed.

Lysander smirked at him. "I thought you said you could spar?"

Zeph gaped, but soon gained his composure. "How long do you

think it's been since I've been allowed to raise a weapon?"

"From your form I would say too long." Lysander handed his kopis back and gestured to the benches sitting alongside the trunk. Zeph sat and waited for the interrogation that always came with a new master.

"So," Lysander said as the weapons went back into their box. "Just how fucked am I?"

Zeph blinked.

Lysander continued. "You're obviously not a slave, Zephyros, or haven't been one for long. So I'd bet either a spy, or a mistake. I'd like to know just how exactly you're going to screw me."

Zeph couldn't help it. He smiled, and decided that he liked Lysander of Laerta.

"Slowly," Zeph replied. "But I might offer you a wine first."

Lysander laughed and clapped him on the back.

"I'd guess you were some kind of commander?"

Zeph nodded. "A lieutenant in the Kurdan Navy. But, my ship was lost and I claimed that I was a nobody so they wouldn't cut my throat then and there."

"Quick thinking. What about before that. Or did you learn Malptian in Kypt?"

Zeph shook his head. "My uncle taught me enough of it. The rest I learnt by comparing texts in Kurdan and Malptian."

Lysander considered him for a moment. "Did you learn politics?" he asked carefully.

"Yes," Zeph replied, inspecting his hands.

"Do you know why?"

He shrugged. "It was an interest of my uncle's."

"How did you know who Nicke was? She told me why you have blood on your chin. That there is something that not many people outside of the Rex's circle know."

Zeph shrugged again. "I know a lot about Laerta."

Lysander hummed at him, obviously unsatisfied with the

response.

"What about you?" Zeph asked. "Nicke said that your father was a slave."

It was Lysander's turn to look at his hands. Zeph followed his eyes and saw long fingers almost designed for strangling. He may be a spy, or an assassin himself. Zeph might have walked out of slavery and into a viper's pit.

"My father was Auntuan. He was born to slavery and sold to Laerta in a skilled-work exchange. He could make saddles and bridles, something Laerta needed for their war efforts. He made a gilded saddle for the then-king and was rewarded with sponsorship to the Credo because the workmanship was so gorgeous."

"Lyon's father?"

"No, his uncle. Galyn Rex. He died in a hunting accident before I was born, his heir following soon after. The sun king they called him. He was meant to have been a hard task master, but almost incorruptible."

"Almost?" Zeph smirked.

"Well when Kallum Rex, Lyon's father, felt the need to bribe his way out of a tricky situation during the Laerta-Malptia war, you could see how that might tarnish the royal family. Even their dead."

Zeph nodded. He could certainly see how.

He knew this story of course. Only when he heard it, it was told like a bedtime story. Eventually the heir returned to Laerta to claim what was theirs.

The sun had begun its descent behind the trees. The earth glowed with streaks of light.

"It isn't just my father's story that causes me to take in talented slaves, Zephyros," Lysander said quietly. "It's in exchange for something precious to me."

"Like a pact?"

"Something like that. I take it very seriously, and so do Sophia, Drakon and Kallias. My siblings, who you'll come to meet. Demetria didn't only suggest you for this because Lyon would wring your neck as soon as look at you."

"Why then?"

"Because it's people like you, with your brash displays and overconfidence, that can most easily see when Nicke needs protection and have the gall to protect her."

"Like they did today?" Zeph replied derisively.

Lysander closed his eyes slowly, his shoulders resigned. "He's never attacked her in the War Rooms. Usually it's sacred ground."

Zeph watched as Lysander's body went through the motions. Anger, fear, and longing all mingled on his face. His hands began to shudder in kept rage.

"I would do it without you asking," Zeph said simply, without pretence.

Lysander almost smiled. "And that's why I choose men and women like you, Zephyros. You don't have any self preservation when your fighting instinct is probed. You'd jump in front of a beast for almost no reason at all."

Zeph nodded. "So it's simple then. In exchange for citizenship, I protect your pretty girlfriend from her shit of a brother-in-law. Do I get a feather bed, too?"

A shadow passed over Lysander's face, and Zeph felt the static in the air that betrayed the small jealousy of his new brother. Then he growled, "I wish she would just marry me and be done with it."

"Why doesn't she?"

"She's Lyon's. His kin in this country. No one can gainsay the king."

"So run away." Zeph shrugged. It's what he would do if the woman he loved was being so terribly treated.

"I can't leave Laerta."

"Is this some misplaced loyalty thing?"

Lysander didn't reply. It was a crap excuse if that's what it was. "Let me show you to your room, and then I'll send letters to my siblings to meet you here tomorrow."

Zeph followed him into the house and up the stairs, turning right at the end of the corridor. Lysander lit a lamp, illuminating a small cot with red woven blankets, a small trunk and a basin in the corner.

Zephyros took his time circling the room, mind frozen and unable to speak. The walls were painted; the floor wasn't dirt; the bed was absent of bugs. Gingerly, he tapped the wood which made the window frame. He'd underestimated the value of a generous place to sleep in the past. His house growing up was luxury; the dog-dens he'd inflicted himself on were not.

But this was something else. Lysander of Laerta held no obligation to him, no service needing rendering. He was simply ensuring Zephyros's safety; his sanity; his sleep.

Zephyros swallowed, and bowed his head to Lysander as he turned.

"I don't deserve this."

Lysander looked at him curiously, probably taken aback by the sudden change in confidence. One's step couldn't always fail to falter.

"Protect that which is important to me, and you will, Zephyros."

"Zeph," he choked, the words unwilling. "Call me Zeph."

Lysander nodded, and took his leave, dragging Zeph into the dark world of obligation to one of Laerta's soldiers.

* * *

The day was fresh and dry when Zeph eventually rose from a fitful sleep. His dreams were full of chains, dead men with vicious smiles, and venturing down wrong paths through jungle. He didn't seek waking, but the sun hauled him kicking and screaming into consciousness.

He waited, listening closely to the early morning of the house. Pigs and goats sounded outside encouraged by what seemed like generous helpings of fodder. So, it was true, then: Lysander didn't really want for slaves.

Zeph rose, rubbing his face. The second day was always the worst. It was when the master left the new servant to the clutches of the middleman or the housekeeper, both of whom usually had a switch in hand. Most slave owners didn't enjoy brutality being visible, so turned their eyes to the west when the sun bled a morning red. Zeph felt a keen need to galvanise himself and make his person smaller; imperceptible. His body was a simple shell through which the world couldn't penetrate and his core-self, the one that screamed righteousness and called for simpler terms to his life, could only be untouched if he insisted.

And he would insist. He lacked scars, lacked the obvious telling of a curt slave, because his submission was unrelated to the vital centre of himself.

He would not yield himself, but, in doing so, yielded everything.

The second day was always the worst.

He began to make preparations for it.

* * *

Lysander met him at the kitchen table: fresh, warm milk and cooked oats ready. He said, "for you," before Zeph could speak. Zeph didn't hesitate to finish the bowl, knowing the trust tests undertaken, but he did thank the Laertan.

"It's no fuss," Lysander replied. "The goats were obliging and Sophia is indisposed today so can't take the milk to the market as she usually does."

Lysander squared his shoulders then, and Zephyros prepared himself.

"They'll be here within the hour, and there are things you should probably—"

He was cut off abruptly by the sound of galloping horses and raucous laughter coming from the east.

"You know what?" he said, mouth twisting in mirth. "Never mind."

Zeph rose from the table with him and followed him outside, one step behind. The view down to the river was obscured by road dust but the scene was unmistakable. Three horses, and presumably their riders, were travelling viciously fast towards the house. The man at the front had a wide brimmed hat which shadowed his dark skin. Behind him, just visible through the dust, was a woman wearing green and another man wearing grey. Zeph didn't smirk, but instead smelt another test.

"I'm sorry you're meeting them all at the same time," Lysander said. Zeph looked at him curiously. "They can be a lot."

Yes, Zeph could see how they could be a lot. Shedding the morning's anxiety and burying it deep into his gut, he wove his trademark arrogance across his shoulders and through his fingers. Let them find him as he was, not as he could be.

The first man, the one in the hat, dismounted and casually removed his cloak from his shoulders, draping it across his forearm. A smile lit his face as his eyes trained on Zeph, the look full of hope.

His two companions stopped and dismounted behind him. The woman was short and slight, with long brown hair and a green peplos. Her eyes were deep and almost black, but her skin was on the pale side of sun-kissed. She shook out her skirts, and Zeph spied the slit in her dress that usually denoted a woman regularly in use of a blade. The second man walked towards them, his grey cloak remaining on his shoulders and obscuring his build. He had the kind of face that was forgettable; like you could see it every day and fail to recall it. Coupled with the grey cloak and the common colouring, Zeph pinned him as the group's spy.

Which was a shame, because Zeph fancied himself for spy-work.

"Zeph," Lysander said from behind him. "Meet my brothers and my sister. Kallias, Drakon and Sophia." He pointed to each in turn as they approached them.

"Zephyros!" said Kallias, his initial enthusiasm unmuted. "I am so happy to meet you. Between what Lysander wrote and Demetria said, I bet you're going to be a great asset to the family."

Zeph shook his hand, his arrogance slipping.

He knew how to survive, how to be sold from place to place, but only very rarely in his life had he heard someone calling him family.

Drakon was next, his grey cloak splitting apart to reveal a pair of woollen gloves. "I hear you're good with language," he said in Kurdan.

Zeph smiled wide, his native tongue spreading warmth between his shoulder blades. "I hope you can teach me more than I know," he said, and Drakon nodded, a smirk playing on his mouth.

Sophia hung back, watching. Zeph turned to her and put out his hand, it looking so much larger than hers. Her hesitation was warranted, he knew. He would have done the same.

"Nicke said you were taller," she said as she grasped his hand.

"One must always seek to seem smaller than their superiors, yes?" Zeph asked, arrogance flooding back.

Sophia didn't smile, but there was an acknowledgement in her eyes. Knowledge they shared, grew, nurtured in the bowels of servitude. He didn't keep her eyes held for long, just enough to identify him as a friend and not a threat.

"Have you all eaten?" Lysander said. Two out of three shook their heads and they all followed their brother into the house.

Zeph originally thought he'd been kidding. When he'd called him brother and gave him a bedroom, he thought it was a lark.

Like when someone offers you a warm bowl of broth that has piss in it, or when you're dressed down by a master for something their children did. He thought it was a gift given then cruelly taken; a prank disguised until an audience arrived.

And an audience had arrived since last night. Prone, ready: waiting for a rug to be pulled.

But instead, Zephyros followed Lysander, Drakon, Sophia and Kallias into the farm house and sat between two men who now considered him a brother.

His breathing grew uneven but he controlled it, letting the need for air grow deep before sating it.

"First things first," Lysander began, divvying up bread rolls. "Any news of last night?"

Sophia was the first to respond, shaking her head. "All was quiet. I think she went from here to her chamber. I didn't get a chance to ask Demetria of her eating."

Lysander nodded slowly, then turned to Kallias. "Alix?" he asked simply.

Kallias nodded. "She was distressed, but not overly so. She was more concerned about Auntu, to be honest."

Lysander sat back. Quiet, contemplative. Drakon drew the conversation elsewhere.

"I'm sure you're keen for the Credo, Zephyros?" he asked.

Zeph nodded. "I have some training, but more is always welcome."

"Do you have an interest area?" Sophia asked.

"I don't suppose? What do you mean?"

She splayed her hands along the grain of the table. "There are schools within the Credo; streams with destinations in different fields. There are five. Three are war, one is Theory, and the last is Trade. Are you good with your hands?"

Zeph smirked. "Depends on the willing participant."

Sophia sat back, smiling small. "He's good for Secondary, I

think," she said to Lysander.

"Secondary?" Zeph asked.

"Yes. It's your confidence: those of the Secondary need equal arrogance and surety while being measured against their betters."

"But the languages?" Drakon asked, eyeing his new brother.

Sophia shook her head. "No, his mouth is too smart to last long in too deep a thought."

Zeph grimaced.

"It's okay, Zephyros," Kallias said. "I did Secondary too. It'll probably suit you."

Zeph looked around at them. "What does it involve?"

Lysander smiled. "You'll be learning strategy and war footing. Lieutenants and captains come out of Secondary, but not generals or kings. Grunts are below, in Primary. Not all of them are stupid, some simply want a farmer's life and being soldiers gives them the time."

"What were you?"

"I started in Tertiary, and moved to the krypteia when the time came," Lysander explained.

"Primary," Drakon offered. "It's easier to watch when no one sees you."

Zephyros nodded, acknowledging the ease with which Drakon offered his position in the family. Zeph, of course, suspected, but was surprised by the candour of the man he'd just met. He tucked away unwelcome thoughts of why Drakon was so trusting.

Sophia sighed. "I'm Trade. Weaver."

"And a good one at that," Kallias said, continuing to smile. It was starting to make Zeph question his sanity.

"That's four," Zeph said. "What is Theory?"

Drakon answered. "Philosophy, law. Human condition and impact. Not many people go that route."

"If they did, Laerta may have found that war was useless hundreds of years ago," Lysander laughed. He cocked his leg so his ankle crossed at his knee and began peeling a pear. Zephyros watched the casual ease, but knew the mind was working. "You'll have to earn the Secondary, though. I can present you today."

"You'll need to know basic strategy," Drakon said. "Do you?"

Zeph opened his mouth to answer but Lysander beat him to it.

"He does," he said.

Drakon's eyes tracked between the two men, astute and questioning. If Lysander hadn't offered Zeph's past, then Zeph trusted his judgement.

Which was a strange turn of events from just that morning, when he'd woken in sweats to wait for the second day of slavery.

Sophia stood then, rotating her shoulders back. "I should get home. I'll be of no use to you at the Credo, anyway. But Zephyros?"

Zeph turned to face her and found her eyes warm.

"Please do come by my house sometime today and we can... ahh," she gestured at his clothing, soiled and worn from days on the road and a few rough nights. "We can get you properly fitted for clothing."

"Thank you, Sophia," he replied, bowing his head slightly.

"I think it's the least I can do seeing as you're wearing gloves for shoes."

Zeph smiled, but with a marked reluctance.

"I'll follow you out," Kallias said, standing too. He nodded an acknowledgement to Lysander as he closed the front door behind them.

Zephyros turned to Drakon to ask a question just as Lysander took a second pear.

"Where do you all live?" Because it wasn't on this farm.

Drakon looked disinterested as he answered. "Kallias lives next door to the king, and Sophia lives close to the Temple. It's easier for her to take students there. I live in the forest near the War Rooms."

"When you're a citizen Zeph, you'll choose a household.

Probably one close to the circle where the king lives."

Zeph mapped what he knew of the city in his head. The Temple was to the west, closer to the sacred mountain and the Credo. The king lived at the city's centre but to the north, where forest came to the back door. He guessed that the War Rooms were in that forest.

"You'll find your place," Drakon assured him. "We all have."

It was then, and only then, that Zeph appreciated the magnitude of the journey he was still to undertake.

CHAPTER THREE

Nicke

Nicke didn't wake well. Nightmares of blades and throats and golden hair plagued her, and the thoughts of it intruded on her waking moments. When the images came, she forbade them root, but they formed anyway. In her mind's eye, the red of the blood couldn't be hidden by his grey cloak. It turned it black, and the abyss always ended up taking him.

Like every day before, Nicke tested for sunlight at her window sill and felt the day dull. Sighing, she dressed with awkward motions and eyed the weaving work she needed to complete before the sun set. She wasn't sure how she would manage it.

A light tap on the door was the only warning before Demetria strode in.

"You look like you've seen better days," she said, dropping fresh linen on Nicke's bed.

"Dreams," was all Nicke provided, unwilling to voice more.

Demetria hummed an acknowledgement. She unrolled a fresh bandage and tidied the space next to Nicke's basin. Nicke placed her wrist in Demetria's hand when it was extended expectantly.

"Did it pain you last night?" the maid asked.

"Yes," Nicke replied. "I woke every time I shifted."

"That's why the dreams would have been bad, then. Usually you wouldn't remember them."

Nicke didn't reply. She'd had nightmares every night since she was a child. The subjects changed but the theme remained the same.

The bandage was thick with dried blood and had to be gently pried from its hold on her. "The wound doesn't feel hot," Demetria murmured. "Perhaps it will heal as normally as it can."

"I expect it to take the full year," Nicke whispered. It was a small conversation within a small room. All she would allow herself; all she would dare. "The burn on my shoulder took almost eighteen moons, though."

Demetria nodded. "Bastard of a power, that."

It was a part of Lyon's magic. Each king and queen came into their earth-gift on ascension and it manifested differently for each of them. The scrolls recorded Kallum Rex, Lyon's father, as having the ability to see the thoughts of his countrymen. Galyn, the king slain by a phantom boar, could run inhumanly fast and heal others. Not himself, though, it turned out.

The pain Lyon inflicted was long lasting and burnt as it healed. When he'd driven the blade through Nicke's wrist and skin, his magic had ensured that the wound would be kept fresh.

"Your sister asked after you this morning," Demetria said, busy with the cloth. "Asked where you disappeared to yesterday."

Nicke swallowed. "What did you tell her?"

"Now Nicke, you know I'm forbidden from lying to her." She worked the skin with the warm rose water she always used, the scent surrounding them. Too sweet; unwieldy and pervading every nook and cranny of the space where it was released. Nicke didn't care for it for more reason than one. "So I told her the truth," Demetria continued. "I told her that you had errands for the war council."

Nicke still didn't quite trust the lady's maid.

She wasn't Laertan, just as Nicke wasn't. Being bought and sold is a terrible thing that can cause unforeseen loyalties in people.

"Thank you, Demetria," Nicke whispered.

She nodded. "But the queen would like to see you before you go to the Temple."

"I have weaving lessons this morning."

"Yes, you do."

They looked at each other then, green catching hazel. Demetria's eyes searched, but likely didn't find what they were looking for. She affixed the bandage with a tight knot and rose to her feet, focusing on making the bed. "Alix is in her quarters."

As Nicke left the room, she heard Demetria whistling a tune of birds and flowers and war.

Nicke found her sister in her sitting room. It was a suite, with a comfortable lounge leading into a bedroom twice the size. Decorated audaciously, with multiple balconies jutting from the room and not a single hard surface bar the doorway itself, her sister had styled it after their home. Nicke didn't blame her, but couldn't ignore the sickly feeling she got whenever she entered here. Alix had been eighteen when their father had lost both his daughters to Laerta, one in marriage and the other in trust. But Nicke didn't begrudge her sister this small oasis of home.

Alix was seated, her hands gliding over the pages of a book without reading it. Her black hair was shaped into a spiral at the back of her head and the right side was shaved completely in the style of a married Laertan woman.

"Good morning," Nicke said buoyantly.

Alix looked up from the book and smiled at her, the sides of her eyes crinkling.

"Hello Nicke," she said, snapping the book shut. "Come here so I can look at you."

Alix had been saying that since they'd arrived when Nicke was only three; since their mother was killed and she took on the task. Nicke stood before her, arms inside the billows of her peplos and warm expression on her face. Alix's eyes trailed up and down, judging her weight, height, hair lustre, cheek colour, lip fullness.

Alix didn't focus on the injury her husband had inflicted. She gave the bandage half a thought before retreating into the safety of denial.

"Are you well?" Alix asked.

An easy question.

"Quite well," Nicke replied.

An easy answer.

"How goes your writing?"

"It's coming along."

"What do you write of?"

"The landscape; history. Theory pursuits."

"I would like to read some."

Nicke nodded, indulging her sister more than she deserved.

Nicke would never share her writing just as her sister would never read it.

"Tell me of the Credo." Alix poured herself some tea. She didn't offer any.

"It runs as it always has," Nicke answered. "Your sons do well. Dannehs is showing promise for the Secondary."

Nicke didn't tell her sister that Dannehs hated war and strategy. That he had what his older brother lacked.

"And Kallum?" Alix asked of her first born.

Kallum, the elder, was sixteen and would be a menacing king once his father died. Whether it was the bluster of a boy trying to impress his sire, or whether it held his character true, was a different question. "Kallum is learning all he needs to know to follow his father to the throne. His swordsmanship is better than his spear work, as it always has been, and he is able to provide solutions to problems quickly enough."

Alix sipped her tea.

Nicke remained before her until Alix's eyes began to shutter and the mood in the room shifted.

"Lyon told me what you did," she said, voice husky.

"And what was that?" Nicke replied, chin rising so her eyes looked over the bridge of her nose. She couldn't bring herself to make her tone cold, but she knew better than to hope.

"You humiliated him in front of his subordinates. He's the king, and you made him a fool."

"If that's what he told you." Nicke wouldn't engage. She'd long before refused to let the hope of a saviour engulf her. Alix was often her only hope as well as being her greatest disappointment.

Alix nodded. "Go now," she said, dropping her eyes and placing her hands back on her book. "I'm tired."

Nicke nodded, but didn't bow, as her sister's eyes glazed over. If you didn't know her, hadn't seen her before their travelling here, you'd have thought her always like this. Small, weak: unwilling. But Nicke remembered the bruises and cuts that had tarnished her sister's skin early in her marriage; saw her eyes go from fierce to sunken. Alix had allowed herself hope of a better life and it had destroyed her. Nicke refused to do the same.

No one was coming for them. No one would dare.

Laerta was the best on land.

Nicke left her sister staring at a page covered in coloured shapes, an appropriation of a mountain scene. The book had words.

But her sister couldn't read them.

* * *

Sophia wasn't home when Nicke called. Flanked by two guards, she'd been herded towards Sophia's house without permission for further stops. Even the markets, with their fresh produce and friendly faces, were barred to her today. She could fool herself into thinking it was because of her arm. The injury was on full display, and her keepers may distrust her ability to deflect questions about it.

But Nicke wasn't a fool.

Ryan was on her left, and Matthew on her right, as they walked through the city. Both were her brother's men, sworn and placed to be guards for her and from her. Helmets covered their hair and their features, leaving the dark in front of their eyes. She knew them otherwise, though. Had learnt with them when she was a girl and had shown promise.

"She may be at the Temple," Nicke said as they walked out of Sophia's front yard. The sun was high and hot, and most people would be seeking the shade until the afternoon humidity muted the day.

Matthew nodded, but Ryan shook his head.

"We're due back at the king's residence," he said, not unkindly. Here, away from their king, things could be easier.

"She'll be at the Temple, Ryan," Matthew said. "I can stay with her. How much trouble could she get into?"

Nicke had no intention of getting into any trouble.

Ryan harrumphed, then sighed. "I'll be back in about two hours. I'll collect you then."

"Thank you, Ryan," Nicke said. He nodded and walked back up the road.

Nicke turned towards the Temple and began walking. Her steps felt lighter.

Ryan was the spy. Matthew never reported.

It was an imposing building. Walking through the gate placed them in the centre of a two metre thick wall, dotted with bronze plaques with embossed names. Bones sat behind many of the names, but others just held flowers, or cloaks, or heirlooms. So many Laertans did not come back from war, but their names were held here all the same.

The fortification hid them from the sun for a moment before a sprawling meadow greeted them inside the compound. Green grass and yellow flowers covered the ground, with scholars and their books dotted among them. It would take ten minutes to walk around the perimeter of the Temple grounds, and there was no break in the wall except for the one they had passed through.

And in the centre was the Temple itself. Only as tall as three men, it housed the texts sacred to the Theory school and the public equipment essential to the Trade. Anyone could use what was held here, or learn something new for a hobby, with experts ready to guide.

"I'll wait here," Matthew said, gesturing at the break in the wall. Nicke nodded, silently thanking him.

She walked to the small building next to the Temple which she knew housed the looms. It was made of grey stone quarried in the north with a deep chestnut wood for the roof and windows. Cloth of all colours and textures adorned the drying racks in the sunroom, making use of the westerly breeze. The weather had been warm and dry for too long and the grass was yellow. According to Theory Masters, the clouds that deigned to make Laerta humid were not yet able to bring the rainstorm she so desperately needed for crops to flourish.

Sophia hummed to herself as she wove, the same lullaby Nicke had left Demetria singing that morning. It felt different in Sophia's mouth: like a promise. Her back was to the door and Nicke sat at a table covered in powdered dyes, watching her.

The song was different in other ways. Here, in the midst of industry, it took on a waulking quality. Sophia threw her shuttle and beat and threw and beat until her foot affected a pedal which disengaged the loom's brake. Nicke knew the cloth was perfect without looking at it. Just as she knew Sophia could weave iron into fur.

"I know you're watching me, dearest," Sophie called. She twisted a mechanism under the loom which brought the fabric onto its beam and gave more room to weave.

Nicke smiled. "I didn't want to disturb you."

Sophia twisted on her stool and gave Nicke a once over, glancing sparingly at where she knew an injury would be. Tutting, she turned back and kept at her song.

Nicke knew enough of weaving to also know that you didn't expect anything of the weaver mid-song. If they were singing, they were in the centre of a pattern and to lose their train of thought was to lose their place. Nicke knew this, but approached anyway.

The cloth was laid out before her in greens and golds. It was an echo pattern, where two warp colours were used in parallel to bring forward an illusion. Parts were golden circles, and others were green, but the overall effect was like an animal's coat. But in silk.

"It's beautiful, Sophie," Nicke whispered.

"Mmmhmm."

Nicke left the loom to walk the room, inspecting the work of Sophia's students. Some of them would make fine Trades, others may have had better luck in the wood sheds.

Sophia's song ended and Nicke suddenly felt a gentle pressure on her arm. Turning, she found Sophia's eyes trained on her with a hand out expectantly.

"Demetria changed the bandage this morning," Nicke explained, holding out her wrist.

"Is it paining you?" Sophia asked, gently rubbing ghostly fingers over it.

"Yes, but I don't think it's infected."

Sophia made an assenting noise and gestured to a table set up with scones and tea.

"So," the weaver started. "Seeing as you're injured, I thought I would let you off the hook with weaving. If you don't flick the shuttle, you won't get enough drive to stop it sinking beneath the warp." She picked up a cup of tea and added a square of sugar, stirring, before putting it in front of Nicke. "But I think you should have something to show for today, so I've dyed some fleece that needs rinsing."

Nicke grimaced. Dying fleece meant urine, the acid reacting with the dye.

Sophia brought a small wooden tub into the room. It was full of blue wool and Nicke didn't dare place her nose over the side.

"How do you expect me to rinse this in here?" she said, looking for the larger tub of water usually used for the job.

"Oh, we'll have to go to the river for it," Sophia said, putting on an apron and holding one out.

"Sophie..." Nicke began, but Sophia tutted at her.

"It's just Matt out there, isn't it?" she asked. Nicke nodded. "Then what's the trouble?"

"The trouble is if I'm found, then —"

"Oh, hush. Besides, you're doing me a favour."

Sophia picked up the fleece tub and left the building without another word.

Nicke tried to breathe. She knew Lysander's sister very well, better than she knew almost anyone else, and knew this wasn't a trap.

It could be worse than a trap. It could be a chance. Nicke didn't fill her days with dreaming of Lysander; of the feel of his hands, or even his mouth. They too soon turned to thoughts of death and punishment.

The sun shone where love bloomed. In an obtuse kind of way; a way that hid it from the lovers. Anyone else could tell by a look what the two thought to thoroughly hide. Nicke knew she was shining.

Sophia knew it too.

Nicke followed her. When she reached the wall, Sophia was talking to Matthew, tub on her hip.

"I can't just," Matthew gestured out of the Temple, "it could get me demoted."

"Oh, come on, Matt," Sophie crooned. "You can come with us actually. We could use someone to take the fleece out of the tub."

Matthew took a step back and looked over Sophia's shoulder at Nicke. "I told you that you were staying in the Temple."

"Yes, I apologise Matthew," Nicke said.

Nicke paused. This wasn't worth Lysander's demise, or Sophia's, or Matthew's.

"Please take me home," she said, face masking her turmoil.

Sophia turned to her. "No, Nicke. You need at least part of a lesson, and I need help with this."

Nicke shook her head. She yearned for Lysander, but between yesterday's travel to his estate and today's jaunt to the river, it was likely to come undone.

She hadn't exaggerated yesterday when she'd spoken to Zephyros. Lysander was the only reason she was alive; the only reason she could face the day. At the War Rooms, she could risk speaking to him in private because that was where her power was held. Here, though, in the city, she was nothing more than a small woman with small talent.

Her chest began to shut down the roaring of her blood.

"You can stay at the Temple, Nicke. There's no need to go home," Matthew said.

Sophia concurred, shifting the tub.

"If we're going to stay here, I'll need some things from home for a different lesson. Matthew?" He turned to her, relieved. "Can you please get some things from my home?"

He nodded, and she gave him a set of instructions. Sophia then turned and walked Nicke back to the weaver's rooms.

"Why are you such a spoilsport?" she asked. "Matthew would have been fine."

"I can't risk what I already have in a quest for more. Yesterday was already dangerous."

"Hmm, yes, Lysander mentioned you'd brought Zeph

yourself."

"Zeph?" Nicke asked, lips turning up at the corners.

"Zephyros? He asked us to call him Zeph."

"That's very familiar for someone who was looking for escape routes yesterday."

Sophia shrugged. "He's going to be presented for Secondary. Kallias tried to reassure him that he'd suit it."

"I thought he'd be better for Theory," Nicke said.

"He's smart, but strategic. As you said, he's already planning his escape."

"I guess I should look forward to teaching him, then."

Sophia grinned. "I'd pay to see the trouble he gives you."

Matthew knocked on the door frame and let himself in. He held small tapestry looms in his hands, the wood shining from a fresh polish. Sophia took them, and asked him if he wanted to stay.

He eyed the fabric in the room, and excused himself. Nicke watched as he sat under a tree outside and pulled a book from his pocket.

"He's strange, that one," Sophia said.

"How so?" Nicke asked, still watching him.

"He doesn't want you to get hurt, but still maintains loyalty to your brother."

Nicke didn't answer, thinking of the purpose of the men around her as Sophie took her through threading the frame loom.

* * *

"No, not like that," Sophie admonished when they were finally weaving later in the day. "Don't pull so tightly. It's meant to be dominated by the weft."

Nicke almost threw the thing across the room.

"Here, try something thicker." Sophia rummaged through the chest where she kept her scrap materials. She picked out a lavender fleece and brought it over. "Spin it lightly, just between your fingertips, and weave it through the warp."

Nicke was trying to manage but found her wrist unforgiving.

"You have to let the form take its own shape. The wool will tell you what it wants to be as you weave."

"Sounds philosophical," Nicke murmured, trying to twist the fleece. Her fingers were stiff.

"Yes, well, there's a reason the Trade and Theory work so closely together."

A knock at the door startled them both, with Sophia dropping a spindle and Nicke dropping the twist. She cursed silently, the pain of her wrist seemingly wasted.

"You can't be here," she heard Sophia hiss angrily.

Nicke turned to find Lysander in the doorway, a bundle of yarn in his hands and a satchel on his shoulder. He was dressed in dark blue, with golden threads embroidered about the neck. It framed his olive face and golden hair like a halo. His hair was half up in the Laertan style men preferred: enough to keep the hair out his eyes but the sun off his neck. She knew he had beads in his hair that his mother had painted when he was a boy. Made up of blues, greens and greys, they were placed through the threads as part of his coming of age. Nicke remembered the day he'd received them, when he had moved to krypteia at nineteen and surprised them all. She thought he was destined for a position beside her at the war table. But, then, how could she have resisted touching his hands when they pointed in the room where her enemy lay in wait?

Nicke had embroidered the chiton herself as a gift, and he wore it more than the others.

"You shouldn't be here, brother," Sophia said, more forcefully than before. It was one thing to meet them at the river, it was quite another to be so brash within the city.

Nicke couldn't speak. Matthew could see the doorway.

Lysander's eyes hardened as he entered. Zephyros came behind him, still dressed as meekly as Nicke had left him yesterday.

"We went to your house, but you weren't there," Lysander explained. "Zeph needs clothes before he's presented."

"Shit, I forgot," Sophia said.

Lysander shrugged his shoulders. "Can you take Zeph to get him sorted?"

"Yes." Sophia turned to Nicke. "I'm sorry. I'll be back as soon as I can." She shooed Zephyros out of the room, slapping his hand like a child when he sought to touch a complicated weaving.

Nicke still couldn't speak.

They were in the city. Inside the Temple walls.

Lysander put his hands behind his back as Nicke rose from sitting.

She swallowed.

"Is everything good with Zephyros?" she asked, fiddling with her peplos.

"Yes, he met Sophia, Drakon and Kallias this morning. I think he'll fit in."

"Sophia said you have him down for the Secondary."

He nodded. "I think he'll suit it."

"I think so too."

They waited, bated breath holding the space where forbidden wants surfaced. She could trace the curve of his cheek bone without touching him, just as she knew he would recognise the profile of her brow anywhere. Neither of them moved, neither of them breathed.

Then a horn sounded from the Credo, to the north and towards the forest that harboured the War Rooms. It was three short bursts, followed by a long wail. Nicke knew the sound. It meant a slave had escaped and krypteia were being called to give chase.

An image of Zephyros and his irreverent grin momentarily

filled her mind until it was swept away by Lysander's swift touch. He'd reached for her and pulled her close, his mouth soft but demanding. She was surprised, shocked, shaken by the ease by which these actions could take place. He so easily touched her. Like it was allowed; like he needed to.

One hand trailed her lower back as the other ran through her hair, loosening the pins that held it. His tongue probed her mouth and she found herself opening for him. Tasting him, dreading him. Each part of her warred against the feelings he evoked and the need that rose within her. It was easy to deny him, to cast him off and out. It was harder to allow him. To permit herself this one thing. Just one thing.

So she savoured his tongue with hers as he brought her behind the cloth draped along the walls of the room. Hung from the ceiling to dry, they effectively blocked the door while the horn howled outside, attracting curious eyes and deafening intrusive ears. Her back found the stone wall, cold under her peplos, and she gasped at the shivers.

He paused just long enough to look at her. He peered into her eyes, seeming to memorise their shape, colour, intensity. Quietly, honestly, and without pretext, she brought her hand to the slope of his cheek and gently caressed the skin. It was rough with a day's growth. It was smooth with sun and air. It was warm like the summer. It was cold like the wind blowing. But it was him. He was all that was in front of her, and all she could ever need.

"Marry me," he whispered, leaning into her hand.

Her body shook as his grip tightened minutely in her hair, dreading the rejection.

Her common-law brother was her master. He was the one that held her mantle, her leash. If they were in Malptia, and she was safe from an unforgiving Laerta, it would be her mother's position. The one that could say no. The one that could say yes.

But here, in the country where they found themselves and each other, her keeper was her brother.

And her brother was a king.

No one can gainsay a king.

Lyon would do worse than have him killed. He would make sure Lysander's soul never rested.

Nicke didn't think of any of that as his eyes searched hers for hope; for release from the fear that dogged him and the brutality that followed her.

But Nicke did the only sensible thing.

She shook her head.

Lysander's breath caught before he kissed her again, this time with wild abandon. The tips of his fingers dug into her flesh, demanding purchase. Again, again and again he sought her skin until the ties that held her peplos together gave way. Briefly, sweetly, his hand caressed her lower back and warmed her skin.

"If you don't want to marry me—"

Nicke squeaked in response, denying the charge. Of course she would marry him. Of course she would revel in his touch and deny every single other aspect of her life if it meant he could unashamedly stand in front of her. Without fear. Without retribution.

"I want to marry you," she whispered, hands running down the sides of his face. His eyes glistened. "But I think you've forgotten that my keeper is a specific kind of bastard."

"Oh, no," he said, voice lilting. "I thought of that, and decided that I just don't care."

She couldn't help it. She grinned at him and pushed her fingers up and through his hair. His eyes closed slowly, enjoying the feeling of free touch.

He'd asked her before. Once. When the moon was full and a bonfire and the drunk masked their conversation. He'd even dared to touch her, then, too. A light feather across the back of her hand. It was the only thing grounding her to this place, to this life. A small touch in a too-large world.

"Then what exactly do you suggest?" she whispered. The horn was still blowing, the distraction elsewhere.

He pulled back, his hand catching hers and kissing each fingertip; each knuckle.

"We go somewhere into the countryside, where no one knows us, and we marry. We keep it a secret until we can speak its truth."

"It wouldn't be as difficult as all that." His eyebrow quirked in question, so she continued. "Well, what are the central needs for marriage?"

He bit his lip, thinking. "We need to be before a Master of Trade who commits the rituals of our joining to the earth. You need to be taken to my house, a prize stolen from your father." She huffed a laugh, but he continued. "Then we hide until that joining is complete." As she smiled, he shook his head. "Doing it outside of the city would be easier. But I need it to be soon."

"And when would that be?" she replied, sardonically.

He kissed the tip of her nose.

"I don't know. But I'd prefer to go to sleep at night knowing you're mine."

"I've always been yours."

His smile blinded her. His mouth wasn't overly large for his face, but when he smiled it was all she could see.

Surely he didn't doubt it. How could he? Every one of her thoughts, her fears, her desires were filled with him.

She hadn't forgotten the hand that ruled her, and neither had he. It was a liminal space, a fantasy land where they could abscond and no one would know her as Malptia's Rose, and no one would know him as the man that loved her.

He was still smiling and she kissed along his jaw, planting her mark.

But then a rushing and a yelling began from inside the Temple compound, and Lysander's instincts drove him to draw his sword and pull Nicke behind him. His hands wound around her lower back as his feet widened to best address the threat.

The horn had stopped, and the braying was vaguely familiar. It was a boisterous, almost short tempered sea shanty that stretched from across the Temple. A lone baritone was singing, half yelling still.

Oh the run and chase
Let us move quick'r pace
They hunt the men running
Enslave the w'men cunning
And work their slaves to their back!

Lysander relaxed, his arm dropping from around Nicke's waist. Then he sheathed his sword and turned to her quickly, desperately bringing her to him. His strength always surprised her. It gave her hope that a king's sword wasn't designed for his neck. Like he would snap the blade before it could take him. His mouth seared hers before Lysander quickly let her go and walked out of the building.

Nicke didn't watch him go. She knew what the kiss meant.

It was a promise. One she didn't know if she could keep.

The singing continued while she stayed hidden, until it suddenly stopped and was replaced by laughter.

"Nicke?" Sophia's voice called, echoing around the space.

Nicke took a breath, and left the confines of her hiding spot.

Sophia smiled at her. "Oh good," she said. "I was worried you'd jumped out the window or something."

"Why would I do that?" Nicke asked earnestly.

Sophia shrugged. "My brother ran out of here like a bat out of hell. He must have heard Zeph singing."

Nicke suppressed a grin. "It was Zephyros singing?"

Sophia rolled her eyes. "My new brother has found a talent for theatre, it turns out. He disappeared, then suddenly he's at the foot of the Temple in his new chiton, proud as punch, and singing a damned Kyptian Navy song! Almost got himself killed. If Matt hadn't have vouched for who he was, he might have been."

It didn't take much for Nicke's mind to turn.

"Matt went to Zephyros?"

"Yes, attention seeking git." Sophia turned to her, face flushed. "You best head home, Nicke. It looks like it's going to storm. But wait." She leant over and gently tied the sash from Nicke's peplos. It didn't require touch, but the movement made Nicke erupt in goosebumps for fear. "There," Sophia whispered. "Couldn't send you home half dressed, could we?"

CHAPTER FOUR

Zephyros

"You're a damned fool," Lysander laughed as they walked the road towards the Credo. "An absolute madman."

"I'm sure I don't know what you mean," Zeph replied, tilting his face to the sun. The afternoon was turning cool, as it had the day before. It was like the midday meal chased all warmth away.

"Matthew almost speared you in the throat to stop your racket."

"Did you have fun at least?" Zeph asked, putting his hands behind his back.

"Yes, I suppose I *had fun*." Lysander huffed out a breath. Zeph didn't know him very well yet, but could hear his frustration.

"Good."

His wrists still smarted from the chains, and a morning's kindness wasn't enough to lull him into a sense of safety. Especially since he knew what awaited him at the Credo.

Reminders of his submission.

Assurances of his station.

Just generally a really bad time.

But Sophia had set him up with clothing worthy of a Laertan soldier, including cutting his hair and tying it half up and out of his eyes. A dark green cloak that complimented his colouring was a gift, she said, one she'd intended for Kallias but he'd rejected because the hue didn't suit him. It helped somewhat; a reminder. He was a slave, but a striving slave. The falsity of the security it feigned was like a well worn joke.

He still didn't trust it. Or them.

They walked until the Credo loomed above, twice the height of the Temple and bricked in with walls five men high and one man wide. The Credo could be distinguished from the Temple's architecture simply by the nature of how the compound was collected. The Temple had many smaller buildings dotted around a main, like most learning institutions, but in a way that was difficult to defend. The Credo, however, was collected around a centre point, for obvious reasons.

A phalanx trained on the only field, with their grunts and hums in line with the coordinated thrust of their golden spears. They wore full armour, complete with metallic helmets that obscured their faces and maroon cloaks on their backs. Next to them stood a tall man with black hair, his own helmet in his hands. He watched them carefully, likely cataloguing their strengths, weaknesses and improvements. If he was of Kurkia, the words would be curt and overwhelmingly unhelpful since that was how that city bore their military.

Or, perhaps, that was why it took Zephyros seven years before seeing progression despite his intensive strategy training as a child. He was not a man who liked being told what to do, and Kurkia despaired of him.

Zeph and Lysander walked through a corridor of olive trees that blocked the glare of the sun from the gravelled ground. It led straight to the wide wooden doors of the Credo, two guards dressed in gold and maroon standing at the front.

"Lysander, you've inherited another pet, I see?" one said, looking down his nose at Zeph.

Or, at least trying to. Zeph was taller than him. It was something he was noticing now he was on his second day. He was taller than everyone he encountered.

"Inherited is such a... disagreeable choice of term," Lysander said smoothly. "I prefer 'acquired', or 'bought'. Or even, 'stole'. Is Sophos in attendance, Rion?"

The one called Rion nodded, still looking warily at Zeph.

"Then he is expecting me."

Lysander moved to walk past the guards, but they held their ground. Zeph's muscles primed, readying for a fight.

"The king knows what you're doing, slave," Rion said quietly. "The more you bring in, the more obvious it gets."

"What becomes obvious?" Lysander barked. "Say it."

"She's only good for one more war, anyway," Rion continued. "Her tactics will become known by our enemies and be useless after that. And then..." He made a slicing motion across his throat.

Why he was trying to provoke Lysander was anyone's guess. Zeph had seen him fight and knew he was exceptional. Perhaps Nicke was an easy target, and Lysander couldn't openly challenge in case it risked her. But that wouldn't have held Zeph back.

Then Lysander did something that surprised Zeph; something he would think back on as an old man, and wonder whether the action changed the course they were sailing on.

He elbowed past the threat to the woman he loved. He ignored Rion and walked into the cool, marble halls of the Credo, letting the danger hang in the air and remain there, stagnant; poisoning.

Zeph would never understand that for as long as he lived. If Lysander had challenged, openly disparaging the city that held his love in such low esteem, and called Rion out for his acceptance of brutality, later events may not have transpired.

Zeph had little time to dwell as the corridor opened up into a gymnasium filled with light. The room was circular and tiled with terracotta underfoot and white marble on the walls. In stark contrast to the multi-building compound of the Temple, the Credo boasted a clear view of the heavens through open ceiling panelling.

Draped green and blue cloth covered resting surfaces, with some Laertans sitting and waiting their turn to be called into the doors lining the outside of the hall. It was warm, despite the outside chill.

Lysander led Zeph to a bench on the western wall, the warmest part of the room. He sat and tilted his head back against the marble, eyes closed and brooding. Zeph watched him only for a moment before tearing his eyes towards the other people in the room. Men, mostly, with chitons in all colours except red. Some eyed him, others ignored him. Many had weapons in their hands, others had scrolls or nothing at all.

After considering his new countrymen, Zeph's eyes trailed higher, to the frieze. The artwork in Kurkia was usually on canvas and only enjoyed by the most wealthy. His uncle had had friends whose houses were adorned with the painted intentions of talented men, but he had never partaken himself. Their house was bare.

The frieze featured war. The faces were grimacing, the swords blood-adorned, the feet trampling foes. Each figure wore a gold cuirass with a short red cape. Zeph presumed that they told the stories of wars past: of hoplites killed or injured and returned as something else. But what stoked his curiosity was the eyes. The figures of the frieze were all painted to have green eyes, a colour that was unusual in this part of the world. His brow furrowed.

"Demetria has green eyes," he whispered to himself.

"Very astute," Lysander replied, deadpan.

"No one else I've met has green eyes."

"You have green eyes?"

"Ah huh."

"That makes two of you."

Zeph thinned his mouth. "Why does everyone in the frieze have green eyes?"

Lysander sighed and squinted up at the artwork. "You can't really tell from here."

"Yes I can."

"No you can't. A man with twice your vision couldn't see that far away."

"Let's get closer then."

"Zephyros," Lysander huffed, frustrated. "Who cares?"

Zeph slumped down. "I was just curious, that's all."

"Yeah, well. Be curious some other day."

Zeph folded his legs under him as they sat on the bench, waiting. His mind turned quickly, watching those about them and the processes he might have to endure. He couldn't think of what would be required of him other than possible questions and maybe a show of his strategic thinking. He couldn't reveal too much, he knew, but some kind of vindication that slavery was an ill-fitting curse would suit him. As they'd trawled through Sophia's house, Lysander had mentioned that Sophos was one of the generals, alongside Nicke and Jonn, whom he hadn't met. Sophos would probably manage his education in the Credo, but he would be mentored by a senior Secondary, yet to be decided, and trained by Nicke in strategy and Jonn in the Phalanx.

"How did Nicke rise so high, given who she is?" Zeph asked, resting his chin on his balled fist.

Lysander sighed again. "She solved every problem they gave her."

"But how did she get educated? Surely she'd be a better prisoner without an education?"

"It was one of her sister's conditions, I believe," Lysander said, resignation in his voice. "She would become a banshee queen otherwise."

Zeph fell silent. Surely it wasn't a long bow to draw. The abuse he plied on the princess could be easily morphed to be inflicted on his queen.

A door opening drew both of their gazes as a large man with sandy hair and pale skin walked into the hall. He wore a silver chiton that washed out his complexion and held a scroll in his hands.

"Another one for me, do you Lysander?" he called.

Lysander stood and Zephyros followed him.

"They drop them at my doorstep. Who am I to say no?" Lysander replied, taking the man's forearm in greeting. "Zephyros, this is Sophos, leader of Laerta's military."

"Zephyros, is it?" Sophos said, taking Zeph's arm in a strong grip. Zeph smiled small, unsure and meek. As Sophos held him, he twisted his arm to reveal Zeph's palm, touching it lightly.

"No callouses here, boy," he remarked to Lysander. "What do you hope to gain from him?"

"Stimulating conversation," Zeph replied before Lysander could speak. "Perhaps I can cook fish, as well."

Sophos scoffed, but a smile graced his face.

"Come on," the general said. "Let's go somewhere less... open."

They followed him into an adjoining corridor, shutting out the noise of the hall, and walked further into the building. Zeph no longer looked at the walls: the art he'd so hungrily absorbed before. Rather, he watched the middle-aged man in front of him, and the slight weakness he had in his right side. He was limping, yes, but in a way that betrayed a problem with his knee and hip. Sophos was slightly swaying as he walked. Zeph tucked this information away, should he need it one day.

"In here," Sophos said, gesturing to a small room. He shut the wooden door behind them and took up a place in an old upholstered chair. The decor was forest green, with hints of dark wood and shelves and shelves of scrolls and books. Zeph suppressed a gasp as his head spun about the room. What he wouldn't give for unfettered access to a Laertan general's library.

Lysander sat comfortably in one of the other chairs and gestured at Zeph to do the same. Just as before, Zeph hesitated. He was still a slave, even if he was no longer dressed as one. His eyes trailed between the faux ease of his new brother, and the stiff back of the commander before landing squarely on the floor. Sophos began without giving any more heed.

"Papers?" he asked, his hand out. "Where did you find this one, eh?"

Lysander began rifling through his knapsack, searching. "Demetria sent him over. Thought he'd not survive the night in Lyon's house."

"Hmm, yes," Sophos answered as Lysander passed him the sheet of paper that seemed to follow Zeph everywhere. He peered down at it, holding it an arms-length from his eyes. "Kurdan. Captured by Kypt. Taken as a slave. Probably navy beforehand." Sophos's eyes ran through Zeph's life quickly and without fuss. When he was finished, he looked up and Zeph held his gaze.

"I'll bet that slavery doesn't suit you, does it, boy?" Sophos said.

Zeph spared a quick glance to Lysander who nodded encouragingly. Zeph was not yet in the throes of trust, but he chanced a bite at it.

"It does not," he said slowly and deliberately, like each word weighed on his tongue in the hope that it would be swallowed.

"What were you before the navy?" Sophos asked.

"A shipbuilder."

"Hmm, so good with numbers too I'll bet. How many leagues between Kurkia and Kypt?"

"Eighty-five," Zeph replied, unhesitating.

"How many mountain peaks between here and Kypt?"

"Thirty-eight."

"Could you climb them?"

"I could climb maybe half on my own; the rest with a friend."

"What was your commander's mistake that got you captured?"

Zeph paused then. Sophos wanted loyalty, and Zeph knew

that, but he probably also wanted to see where mistakes were possible within Kurkia's ranks. Zeph could tell him of the too-late pigeon, sent when the blood was already in the water. Or the way the wind drove them into a shallow cove so that arrows could pick them off, one-by-one. He could hear the screaming again: his men, his friends, the ones he'd sworn with his life to protect and had instead left behind in the wake of a Kypt vessel. He could tell Sophos of Gelos, his best friend from childhood who had become his lover and then become dead.

But it was more what Zeph couldn't say. How it was his mistake. It was his foolishness and hubris that had meant the rowers were not engaged when Kypt advanced. How, instead, the wind had driven them into shore and Zeph could only watch, helplessly, as his blue plume became scattered in the wind. They were his men. It was his mistake. He couldn't tell Sophos that, so, instead, he told him a half truth.

"We were directed into a neutral cove, and then set upon. The maps were wrong."

A half truth, but one that made the commander smile.

Lysander sensed the shift, and leant forward. "I thought Secondary?"

"I suppose it's the only place she isn't covered," Sophos replied, still looking at Zephyros.

"Except the War Rooms," Zeph supplied, voice strong and heavy, the fight that he so often buried rearing its head. It was impossible to quiet completely. Like an instinct, the words spilled out.

Sophos didn't break the stare, but instead thinned his mouth and stood. He came up to Zeph's shoulder, he still taller than any man yet met in this city. Then Sophos did something Zeph did not expect: he searched his features. His strong chin, his olive skin red with too much sun, his auburn hair that turned red when the light hit it. It was like he was looking at a past packaged and shoved down; like he was pinning Zeph's character through the slips of gold between the green.

"Your colour eyes are unusual in Laerta," Sophos whispered.

Zeph didn't answer, but continued to look into the general's brown eyes as he searched and searched and searched and seemingly came up empty. He leaned back with disappointment rolling off him.

"Yes, I think Secondary," he said, going back to the table and signing a piece of paper. He held it out and Lysander took it. "A word of advice, Zephyros?"

Zeph squared his shoulders.

"Stay away from the king. The general's maid is right: he may kill you on sight."

* * *

It was late afternoon by the time Zeph and Lysander left the Credo. The air was cool and the humidity had disappeared like a phantom.

"Usually in Kurkia, if it was humid in the afternoon, it rained that evening," he offered to Lysander.

Lysander nodded. "Laerta has been in drought so long that it can hardly be called so anymore. The records record weather similar to that which you describe. The city had to push further into Boornea's autonomy because the rains stayed away."

Zephyros sniffed the air and couldn't scent the telltale signs of storm. Frowning, he continued to follow Lysander along the city path until rolling hills surrounded them.

He'd been instructed by a lieutenant in the phalanx, and had his spearwork improved through grip and shoulder stance. He'd been given a kopis of his own to carry with him, as well as a navy cloak to denote his status as student.

"Don't worry," Lysander had said when Zeph had pointed out

the teenagers also wearing navy. "You won't be a pupil for long."

The sun dipped behind the mountains as they walked back to the farm, and the chill became overwhelming. Zephyros's mind was wiped clean by the sheer amount he had to remember, and Lysander was being equally quiet. So far, no axe had fallen; no rug had been pulled. It was almost as if Lysander intended on keeping his word.

"Can I have a look at your kopis?" Lysander asked suddenly, with a brightness in his tone.

Zeph eyed him suspiciously, but passed him the weapon. It gleamed in the twilight, though the handle needed waxing. Lysander was looking between it and the forest at Zeph's back when the world went dark.

He immediately reacted, fisting the thick canvas bag that had been pulled over his head and trying to wrench it away. It smelt like horses; like the sliver of trust he'd afforded had been blackened. He called out but found himself drowned out by the sound of running feet. He was lifted unceremoniously into the air and onto the shoulders of at least two people. Both were laughing, but it sounded like sniggering to Zeph's ears.

He writhed, thinking only the worst.

"Earth, he's heavy," said a not-unfamiliar voice.

"It's all the oats he ate this morning."

Zeph twisted, using his dropped shoulder to dislodge from the arms of one of them.

"Be quiet, Zephyros," they grunted. "And we won't drop you into the fire."

He stiffened then.

"I don't think carrying a board is much better."

"We're almost there."

Zeph ran through each scenario in his mind, each twist getting worse and worse until his mind built an image of them tending towards the cliffs and him being thrown into the river below.

After a five minute struggle, he was dropped, hard, onto a grassy patch. The canvas came away from his face and he blinked, trying to find his vision in the dark.

Instead of demons, he instead stared into the faces of his new siblings, though the difference was slight. The shadows played, and they were all smiling maniacally. Sophia shoved a cup into his hand.

"Drink up," she sang, giggling.

"Why would you do that?" Zeph huffed, ignoring the cup. "I could have murdered you!"

Lysander laughed, and passed him back his kopis. "I thought of that just before they came over the hill. I thought: 'bugger, all this careful planning is going to come to naught.'"

"Careful planning?" Zeph replied. He let the breath he'd been holding escape, the stress in his shoulders releasing slowly.

"C'mon, Zeph," Kallias said. "You didn't think we'd let your first night not-a-slave be a home affair, did you?"

They were all grinning at him like mad. Sophia still held the cup, brimming with wine. Kallias moved towards the centre of the clearing with flint and some kindling, a pack already beside a fire pit. Lysander busied himself with putting a grey cloak about his shoulders, his face alight with mischief.

"Where's Drakon?" Zeph asked, taking the cup from Sophia. He sniffed it, not that he would be able to sense poison in such a pungent aroma.

"He's seeing to some errands," Kallias replied. "No doubt he'll be back soon."

Zeph couldn't help it. He was swept up in their energy; their carefree benevolence. Suddenly, he was transported to a place where he didn't have to constantly shift his stance or words to seem smaller; milder; more agreeable. Kypt rewarded him for it; made him a fitting target and a worthy slave. But here, among the woods near his new brother's farm, perhaps he could be the man his uncle had raised. The part of him that had been beaten down with a sharp stick since his ship was sunk had already reared its determined head, and Zeph had allowed it. It wasn't the surety of misplaced and falsified arrogance: it was real, and true confidence.

He drank deeply from the wine.

Kallias started the fire and Lysander gestured Zeph to one of the logs along one side.

"You four come here often?" Zeph asked, gesturing at the woodpile.

"Usually in a different season," Sophia responded, pulling her cloak tighter. She poked at the fire as Kallias hissed at her to stop. She giggled, pleased with the effect.

"We're still on my lands," Lysander said as he began to prepare the food.

"How far do they extend?" Zephyros asked.

"To the blood creek. Over that it's city lands; the commons. Many a Laertan met my father's ire when they inadvertently poached his goats." He placed the meat of the aforementioned animal onto a searing pan and its loud crackling paused their conversation for a time.

Once it had quieted, Kallias relaxed back on his elbows. "Dannehs knocked the staff out of my hands today," he said proudly.

Lysander sent him a smile. "He's growing well."

"Alix thinks he'll be tall, not unusual in her family, of course," he continued. "Apparently his brother told him a particular tale of how yesterday happened."

"Of course he did," Sophie said with rolling eyes.

"Apparently our general deserved it for speaking out of turn," Kallias continued, ignoring his sister. "Apparently speaking out of turn enables such punishment."

Lysander growled. The conversation moved around Zeph like a river without a bank. He understood that they were discussing

Nicke, her bandaged arm that still sent a spike of malice through his blood, but the rest passed by his reckoning.

"Did you set him straight?" Sophie asked. "It's not the first time Kallum has shown his arse."

"Sophie..." Lysander admonished. "He's fifteen."

Sophia shrugged. "Many of us were once. In more dire circumstances."

Lysander hummed, and Zeph finished his wine and reached for another.

They drank in companionable conversation until Drakon appeared through the trees an hour later. The first thing he did was yell hello, the second thing was to accuse them of being drunk.

"We are not, how dare you!" Sophia laughed. Zeph joined in, her soprano joining with his baritone. The trees swayed with the melody.

Drakon lifted three now-empty wine skins. "You most certainly are. What if you were set upon?"

"Only a coward attacks drunks," Zeph offered, Kallias joining him by nodding. "And besides, this is private land."

"I guess I'll be the adult then," Drakon said. He sat down next to Lysander who, having finished cooking them the meal, had lain back to watch the stars.

"Leave them be, Drakon," he said. Zeph thought his words were spoken in contemplation; of not wanting to be disturbed lest his thoughts vanish. He had a gleam to his eye that had nothing to do with alcohol.

"Isn't this your wine?" Kallias asked Drakon, pointing to the empty bottles.

"Doesn't make it my fault," Drakon hissed back. Kallias just laughed in response.

"Zeph," Sophia said, sitting down cross-legged in front of him. "You owe us your life story."

"I absolutely do not," he said, sure of its truth even as the dread of the things he'd experienced reared just behind his tongue.

"Well, let me tell you that I was born in Boornea, and sold by my father to a pleasure house before being shipped here as a certain type of slave." Zeph's mouth had fallen open slightly, belying his surprise. She nodded, satisfied that she had now cornered him. A fact for a fact; a lie for a lie.

"I was born in Kurkia and raised by my uncle."

Sophia rolled her eyes. "We already knew that. Why did he sell you into slavery?"

"Oh, he didn't," Zeph corrected. "He died when I was fifteen. He had a heart attack."

"What shocked him into that?" Kallias asked, feeding the fire a log too big for it.

"I... ah. You know what, it doesn't matter."

"If it helps, Zeph," Lysander said as he sat up. "None of these fools will remember this in the morning."

Zeph looked over at him, and even through the fog of drink, he saw a hunger for knowledge forming in Lysander. Zeph wasn't safe, but he had taken the cup despite that.

"He had a heart attack when I told him I was joining the navy."

All their mouths opened, except for Lysander's. He already knew, of course. In his eyes, Zeph's loyalty had been tested and he'd been beguiled by sweets and honey into a new country's loyalty. But he may have underestimated Zeph and his iron morality.

Zeph would never be loyal to Laerta so long as that country held slaves by the throat and women on their knees. He wasn't loyal to Kypt for marrying girls to old men and killing them with raped births. He wasn't loyal to Kurkia for the finite heed they paid to feminine personhood and strict class structures. His mind flashed of dark hair, tied tightly, and wounds bound even tighter. A new mission was quickly forming in him. If he was brilliant at anything, it was bending men to his will. His loyalty to Laerta would be bought with Laertan change.

Zephyros swallowed, punching the treacherous thoughts down. "But I only joined the navy to follow Gelos, my best friend. He was leaving, so I did too. It wasn't what my uncle wanted."

"Screw what he wanted," Kallias declared. "It's your life."

"Hush," Sophia admonished.

"I thought it was too, then we were sunk and I became a slave. If my uncle had lived, the advent of my slavery probably would have killed him anyway. He hated slaves and refused to have them. Thought the world could do without them."

"Man after my own heart," Lysander drawled, eyes still on the heavens.

Zeph went silent, his own eyes looking to the stars. They were brighter here, somehow. Perhaps it was because they were away from the city. Perhaps it was because they wanted to shine brightly on Laerta, never defeated on land.

When Sophia, Kallias and Drakon were speaking of the next festival, and their plans within it, Zeph made his way over to Lysander and sat down.

"Something's eating you," Zeph asked, his feet tucked under his knees.

"You don't know me well enough yet to know that," Lysander replied. "Can't I just be relieved that today was easy, and that you are now where you're meant to be?"

"You could," Zeph said. "Or you could be truthful."

"A truth for a truth," Lysander proposed. "You tell me a truth, and I will tell you one."

"Okay, but it has to be the one I asked for."

Lysander smirked at him, then nodded. He thought for a minute, pursuing the question through his mind.

"Are you going to run, eventually?"

Zeph smiled, small and knowing. "Eventually, yes. I will run.

Whether it's from here, or to somewhere else, I haven't decided yet. Your turn."

Lysander quirked a brow. "Just know that it's within my power as a krypteia to hunt you down and chain you to my well-pump."

Zeph smirked at him. "If you can catch me, that is."

Lysander returned the smile, then lowered his eyes and began to draw figures in the dirt at his feet. "She said yes to me today."

"Nicke?"

He nodded. "She's going to marry me, or wants to, at least. Preferably before this war begins."

"There will be consequences for her."

Lysander nodded. "But, as my wife, she'll be part of my household and I can protect her. Laerta's laws are strong."

Zeph suppressed a snort. It didn't seem the place to laugh, when the air was full of truth and repelled by lies. But it was a farce. A joke. A hurrah. Marriage would not stop a king from his due, when a war brewed in the north and that husband was just a soldier. Laerta was their war.

Zeph could see it play out before him, the sight coming easily as it had when he was a child. A push to a wall, a flailing spear, a cold note in his hand to mark the death of his brother on a field far away. He pushed the vision back, discounting it and giving it no power, but it forced its way into his mind's eye easily and the result was a flare of silver tears on a brown face, skin bruised and bloody from blows not yet marked. He knew what it meant. But, as it usually was, they were already hurtling towards that reality.

The silence filled the space between them, getting lighter as the words they'd spoken floated away.

"I feel guilty," Zeph said after a time.

Lysander smiled at him. "Why?"

"Because if it does turn to war, then I started it."

"What?" Lysander gasped. It drew the eyes of the other three, waking Kallias from a stupor.

"I... look, do you promise not to tell?"

"Depending on how funny the story is, I might."

"Okay fine. It was a neutral bay, we were anchored. Kypt was about three leagues out to sea. We were instructed not to engage, but a lone Kypt ship began offensives. We responded with arrows, but our rowers weren't able to get to their positions quickly and we were sitting ducks. My ship was sunk, with me being pulled from the water and then sold into slavery. The rest of my men drowned. Including Gelos. Kypt claimed we were the aggressor, and made the final push to retake Kurkia."

Lysander's jaw had slackened as Zeph spoke. Zeph watched his eyes go from shock to dismay. He waited for the judgement, for the knowledge that it was his shoulders' burden. But, instead, Lysander gripped his upper arm and whispered his apology and an assurance that it wasn't his fault.

"I don't want your pity," Zeph said, shrugging him off. He stood to his feet, unshaken by the wine, and bid them goodnight.

"There's a bedroll for you here," Drakon called after him, but he waved them off, needing time to be alone and to think.

Zephyros made his way down the hill towards the sound of rushing water. He figured it would clear his head and should he walk south, he'd come to the farmhouse.

The water was cool on his feet, like a balm. He didn't know why he opened himself to Lysander. He knew almost nothing about the man. Except for his general mercy and intricate plans, he was a stranger. And Zeph was simply a cog that kept the wheels of safety turning. He was nothing more, and if he proved himself incapable of protecting that which was most precious to Lysander, he'd probably find himself cut adrift. No anchor other than his own self and the knowledge he held of the world.

Sit straight, do not be cowed, his uncle had repeated ad nauseum. To a boy who was taller than the rest, stronger than the rest, quicker than the rest. With his training in the spear and the kopis, Zeph thought his education well rounded, until the Kurdan Navy taught him otherwise.

He still missed Gelos. His best friend, and his first lover, but he wasn't really Zeph's to lose. The rank had gotten between them. Why Zeph had mentioned him was beyond reason. It was many years ago now that his blood had stained the sea, but he could still hear the thud of the arrow that had ended his life, and could still see the light of his eyes as he was thrown overboard. He'd been beautiful, and now he was gone.

Zeph walked further into the river. It grounded him in space and time when his mind wanted to wander. He couldn't allow it. It was always so difficult to get back from that place.

He rounded a bend and looked up at the house, braziers on the front porch empty of fire. The wind had picked up since he'd left the camp, and he bundled his navy cloak around him to ward off the chill as he approached his new home.

A figure, small, almost unnoticed, flitted across the verandah. He could barely hear the tapping on the doors and window shutters, but he could sense the desperation in her voice as he approached. It was a woman, yes, and she was simply dressed, without a cloak.

Ice froze his veins as he recognised her gait like he could recognise his own. He picked up his speed, yelling for her as she turned to the woods.

"What's wrong?" he called, trying not to frighten her.

With no torches, and only very small moonlight, he couldn't see her face until he was upon her. It was then that he saw the grim line to her mouth, the sweat framing her brow, and the tears in her eyes.

"Demetria?" he said, gaze wide. "What's wrong?"

"Zephyros," she replied, shock and fear in her voice. "Oh thank the earth. Where's Lysander?"

"In the forest with the rest of them." He gestured behind the house.

"She's ill."

"Who's ill?"

"Nicke," Demetria gasped, like it was obvious. On reflection, it probably was and they were wasting time. "She needs Lysander."

"I don't know where they are," he bayed, gesticulating. "I was blindfolded."

She rolled her eyes, making Zeph's irritation skyrocket.

"Take me to her, I can bring her here."

Demetria laughed right in his face. "I thought you were smart."

He grimaced, trying to calm down. "I *am* smart, busy-body."

She groaned at him, her green gaze bright with aggression. He began to laugh at the ridiculousness of it all. Later, he thought, he'd ask her about her eyes, and why they were the only ones with eyes to match the frieze.

"Take me to her," he demanded, authority overwhelming him.

She studied him, seeming to weigh up their chances. "She's in a bad way. I worry that she'll…" She paused and shuddered. "I think she would prefer Lysander."

"Of course she would. Once we move her to this house, we will go and find him."

"She's in the queen's rooms."

"Then we move her here. I don't understand the problem."

"Because she's not married to you! Or Lysander! She needs to be with her kin. Lysander needs to go to her."

"Then play chaperone, Demetria. But if she's in as bad a way as you're suggesting, we need to go to her quickly, yes?"

"Yes!"

"Then, by all means." He gestured towards the road, inviting her to take the lead. She acquiesced, grumbling under her breath. He ignored it and followed at a run. She began to shiver when they were on the main road and he took off his cloak and passed it to her, he still warm with drink.

They reached the city major and Demetria directed him to the outdoor kitchen of the king's residence while she went inside. It was where she had processed him, deemed him unfit for the king's house, and shipped him to a place where he'd be useful. It had been a weird afternoon. She would barely look at him.

Demetria returned, a bundle of cloths in her arms. "She's in the queen's bed," she said. "Come."

Zeph followed her through the house, keeping his heels off the floor so as to not disturb the quiet. It was dead, like a switch had been flicked. He entered the queen's rooms to find it outfitted very differently to the rest of the house. His eyes flew around them, first registering a woman who could only be the queen, plus a younger child just entering adolescence.

"Who are you?" the queen asked, her tone sharp and accusing.

"My name is Zephyros, lady. I am here to take Nicke to Lysander's."

The queen looked at Demetria, assessing; judging. "You think he can help her? No one can help her."

Zeph looked away from the queen towards the bed, a sunken mass in the middle of it. White sheets were darkened by vomit, her hair an almost black halo around her head. He approached her and, gaze turning to Demetria for guidance and receiving it, he placed his palm on her forehead. It was hot, burning, and Zeph almost recoiled. "What happened?"

Demetria replied: "An asp. We think it was meant for the queen."

The boy standing with his mother gasped, this information new to him.

"Slipped into her bed?" Zeph asked. Demetria nodded.

"If we take her to Lysander's, we can look after her."

"Why not leave her here?" the queen shrilled. "She's my sister."

"Zephyros is an expert in these things," Demetria said gently. Zeph almost scoffed, but held it inside. In his mind, their path of action was decided, but of course they would have to convince the queen. The king, too, if he was here. Zeph quietly thanked the gods that he was absent.

"Then he can work his knowledge here," the queen said.

"Alix, we need to take her," Demetria said, her tone changed. No longer coddling, but firm and sure. Zeph moved towards the bed and picked Nicke up, her breath escaping in a groan. He tucked her head into his shoulder, and waited for assent from Demetria.

"And what happens when he finds her gone?" the queen asked. Fear laced her tone, and Zeph instinctively glanced at her upper arms, her neck, for bruises or scratches.

"She will be back when she's been tended to," Demetria assured. "I will stay with her."

"If it saves her life, ma, we should let her go," the boy said, his voice only a little wobbly.

Alix squared her shoulders, and nodded. Zeph didn't hesitate before leaving the room with his charge embedded in his arms. She was lighter than she looked, like her bones were of a bird. They stole into the night before the king could see them, follow them, find them. His wrath would be great, but not greater than the danger Nicke was already in. Zeph could feel her quick heartbeat, her sweat-ridden skin, her cold hands.

"And when she dies?" he asked as they half-ran to the farmhouse. "I am no expert in venoms."

"The queen doesn't know that," Demetria said simply.

* * *

"It is suspicious," Lysander said, his feet curled under his legs as he perched on a trunk in the corner of the bedroom. Ready to pounce, he reminded Zeph of a mountain lion.

"No shit," Drakon replied. "Why was she in the queen's bed?"

he asked Demetria.

She shrugged. "Nicke's sheets weren't dry and the queen was out. Nicke often slips into Alix's bed when she's feeling down."

Lysander's brow developed a deep line. "Feeling down?"

Demetria shrugged again and her gaze turned to the lightly breathing woman in the bed. "She's feeling more trapped than normal, I think."

Sophia and Kallias joined them then, bearing food and water. It was just before sunrise and the mountain was starting to sing its morning song.

Drakon continued his questioning; it wasn't yet an interrogation. "Who had access to the queen's bedchamber?"

Demetria sent a pointed look in Kallias's direction, before answering. Zeph missed the second part of the exchange, but Demetria must have received the information she needed.

"Me and Kallias," she said. "And Dannehs, and Alix herself. It could always have gotten in there itself. Snakes sometimes do that."

Sophia shivered, pulling her cloak closer around her. She pressed her arms into her chest and tucked her knees up, becoming a small ball. Zeph wondered why. Nicke wasn't in danger of dying, she'd passed the worst of it now, but Sophia acted as if this had been a physical blow.

Drakon sent a worried eye to Sophia before rounding on Kallias.

"Were you there earlier today?"

Kallias shrugged. "I'm there everyday."

There was resentment there, deep and driving. Zeph didn't know if it was directed towards Lysander or another yet unnamed source.

"But no," Kallias continued, sitting back in his chair and crossing his arms. "I didn't see anyone place the snake."

It was quiet for a moment while everyone's gaze was drawn to

Nicke's small whimper. Her forehead was still shining with sweat, and her heartbeat was too fast, but she'd been able to take down some food and drink.

"You really think it was sent on purpose?" Zeph asked.

Drakon nodded. "It's a classic. Excused as an accident," he nodded to Demetria, "but usually deadly."

"To Laertans," Zeph said. "Snakes are deadlier in Malptia. The asp may be docile compared to what her blood was bred for."

Lysander sat up a bit straighter then. Like he was given hope in a desolate wasteland.

Drakon drew the bridge of his nose into a pinch of his fingers. "It doesn't matter. It didn't work, something else might."

Zeph suddenly felt exposed. He'd thought Lysander's request to protect Nicke to be an easy thing. She lived well enough; looked healthy enough. But as his gaze travelled between Lysander's tension and Nicke's sleeping form, he felt like he was standing atop a high precipice. Like the world simply needed to tilt, and he'd go tumbling to one side.

CHAPTER FIVE

Nicke

Nicke wished she was unconscious. She wished that she could feel something other than the fire drenching her veins. Every action was coarse, every whimper was strained. Vaguely, quietly, she heard voices and felt warm hands about her leg. Often enough, they gave her broth and water, but nothing stopped the burn except sleep. Elusive, illusory, sleep. Like she could rest; like she could call back the blankness of mind and revel in its depth until her fingers could move or her eyes could open. No, it was false. And a cruel falsity, at that.

So she sank, quietly, into the agony of burning.

* * *

Gentle snores broke the air first, followed slowly by birdsong and the sound of running water. Snuffles, grunts, shuffling: the noises of people moving in sleep lulled Nicke from hers. It was a comfort, like the mundane of mortality was singing, finally, the song of blissful life.

But then the drop. Her stomach swooped in a way that her mind wanted to forget and she was hastily handed a bowl before she vomited.

"There you go," Demetria said soothingly as she drew Nicke's hair behind her head and gently rubbed her back. "Get it out, love."

She did as instructed and Demetria took the bowl away. Nicke opened her eyes to dazzling light; a marked change to how she usually woke.

"Where am I?" she attempted to say. It was grizzly, and difficult. Demetria shushed her.

"You're at Lysander's," she said gently. She shushed again when Nicke almost jumped up from the bed, startled. "You were bitten by a snake. We agreed that you'd recover here."

Her mind turned sluggishly. The pain receded but her muscles were stiff to move.

"Who agreed?" Nicke said without her signature sharpness. She wasn't safer here; the time spent in this bed may be her undoing.

Demetria hummed, avoiding the question, and Nicke could guess why, even in her weakened state. She couldn't imagine a situation where Lysander or his circle of protection would endanger her so, leaving only few options.

"I think I'm going to ban you from making decisions with Zephyros," Nicke said. Her voice was still difficult to discern, but Demetria's small laugh meant her words hit their mark.

"Alix knew, and let you go. Turns out Zephyros is versed in snake venom."

"Is that the rumour you'll spread, is it?" Nicke said tartly.

"It is already done. Now, I'll be back with some broth and Lysander. He's been at the War Rooms all day and is very frazzled."

Nicke watched her go and sank further into the blankets. They were soft, blue, like a spring flower just after a cooling rain.

A light huff originated from a deep chair in the corner of the room. Zephyros was watching her closely, his eyes red from what was presumably only a short nap. If she knew him better, she'd confidently guess that there was anger brewing beneath his brows, but, as it were, she simply wondered so.

"You brought me here?" she asked him when their stare down had become too intense for words not to break it.

"I did," he replied. His limbs unfurled slowly, like they'd been curled too long. "Do you remember anything of the incident?"

Nicke gently shook her head, blood quickly rushing to it. "I fell asleep in the queen's bed with Dannehs. Is he okay?"

"The boy?" When Nicke nodded, "Yes, he's okay. Looked a bit shaken."

Once her larger fear was abated, she let her smaller one shine. "Why am I here?"

He indulged in an arrogant shrug. "You were dying, Nicke. What would you have had us do? Prevent my new brother from seeing you off?"

Nicke's temper was inflamed by his ease. He spoke as if it was a given that her place was here, in this stone house, and that dignity in death, surrounded by loved ones, was her fate. It wasn't, but she was too tired to set the record straight.

He continued, taking her silence as agreement. "You're safer here than there."

"No, I'm not. And that you think so is key to your misunderstanding. Lysander never should have agreed to it."

Zephyros laughed, his mirth filling the space. Not for the first time, she felt it spread heat through her blood.

"We took the decision out of his hands."

At that, Lysander entered the room and the air felt still. First, her eyes caught his, the deep blue resonating into her soul and urging it calm. Then, she drew a breath that sounded too close to a sob to be mistaken. She knew he was dirty from the road and likely smelled sweetly of sweat, with his hair matted by wind and his actions singularly purposive. She was stuck, unable to breathe lest her world lose itself to a howling wind. He obviously thought differently, because his pause was short and frustrated at the distance between them. He crossed the floor and sat on the bed which Nicke was only just realising was his. Closer, her stare began to track the evidence of his stress: hollow eyes, a two-day-old scruff, and a gauntness that spoke to dehydration. The day wasn't hot, but she felt suddenly heated by his close proximity.

"Zephyros said I was bitten by a snake," she whispered.

Lysander nodded. "An asp. Drakon is taking the measure of it." His hand drifted to her face, and waited, as always, for her assent to touch. She scoffed: they were well past that now. He pushed her hair behind her ear and rested his hand on her lap. "How are you feeling?"

Her mouth was sandy, her ears were ringing, and she needed water. But, otherwise, "fine," she said. Demetria entered then, a bowl in her hands. Nicke took it gratefully and began to eat, calming her roiling gut.

"What time is it?" she asked.

"Afternoon. You've been asleep all day."

She looked around the room, noting the mess it was in. Blankets were strewn, mugs were scattered, and the evidence of invigilation surrounded the bed. Zephyros and Demetria were gone, so her gaze turned back to Lysander.

"Someone tried to kill me."

He took a breath even though he must have been aware of the possibility. "It may have been an accident."

She shook her head, the air still pregnant to bursting with tension. Nicke's movements were slow, measured, as she pushed the blankets away from her waist and rose to her knees. Even though her muscles were weak, her wrist was painful, and her head swam, she edged towards him on an unyielding pull. It was an easy thing, in a house that had only shown her what life could be like without the fear that permeated everything else. He watched her come, eyes wide and needing.

"My brothers are guarding the house," he said gently.

"Good," was all she said before she kissed him. It was unhurried, unlike their last one. It was neither a promise, nor retribution against those that sought them ill. It just was; it was just what could be.

There were laws in Laerta, Nicke thought quietly as his tongue gently probed hers. Laws designed to protect, to assure, to prove the might of their military and the providence of their children. Women could usually choose their suitors and their husbands, with fathers and mothers simply being the bind on a contract that could not be made without family approval. All else equal, Alix would have been the seal on Nicke's marriage in their parents' absence. As it was, Lyon was the one standing between her and happiness. No one could gainsay a king.

The king only brutalised her because it was within his power. She was in his household and his power was state-sanctioned; state approved; state encouraged. So movement away from him, his house, could prove the value of her safety. When she married, she would move to a different household. One with love, and kindness, and trust, and children. It would mean she never had to be under his power again.

Lysander broke the kiss and looked at her through hooded eyes. "You want to say something," he mused, smiling wryly.

"I would be happy here, with you, in this house."

His smile widened, losing its mocking, and made the scar across his nose stretch.

"When you marry me, you will be."

She rested her forehead against his chest and he circled his arm around her waist. Tenderly, he picked up her still-bandaged arm and kissed it. "Does it still smart?"

She nodded. "The sharpness has dulled, but not abated."

He kissed her forehead, the action causing her to shiver.

They stayed like that for a while, just revelling in touch and each assuring the other of their presence. After a time, a knock sounded at the door and Sophia called for admittance. Lysander let her go and Nicke let herself out of his lap. She was still uncomfortable touching under the eyes of others. It would come with time.

When Sophia entered, she wore a look of resignation. Her actions were strictly controlled, like the afternoon's events were simply unbearable.

"Some clothes for you, my dear," she said, placing a pile on one of the trunks. "For day and night wear. Demetria went to retrieve some, but was barred." She chanced a glance at Nicke, looking her over. "I think a wash is in order."

"I'll see you soon," Lysander whispered, kissing her gently on the nose. When he'd gone, his feet almost bouncing down the stairs, Nicke turned her attention to Sophia. She began to swash soap around the tub, creating suds.

"Sophie...?"

"I've just had enough of this," she said, resigned and agitated. "First you're injured because you spoke the truth in a war room where that's meant to be rewarded, then you almost die from snake bite."

Nicke pondered for a moment, letting the words seep into the air.

Sophia sighed. "I'm sorry. It is just a lot."

"I know," Nicke said gently, swirling her fingers through the too-warm water.

Sophia had been under pressure recently, from her own Master role in the Trade. She still received disdain for her origins in slavery, and the type of enslavement she'd endured.

"And to know that Kallias could have been in danger too, it's just too much."

Nicke nodded. She understood. Kallias was by far Sophie's favourite brother; her best friend if they were honest about it.

Nicke's fear for Dannehs was similar.

"Do you think Kallias may have been the target?" Nicke asked.

Sophie shook her head. "I think the target was you, certainly. But he might have been collateral. The king is becoming more controlling of you and his family, and Kallias might be in the firing line too."

"Laertan queens are allowed to keep lovers once there is an heir," Nicke said.

"And Dannehs is his son, but that doesn't change a husband's possessiveness."

* * *

The letter came after she'd washed and dressed. Lysander came into the bedroom as Demetria twisted her hair into plaits.

"Lyon's sent for you," he said, throwing the letter to the floor. "He had the gall to threaten my brother with the sword for kidnapping!"

Demetria tugged Nicke's hair at Lysander's words, and Nicke felt a question rise within her, but quashed it to address the matter at hand. She looked at him calmly, expecting this as soon as she'd woken. He was often furious, though without an outlet for it. Fury gave an energy to this house; almost giving it life.

"I should have just left him there," Nicke said flippantly. "It would have saved time."

Lysander thinned his mouth.

"He's not going to kill him, Lysander. He's your household. The ephors wouldn't stand for it." She stood then, Demetria having finished. It was dark and the moon shone upon them, leaving the wilderness stained silver.

"Is the messenger still here?"

Lysander nodded. "Matthew. He won't leave without you, apparently. Sophia is with him."

"I'll speak to him."

She edged past him to enter the hallway. He reached out, his palm catching her cheek.

"I'm sorry, my love," he whispered. "I'm sorry I can not protect you from this."

She nodded gently.

Matthew was in the living room, sitting uncomfortably under the eyes of Kallias and Zephyros. Sophia was busying herself by slicing some bread and cheese.

"No, no, that's not the best way to gut a man," Zephyros said loudly, apparently to Kallias as Matthew sat between them. "You have to start from the bottom, on the left front."

Kallias shook his head. "No, on the right. It means he dies more slowly."

Sophia was giggling as she watched Matthew squirm.

"Nicke!" he said, standing quickly and striding towards her. Lysander growled, warning him off. Matthew wasn't frightened of Lysander, Nicke knew, but he still hesitated before speaking.

"You have to come back," he said.

"I am well now, and can return tonight."

Matthew shook his head. "You need to return now. He's in a temper."

"Then why would I let her go if that was the case?" Lysander snarled. Nicke felt his presence behind her like a wall of surety. He was sure of his life; his feelings; his place in the world. But he was wrong this time. He ran his protection racket, and she ran hers.

"It'll only get worse if I stay," Nicke admitted to him.

Matthew's shoulders relaxed and he nodded. Sophia rose from her place behind the table and gestured for him to wait outside, giving the family time to speak. She turned on the threshold, her eyes seeking out her eldest brother for guidance. Lysander nodded almost imperceptibly, and Sophia followed Matthew out.

"This is a bad idea," Zephyros started, but Lysander hushed

him sharply, wanting none of their voices to interfere. The noise was already too much, the white flashes of each interruption building to blind them. Nicke didn't want to delay.

Lysander took her chin gently and met her eyes. "You will be back soon. I expect no less than to be your husband. You will go tonight, but be back here, safe with us, soon. Yes?"

"Yes," she lied dutifully. He nodded, swallowing the falsehood, then his grip on her chin tightened and he kissed her softly. She didn't revel in it, the touch under watchful eyes new and as-yet unformed, and pulled away to see Lysander's gaze harden. He let her go reluctantly.

Nicke's spine grew stiff with the prospect of returning to her brother's house on this day: the day after she was almost killed in it.

* * *

She knew Lyon would be waiting in the receiving room, seated on one of his ornately carved wooden chairs. She dismissed Matthew at the door and was relieved when he went without question.

Kallum was standing at his father's elbow, likely watching the exact brutality that necessitated a king. His brown hair was swept back in the Laertan style, the ribbon that held it a blood red; the same as the cloak. His beads, jealously given by only his mother until he found himself married off, caught the light and told of his spoilt upbringing. He was a child who was rarely chastised and handled challenge poorly as a result. A small pin declared him heir, and it reflected the light of the braziers. He was following how his father worked, and Nicke felt like she was drowning in a rising tide. She fell to her knees on entry.

"Sister," Lyon crooned. "Are you well?"

Nicke nodded, her eyes downcast. "I was bitten by an asp, but a healer tended me and I am well."

Lyon stayed seated, but Kallum started. Was he not told of

why she was absent? Of how someone in this house likely sought out the bed she was in to slip a snake inside?

"A healer?" the king asked. "Which one?"

Nicke's throat was parched, and she swallowed down her large fear roughly.

"Zephyros."

"I don't know anyone named Zephyros." He turned to his son, question in his eyes.

"He was offered to the Credo as a Secondary, father," Kallum replied. His gaze darted to Nicke before he continued. "One of Lysander's."

Nicke's heart dropped but she did not falter in her submission. Her chin was lowered, and her eyes soft. Earnest. Plotting.

"If he is a healer, why was he recommended for Secondary?" Lyon asked, likely to the air. Nicke didn't answer. "No matter. What I wanted to know, dear Nicke, is why Matthew had to fetch you from Lysander's house, but I suppose that's answered now."

He rose from his position and swept out his red cloak. It dwarfed him, but Nicke would never tell him that. She was subdued here: her tongue tied to the fear he invoked. This was his house and she was his household.

Lyon approached her and gestured her to stand. She kept her chin down, but he lifted it, not dissimilar to how Lysander had just earlier in the evening. Their eyes could not have been more different. There was dark fury in the king's, the depths of fire reflected back. He was angry, yes, but there was something else: some notion of propriety. If anyone was to kill her, it would be him; if anything was to cause her blood to flow into the depths of the underworld, it would be his doing. The asp almost stole the opportunity from him, the one he'd bought and paid for on a Malptian field twenty years prior, and he was jealous of the power such a thing had over and beyond him.

She had wondered if the asp was him, but the absence of his

kingdom gift's power to make her burn for months had answered that question. Possession poured from his touch and her face began to smart in his harsh grip.

He turned her head sharply to the left and whispered along the shell of her ear. "Did Lysander take you, Nicke?"

Her shock almost pulled her completely from his hands but he held firm.

"Of—Of course not," she stammered. "Zephyros knows of venom, and that I am standing before you is testament."

"Hmm. Or maybe it was a ruse designed by one known for their strategy?"

He moved too fast, releasing her then hitting her squarely across the face. She stumbled to the ground, the stone meeting her hands and collapsing her weak wrist. She screamed in pain, the dull ache turning into a fierce throb as the break cracked through the room. Kallum moved towards her, but listened to his father's halting hand.

"You're not to see Lysander again," the king said gently. "Even in strategy, even in the War Rooms, even in the Credo. You're not to speak to him, hear him, or acknowledge his presence."

Nicke gasped but he continued.

"If I hear a whisper, a word alone, of your disloyalty in this matter, it won't be you I kill. First he will see his stupid brothers perish, in front of him if not because of him, and then his sister will follow a similar path. All he loves, dead, then his own head joining them."

The threat hung in the air, weeping.

A war was coming. It would be easy to do.

"Yes king," she whimpered, trying to hold in the sob.

"There," he whispered, running his clammy fingers over the back of her neck: the promise of her circadian nightmare made real. "That was easy, wasn't it?"

He left her there, in a puddle of fabric, on the floor of his receiving room.

It was then that Nicke's resolve sharpened. For some reason, she'd descended so far into the safety of Lysander's touch that she ended up feeling him solid and out of the leagues of danger. She'd thought only for herself, and the way Lyon would instil his power and control onto her.

But he was king, and she was no one. Her husband would be worth even less.

She was still polishing her will when Kallum approached. He was tall now; not as tall as his father, but tall still. He put out his hand and she took it.

"I was worried when Dannehs told me you were gone, but didn't tell me why," he said, eyes troubled. His voice was low and difficult to hear. He took her wrist and she took a breath through her teeth. "It may be broken," he said. "That's just what you need on the eve of war, isn't it?"

"Be wise, Kal," she said, grimacing through the pain. "I'm not worth angering your father over."

He tilted his head then, staring at her. Like he was weighing his options. "I am the heir, aunt."

He was sure of his place, and sure that the king would not mark him. But he was growing, and Lyon liked control.

Nicke simply nodded. "I will be at the Credo tomorrow for yours and Dannehs's strategy session, don't fret. But please go straight to your room now. I don't want to think of danger coming to you."

The boy nodded, and made his way down the corridor, away from her. She turned towards the women's side of the house, where hers and her sister's rooms were.

When she got there, she found a bowl of almost cold water, a mint numbing gel, and the sweet oblivion of sleep. Tomorrow would come, either way, and she would meet it when it did.

* * *

When Nicke was summoned to the War Rooms, she almost didn't attend. She almost hid the missive under her mother's carpet to forget the looming duty.

Because Lysander would be there, and she would have to ignore him.

It ached already.

But she made the walk to the forest, her cloak of Rex on her back and her wrist held lofty in a sling hidden under her clothes. Her determination had hardened in the darkened hours of night. She must protect Lysander. She had to forget about the stupid, childish romance she thought they had and focus on keeping him alive. It was the only way to bear it. Marriage was but a lofty cloud dispersed by harsh sun.

When Nicke attended the huts among the woods, she already knew it was for naught.

Lysander was krypteia. He'd left the Tertiary, where their generals were made and honed, into the Rex's protection. Foolishly, they'd hoped that he would be assigned close to her. Nicke was young at that point, only seventeen, but even then she knew that Lysander was a flame ignited in a darkened cave. He illuminated a life that she couldn't even dream of.

Krypteia do not go to war. They do not march, and they do not join the phalanx of hoplites protecting Laertan honour abroad. They stay in the city and protect the people, the crown, the homeland from incursion should an enemy's sights be set while the primary army is away. Lysander wore a cloak of grey to designate his place among the only Laertans the majesty could guarantee loyalty from.

When Nicke walked through the archway from jungle to compound, she absently sought his golden crown right away, but saw it through a haze of maroon. Because Lysander was wearing the old-blood colour of the general hoplite, and not the grey of a hidden blade.

She almost choked back a sob, but it escaped through her hands anyway. He looked at her sadly, leaning on his spear and surrounded by countrymen who shared a similar fate. Nicke didn't focus on anyone else, though if she had, she would have noticed the particular flavour of the new, numerous krypteia-turned-soldiers. They were her spies, mostly, who would be treading the field far away. But she didn't look; didn't see.

This was her brother's revenge. To send the man she loved to his death, clean and right, on the fields of Auntu. Dead by an Auntuan spear. She could see the blood seeping from his shoulder, and the red slipping from between his teeth. His eyes shifted their intensity when she met them. Turning from grim to resigned. He'd maybe made the same decision as she had in the darkest hours of night: to protect each other, they must stop their hearts.

"Nicke?" she heard from an older and friendly voice. "We're beginning."

She followed the voice into the chamber that held their maps and their markers. She saw none of it. Just his dark blue eyes, closed forever.

"Kypt will wait no longer. They have been further slighted by Auntu. They lost three ships in the Auntuan Sea, and Auntu enabled their colonies to break free of their hold. Kypt is going to war, and Laerta with them."

He was going to die, by her hand if by another. How could they have been so stupid. The sun was shining from them, even if they had tried to cover their blinding love.

"It is spring. Who does the sowing when it is needed?"

"Kypt has demanded speed."

"We need a way to breach their long wall. There's no point in taking the plains if they can access their port for supplies."

"And I bet they have their own war chest to work against exactly this kind of campaign."

His hair will be brown with the dirt of another nation, his bones not even permitted to be placed behind his carved name in the wall. Lyon will ensure she has nothing to mourn, no one to hold on to. It was already done: her gut knew it.

He wouldn't survive this.

"Nicke? Any ideas?"

Her thoughts were muddied and fraught, and she looked at Sophos like she was seeing him for the first time.

"I've already developed a plan for the wall, Sophos," she said. It involved an almost sacrificial distraction and a bevy of spears, but it would be effective. "Use that."

His mouth thinned, and she realised that the conversation had moved on. "Any ideas for what?" she sighed, keeping her mind away from the cold touch of death.

"About the troop movements towards Auntu?" Jonn said, frustrated with her. "Summer is harvest."

"The slaves and krypteia can stay to harvest," she said. "And the breeding women, as they usually do as well."

Sophos nodded, noting it down. "Should we call on Malptia?"

"No," Nicke said, at the same time as Jonn's "yes". This gave Sophos the final vote.

"Why no?" he asked.

"Malptia has ingratiated the Laertans that stayed and many of them consider it their home now. You would place such a question of loyalty among the soldiers of the march? And besides, Laerta has enough soldiers."

"No, she doesn't," Jonn grumbled. "Our numbers haven't recovered from the Boornean rebellion. And the numbers of the Trade and Theory have been increasing: useless at a time of war. It should be capped."

"So we travel along with people who hold us in no esteem, and hope that fear does not turn to violence? No. If we assist Kypt, it will be on Laertan terms. What do we owe them that we have not already paid?"

Jonn and Sophos exchanged a glance.

"What?" Nicke despaired. What had Lyon done?

"Kypt's Princess Princi will marry Kallum when he comes of age," Jonn said. "He didn't tell you?"

"No, he didn't tell me." That changed things markedly. Laerta would follow Kypt into the sea to hold onto this alliance, then. "I suppose involving Malptia shows good faith; shows that Kallum is supported in his proposed marriage by both of his parents. I'll write the missive to my father, in that case."

Both men relaxed.

They talked at length, until the sun in the sky trailed over to the western wall. They were not joined by their lieutenants, nor by their king, until their plan was worked. Nicke was fatigued by the end, and in pain in most places over her body.

"They need to be marching soon to fulfil Kypt's War terms."

"I need some time, Sophos," Jonn said. "We need new arms smithed at least."

"How long?"

"Three months? Maybe more?"

Sophos shook his head. "I can maybe give you three, but not more."

Jonn left them first, he the leader of the bloated Primary and with the most work to do in order for them to march. Sophos and Nicke stayed behind to work out rationing and timetables.

"Nicke?" he whispered, when she was shuffling through scrolls, creating enough noise to cover his words. "He forced Lysander from my krypteia. I'm sorry."

Nicke continued shifting the paper, her movements jagged and hard.

"But I will keep him with me in Auntu. Keep an eye on him."

Her tears were silent and tickled as they rolled down her face. It was hopeless.

"He's not your man anymore, Sophos. He's general army now, same as Kallias."

"It doesn't matter, pet. I'll bring them into my fold. This old dog has some tricks."

Nicke laughed quietly. It built tension in her, rather than dispelling it.

But as she walked home, she felt a coldness that fed her fear. Lysander was to march in three months. And he'd probably be dead in four.

When she entered the gate separating the forest from the garden, she heard Demetria and Sophia in the kitchen, speaking in low voices over the stove.

"I don't think it's wise. You barely know him."

"Yes, but he's sweet enough."

"Don't fall into the trap of thinking kindness is love. It isn't."

"What are you two talking about?"

Demetria didn't start, but Sophia swung around wildly. "Nicke! You're back! I've been waiting all day!"

"Why? What's the matter?"

Sophia looked beseechingly at Demetria, but the older woman didn't seem to want to make this easier on her.

"Lysa—"

Nicke shushed her violently. "Don't say his name," she breathed, almost silently. "The king has forbidden it."

Sophia pinkened and then hardened her eyes. "So that's why he was moved from krypteia then."

"Sophia, don't do that," Demetria snarled. "None of this is Nicke's fault."

"But it is," Nicke murmured. "Lyon threatened him only last night."

"No, Nicke, it is not. Sophia is just bursting with news and doesn't know better."

Sophia blushed further, but shook her head.

"They march by the end of next season," Nicke provided. "Speed is part of Kypt's war-terms."

"Yes, that's why I'm here." Sophia looked again for help from Demetria, but she continued to stir the stew.

"I'm getting married," Sophia said. Nicke's mouth dropped open, her breath caught.

"Who?" was all she could provide.

"Matthew."

"Matthew?!"

Sophia nodded. "He asked me this afternoon. He knew about the march, and said that he likes me, so we might as well."

Nicke's mouth gaped open and closed until she finally shut her teeth with only her iron will.

"And he really is a nice person, Nicke. You've seen that. He's considerate and actually quite funny and—"

"I don't have any objections to Matthew as a person, Sophie. But he's going to war. Doesn't this feel rushed?"

"That's what I said," Demetria interjected.

Sophia rolled her eyes. "Not all of us can have an epic childhood love, Nicke. Some of us just want to be out from their brothers' gaze and enjoy life in a partnership."

Nicke's mouth hung open again. She knew Sophia was simply being daft, but to think she pined for what she perceived Lysander and Nicke had. Nicke and Lysander couldn't touch in public. He couldn't even speak her name lest the sword fall.

Nicke shook her head. She wasn't going to make this the bed to sleep in tonight. Sophia was a dear friend, maybe her closest, and she needed to support her.

"Did you want me to attend you?" Nicke asked instead, shoving the anguish Sophie had caused down into her gut.

Sophia beamed. "Yes, please. As my main."

Nicke nodded, then smiled. A wedding might be just what they needed.

CHAPTER SIX

Zephyros

Zeph was navy at heart. He yearned for the spray of the sea and the call of the gulls more often than he wanted to admit. It was culture, this yearning.

Kypt had torn him from a world that was entirely his own; a world that had belonged to him just as he had belonged to it. Though his uncle had despaired of him, and had disowned him for his involvement, Zephyros had followed his friends into the mouth of the sea and all of the teeth it held.

He remembered, with no small fondness, the frenzy that decided the days following a call to arms. How the bronze smelting made toxic air; the waulking of a thousand weavers singing in tandem as sails were folded off their looms; the wood cracking under strain of human and beast both. Zephyros had managed his own ship and his own men to a refined precision of hours preceding a bout.

But it wasn't like this. He'd been in Laerta for little more than a season, and the city had been only quietly preparing for war in that time. Perhaps it was the difference between Kurkia's defensive nature and Laerta's aggression. Or, more likely, it simply spoke to Laerta's efficient prowess.

Spears being turned; kopia being sharpened; maroon cloaks darned, sewn, placed with the hoplites marching north. He knew that as little as a hundred slaves would probably not invoke such speed. Only three months ago they'd received the order to march, and they would be gone within the week.

He sat quietly among the soldiers, his navy contrasting with their maroon. It designated his other: he was not yet qualified to let Auntuan blood. Though his spearwork was now excellent, his phalanx training passable, and his speed eclipsing the norm, he would stay in Laerta to finish his education. He was frustrated by it, certainly, but all wasn't completely lost: his quiet ability to turn loyalties to his cause would benefit from him remaining in Laerta, even for only a little longer.

Lysander sat next to him, with Kallias on his other side and Drakon sitting opposite. Drakon quietly rolled tobacco while Lysander sharpened his second short sword, the one that sat on his right hip if he got into a tussle. Kallias had eased back onto his elbows, watching the crowd of people around him. Zeph watched too, but likely for a different reason.

His new brothers, the ones he'd been living with, striving with, sparring with and who were beginning to see his full self, were going to war without him. He couldn't help but think that if he'd tried harder, worked harder, become a better swordsman or not held back his acute knowledge of strategy, he could be going with them.

Kallias scoffed lightly, drawing Zephyros's attention.

"Look there," he said, pointing to the other side of the compound. Zeph saw the argument he meant: between two lieutenants who should know better than to come to blows in front of their subordinates. "Looks like Rion is unhappy with the expectation of walking."

Zeph grunted in acknowledgement. "It's a march, isn't it? Does he expect to be astride?"

"I suppose so," Kallias said. "Caitlin will put him to rights. He'll be walking like the rest of us."

Lysander paused a moment in his sharpening, then continued as if without interruption.

"Yes," he said. "Everyone marching north to their demise."

It felt like a slap to Zeph, even though he knew that Lysander was relieved that he would be staying. Someone had to keep up the farm, the holdings, the hope. Lysander's ire was for himself. For the maroon cloak that was swapped for his grey: for a king's word on the change.

When the news had come through, Lysander had accepted it quietly and knowingly. It was inevitable that he would lose the protection of being the city's last line and instead be put in a place where he would so easily die. There were always consequences, even if the actions themselves were right.

Zephyros, however, festered in the knowledge that it was one life for another. Nicke had been gravely ill in Alix's bed when Demetria and he had taken her to Lysander's house. Though Zeph was no expert on venoms, he did know a little of the aid he had to supply in order to keep her breathing and hydrated while her body fought. But she could have stayed and Zephyros could have tended to her at the king's house, Lyon's jealousy mooted.

Demetria had tried to set him straight on the idea, but he knew it was his fault. His hubris, assurance, and hatred of Nicke's position endangered his brother to the point of death. Lysander had only wanted safety for the woman he loved, and Zeph may have killed him for it.

"Rion deserves to walk," Zephyros offered into the silence. "I don't like him."

"I don't think you actually like anyone, Zeph," Drakon laughed, putting the cigarette into his mouth.

"I do so," Zeph retorted. "I like you."

Drakon laughed again, and Lysander's lips curled in an appropriation of a smile.

"And I like Sophie, and Demetria, and Nicke. I like Sophos."

"Wow, a whole seven people," Lysander joined in.

Zeph worked his mouth, thinking. "I like Matthew."

"You have to like Matthew if he's marrying your sister," Lysander replied. "It's one of the rules. And besides, he didn't ask for a dowry and has offered her every comfort. It would have been wrong to stand between their happiness."

"I would have paid to be a fly on the wall during that conversation," Zeph murmured. Watching Matthew squirm under the eye of Sophie's most senior brother as he discussed for her hand would have been theatre. Not that it was within Lysander's rights to decline him: Sophie hadn't known the offer was coming, and Matthew had needed Lysander's help to make it special for her.

"I like how he isn't afraid of us," Kallias said. "Though I don't love how quickly they're rushing into this."

"It's war. He'll be marching with us. You can't begrudge her for wanting to marry quickly. And I think most people would be afraid of the queen's lover," Drakon said sardonically.

Kallias laughed, his chin pointing upwards. "Didn't save me from the march though, did it? Alix didn't get a say in that."

Zeph paused, wondering. "Would it normally have saved you?" he asked quietly, leaning over.

Kallias shrugged. "I've never been sent abroad before, if that's what you mean. I suppose Alix had something to do with it."

"Was she upset?" Lysander asked. They'd huddled together for the conversation. Alix was allowed lovers, but it wasn't necessarily common knowledge.

A shadow passed over Kallias's face. Fear, grief, or anger; or any combination of the three. "Not that she would show. But Dannehs was upset."

The whole situation baffled Zephyros. Alix was a queen, and her second son was the get of a man borne of slavery even while her husband the king remained breathing. It was unheard of in foreign lands, but Laerta permitted it of her queens with the understanding that they were equal in their role with the king. The women and men who became the leaders of Laerta were their majesty first, and themselves second. So, when a monarch came to choose a partner, it would be one that could perform the position rather than one that would provide the companionship otherwise valued in Laerta.

Though, of course, kings and queens could choose for love, and remain committed to each other, but it wasn't essential. Zephyros doubted that Alix was one to love her husband. He didn't doubt that Alix loved his brother, though.

In Kurkia, Alix would have been strung up by her wrists for the privilege of loving a man other than the king. But here, since she'd given the Rex a robust heir who was almost of age, she could dabble in her love.

But, funnily enough, this didn't instil a feeling of comfort in Zephyros. Instead, he thought that the chains from which Alix had been released had instead enslaved her sister. He was glad for Kallias, in his happiness, but thought of the way the behaviour of the king was turning.

Lysander was stripped of his role as protector of the city and given marching orders.

Kallias was removed from the queen's arms and similarly, was going north.

While Zephyros was staying in Laerta. Sophos's warning not to become known to the king surfaced, and Zeph wondered if this was why: so he could quietly provide refuge to Nicke should she need it.

The wind began blowing in earnest and it whipped Zeph's hair around his face. Sophie had cut it three months ago but it was growing long again.

Lysander turned to him seriously, his beads tinkling in that same wind, and Zeph flinched. His brother's gaze bored into him, and he knew the instruction that was coming.

At a look, Lysander leant back. "You know what I'm going to say?"

Zephyros nodded, digging a stick into the feet-worn ground.

"Sophos has organised for you to scribe Nicke's strategy sessions. Can you write Laertan?"

Zeph nodded again.

"Good. You're to go to the Credo everyday, and sit in."

Noise burst from Zephyros, unable to be contained. "I should be going with you! I should be marching too!"

His brothers looked taken aback, and he'd attracted the attention of those around them.

He leant forward and lowered his voice. "It's not fair that I sit here when I'm more use out there."

"Use to whom?" Lysander said. "You're no use dead."

"And you think you'll die in this war." A sadness passed over Lysander's face, a resignation that infuriated Zeph. "Why won't you fight for what you want?"

"It creates risk," Lysander said, voice dangerously low.

"Bullshit. Apathy creates more danger than righteousness."

"And how did that go? How did the decision that you and Demetria made affect Nicke?"

Zeph didn't reply, his breathing laboured.

"Her wrist was broken, Zephyros, and because of the king's magic, it is still healing. That's where brashness gets us. She gets hurt, and I get sent north to die. Those are the lives we lead."

"You're not going to die!" Zeph seethed, each word its own arrow.

"Lyon has all but promised it."

"Sophos won't allow it."

"I think you forget where you are, pup. Here, we don't matter. We're sandals on a foreign land and we'll be killed and burnt on the very fields paid for in blood."

"Now is not the time for quarrel," Kallias interjected. "We're all stressed, even if it is for different reasons. For now, we need to focus on Sophie and the march. I refuse to let this family degrade into squabbling before war."

Zeph stayed silent, but nodded when Lysander huffed, suitably chastised.

He was still quiet, thinking, when a hush descended around them. Each Laertan turned, facing the dais for direction in their final days at home. Sophos and Jonn ascended the steps, each with a scroll in their hands.

"We thank you for your patience," Sophos started. "We regret to say that the harvest was lower than expected due to drought, and your rations will have to be supplemented on the road." Lysander scoffed quietly as the general continued. "We will run a plains campaign, with aim to force the Auntuans into their city. Then, we will cut off their access to the port, effectively starving them."

Kallias nudged Lysander in the arm with his elbow, a knowing look crossing his brow. Zeph didn't pry into it.

"We march in four days. For now, take your leave to your families. There is no need for further from you. Good day."

Jonn stood forward then, unrolling the paper in his hands.

"The following people must attend me before going home. Bryan; Lily; Harold; Jyn; Lysander; Catherine; Sara; and Zoe. Many thanks."

Lysander's brow furrowed, and Drakon whispered something in his ear before he made off. Zephyros watched the hoplites called to assemble, trying to find something similar in them. Their build was alike, but not enough to be the point. Perhaps they were ex-krypteia called to a specific purpose.

"I'll see you later," Kallias said. "I want to see my son before I die."

He whirled away before either Zephyros or Drakon could

answer.

"I don't know where these two have gotten it into their heads that they're going to perish on this march," Zephyros said.

Drakon looked at him sadly. "Because Lyon has told them," he said simply.

"How?" he asked, trying and failing to keep the hopelessness from his voice. "How could he guarantee it when he himself doesn't take the field?"

"He can't, but it's why neither of them are staying in the city. Something's changed in Lyon in the last season or so. He's become more rigid and possessive."

Zeph had kept clear of Lyon, but he'd seen him in passing. He was a small man, unkempt. Or perhaps that was just what being a king was.

"And this is the result," Drakon sighed as he watched Kallias walk away.

"Why was Lysander singled out?" Zeph asked when they began to make their way out of the city.

"The wall solution. Sophos made him a lieutenant, and he can single-handedly take down multiple adversaries. They'll need that for their plans probably."

"And your part? Or are you just a grunt on this march?"

Drakon looked at him levelly. Of all his brothers, Zeph probably shied from Drakon's work the most. Spy-work was difficult, and uncanny, and the pockets of knowledge that Drakon carried with him at any one point was disconcerting. Zeph wasn't adverse to partaking in it, but couldn't find himself fully trusting this particular brother.

"I go as a grunt," Drakon said. "At least they aren't taking as many slaves this time."

"Do they usually?"

Drakon nodded. "As supports; as fodder for the front lines. It's disgusting how Laerta treat their enslaved people."

Zeph was surprised at the vehemence of Drakon's words, but couldn't deny that he spoke truth.

At the fork, Drakon was to continue right while Zephyros went straight.

"I'll see you tonight at home," Drakon said. He continued walking without waiting for an answer.

Yes. Tonight. It was to be the night for Matthew's welcome into the family. Zeph had to go home and prepare the house.

Home.

When had Lysander's house become home? When had his expectation of waking safe and warm surpassed his fear of a quick master's sword slice? When had he been so willing to call these men brothers? A shiver of knowing went up his spine, even as tears slid down his cheeks.

It was home, but he was losing it again. It was slipping through his fingers because of one man's megalomania. Instead of revelling, enjoying, and relaxing into a family that had chosen him, he was sending them to far-away plains with the promises of a killer in their ears.

Could he save them? What would it take to finish this, and protect his brothers once and for all? Murder wasn't new to Zephyros. He'd seen war and knew what it looked like to cut a man about the throat and watch the blood escape. He knew he could do it, but whether it would serve to save his brothers was another question. It would have to be quiet, unknown, in the darkest night.

A laugh escaped. Completely *mad*. Even if he wasn't busy every night preceding the march, he would be found and killed himself, without saving his brothers anyway.

He stopped at a field of yellow flowers next to the road. It twinkled in the closing of the day, swaying and calling him.

Sometimes, just sometimes, he heard notions of worlds adjacent to his. Perhaps moving in tandem, perhaps past and calling, or future and telling. This reckoning was gentle, like the breeze through his hair or the purring of a cat about his ankles. His knack, as he called it, was a warm hand on his shoulder that shifted his direction when necessary. It called his name, but not the name by which he was known here, in his slavery. Rather, it was the name his uncle had sometimes muttered in anger; the name inherited from his father, if his insights could be trusted.

Galyn.

The flowers swayed, and the name was on the wind.

He looked at the sun, and deemed he had time. So he walked into the field and sat among the flowers that spoke to him, and he wept. Some of the flowers made their way into his hands. Tied together with a spare, they formed a bouquet that could be placed at the stones scribed with his parents' names. It had never really hurt before. He'd been raised and cared for by his uncle's fist, and had been told that his father was killed for his strength, and his mother died because she ran.

Though they weren't born slaves, why else would two people be killed for such reasons? Why else would his uncle move to a foreign city with a young baby?

His tears moved into the ground, seeping through cracks to the underworld below. For no one to see, for no one to hear. His name was still on the wind and he took it for the warning it was.

* * *

The food was cooking, Demetria lending her expertise to it.

"No, not like that," she said, taking the knife from him. "You have to cut lateral to the spine. Like this."

She showed him too quickly, and passed the knife back to him to copy. He cut slowly, glancing between Demetria and the chicken to ensure she approved. For some reason, her approval was important to him. She smiled a little, and he relaxed.

"Thank you for helping me with this, Ria" he said, putting the meat into a pan.

"You're welcome. Better than you being known as the *worst* cook in Laerta."

"In all the continent, probably," he laughed.

"And Kurkia." She paused, looking at him sidelong. "You said your uncle raised you? Not your parents?"

He nodded. "They were dead by the time I walked, according to him."

"I'm sorry to hear it."

Zephyros shrugged, but Demetria insisted. "If it helps, I remember only glimpses of my parents. I was young when they died."

He looked at her, and found her eyes glistening. It must be the day for it. He put his hand on her shoulder but she shrugged it off. "What do you remember?"

Her back stiffened, then she seemed to make a decision and continued. "My father was the largest man I'd ever seen. He was a giant." Zeph laughed, and was rewarded with a small smile. "Of course you'd laugh, idiot," she said, rolling her eyes. But something seemed to unravel in her, and she spoke more freely.

"And your mother?" he asked. "What do you remember of her?"

"Just how much love she had." She paused, considering her options, then she spoke in nothing more than a whisper. "And that her name was Chrysanthe."

Zeph nodded, but felt a knowing shiver overcome him. Yellow fields of yellow flowers calling his name flashed, but he dismissed it. It was fancy and he was fanciful.

A holler came from the front verandah and Demetria looked at him pointedly. "I'll stay out here and finish. You go and get changed and enjoy your night with your family."

"I owe you one."

"You owe me many, at this point."

When he'd dressed and gone downstairs, Kallias had his arm

around Matthew like he already belonged.

"Zeph!" Kallias called, drawing him over. "Tell Matthew here what will happen while we are away."

Zephyros looked at him like he had a third head. "The usual, I presume," Zeph said.

"No, no. You'll look after Sophie, won't you?"

"She's my sister," Zeph said, still confused. The term came to him easily now, never avoided and always voiced until it became true. "Of course I'll look out for her."

Matthew smiled gratefully. "I feel terrible to be leaving her so soon."

Zeph put his hand on his shoulder. "Don't stress. You'll be back soon enough."

"By solstice, eh?" Lysander provided, entering with a small wine barrel over his shoulder.

"That's what they're saying, is it?" Matthew replied.

Lysander shrugged, dropping the barrel into his arms. "There has to be something to tell our wives."

Zeph took the wine and placed it on the table, collecting mugs. He was still unclear on how Sophie and Matthew had worked themselves out, but he also knew it probably wasn't any of his business. Sophie was happy when he'd spoken to her, and he knew Matthew well enough that he didn't have many qualms.

Matthew was Primary while being a guard for the Rex, but he wasn't stupid. He probably wanted a quiet life; a way to have a farm and family while fulfilling his obligations to Laerta. And he would probably get that with Sophia. She was a Master of Trade, the Master Weaver. Not only was weaving a revered skill, it made Sophia part of the Senate: giving her vote over the chosen ephors. Matthew was marrying quite a powerful woman.

The night passed easily. Matthew relaxed into their dynamic. When Sophia's past came up, Matthew stiffened, and Zeph watched him prepare to defend her enslavement. Lysander reacted almost angrily, not realising the reason for Matthew's posture was not because he was ashamed, but because he was proud.

Zeph went to bed that night calmed by drink, comforted by the knowledge that even if he died, even if he was taken from this world to seek solace in the next, he would be remembered. There would be someone, one person at least, who would carve his name into a stone to ensure he could be recalled for years to come. Something his parents hadn't had. Something he was sure he had given up when his last love had walked away from him.

But instead, he was real, and tangible, and living.

* * *

The sun blinked at him through the eastern window. It was bright, harsh, and probably earlier than he'd expected it. The bed groaned as he rolled, pushing his pillow over his eyes and the knowledge of the day's break out of his mind. Blinding, and unwelcome. The night before's drink still echoed through his head and bounded between his ears. The soft covers helped, and he relaxed almost back to sleep.

Shit. Shit. *Shit.* Zephyros jumped, tripping over blankets as they pooled on the floor. The thick wool carpet broke his fall, but he was already up and dressing before either of his knees could smart. He'd gone to bed in a chiton, but it was stained with wine and food and would be completely unacceptable.

Nicke's strategy sessions began at daybreak. And the day had broken.

She was going to be very cranky.

A yell from an adjoining room broke through his hysteria, accompanied by a *thump, thump, thump* on the wall. Zeph ignored his hungover brother, as he made more noise rummaging through his room looking for his sandals. He'd placed an iron nail in the candle to wake him as it burnt down, but obviously that hadn't worked.

He made it out of the house in record time, but thought briefly about whether preparing a horse would be quicker than running. Seeing the lazy turn of the gelding's head, he decided on the latter.

The run was probably a good idea, anyway. It let the wind take his hair and make it somewhat presentable, and it released the hangover that was looming over him. Matthew, it turned out, liked wine and they'd drunk the entire barrel.

Affable, was how Zeph would describe him. He'd fit in easily, though whether he could be fully turned to the family's purposes was another question. Sophia was fiercely protective of Nicke, and soon her husband would be one of the king's guards. Whether that would become irreconcilable remained to be seen.

The Credo was still waking when Zephyros ran through the wall. Only a small objection erupted from the guards on either side when he shot past, but a wave of his hand had them yell mockingly instead. "Where are you needed so badly, Zephyros?" He ignored it still, running.

It was quieter than a normal day, when Primaries and Secondaries would be training or milling, laughing heartily or resolving gambling debts. Instead, there were messengers here and there, and the navy blue of the students dominated rather than mingling with the maroon of the soldiers. The sun blinked through the compound and made the stone shine, and it became hot when he entered the hall in its centre. It was like a sink, the windows at the roof allowing in as much sun as the earth saw fit while the stone simply absorbed the heat given to it. He wasn't entirely sure which door the heirs and their tutor would be sitting behind, but knew where the strategy rooms were and began in that corridor.

He knocked on each wooden door until he heard her voice, tight and controlled, bid him enter. The room they occupied was like any classroom. A map of the continent dominated one wall with various coloured pins covering it, waiting to be moved off. The sun shone through a window and was redirected with mirrors to fill the space with light. It was warm, too, as Zeph realised he'd left his cloak at home.

Nicke was standing near to a chalkboard, her hands empty and held behind her back. She wore a forest green peplos that made her hazel eyes glow, and about her neck was a gold chain with a small sword pendent hanging towards her centre.

"I'm sorry for my lateness," he said as he closed the door behind him. A small nod was all he received from the general, and she turned her attention back to the heirs.

The elder, Kallum was his name, was seated carefully. His ankles uncurled from under his seat and took up a stance, feet flat on the floor, denoting him thinking he may need to be quick. He looked like his mother, Zeph remembered quietly, though he'd only met the queen briefly. There was a vague resemblance between aunt and nephew: in the way their chin jutted, and the expression of concentration they adopted when cornered. Because Kallum did look cornered: a mouse caught in a trap.

Dannehs, contrarily, looked carefree. He was much younger than his brother, Zeph noted, but with the same brown hair. That was where the resemblance ended. His chin was not a proud one, and his gaze darted with the innate knowledge that children eventually grow out of.

This was Kallias's son, Zeph thought solemnly. There was no outward resemblance except the boy's general dark complexion and his eyes, which could easily have been inherited from his mother.

Both boys turned towards him as he entered and sat at a desk in the corner of the room. Kallum scoffed and said to his aunt, "Why is a slave allowed into heir training?"

Nicke ignored him to speak to Zephyros.

"I trust you don't need any writing implements?"

"No, commander," he replied, pulling out his ink and quills. The scrolls had been provided by the Credo. They were vellum, making them hardier than parchment and more likely to survive when needed in the future.

"We have, unfortunately, already begun, but you can note that please."

She turned back to her nephews and Zeph began writing furiously. The scrolls would be used for the younger students in Tertiary and Secondary who did not have enough promise to be taught by Nicke herself.

"You have a group of men," she said. "They have procured all of the weaving looms in town, and refuse to weave cloth until the king agrees to a set price for it. The shepherds will be affected by this, as their fleece will only be bought by the weavers. The weavers have told the shepherds that they will pay only a small amount for fleece. Masters are unable to weave as they no longer own looms. How do you react as king?"

Both boys pondered their answer, then began writing as Zeph finished. He sat, quietly and contemplatively, looking again to the frieze that shared his eyes. He'd not thought about it much since he was first here, as he became blind to the general decor by familiarity, but the colour skewered him with questions.

The circumstances of his parent's death had never really occurred to him. What difference did it make to the price of fish, or to the way a blade was honed?

"Your answers please," Nicke said, gesturing first to Kallum.

"I would kill the weavers," he said simply. "I would give their looms to the Temple, and the Masters can weave. No set price; wool is bought from the shepherds as normal."

Nicke considered him through hawk's eyes. The answer wasn't one that Zeph would have given.

"Dannehs?" she prompted the younger boy.

He looked down at his paper slowly, intimidated by his own brother's brutality. "I would set the price low to encourage them away from the idea," he eventually said "The price will be so low that they will be forced to abandon it."

Nicke simply looked, her forehead high and her mouth thin.

Zephyros could then appreciate how she commanded rooms full of hoplites; how she could inflame them. It wasn't in the fold of skin next to her eye that was shouting her displeasure at her nephews' responses, or the way her mouth curved slightly down, denoting her disappointment. Rather, it was the way her neck tilted her head to the left: a question asked then unanswered. Like an ill-fitting woollen hat on a proud head, or a high musical note absent the correspondingly low finish. It was undone, and Zephyros suddenly saw the answer she was seeking.

"Who gave the men the looms?" Zephyros blurted, taking the heat of three sets of eyes and banishing the way they made him feel: small; unwelcome. But he had been a lieutenant, and he was almost a Laertan.

"Slaves need permission to speak here," Kallum growled, glancing quickly to his tutor.

"Quiet," Nicke admonished, the word a whip. "What do you mean, Zephyros?"

He weighed his answer. Whether he should stay small, silent, out of the attention of the king and his son in order to best protect the woman currently looking at him like he may be more than his green eyes betrayed; or whether he should lean into his teaching: the world of politics, etiquette, and war, in which his uncle ensured he was not only learned, but expert. His brothers were going to war anyway. What would be the difference?

"Preventing a group of people monopolising a resource should be a priority for a king, if he was to stop short of killing his citizens or crashing their economy."

As the words escaped, he saw the intensity in her eyes grow, like her hopes were dashed then pinned.

"See, nephews. Sometimes all it takes is a pair of fresh eyes."

"You're joking, yes?" Kallum said, violence in his tone. "You can't prevent every problem."

"No," she replied. "But you can prevent this one. What would you do after the fact, Zephyros? If they gained the looms anyway."

"Are the men that have the looms powerful?" he asked eventually.

"Yes," she replied.

"More powerful than a king?"

A shake of the head.

"Then I would name them the new weavers, and make it their only worthy skill. They can set up their looms in the Trade, and weave cloth everyday, all day, until they decide it is beneath them. They will be employed by the state, and receive no profit."

He swore he saw a smile, but it vanished much like his humility.

"And when those men revolt?"

"Ahh, that's the beauty part," he said with a smirk forming on his mouth. "Who would listen to men with no money, no farm, and no bronze to call to arms?"

"You rely on their disenfranchisement," she breathed. "By giving them what they want, you strip them of what they need."

"No one revolts in my city."

His eyes turned down, to the vellum where the problem was written. He didn't wish to engage further, lest the gaze of vengeance come too close to glimpsing him. The heir was already breathing heavily in his direction.

He was a little tired of living in a world where power eclipsed him.

Nicke cleared her throat, and continued the lesson, not addressing him again.

When it came time to finish, Kallum, characteristically, shoved past him as he cleaned up his inks and nibs. Nicke hesitated, righting some aspect of her materials until both boys had filed out.

Zephyros knew what she was waiting for.

"For you, rose," he said quietly, handing her a note from his brother. It was small and all she would allow, Lysander had told him. "Do you have one to return?" he asked.

"Yes," she said before she reached into her pocket and passed it to him. It smelt of vanilla. It smelt like her.

"Will you be attending Matthew at the wedding?" she asked.

Zephyros nodded. "All of us will be. Poor Sophia was blessed with only brothers."

There, a small smile. It's a tricky thing to smile when your thoughts are already on foreign soil.

"I will see you there, then, Zephyros." She turned away, and he thought only a little before gifting her familiarity. The sign of a friend, how such intimacies were established in the land that was claiming him as its own.

"Call me Zeph."

She glanced back at him, nodding slowly. "I thought we were beyond such informality, since you use my title instead of my name."

He shrugged. "If you minded, I think you would simply punch me again to show it."

He saw a glimpse of teeth as she smiled. "Thank you, Zeph."

He bowed his head, and left her to the room.

CHAPTER SEVEN

Nicke

She wondered, sometimes, about the flowers in the trees. Green haloed a pink close to red, with a trumpet that held precious golden nectar along its tongue. Why they bloomed so late in the season when their companions were already dirt; why their colour was brighter the longer they lingered on the branch before falling to the hard ground. They weren't crushed underfoot, for their juices to stain and raise a stink as the summer sun beat down. Rather, they were collected and collated: most weddings happened in late summer.

It was a fine coincidence, then, that the hoplites were marching and Sophia's nuptials were happening before they left. Like the birds in the sky and the bears in the mountains, marriages were made when seeds were sown and cubs created: to buckle down in winter and grow new life to be born in spring.

That's what Nicke told herself as she collected the red flowers sunning on the ground. That they were promises: of things made and of the world righted.

Three days until they march, and there would be a wedding tonight.

First, they would feast. Sacred goats that were grown for that exact purpose roasted and shared among the group. Then, the ritual would be performed at Sophia's brother's house: a Master of

Trade to join them in a show of solidarity with Laerta. They would sacrifice blood, say their promises, and their will let to the air to be bound by each breathing soul in attendance. They would all stand witness, and cheer as a strong partnership was made.

Laughter would chime, and drink would make the talk loud and boisterous. Then, later, before the yard of people quieted and looked among themselves for the married couple, Sophia and Matthew would slip away. Silently, hand in hand, to go from wed to married in the space of what could be a single breath. Nicke and the other attendants would look for them. The mocked search would span from a few minutes to a few hours, Lysander slighted by the stealing of his sister and Matthew vindicated by keeping her. It was a silly tradition, truly, but one Laerta held onto. Nicke didn't know the marriage traditions that occurred in Malptia, but she assumed they weren't so ostentatious.

The flowers collected, she returned to Sophia's along a busy road. Shadowed by Ryan—Matthew's usual partner, but solo today—Nicke flitted between the crowd so as to ensure she touched no one. Though it would be accidental, word would get back. Word always got back.

Once, she had tried to give Ryan the benefit of the doubt: tried to gain whether he was a singer, or a dancer, or liked skipping rocks. But he was a hard wall, down to the scowl he employed to keep the populace away from her. Not that they would come near anyway: she was a general and generally untouchable. They simply didn't realise how close to the truth it was.

Sophie's was a riot of sound. Laughing, singing, gaiety spread down to Nicke's bones and released the tension along her shoulders.

"May I go in by myself?" she asked Ryan, not turning to him, but still studying the house.

"I will be at the entrance to the yard," he said gruffly.

"You could always go and join Matthew's entourage?" Nicke

replied, finally looking at him. He was surveying Sophie's house with a whimsy she didn't think possible for him. "He's like a brother to you."

"That he is," Ryan replied. His brown hair chittered with the beads throughout it. "Do you know everyone in the house?"

Nicke nodded. She knew most of them, at least.

He turned to look at the busy road. "I better not. I'll wait for you."

"Ryan—"

"It's just easier this way, Nicke." With that he turned and walked away. Nicke thought of his reputation as a spy, and how she would be punished for this perceived mercy. Rather than considering it, she entered the house with her chin high, embodying as close to joy as she could. If she fancied that the dread churning in her gut was false, then candour might follow.

But she didn't have to force a smile when the bliss of unheeding conversation swam over her. It made her blood hum; made her skin tingle. Flower garlands decorated the receiving room, the main one of the small house that Sophia occupied. A hallway led off the back, to her smaller bedroom, with a dining nook embedded in the wall to the east. Usually decorated with ocean greens and sandy whites, obnoxious colour greeted Nicke as she entered.

Lysander built this house for her when she became a Master because she was considered independent in her craft. She was no longer under the wing of her senior sibling. Usually, people married before they received their credentials: Sophie before she was a Master; Nicke before she was a general, but it didn't work out that way for either of them. Sophia had her mind elsewhere: with her work, with her brothers, with the posse of students that she acquired annually. Marriage was not even a figment, but war changes things. Sophia had known Matthew for a few years, so this turn was not in itself unsurprising. That Sophia had chosen one of

Nicke's guards, one of her brother's men and one who could report subterfuge to the Rex, was. Though Matthew had shown leniency, he was still Lyon's man.

Only now, perhaps, he would be Sophia's.

Alice met her first: a Master of Colour who worked at the Temple. She was a small woman with a plump middle, made so by her husband's high yield farming. Brown hair and a sharp nose that was typically Laertan met her widow's peak. She was a mother hen among unmarried maids.

"General, how are you?" she said, beaming widely.

"Well, thank you Alice. The house looks beautiful."

Alice nodded. "We can only take small credit for that, the slaves did most of it." She turned back to Nicke. "Here, for you. Everyone is to wear one."

Nicke took the flower garland from her and draped it over her hair. It complimented the navy blue of her chiton nicely. The weather was warm; Nicke didn't wear a red cloak.

The room opened up before her as Alice moved away: people sitting, eating, lounging and laughing. It wasn't only women, with the song of the event attracting with indiscriminate regard for gender. It was more important that this style of celebration spoke through the attendee's blood, and such a thing made anyone welcome here.

Sophia sat in the middle in a plain white peplos of the finest wool. Most of the group were friends, people of the Temple. Some of Matthew's family were here, too, and Nicke's eyes roamed over them trying to remember their allegiances.

But when Sophia spotted her, she gestured her over excitedly. She didn't stand, and she didn't touch, but Nicke appreciated the excitement she bestowed. "Oh, I'm so glad you're finally here," she said.

"I know, I'm sorry I was late."

Sophia shook her head. "You're busy at the moment. If I was

you, a wedding would be the farthest thing from my mind."

"It isn't just any wedding, though," Nicke smiled. "It's yours."

Sophia nodded, satisfied. "And you'll be my main attendant." She leant in to whisper, "I had to bat away Matthew's sister for the honour, but she holds you no ill will."

Nicke nodded. No one ever held her ill will, almost like pity.

"There is a small problem that I needed to speak to you about," Sophie said as she accepted a plate of food from an older woman. Nicke recognised her from the Credo, but couldn't place her.

"It requires touching," Sophia continued. "Just a little. You have to adorn me with ash from Lysander's hearth."

Nicke felt her blood thin, but maintained calm. It was an old and harsh reaction to the truth of her isolation, but with it came the heady rush of acceptance.

Because that role was usually played by the matriarch of the bride's family. It was their mother, older sister, aunt, or, as it were, the wife of her older brother. And Lysander was Sophia's older brother.

"Sophie..." Nicke whispered, and Sophia looked about them momentarily before she grasped her hand.

"You're my sister in all but name, Nicke. Always remember that." She released her just as quickly.

It took a few moments for Nicke to catch her breath and remember her gift for her friend.

"Here, for the adornment," she said as she retrieved the satchel of red blooms. They'd travelled well, and their colour was intact. A trail of them would fall down Sophie's back, each placed by a loving hand in recognition of the joy that the union would create for the city. Laerta approved. Laerta was joyous.

"Thank you, Nicke," Sophia murmured. Her hands delved into the flowers and began to sprinkle them around her in a circle.

Nicke looked at her friend in wonder, awe, amazement at the vision she made. The flowers were her earth's blood made useful in radiance, just as her unblemished woollen skirt was the promise she made to the country of her adoption. She would be married, as pure an act as she could undertake as a Laertan, and present Laerta with children worthy of the risk of sacrifice. She may die, and the white wool was the protection she sought if that was the case.

Nicke's song started with a hum, easily found and repeated throughout the group. It was instinctive, but she had been shown it by Demetria who knew all the songs of this country. They'd practised together in the time since Sophie had asked Nicke to attend her.

It was a lilting lament: a family losing one of theirs into a new life of domesticality. That was why Sophia's matriarch began the song and would adorn her with ash from the hearth. A goodbye from the house that had loved her, cared for her, grown with her, into the care of the people who would nurture her still.

After a verse, Matthew's mother came alongside Nicke and took up the song: their voices filling the space in harmony. It turned from a hymn of grief to one of resignation, a family member passed from one side to another, but generous in the passing. As they sang, other voices joined until the music turned light. Each person, friend or family, picked up a flower from Nicke's basket and, taking turns, affixed it to Sophie's veil. Pops of red on white. The elders knew what the red was: the blight that cursed marriage and the womb that bore it, but the youngsters only basked in the display.

Nicke went last, her flower finding its place as she closed out the song, and they all laughed and applauded once it was done.

"You're ready," she said, as she pulled the sheer veil over Sophie's head. "Are you nervous?"

Sophia laughed a little, then shook her head. "No, I'm sure."

"Then let's get you there."

* * *

They waited for Matthew's procession in the yard of Lysander's house. Apple trees, close to the river, swayed in the breeze and released the scent of a summer worn beyond its welcome. Nicke stood at Sophia's shoulder and held the basket of flowers that would be thrown in triumph when the time came. She could hear Sophie breathing, in and out, releasing the nerves Nicke knew would be bubbling under her skin.

It was no small thing, marriage. To tie yourself so completely and be bound by another's wants, needs, their soul and body, was intimidating. It wasn't that it was a necessity, both Sophie and Nicke had proven themselves able to hold their ambitions to Laerta's account without the cut of a man over their names, but that Laerta was, at its core, a war machine. It let boys and girls into combat training; it placed them with the beasts of the mountains so the children who could not set their spears against a monster's heart were weeded from the others. Sometimes, more often than acceptable, in Nicke's opinion, children were not permitted to descend the sacred mountain when their kills went badly. If they did not come down with the hide of a lion or a wolf or a leopard then they were unceremoniously branded with a mark and given over to slavery or to death.

This horror, this tragedy of precocious treatment, could only work if children were plentiful. To delete every third or more child from Laerta's systems would cripple its war prospects if it had the same fertility rate as Malptia, or Auntu. But each marriage here not only produced many children, but ones that were strong and healthy and robust. The only way to achieve that was to ensure that the parents were a true partnership, and that the mothers were beyond the age of growth. There were laws around it: women had to accept an offer before thirty years of age, and men before forty. If they did not, then slavery would welcome them with arms open.

When Nicke had come of age at twenty, she could have accepted offers of marriage, but only one would ever offer.

With the other attendant's eyes forward, Nicke took the opportunity to bask in being at his house, his yard, under the watch of his almond trees with his hand-seeded grass under her feet. Just a little; just enough to remember the intoxicating feeling of his breath against her neck, she let herself imagine smaller feet playing among the grass. Ones with her tightly curled hair, and his ocean eyes, and her straight spine, and his deft hands.

She stopped abruptly when the imagined child disappeared beyond the low wall that bordered the garden. This was not that life, and her melancholy threatened to choke her.

It began with a small roar, then the jingle of bells started over the hill towards the road. The group of Sophie's attendants hadn't been waiting long, and if war was not on the horizon then they may have waited longer for the men to crest the brae. They came dressed in deep blues and crisp whites, with green laurels in their hair and Matthew at their front. A procession of people from both families, mostly men, but also others who preferred the men's idea of pre-wedding festivities, spread like rivulets of water through the valley. Sophie laughed and others joined in. Quickly, Nicke stepped towards her and set her veil to rights, whispering, "You look beautiful." She then stepped back and heard as the collective's voices rose as Matthew approached. Lysander was at the groom's right shoulder, a mug of wine in his hand and a look of complete adoration on his face. Nicke blushed and turned away, stepping from foot to foot.

A hush fell as they entered the yard, this moment the one that ensured consent, willing and full, for the partnership to be achieved. Matthew walked gingerly toward Sophia as she stood still: untouchable sacred. And she was. A woman, a Master of Trade, a slave risen to value and a kindness that flowered despite it, may have been more than a guard like Matthew could have hoped for. His hand trembled as he reached out to touch the embroidered oxen along her veil. He hesitated only a little, before throwing the material over her head and revealing her smile. Her eyes shone with her sun-bathed skin. A vision, Nicke thought, as Matthew huffed a quick laugh and kissed her. His strong arms wrapped around her shoulders and waist and lifted her towards him. A cheer went up as they spun, her hands disappearing into his brown hair as he clutched her for dear life.

This was the point of it all. To find the aspect of life where a contented soul can leave the weary body and gain the peace of happiness, and living would begin.

Nicke's eyes flitted back to Lysander as he stood stronger than she'd ever seen. Just another day in his sun would be all she would need, and she would be satisfied. Just one more touch, one more stroke from his fingers along her skin, and she could swallow the rest. A loving touch would be the equivalent of ten strokes with a baton, if only she could have one more.

She didn't shy from his gaze when he next looked at her, and she saw a change come over his face. His regard swam towards her like they were underwater and all else was muted, even though the congregation sang their approval.

The singing could have been for them. The shouting could have been for their partnership, for all they knew. But as she looked at his face, usually so close to resignation or forbearance, and now closer to determination and growing power, she knew his mind, and she knew he would have to be sworn off. They hadn't stayed apart for the better part of the summer for it to fall to naught today. His life was his own, but she felt like she held it in her smaller hands. Enough to kill. It was all but promised, should they fall into the oblivion of love together.

They were passed along with the crowd into the orchard behind Lysander's house where tables and benches had been set up. Candlelight swarmed the trees and a lilting tune came from the far western corner. Nicke knew these trees, but had never seen them look so hauntingly beautiful. As dusk settled into night, she knew the magic would increase with the drink available.

Matthew and Sophie sat together, Nicke on her immediate side as her primary attendant and Matthew's brother on his. Her eyes sought Lysander, it only natural for him to sit near his sister, but, instead, the seat next to her was pulled out and occupied by Zephyros.

Nicke was again reminded of the politics that sometimes seemed to preoccupy his mind. No one would have told him to take that seat, but he did anyway.

"You think we're going to do something foolish tonight," she said to him. He was wearing the white and blue of celebration but had already abandoned the laurel that sat atop the other men's heads. The green would likely have matched his eyes, but he seemed to reject the assistance to his appearance as easily as breathing. His fingers ran over his face, rubbing along his chin and eventually following the grain of his day's-growth into the strands of his hair. It was tidy, but without the usual tinkle of beads. Nicke quietly wondered why Sophie hadn't gifted him anything, as his sister.

"Good evening to you too, rose." He smirked at her then passed her some pork with a corn and rocket salad. "And yes, is my answer. I get feelings that sometimes turn out right. Besides, Ryan's here somewhere getting merry himself. I would hate for him to misinterpret Lysander seated next to you."

"Like a wife?" She took a sip of wine with challenge in her gaze.

He eyed her sidelong, then his gaze flicked to the goblet which he then swapped for water. "Best not tempt it, eh?"

She scrunched up her nose. Perhaps the drink had made it to her bones already. As Sophia was engrossed in Matthew, Zephyros was the only one she could speak to.

She had to admit that she'd not really considered him much. He'd been a slave for less than a day, and had been a student for a season. He scribed her lessons now, but otherwise they'd rarely spoken. Other than him causing her stiff wrist and her sometimes being reminded of his eyes when she studied the likeness of Laerta Rex as it danced across the Credo's frieze, his existence exited her mind as soon as she thought of him.

"Would you like to get married someday, Zephyros?" she asked, purely for conversation. Nicke gestured to the feasting party, laughs and shouts amounting.

He looked around, eyes swallowing all as he considered his answer. Then he turned back to her and his expression muted; almost deferential.

"Only if someone both willing and worthy were to come along."

She scoffed. "You don't see many as worthy? By the way you spoke to me when you first arrived, I'd have thought you were fast and hard in such a department."

"Oh yes, I will simply marry the first Laertan who will have me. Or Malptian, as it were." He took a sip of the goblet he'd taken from her and shook his head with mirth written across him. "Not so much their worth, rose, but mine. Either way, I imagine that war will claim me in the end."

Nicke internally cursed. Her own mood was for the ease at which such an event as a marriage could occur for others, but that wasn't Zephyros's fault. She suddenly felt responsible for his poor humour.

"War claims fewer than you may think. Especially if you were to be made a lieutenant or a captain, then I'd have to ensure your life with my plans."

He laughed then. The sound coursed through her, easing her own troubles. After all, weren't they all simply collected to the needs of their city? He was Laertan now, just as she was.

"I would hope you wouldn't aim to put me in danger anyway, no matter my station. After all, my brother says he will marry you, so you're basically family now."

"He said that, did he?"

Zephyros nodded.

Her eyes were then drawn to Lysander, sitting at the curve of their table, five people down. He was laughing with Drakon and his laurel, too, was sitting in front of him rather than on his head. The force of the warmth in her chest almost combusted.

"Can I tell you something?" Zephyros asked. When she nodded, he said, "I think you would be foolish not to do exactly as you please before he marches. You might regret not."

"Is this another one of your premonitions?"

Zephyros shrugged. "No, but it is something I can relate to. You have to grab love with both hands, Nicke. If you don't, you may find that it will slip from your grasp for the rest of your life."

"But it's dangerous."

"Life is dangerous. Doesn't mean you give up because of it."

"I don't think I could live with myself if he died because of me."

Zephyros sat back and eyed her, knowledge circling in his gaze. She knew then. She knew the extent of her brother's threats and where the ire had landed. Nicke looked at her own hands and saw the figures of red soldiers moving across maps and into position. Lysander was one of a hundred that would be placed by her own fingers and her own machinations. No matter what she did, he would fall.

A feather-light touch held her chin and raised it. It was like when Demetria reminded Nicke of her birthright, a princess born and stolen. Zephyros's eyes bored into hers and she felt the earth shift into surety.

"Never think it, rose," he breathed. "Never think of the impossible action belying an untenable position. This isn't your doing any more than it's mine, or his."

"But I didn't stop him loving me, Zeph."

Zephyros shook his head. "You never could have. I've met lots of people, and Lysander's the most tenacious of them."

"That's why I love him." As she smiled, she saw it reflected in Zeph. He curved his lips in warmth, eyes bright.

He stood and put out a hand to rub her shoulder, but must have thought better of it.

"I'm going to go and spike Ryan's wine," he said confidently. "In Kurkia, the rites come before the feast, but I can see here it is different."

"It is. The rites come when the feast is put away."

"Then you best get ready to represent our family, rose."

He walked away and she watched him disappear into the trees, his shoulders tall and his pace sure. She felt a spike of anxiety when she thought of Ryan's fate tonight, but she knew Zephyros wouldn't kill him. It wasn't within his character. But, then, she barely knew him at all.

Sure enough, the tables were being cleared away from the centre of the grove and plush carpet was being rolled out. It was probably red, but it seemed like an inky pool in the dark. Nicke drank the water Zeph had left behind, grateful to him for the first time since she'd met him. Her broken wrist was partly his fault, but, then, so was her recovery from the asp.

A Master of Trade approached. "Sophia, Matthew, it is time for the rites."

Nicke rose with Sophia and walked behind her. She stopped next to a table of various implements: a knife, a white rose, a flint, a bowl of ash. Nicke took the bowl and watched as Sophia knelt in front of Matthew.

"Nicke, Samuel," the Master said. Nicke took her cue to step forward as Matthew's brother did the same. She went to Sophia and stood before her. Nicke mentally shook herself, swallowing through the fear such touch would cause, and began to rub the ash from Lysander's hearth into the skin of her face. In this light, her countenance could have been a death mask for how the shadows played. Zephyros's comment about his intuition turning to premonition gave her pause, but then Sophie smiled. The ashes were Nicke's, and by extension, Sophie's family's parting blessing.

Just as Nicke was adorning Sophie in grey, Samuel had cut into his palm and was smearing blood onto Matthew's face. Nicke's was a blessing, and Samuel's was a reminder of duty.

They both stepped far back, melting into the crowd that had come out of their seats and stood quiet.

As they knelt, Sophie and Matthew whispered their promises. It was not for mortal ears, but for the smoke that sent their words into the world. The earth witnessed unions in Laerta, and kept them accountable.

As they finished speaking, the Master approached again with a different knife. The couple stood and Matthew took Sophie's hand. He sliced open her palm and she squeezed her own blood free over the offered white rose, turning it black. She then cut her husband's skin, and when the rose was drenched, the Master threw it into a brazier. It sizzled and the smell of iron leached into the air.

Matthew didn't hesitate, then. Just as he had done that afternoon when he'd first happened upon her, he took her into his arms and held her fast, kissing deeply. The crowd, so quiet before, yelped in harmony with the joy of the couple. Those closest to the bride reached her with congratulations first, Zephyros and Kallias mocking a fight over who of them had the right. Nicke giggled when Kallias won and Zeph just embraced them both together. More people moved past Nicke and she was pushed to the back of the crowd to avoid touching. She watched as Sophie and Matthew were swallowed by well-wishers, and a stab of jealousy pricked at her. She knew what would happen next, and why the crowd were giving their congratulations now.

The newlyweds would disappear, and the revellers would mock a search.

It was an old tradition, but one Laerta held on to. When men would steal their wives from under their fathers' noses, and both would wake in the morning married. This was just the tradition modernised.

Eventually, Nicke saw the crowd begin to turn away from Matthew and Sophie, even though they had been separated into different sides of the party. Matthew began to circle the group, quietly, taking his time to find his now-wife.

"Nicke?" said a small voice called behind her. She turned to the trees but couldn't see through the gloom.

She stepped into the darkness, listening for the rustling of leaves and feet against bare ground.

"Nicke..." he called again, lending a singing quality to his voice.

"You do know it's rude to call out to women in the dark?" she replied.

"I don't think it is," he said. "In fact, I think it's very polite."

She giggled, the sound unfamiliar. Turning to find him leaning against an almond tree, his eyes gleaming with mischief, she couldn't help but laugh outright.

"This is no good," she said. "Who is going to lament the loss of your sister if you're playing hide-and-seek in the trees?"

Lysander leant forward then, so their noses touched and he could look directly at her. She was surprised by what she found: he was completely sober. Coldly so.

It had been more than a season since she'd let herself speak to him, to love him in the small ways she could. The letters exchanged were all she would allow lest the sword fall. So, with the city's gaze elsewhere and Lysander right in front of her, she put a sure hand on his shoulder.

"She has other brothers," he whispered.

His lips touched hers lightly, like they had all the time in the world. She'd always found his hesitancy frustrating, never more than now. Usually, she held back, gave herself a moment to remember what was at stake. But he was going to war, and Zeph was right: opportunities were fleeting. Like a dandelion ready to seed in a child's fist; like clouds on a mountain peak.

She pushed him forward and against the tree, pinning him there. He responded quickly, easily, like her body fit his and nothing would prevent the key from opening the lock.

His tongue seared her mouth, prompting a familiar heat. She'd only kissed him like this once, and her heart constricted with the thought of ever letting him go. Lysander's hands explored under her peplos, finding her skin cold and yielding. His thumb dragged mercilessly up her ribs in a chorus of sensation and a groan escaped. Each strand of hair felt coarse in her grip, each bead its own testament to the love of his mother and sister. Nicke brought him impossibly close until she couldn't think through the fog.

"Nicke," he crooned, resting his forehead against hers.

A yell from the crowd went up then, probably Kallias, lamenting the disappearance of his sister. Lysander grinned. "See," he said. "She has other brothers."

Nicke thinned her mouth. "They might come looking for you now, too, you know. Now that you've proven missing and unable to fulfil your brotherly duty."

He looked at her seriously, the turn startling her. "Do you want them to look?" he asked. "Do you want them to come looking for you at my house?"

Nicke stared at him.

That wasn't the question he was truly asking and it wasn't the one she would answer. It wasn't a question of wanting, but a question of consequence. Did she want him to spirit her away, under cover of a moon-silvered night, and claim her as his? It was the old way of doing things: without rites, without consent, without the joy of their city cheering them on. Just a man who took a willing woman from daughter, or sister, to wife.

She knew her answer. If he had to ask, he might know it too.

Zeph had likely dealt with Ryan. Zeph had an uncanny ability about these things.

"Yes," she whispered. She tried to capture the word before it escaped but found herself unable to put her heart into it. "Yes," she repeated, firmer; sure.

That was all he needed. He grabbed her hand and drew her through the trees, the ash of his hearth still about her hands. The orchard was not next to the house and there was an empty field of about a hundred paces between them and it. He pulled her forward, walking purposely. They could simply be searching for Sophie; they could simply be searching together.

Once the door closed and was barred behind them, Lysander picked her up and kissed her against it. Her legs wound around his waist, appreciating his strength and might. She tilted her head back as his tongue found her pulse hammering in her throat.

For the first time, she didn't feel the inane dread that usually accompanied his touches; she just felt the warmth spread and collect. Damn her to the underworld, but she simply couldn't care.

She was still clasped around him when he moved them up the stairs and into his furs. It was effortless, like he'd been made for this exact moment. Once she was down he knelt above her, drinking her in. Each place his eyes touched was branded, and she felt itchy in the places he could not yet see.

"You're so beautiful, Nicke," he said, awe in his voice. "Every part of you. Your mind, your voice, your eyes. Every part."

She thought of all the times she'd dismissed him: told him not to hope, to not rely on her love. How often had she scorned him for fear?

"I love you," she said, the words coming easily. "More than I could hope to breathe."

He nodded, like he knew already and didn't need confirmation.

His finger trailed her shoulder and looped around the golden-leaf clasp that held her peplos together. A question rose on his face and she simply nodded, refusing to hesitate any further. He clipped them open and placed them reverently onto the floor.

His mouth traced where the fabric had covered, and she shivered.

"Tell me you love me again," he murmured, kissing down her neck.

"I feel like I've loved you all my life."

He sighed when she gasped, his tongue finding the space at the base of her throat.

"Tell me you'll marry me again."

"I will be your wife, Lysander."

His exploration continued, first her collar, then down to her wrists, until he finally peeled the fabric covering her chest away. Scalded by his gaze, she almost squirmed away but he placed a firm hand on her cheek, bringing her eyes back to his.

His grin was blinding. Nicke knew that this was a different Lysander to the hesitant, resigned man she knew as a girl, as a teen, as a commander. He wasn't waiting anymore. He'd made a choice, bending the consequences to his will and forging them anew. Lysander had been emboldened, and Nicke knew why, even if it was unthinkable.

Refusing to let the thought sour her, she pulled him down to kiss him fiercely, like she could hold onto him for the rest of her life.

For the rest of his.

She made fast work of his own chiton, drawing it down to the belt at his waist as he unfastened it. She had never seen him naked. She'd seen his chest gleaming with sweat as he trained, his bare legs tilling the fields with slaves, his shoulders flexed and straining under a water bucket. But the view she had now made her blood sing.

Daring, Nicke licked down his chest and was rewarded with a chuckle as it tickled him.

"It's rude to laugh when in bed with someone," she chimed.

He laughed again. Then, another already answered question in his gaze, he pushed his fingers down under her belt to slip it free of her body.

Easily, like breathing, she was before him, with every part of her touched by his eyes. His hands, loving and generous, roamed her skin as she drew him down to kiss him.

He broke off suddenly, pausing.

"What?" she asked breathlessly.

"I just..." he hesitated, flicking his eyes between her eyes and her mouth. "It's just that I've never done this before."

She couldn't help it. She laughed. Mirth skirted around the room, stopping at the look of bald-faced fear he had.

"Oh Lysander..." she said, kissing him gently. "Did you think that I've somehow got experience?"

He shook his head. "No, I suppose not. But just... just tell me if anything hurts or isn't good or—"

"I love you, but sometimes you can be a real idiot."

He moaned, exaggerating his face. "Tell me you love me again."

She laughed and he didn't hesitate or wait or delay or ask permission again. She'd never been touched like this, when she could feel his life force like electricity.

She wondered, after, if all claimings were like this. If each wife or husband felt the hand of providence when they were matched to their spouse. Fate always felt fragile while being unyielding: the arrow that had defeated her father, the contract that had caught her sister, the mind for strategy that she had inherited. But even fate couldn't take credit for Lysander's and her partnership. Both of them had fought against their binds to be in each other's arms now.

As his gentle snoring continued behind her and his arms tightened around her waist, she knew that the biting consequences would be shown light in the morning.

When the king came looking. When the power of the Rex stripped her of her largest love.

But now, she slept, comforted in dreams of unwilling hope.

$$* \quad * \quad *$$

When Nicke woke at dawn, it was to Lysander's hum in her ears.

"You need to get back before they find you missing," he whispered, sleep still in his voice.

She turned to him and traced the scar across his nose with her thumb, as she'd wanted to since he'd received it.

"I think I'll stay, actually."

He mumbled a reply that she didn't catch.

"You march tomorrow. Let me stay the day."

He shook his head with suddenly bright eyes. "I've not yet been responsible for your demise, and I'll be damned if it happens while I'm half a world away."

"Then be damned, Lysander," she said fiercely. "How can I go back to that house with its sealed windows and echoing footsteps with this knowledge of you?"

"Because you have to, Nicke. You have to hold on, just for a bit more."

She shook her head.

"Please," he said. "For me, you'll do this."

Her eyes became hooded, suddenly scheming. "You would send me away?"

He kissed her knuckles and didn't take the bait. "I would, yes."

"Then you're not thinking straight yet. Still drowsy with sleep."

"The best sleep of my life, lying next to you."

She shook her head, temper fleeing.

"Then let me take you to Matthew's," he said. He rolled onto his back and put his arm under his head, eyes closing. Her mouth opened in surprise, but her gaze snapped to his shoulders and the strength within them.

"What do you mean?" she asked.

"Sophie."

"Sophie?"

"My sister is a Master of Trade, is she not?"

"She is," Nicke said slowly.

"Then let us find her before you venture back to the king. Let us impose on my sister as she wakes just as you have."

Nicke yielded, earth damn her and all that she was. By the time the sun had fully emerged from the east, she was kneeling in front of him, the ashes of her sister's hearth quickly fetched just as Sophia cut her own hand to adorn Lysander's face. His words were simple, protective, just as hers were easy, nurturing. It made liars of them both, but as the saccharine scent of old-summer flowers caught the air, Nicke found herself able to believe it. That he would hold his sword to her threats and she would be the laugh he heard in a midwinter storm. Hopes, tied to a fate that was beyond them, let to the world's reckoning.

And after she'd made her way back to the king's residence, clean and happy, she found herself tucked easily into her own cold bed. Pretending she'd never left. Acting like her soul wasn't currently over the river, to the south. Her grief was palpable, but her wariness belied the truth.

She'd always be his. And he would always be hers.

CHAPTER EIGHT

Zephyros

Zeph had never been so cold. Despite his warm cloak, still navy blue, and the stockings Sophia had woven, cut and sewn for him, he felt the wind's bite down to his bones. Winter in Laerta must be something else. A beast which, if left hungry and determined, would eat him whole.

The Credo was perhaps the worst for it. The wide expanses of field needed for phalanx training, as well as the hill the compound was hoisted upon, meant the wind was both unbroken and cutting. And Zeph *hated* it. Each day he would walk here, greet his friends, his mentors, his tutors, spread hope of a day when the king didn't affront Laerta's bounty, then trudge to the square of grass down the very back of the wall where Nicke had decided her classes would now be held. Each day was colder than the last; each morning brought with it his expectation of snow. When he'd mentioned such a thing, Demetria had set him straight. *It only snows on the mountains here, silly*, she'd said.

Perhaps Nicke thought the cold would humble them. Or maybe she wanted to feel the sparse sunshine on her face.

Maybe she felt the walls of the Credo closing in every time she was inside.

Zephyros felt the inevitable survivor's guilt stirring, but quashed it. His airs of escaping Laerta were but a distant fancy, him kept firmly here by a single promise to his brother. Despite them leaving him here, the sole lookout for Nicke's safety.

Lysander was not yet dead, surprising the lot of them. His letters were regular and long with Kallias's scrawl and Drakon's scratch at the bottom. One letter every seven days, or thereabouts, and there had been twelve letters. Sometimes there was something for Nicke inside, as well.

He walked to her now, in her claimed territory at the back of the Credo. Her nephews still received their education despite the war.

The sun crested the hill just as he did, and he settled his scrolls and pots of ink on the soft grass and waited.

It was an hour later that he gave up. No one was coming. His fury had increased with the wind's bite but he could hardly blame anyone else. Usually Nicke would have sent a note telling that she was indisposed, and Zeph not receiving it made his usual premonitions scream at him. The nature of them was changing, like a whisper in his ear rather than the visions that had plagued him since he was a child. It made their intent clearer.

He packed his things into his rucksack and walked to the Credo major, slipping into the atrium and towards the strategy rooms.

Quick voices met him as he walked along the corridor. His knack could feel the menace in the air and his anger suddenly took a different turn.

"Write it!" the man said, like the crack of a whip.

"No, I will not," Nicke replied. There was steel in her voice; a determination that acutely terrified Zephyros.

"The order must come from you, general," the first sneered. Zeph didn't recognise the voice, but knew only one person that would speak to the commander in such a way.

He slowly rounded the corner into the strategy room, a bookcase obscuring his figure. Nicke was pressed down into the table, her face towards him, and rough with bleeding. Lyon stood behind her, the full strength of his grip focused on her almost snapped neck as he pushed her cheek into the desk. A piece of paper sat on the surface and the trademark red ink, denoting a direct war order, was dripping from the tip of the quill in his hand.

Nicke's gaze met Zeph's, widened, and infinitesimally, narrowed her command.

The '*No*' was unspoken, but abundantly clear. He wanted to ignore it. Needed to ignore it and tear the king's hands from her. Perhaps he would like such treatment, and Zephyros would be glad to give it to him.

"Write the order, Malptian brat!"

Her focus returned to the man standing behind her, and Zeph watched her will strengthen.

"No, I will not."

"And why is that? Still hold hope that he will come home, fresh as the day he left? He hasn't been writing you, I've made sure of that, so perhaps you don't know about the injuries to his leg, the tendon cut through? Or how Jonn forced him onto the field despite it."

Zeph stayed where he was. He had enough guilt of his last challenge to the king's authority without adding more. But the man spoke lies. Lysander hadn't been injured. His letters would have mentioned it.

The same thought must have occurred to Nicke, but she stilled at his words.

"I will not condemn him," she whispered. Even with her throat against hardwood, she was clear and strong.

He pushed harder and she began to choke. Short, punctuated breaths were all that could escape. Zeph watched her eyes shutter, the whites dominating, and he acted: only this time, he had a plan of action that wouldn't pour oil onto the fire that was the king's fury.

"Commander!" Zeph yelled, directing the sound down the

corridor. It would bounce on the stone and be different to different ears. The effect was almost other-worldly, and Lyon released her, eyes tending to the frieze. Zeph yelled again, the same word, and Lyon gasped, eyes still high. Like he thought the art that surrounded him was ordering him; like the murals of Laerta's fighters stood to condemn.

"Galyn," Lyon gasped, before he fled the room. He didn't see Zephyros as he passed, but Zeph would hold onto the king's distinctive terror.

Nicke was slumped on the floor, chin to chest, when Zeph reached her. His hands were gentle along her jaw as he tilted her head high to allow air to flow.

Inwardly, he was screaming. How such an open secret of brutality was allowed was inscrutable. How the marks upon her body, always red and raw, were like a bastion of propriety. Lyon owned her, body and soul.

But not her heart, which was currently engaged on a field in Auntu. So far away but always hers. Lysander knew the risks and fought for her anyway.

Nicke gasped a breath but didn't wake straight away.

"Rose?" Zeph murmured, whispering almost. He didn't know who else was in the building. Who else would help, or hinder, him.

The urge to carry her home was overwhelming, but he snuffed it like he did his guilt. The impulse lay in wait, though, for a time when he was at his weakest.

She began to stir after a minute of difficult breathing. Her eyes fluttered open, taking in first the light of the high windows, then the deep blues and reds adorning the walls, then the worried face staring down at her. He was angry, and it was misdirected, he knew.

"Why didn't you come straight to the strategy session?" he snapped. "I was waiting and instead you were here."

It took her a few glances about his face to respond, and his concern tripled. His anger didn't abate, however.

"I was collecting things," she replied slowly, like it was difficult. She was propped up by his arm around her lower shoulders, where he'd supported her breathing. She moved away now. He almost didn't let her go.

"Where was your guard?" he barked.

"Ryan? I don't know. With Kallum, I suspect."

"Convenient."

She hummed in response. A light tinge of pink wove over her features and into the darkness of her tightly curled hair. It was the design of the grain of the wooden desk made flesh. The imprint was most prominent on her cheek, where the bones that made her appearance delicate protruded.

He simply had to know that she was okay, more than physically. More than he could feel or regard or see.

"And I suppose it was easy for him to follow you in here. Don't you have any weapons training?"

"No, you know I don't."

She was getting more frustrated. Good.

"You can't be found alone, rose. It will always end badly."

"I wasn't alone. He sent the boys away. They can't disobey their father."

"They could if they had any semblance of decency!"

She growled, low in her throat as she pushed gingerly off the floor. He caught her again as she stumbled and she pushed herself out of his arms.

"It isn't my fault."

"You not knowing how to defend yourself is! Even how to turn your body when you fall!"

"I don't care how I fall."

"And your nephews just disappearing when they know what your father does to you is inexcusable."

Her gaze was like a knife, pinning him in place. "They are

children!"

"And so were you, once. It didn't matter then! Why should it matter now?"

"Because it's my job to protect them!"

"And you're teaching them that this is allowed. That when they are king, brutalising who they want is permitted."

She leant back, her hand on her chest but he didn't feel done. Didn't feel like he could stop the tirade. Originally, he'd just wanted to see the light back in her eyes and for her to fight him; back to her usual self rather than the shell she'd been for months now. Waiting for the letter that would confirm her largest fear.

"Kallum isn't like his father," she replied softly. Her gaze flittered down to the desk where the missive lay. Auntu's port was the next prize.

"Apples and trees," Zeph said bitterly. Nicke shrugged.

"It's fine. I'm fine." She spared him a glance as she picked up the order and threw it into the fire. "You should probably go."

He nodded. "I'm going to go and find Ryan. Can you please wait here for him?"

At her assent, he left the strategy room with his fury building.

He found Ryan on the grass standing above the heir who was sharpening a kopis.

"The general needs to be walked home," Zeph said. Ryan straightened at his tone.

"Why?" he said.

"Because that bastard of a king had his hands on her, and she needs both Demetria and rest. Please see to it."

Ryan was quick to acquiesce. That left Zephyros with Kallum, the boy who would become king. He was lanky as most youths were: childhood verging on adult. His eyes, almost as furious as Zeph felt, were dark, probably from his Malptian side.

Kallum stood up and poked Zeph in the chest.

"You shouldn't speak about my father that way."

Zeph wanted to laugh at this child playing at power, but he held his poise.

"Tell me, boy, do you care about your aunt at all?"

Kallum's eyes flashed and his grip on the sword he'd been sharpening tightened.

Zephyros could see how it would play out. Zeph would goad the heir some more, then Kallum would attempt to pierce his flesh in a display of his inexperience. Zeph would then be bound for lifting a hand to their prince and Nicke would be in a worse place than she was. Sophie, with her husband on the plains far from here, would be worse off without a brother at home, too. Even though, in his sister's immense competence, it would probably be unfair to categorise it as her needing him.

"Of course I care about her," Kallum said. "But she doesn't listen. She disrespects the king and the queen daily. Disrespectful women should be punished."

Zeph felt like engaging him simply to spare his future Kyptian bride his views, but no.

"Good day, heir." Zephyros bowed slightly, ill-mannered, and walked towards the Credo's entrance.

The day had turned warm for winter, and he'd been on the road home for twenty minutes before he felt the first coward's punch.

"You'll pay for disrespect just as she does, slave." The flat plane of Kallum's sword knocked Zeph on the back of the head and he fell to the dust of the road. His cloak, still navy blue but close to being maroon, dulled with dirt and debris. "You'll pay for your words."

Zeph was too surprised by the assault to do much other than stare. Kallum circled him and attempted many glancing punches. Some made it to a sensitive part: a lower rib, a collar bone, the meat of his left flank; but most had no power behind them.

Zephyros recovered and stood tall. His own kopis remained in his belt.

"Perhaps you're too much like your father after all, child. I imagine he would only hit from behind also."

Kallum's face went red and he attempted a punch to Zeph's mouth, but it was blocked easily.

"My father is not a coward!"

"And my father was a king, since we're sharing falsehoods."

As Kallum, his sword rippling and his anger too fleeting to put strength behind the blade, launched towards Zeph, he had a sudden revelation.

Of children coerced and left to dangle by their own unworthiness. Of the way the strongest sunflower would follow a drought-inducing sun, even though it meant its death. Of how a spider, caught, envenomed, and planted with the eggs of a wasp, would still build webs and eat flies towards its own doom.

Zephyros had had a hard hand as he'd grown and more than once he'd begged the stars for a different lot: for his parents to come back to him and tear him from his uncle's grasp. It was every orphan's dream; every beaten child's fantasy: to be more than the circumstances that dictated their life and for family to come and claim them back from it. And when the phantoms never showed, they wouldn't wither and shrink because of it: they would try their best to be that family for other children.

Zephyros knew the marks Lyon left on his wife's sister. Even if Kallum was free from blows, he could be harmed in other ways. The speed at which he defended his father and engaged a man almost twice his age may have been testament to it.

Fear does funny things.

Nicke was right. Children are more than the simple parts of their upbringing. They deserved protection, moreso even than his brother's choice.

Zephyros blocked the blows, but didn't engage further. He looked at Kallum with sad eyes, and hoped to gods that his mother loved him enough. Nicke shared enough casual, loving touch with both boys to amount to love, at least.

The heir eventually gave up, panting.

"Why are you looking at me like that?" Kallum snapped.

Zeph shrugged. "I remember being sixteen, is all."

Kallum tried to laugh but it came out more like a scoff. "Don't let me hear about you talking shit again," he said. "Or it'll be worse for you."

Zeph nodded, then skirted around the boy and walked home.

* * *

"What the hell happened to you?" Demetria yelped when Zeph pushed open his front door. His face had swelled under the biting wind and he couldn't quite feel his lips.

He shrugged.

She tisked. Her hair was severely away from her face and she wore a soft woollen jacket, even next to the braziers that gave off ample warmth. Zeph was glad she was here.

She was holding a grey folded cloak in her arms and put it into a pile on the table while Zeph sat. Piles of clothing covered the counter, sectioned into mending categories. The grey cloak went on the 'low priority' pile.

Demetria had been at this task since the Laertans had left for the war. Her duties at the king's residence were fewer now that the queen had taken on further slaves, so she found herself wanting something to do. Zephyros appreciated the company nevertheless.

She gave him a wet cloth. It doused much of the pain.

"Thank you," he whispered.

"What happened?" she asked again, softening her tone.

"I intervened on the king beating Nicke and his son didn't appreciate it when I called his father a bastard."

Demetria was silent for a moment. Then, "Did the king hear you say this?" Zeph shook his head. "Well that's something at least."

"He was forcing her to sign a war missive and she refused. So he began to choke her."

She didn't reply straight away but he could feel her trembling. He took her hand and gave it a squeeze. "She's okay, Ria. I made sure Ryan walked her home."

"Ryan is Lyon's man."

"He is, but he's also terrified of me, so would have done what I said."

She nodded and took her hand back. He wasn't done talking about what had happened, about how the rage overtook him, but he didn't want to push her.

"Now," she said. "Is there anything in these piles that you want to keep?"

He pointed to two or three things and she put them aside.

"I thought I could teach you how to make a lemon loaf? There are so many beautiful trees in the orchard going to waste."

"Are you calling me a bad farmer?"

"Zeph, you're the worst farmer I've ever met."

He furrowed his eyes in offence. "I am not."

She rolled hers. "Come on."

When Sophie found them, Zeph was just putting the final drizzle of lemon syrup on the cake. Their heads were together as they attempted to avoid the hot honey touching the cold cheese icing, and they were laughing as the flow caused the icing to slide off.

"You'll never make a cook at this rate," Demetria said.

Zeph grimaced then tried again. This time, the syrup was accepted by the cake with minimal spillage.

"It simply takes a deft hand," he said triumphantly.

"And you certainly are triumphant, brother," Sophia said.

"Soph," he said brightly. He took her in, quietly cataloguing her health and mood. The shaved side of her head denoted her change to wife even as the rest was caught in a bun at the nape of her neck. "You can taste it for me!"

Sophia's gaze flicked to Demetria before turning back to Zeph. He felt the slave make a sharp movement from behind him. "Maybe later, Zeph," Sophie said gently.

He grimaced at Demetria again. "It won't poison you," he said, a bit deflated.

"Because that's the standard food should always be held to," Demetria deadpanned. She still cut a slice from the end and offered it to Sophia.

Sophie took it gingerly and took the tiniest bite possible. Zeph deflated further.

"I'm just not feeling well otherwise," Sophie said. "Nothing to do with your cooking, Zephy."

"Zephy?" he said. "I feel like it's time to remind you that I'm older than you."

She patted him patronisingly on the shoulder. "Of course." She turned to Demetria. "Are the clothes ready?"

"Oh yes," she replied, heading into the dining room. "I'll show you what I've found."

They left Zeph outside to clean up the mess he'd made of the kitchen.

When he went back inside, Demetria was gone and Sophie was sitting in Lysander's chair, patting one of his cloaks.

"Demetria went home?" he asked.

She nodded. "She was called back. Something about Nicke."

Zeph knew what it would be, but didn't want to burden Sophia with it. "Have you received anything today? I saw the messenger making the rounds."

"I got a letter from Matthew, nothing from the others. He's bored now that they've taken the plains, but is glad that it means he'll probably come home for the sowing."

Zeph nodded, and sat at his usual chair.

"I miss them all so much," she uttered. "I've finally stopped expecting them to crest the hill behind my house. I don't have anyone to sing with, or who wouldn't judge my weaving theory if it sounded crazy. I miss Lysander's surety." Her eyes turned to him then, tears collected. "He's been the only person I could rely on for years. He cared when no one else did, when no one else would come near me in case I tainted them. And I'll probably never see him again."

Zeph made a pained noise and stood. He wrapped his arms around her shoulders. "He's still alive, Soph, they all are."

"As far as we know. The letter could be on its way here as we speak."

"Don't wish fate closer. It doesn't need help."

He held her for a while, until her sobs lengthened and her breath came more easily. She patted his hand and he returned to his chair.

"I married them," she whispered. Letting the truth into the air stirred it, like the world was planting itself as witness.

Zeph stilled. He felt the slide of dread crest between his shoulder blades, just as it did whenever he was faced with insurmountable odds on a battlefield. "What?" he breathed.

She sniffed. "I married them the day after I married Matthew. I presided as a Master of Trade."

"Why?"

She looked at him with one eye cocked.

"Oh," he said.

"And it was what they wanted; what they needed. Even if he never comes back from Auntu, he shouldn't have gone to his grave a bachelor."

"I'm glad you did. But I wish you would have invited me."

She laughed softly. "That's fair enough."

Zeph had long since retreated from his first impressions of Nicke: of her beauty and fire. Once it had become clear that she was in love with Lysander, he put a firm clasp on the part of himself that coveted her. His need to protect her was borne out of love for his brother and deep appreciation for everything Lysander had done for him. Echoes of that deal wove through his letters from the battlefield, and Zephyros kept himself keen to the creep of desire for his brother's chosen.

Now that he knew that she was his brother's wife, the creep would have to be more tightly controlled than before.

"Zephy?" Sophia hesitated in saying, bringing him out of his reverie.

"Yes?"

"You and Demetria. Before, when you were trying to get the syrup to seep into the cake... Well, you looked alike."

"What do you mean?"

She paused, looking unsure. "I mean you have the same features. Same eyes and the same chin. Are you sure you're not of Boornea?"

He laughed, nervous but trying to hide it.

"You've noticed, haven't you?" she said.

"Yes." His head tilted back, like he was praying for strength. "We're the only ones with green eyes."

Sophie looked more relaxed, impossibly. Perhaps this was a safer territory than her grief at her brothers and husband being at war, or maybe it was something that had been nagging her. Zephyros wished she didn't look so interested in his possible connection to Demetria.

"That's not all," she said with a bit too much enthusiasm. "You sound the same when you laugh. Have you spoken to her about it?"

"No. I don't know how to bring it up."

"I don't know either," she conceded.

Demetria was as close to a sister as Sophia. She was one of his biggest supporters: reliable and constant. It wasn't only their similar look that had him wondering, but how his knack calmed him whenever she was around. Like it knew her from another life. A cousin, maybe.

"It's weird that you both ended up in Laerta," Sophie continued. "And with your training in the spear being so similar to the Laerta style rather than the Kurdan."

"My uncle taught me. We travelled to Kurkia when I was an infant. I wasn't born there."

"Did he ever say anything about your parents?"

"Only how they died. That he was killed for being strong and she was killed for running. I don't know what actually caused their death."

She hummed. "Krypteia hunt slaves here. The ones that they deem a threat to Laerta and can't be successfully sponsored, they slaughter. That's why Demetria first brought you here, because otherwise you would likely have been culled."

"Is that why Lysander became a krypteia?"

Sophie nodded. "One of the reasons; to get to the slaves before they were killed. He saved Drakon that way."

"You think my father was a Laertan slave?"

"I think it merits looking into. Do you have a name for your uncle?"

"Brynne."

"Maybe take that to the slave villages. They might know him. But maybe speak to Demetria beforehand so you can take her with you. I have the feeling you poking around on your own won't be as well received."

She was right, he knew. Him turning up to a slave village with a citizen's cloak and a sharp knife to ask difficult questions wouldn't get him very far. Demetria, though, was known to the people there.

Whether he had the nerve to discuss his thoughts with Demetria was another question entirely. He wasn't a coward, but he didn't want to raise the possibility when she was so reticent to discuss her own past. The only time she'd mentioned her parents was with overwhelming sadness.

"Zephyros?" came a call from the front door. Both of them looked to the messenger rifling through his bag.

"Bryan," Zeph said as he stood to retrieve the letter from him.

"A thick one today. No scroll, you'll be glad to hear."

Zephyros nodded and took the padded envelope. A scroll was from a general, Jonn or Sophos, to notify a family of loss. No scroll was good news. Another week.

He sat as Bryan left the yard and dragged his chair towards Sophie.

His hands were shaking, inexplicably. It was just a letter. It would be similar to what Sophie heard from Matthew.

He read it to himself first, then out loud to Sophie.

Dear Zeph,

Happy winter. I'm sure you're enjoying just how cold Laerta can become when the wind travels off the snow. You'll be glad to hear that it only gets colder from here.

"He's right, that's why I made you the stockings."

"Don't interrupt."

Sophie harrumphed and Zephyros turned back to the letter.

We've started our own winter sow using the fields of Auntu. It's made it look more like home. But the mountains are less sharp here and the weather more predictable. Many of the farmers left their fields intact, but some salted the soil as they ran from us. Terrible choice, I think. It's not like we'll be here forever: they might gain the land back eventually. Either way, it makes a patchwork of chance. My company were lucky in that we have shoots growing now. Others have found the earth hostile.

Sophie was tapping her foot, so Zeph paused in the telling.

"Matthew got a salted field," she said. "That's why he's coming home for the sowing."

"Huh," Zeph said with interest. "I wonder what decided which ones got which fields."

She shrugged. "Part of me wishes it was all salted."

Zeph laughed. "All of me wishes that."

We got drunk the other night, uproariously.

Zeph stopped again and looked at his sister sidelong. "This isn't for your ears."

She scowled. "Why not? I want to hear what he said."

"Don't you get your own letters?"

"Yes, but they're not as long as yours. And they don't tell me what they get up to when they're drunk."

"Probably because they drink with your husband."

Her scowl turned into reservation.

"There are some things that men don't want their wives to know."

"But it's okay for their brothers?"

"Yes! It's different."

"It isn't, and you know it."

"I still don't want to read it out to you."

"Fine."

He skimmed over Lysander's telling of how he, Matthew, and Kallias got into a faux fist-fight over which of their respective partners were the better. How Nicke was the smartest, Sophie the most practical, and Alix the beauty of the bunch. They apparently fought about other aspects of marriage too, which was why Zeph felt the tips of his ears redden at the thought of telling his sister of it.

I'm hoping the campaign won't last until Maios, your first in Laerta. I want to show you the festival myself because it's one of my favourites. I didn't think I'd see another one, so here's hoping.

When you write back, I want to hear from you that she's okay. She always writes that she's well, but it's almost as if I can hear the whisper in her voice that it is not so. I'm worried that she's acting like I'm already gone.

Please remember your promise to me that you would protect her. Keep her safe for me, Zeph. But, aside from that, please try and make her happy. I can't sleep for the worry that she's withering.

Zeph's voice hitched at the words and Sophia placed a comforting hand on his shoulder. The sooner the two of them could live their truth, the better the world would be.

I owe you much, brother. More than you could know.

Love to you, and Sophie who is probably there with you,

Lysander.

"How do you reply to a letter like that?" Zeph said, suddenly angry. "How do you assure someone so far away that his loved ones aren't in pain without him?"

"You don't try to do that in the first place." Sophie brought her hand to his cheek and directed his eyes to hers. "You tell the truth. That we're not okay. That she is a shadow without him. That you are."

Zeph didn't know what was worse: Nicke's true condition, or telling Lysander the truth of it. He suspected that there wasn't much tethering her to this world. If he could turn the resignation to fury or the stoicism to hate, then she might stand a chance when

Lyon fulfilled his promise. Even if she hated Zeph, to channel an emotion that didn't leave her bereft of feeling would be worth it in the end.

A letter to her slipped out, explaining the padding, and it looked longer than Zeph's had.

"I can take it to her today, if you want," Sophie suggested.

Zeph shook his head. He felt the sudden burst of feeling that threatened the leash on his need for the commander. He held it still then pushed it down, far enough below his reckoning, to make acquaintance with his fear.

"I'll take it to her tomorrow, when I scribe the strategy lesson. It'll be less obvious."

Sophia nodded, then took up vigil at the head of the dining table and began to sew, as Zeph wrote his reply back to his brother.

*   *   *

Nicke spoke with a cadence that denoted that her mind was elsewhere. She prescribed the work fluidly, proscribed their limits, and let the heirs run their minds into the rut of impossible odds. It was a war scenario, even though Laertan kings were not required to be warriors. That was one reason their education was separate, apart, from the rest of the children and teenagers. They were not subjected to the mountain that so often killed kids for sport, nor the viciousness that was encouraged by rival families seeking the Tertiary for their sons and daughters. It only took a certain number an annum: places were coveted.

Zeph transcribed it using Credo inks and Temple paper. He'd run out of his own supplies.

"Solve the cipher," Nicke said, writing it quickly on the wax tablet and placing it between them. "And learn war's fate."

Zeph wrote it into the dossier and then reclined, his shoulder flexing under his increased bulk. He'd moulded himself to his new city's expectations for a soldier, even if he was barred from war. Soon, though, he'd be a citizen, and his new physique would be put to use.

"Do you know how to solve a cipher?" Nicke asked suddenly, on his side of the grove. His eyes had been closed and she'd surprised him.

He shook his head. "My uncle used to receive letters in it. I suppose he didn't teach me so I wouldn't pry."

She nodded, like she'd expected him to be lacking in this department.

"I could teach you," she offered. She gestured at her nephews, hard at work. "It's often how royal correspondence is given and sent."

"So why would I need to learn it then?" he countered.

Nicke shrugged. "Who knows when it might be useful."

"Finished!" Dannehs yelled, waving his results in the air.

Kallum glared at him, grumbling about vowels.

Nicke moved away and Zeph went back to his tools in order to write down the answer.

"Very good, Dannehs," she said. "That's right."

They waited, until Nicke finally gave Kallum a measured look of disappointment and dismissed him. "Do better," was his goodbye as the two boys left the Credo.

She took three or four deep breaths, sounding like she was holding back tears. Zeph had never known her to cry in the over half-year he'd been in her life. He moved towards her gingerly.

"What was the solution?" he said gently, taking Dannehs's paper from her grasp.

"A fragment from one of the songs. *Once spoken and twice lost; you will be aimless. Another shade singing silently with shades of no worth.*"

His face crumpled and he was suddenly silenced. Usually a man with much to say, for the first time in his life he felt like his voice wasn't what was needed to fill the space. It must be the season for revelations: first his sudden realisation that Kallum was a boy in need of love, and now that he didn't have a solution for this particular problem. No amount of arrogance, facetiousness, or galling hubris would lift the burden that Nicke carried. She'd been laden with a lion's share in her short life. Born a princess, sold for a city, raised a traitor, and likely killed a wife.

Zeph's skin itched with the injustice of it. Nary a situation had not been solved by his surety. But this was just that: something he couldn't solve.

His grief surprised him, because he'd always held on to the prayer that Lysander would come home. The truth of it hit him harshly. He swallowed thickly and gave in to the instinct to draw Nicke to him and envelope her in his arms. The trees shielded them from the rest of the Credo, her guard was waiting for her at the top of the wall, and he felt her collapse against him. She didn't cry loudly, other than a small intake of breath before his chiton muffled her. He held her until the shuddering stopped through sheer will and she extracted herself from him for the second time in as many days.

"I have a letter," he whispered, retrieving it from his cloak pocket. "I'm sending my reply back tomorrow, so you have time to include yours."

"Thank you, Zeph," she said. "I don't know how I could continue without you."

He shrugged. "Sophie told me yesterday, you know. Of what happened." She looked at him sharply, daring him to voice it. "And I'm a little upset that I wasn't invited."

Almost against her better judgement, it seemed, she laughed lightly. "It was a short guest list."

"What it means, though, is that my house is yours. If anything were to happen—"

"No, Zeph. I'll be in more danger if I gave in to the notion."

"I mean if he's going to kill you, like he tried to do yesterday, then the house is legally yours. The ephors would agree, and Lyon wouldn't be able to touch you."

She sniffed a little, then moved away to clear her supplies. He didn't wait, but transcribed the solution to the cipher and left her to it.

CHAPTER NINE

Nicke

Nicke felt a sombre breath of truth when she put her name to the specifics of her battle plan and folded the thick piece of scroll. She was signing death warrants of some of their bravest, of the ones who had been told of the insurmountable odds and had volunteered. She'd given explicit instructions that Laertans with families, children, were not to be accepted for the task. Those with the skills, but not those whose absence would fester in the grief of people left behind. It was a fine balance between age and experience. She knew for certain some that Sophos would choose. She suspected others.

The strategy was deceptively simple. Auntu had a city wall five men high, and that wall stretched from the perch of the polis towards its port on the eastern tip of the land. Auntu was an importer. The city fields, though abandoned and many salted, were not the key to the strategy that city was currently running. It had a war chest for exactly this type of campaign, like they'd been the ones goading the war and knew that Kypt would be incited to call on their much more powerful ally. Like Auntu had something to prove to Laerta on the battlefield.

They hadn't yet succeeded. Auntuan farmers and slaves had been overrun. Only minor skirmishes dotted the field. But Nicke was cautious to be optimistic in the way Jonn and Sophos were.

Because she was here, in the city, and saw its own empty fields needing sowing while hoplites fought abroad. She saw the grumblings among the slaves at the backbreaking labour, usually shared with Laertans from the Primary. She heard the way families missed their members, so far from here for so long. If the plains had been easy to take, it was simply so Laerta was weaker when the push back came.

Her own grief intensified this. She had wanted the hoplites back for the winter sowing, now a moon past its beginning, for her own reasons. But Lysander wasn't Primary, and he wasn't coming back.

A gust of wind pushed the missive onto the floor, close to the fire. If Nicke had been the type to see such signs she may have discerned the omen in it. Sometimes wind is just wind, and sometimes her needs were below the reckoning of a war machine.

The group chosen would be small. Around thirty of them, ones who could think for themselves and act like a unit. Ones that had been trained to reason, to look to their fellows, and work and fight with only the band in mind. Spies, and those specially trained by the Rex to be their guardians. They would move away from the main force under the cover of night and change their clothing. Laertan colouring was similar to Auntuan, and they could blend in.

The main part of Laerta's army would then assault the wall's weakest point: where the foul water of a city escaped. Laerta had steered very clear of that part of the wall so as to not draw attention to their knowledge of it. It was a secret thing that was known to the engineers, and their slaves.

A planted slave could mean life, or death. Something Nicke took to heart when she thought of her own daily rituals. She no longer thought of Demetria as a possible threat to her. As Nicke had opened like a ripe peach to the inexplicable warmth from the slave, so had Demetria earned her trust. She was probably the one who could do the most damage, should she turn. But Nicke didn't think she would turn.

As the army pushed that weak point in what looked like a common assault, the small band would infiltrate the city and open the then lightly fortified gates wide.

It was dangerous, suicidal even, for the hoplites chosen. That's why they didn't have families. That's why she'd desperately wanted at least them to come home one last time before her signature sent them to their deaths. It was a weakness unique to her in the War Room: she didn't see simply the tokens that denoted a phalanx moving across a map. She saw each of their faces as they were moved into position. She saw their frowns, their smiles, then wiped clean in death. It wasn't empathy as such. She was a great despiser of waste, and war wasted good people. Perhaps it was because she was brought to this place as a war prize. Perhaps it was because she'd been the beneficiary of war; the receiver of war's bounty of blood.

Or perhaps it was because war was about to take her husband's life as he led the band of Laertans to that long wall. Sophos had promised that he would protect him, but even if it was possible for her to be objective, Lysander was uniquely placed to lead them. He was well liked and clever. He was strong, and not resistant to new ideas from his compatriots if the plans needed changing. He was good with words should they be questioned by the gates men, and exceptional with a sword if the answers he gave were wanting.

He was uniquely placed to fit the position. But others were too. Others with better words, or more training.

The letter fluttered in the wind again, closer to the fire, and she caught it between her fingertips like it would burn her. Anyone else and it would already be away. Nicke was adult enough to recognise her own limitations. It was the untenable position, and she would forever be begging the earth for forgiveness. Lysander was uniquely suited, yes, but being thrown around by fate was an impossibility in her mind, where every aspect was unaccounted for.

She would place him there. Then, at least, if he died as a leader of Laertans, it would have been for a purpose other than punishment. The existence of Nicke's love causing his demise was unthinkable enough to cause her to assign him a suicide mission to assuage some of her own guilt. She despised waste.

"Commander?" a voice said from the corridor. It was one of the runners sent for her instructions. She couldn't run the war from here, but using the information the other two generals sent her, she could try.

"Here," she said, her voice flat. Nicke didn't look at the man who took the missive with her seal keeping it intact. She knew he'd be some boy of the Secondary whose first war would be one of sidelines and learning. She didn't much care, either. She felt the air move as he bowed and left the room.

Leaving her alone with the fire that she wished would consume her.

* * *

Nicke didn't often venture into the mountains where children sparred and trained. Once they were literate and had enjoyed a childhood of philosophy and arts, they were stripped of their hair and exposed to Laerta's specific brand of brutality. This was where each stream was weeded out. It was a mistake to think that if a child was poor at war, then they would be sent to the Theory or the Trade. Those two schools only took the children with talent in their craft, not simply the ones that were mediocre elsewhere.

The children that had no talent in woodworking or theology were sent to the mountain to thrive or become slaves. Many of them simply died. It was a shameful thing.

Nicke rode her small, almost lame horse with Ryan trailing on his larger one. Even if she had airs of escaping into the countryside, it would stop her. And besides, the weather was so fiercely cold that it would stop the devil himself from leaving the protection of the trees.

They came to the crest of a hill at the base of the sacred mountain and Nicke dismounted. The camp was spartan and shimmering with water made steam by the fires dotting the space. Children from nine to thirteen spread amongst the canvas, desperate for warmth. Of course, to make them strong, Laerta did not provide them with cloaks or with blankets. They wore a chiton and some leather on their feet for shoes, but otherwise they could only be made warm by each other, or by the cooking flames.

"General," their teacher said as Nicke entered the camp, bowing his head deferentially.

"Samuel," Nicke replied. She walked to him and was comforted that there was at least warmth in his expression. Samuel wasn't one of hers, one she could rely on, but nor was he one of Lyon's. Like Matt, his brother, Samuel enjoyed the space between loyalties. If Nicke was thinking truthfully, the only loyalty Sam would afford would be to his almost-royal mother.

"The children are enjoying their breakfast, so I thought we could brief you on their progress before the demonstrations."

Nicke's skin itched at the implications of the scene before her, but she nodded her ascent. There were far more older children than younger ones, when usually the ratio was reversed as the difficulty of the camps came to the fore.

She entered the canvas tent by ducking her head slightly. She was tall for a woman, but not taller than the average Laertan man. The tent was made a comfortable height for the tutors here. There was a singular long pole in the centre of the space, and a circular oak table placed it in its middle. Three Laertans stood to attention as she approached, and her eyes slid to the slaves at the edges of the room. Some held water jugs, others had their hands free to assist the citizens with what they needed. Food was already set out, as were the wax tablets that the Credo relied on to mark down their progress for these review meetings.

Nicke had attended them in the past, but found the work was not really her forte. She was harsher in her criticism than warranted because she did not want any part in the cog that was children dying. It made her a hypocrite, she knew, but the alternative was her compassion absconding completely.

She sat at the round table and waited for them to begin. The three facing her, made four by Samuel, looked at her with varying expressions. One, Jane, sly by nature, openly glared at the tablets before them. Another, Karl, had what he likely thought a neutral expression painted across his face. The third, the one who Nicke knew could throw a javelin clear across a field and strike an enemy in the neck, was her second, David. He looked at her with a serenity that spoke to his distrust of the Laertans around him, and she heeded his unspoken warning. She would follow his lead. He usually wasn't stationed on the mountain, but was here to place the older children he thought would thrive under his care.

"Commander," Karl said kindly.

Nicke was passed a parchment summarising the numbers. It sent molten lead to her stomach and she almost vomited. At the top was the number of children who had climbed the mountain, and below it, the number of children who would never descend. A hundred and fifty-two who would never leave this place.

"Is this normal?" she asked, swallowing her revulsion.

"No," David replied. "That's one of the reasons I was called up here before Maios. It's an unusual number of children who have died."

Karl huffed a little, probably because this overrode his authority. "It's not so many more so as to invite scrutiny."

David glanced at him but kept his attention to Nicke. "It's about thirty percent more. Some who had promise when they left the children's training at the Credo."

"So more of the younger ones?" she asked.

He nodded. His glance to Karl left much unsaid and Nicke

wished he would speak freely.

She looked at the paper in her hand to study it more closely.

Of the hundred and fifty-two children that had not lasted the season, a hundred and ten of them were under the age of eleven. The rest were twelve and thirteen, the ages beyond what was considered unsafe. So many children dead for a country's warmongering. But there was more than that, here. Something piqued her curt mind, a fear unwilling to be spoken.

"Do you have a list of names?" she asked.

Samuel passed her another piece of parchment, this one curling because of its length. Nicke had little to do with the children, with her focus on the older teenagers of the Tertiary and her nephews, but some of the names stood out.

"These are the children of sponsored slaves," she whispered to the open air.

"Ones that earnt their status of citizen in either the Boornean uprising or the Malptian War," Samuel explained. "Some have been citizens for longer than the king's been on his throne. All of their warring parents are currently in Auntu."

She looked up sharply. "All of them?"

Samuel nodded.

She held the paper in a clenched fist, then she looked at the people around her. All were comfortably Laertan, with no slave or foreign blood. Laerta's practice of killing slaves that had proven too strong, or smart, or cunning, was leaching into the children of the state.

Nicke's instincts had always been sharp. It was one of the reasons she'd been successful in her rise to general. And they were screaming at her now.

"David, I want the remaining children moved down to the plains for the rest of their training. Where I can keep watch on the situation."

"But general!" Karl started. "Part of it is the winter cold and surviving it. If they don't survive it here, they won't survive it on the field."

"It's less about keeping them alive and more about the winter sowing," she placated. "Sophos and Jonn won't release enough hoplites for it. Only those who are of little use in Auntu are coming back. We need the strongest children to help with it."

He receded from his initial outburst and nodded.

"I'd like to see the demonstration now. David, Jane, if you please."

Samuel and Karl took it for the dismissal it was and didn't follow them out of the tent. Nicke took a breath and knelt down to retie her already tight sandal.

"David?" she murmured.

"Karl's trips up the mountain have double the amount of dead to the rest of us. Always a stray animal that catches them."

"It's worse than that," Jane continued, obviously in David's confidence. "He doesn't bring the bodies back for burial. They're all slave children, commander."

"Yes, I know."

"My nephew was one of them," Jane said plaintively as she straightened. "And I couldn't do a damned thing to stop it."

"Some plot is afoot," David confirmed. "Perhaps he knows about..." He looked to Jane and Nicke saw her shake of the head, preventing David's further commentary.

Nicke hummed. "Move the children to the plains and I'll update the procedures so you have to report more often. Maios is only a few moons away and they'll return to their homes for the festival."

"Nicke, I don't know what is behind this, but I don't know if moving the children will help," David said. "Karl will still be their tutor. I thought maybe bringing in an older student under the guise of learning directly from him would maybe calm the situation."

"You mean Zephyros," she replied quietly. "But I need him at the Credo."

"He's almost finished the theory of war," her second continued. "He's damned good at it, but he's more brilliant with children. I've been using him to teach as much as I've been teaching him."

Jane nodded. "That he's a slave himself, too. And Karl is terrified of him."

"Most people are," David agreed. "He already acts like a—"

"If you bring the children to the plains, I can spare Zephyros," Nicke interrupted. Her instincts were sharp, knowing.

If anyone could rise to the top of the military, and had the wits, charm, and drive to recruit these Laertans to him, it was Zeph. It sounded an awful lot like work he was already undertaking, and Nicke needed to nip it in the bud.

Both of them nodded, and directed her to watch the children play at war.

* * *

He wasn't happy when she gave him the order. He was to stick to Karl like butter, following his moves so he could prevent the piling up of the bodies.

Nicke went with him to where the new camp had sprung up. They shared a wagon with food supplies, her watching the scenery pass while trying to prevent herself from vomiting because of the rutted road, and he with a knife and a small block of wood in his hand. When she'd asked what he was carving, he'd said something asinine and trite, his mood sour. She could almost cope with the pain the wagon wrought if it wasn't for Zephyros's needling.

"When are you going to permit me to teach you the spear?" he asked, the whittling eventually producing a small figure.

"I'm not," she said. "When are you going to permit me to teach you war codes?"

He grimaced. "I don't want to learn war codes."

"Why not?"

"Presumably the same reason you don't want to learn the spear." He blew the shavings away, studying his work. "Because you might be terrible at it, and you're used to being good at things."

"Spoken like a true Kurdan," she murmured.

"What was that?" he said loudly, cocking a brow.

"It doesn't matter."

They sat in silence for a while, listening only to the calls of the birds and the grunts of the horse as it traversed the gullies and hills. Three slaves walked next to them and, though Zeph had offered, all said they'd preferred the predictability of their own gait to that of a wagon. Nicke envied them, and had tried to join them before Zeph had insisted she be close enough to his blade should he need to use it. Ryan was behind the wagon, guarding it as much as guarding her.

"Do you know the story of the mountain?" she asked, needing distraction from her roiling gut.

"Yes."

She stared at him open-mouthed. "How?"

A shrug. "My uncle taught me all the stories."

"Your uncle," she deadpanned. "Taught you *all* the stories of foreign nations in the off-chance you ventured there."

"Yes. I know the story of Malptia's founding queen, too, if you want to hear it."

"No thank you."

Mirth travelled across his face and she was tempted to push him from the cart. "Her name was Petra, and she was married against her will to a foreign king who abhorred her culture."

"Zeph..." she warned quietly. No one was in hearing distance, but he ignored her anyway.

"And in revenge for him cutting their sacred blooms and felling

171

their sacred grove of olives—"

"*Zeph.*"

"—she gutted him on their wedding night—"

"Zeph!"

But he continued, ignoring her protests. "—and from his blood, she made her crown. His hair adorned the city's first amphitheatre and the wind blew through it whenever the sister-gods were pleased." He turned to her, then, his eyes fierce and she found that it centred her; brought her breath out of her body. He knew the effect of her homeland's stories on her, he must, because the way he catalogued her reaction was as if he was looking for a fury building and blinding. But she wasn't angry. These stories were only hers in secret, a burden shared between sisters only on the darkest nights of the winter solstice, Malptia's main festival event.

She knew that Zeph worried; knew that he worried as much for her sake as for his brother's. And that these needlings were par for the course of him trying to bring her back to her old self.

But then, he hadn't really known her before.

"And then," he continued, his gaze capturing her and refusing to relinquish its grip. "She passed her crown to a daughter, who then passed it onto a daughter. Different to other places I know of. Lyon didn't just remove a princess from her home and marry her into submission, he stole both heirs too."

She stayed silent. This wasn't common knowledge.

"And further, he only gave the king of Malptia, your father, his consideration in negotiation. Despite your mother, Helen, being queen and he simply being her consort."

"It was Lyon's father, actually," she whispered. "The negotiations were Kallum Rex's doing before he was sentenced to death for taking a bribe in the same conflict."

Zeph paused and Nicke wondered why he hadn't heard of it.

"He negotiated the marriage contract with my father. Then he took a bribe from my mother's general and threw one particular battle in order to gain the lands he wanted for Laerta's farmers. The battle went worse than the ephors of Laerta would tolerate, and when the bribe came to light, he was sentenced to death. He died here, given hemlock and told that he would either take it, or starve to death. He chose the former. It was Lyon who negotiated me into the contract because Malptia was on their knees. My mother was dead and my father took the only available option."

She swallowed roughly. She'd not spoken about this to anyone, not even Alix. It was a cavernous part of her that knew how much she was worth, and that it was less than control ceded.

"That's why he acts like he owns you," Zeph said.

She nodded. "Because he bought me, just as he would a slave."

"But you're not a slave, rose. You never have been and you never will be. What happens to Malptia when your father dies?"

"It gets absorbed."

"And you're okay with that?"

"Of course I'm not okay with it. But there's nothing to be done. The woman who was groomed for queendom became one."

"Sounds like the royal line of Laerta needs to be cut down to size," he grumbled.

"You can't say that Zeph. It'll get you killed."

He grumbled again and went back to his whittling. The horses were taking care of themselves on the narrow trail, so there was little need for his hands to direct them.

He sighed loudly and she knew enough of him to know that this conversation wasn't over, just paused.

They travelled in silence until a lurch in the road. A thundering crack broke into their tentative silence and Nicke felt the body of the wagon break under the strain. She was thrown from the seat, head first, and landed poorly onto her right shoulder. The shuddering of multiple sacks of flour and beans tumbling from the wooden bed sounded and she turned in time to see Zephyros pushing her out of the way of a cask barrelling towards her.

Screams rent the air and Nicke stood among the chaos, trying to find the source.

"Lily," Zeph said from behind her. He rushed to the side of the cart where the sacks had fallen. Quickly, with a strength that surprised her, he began to throw the sacks away from the crying woman. Nicke ran to join him but ended up superfluously fussing over Marie and Stefan, who were uninjured, while Zeph worked. Ryan joined him, moving the grain further away from the pile.

Eventually, the brutalised figure of the youngest slave was revealed from under the food. Nicke took off her cloak and offered it for warmth, the red hiding her injuries. Then she hung back, letting the slaves who knew her better to assist her in her pain. To Nicke's surprise, Zeph stayed with them. Marie had Lily's head in her lap and was murmuring quietly. It sounded like a prayer; like a promise of a life beyond what had been offered here.

Her chest was weakly rising, slowly falling with each breath.

Then the movement stopped, and she died there under a winter sun.

Nicke moved back to give them some privacy, but Zeph caught her hand.

"I think some daisies, Nicke. White, if you can?"

She did as he said and brought them back. Marie thanked her quietly and placed them into Lily's hands. Zephyros stepped away then, standing beside Nicke as they gave the others solitude.

"It's an old story that they still tell, not in the city, but in the outskirts." He looked down at his own hands and clenched and unclenched them. "Of payment needed at the moment of death for a peaceful crossing. Something alive and coveted by those who enable the passing."

Nicke nodded, and they waited together until the sun had dipped lower than was necessarily safe in this part of the countryside. Stefan approached them.

"Zeph, we need to bury her. It could take a while."

"Whatever you need, Stefan." He looked quickly at Nicke. "But I have to get the general to the camp."

"I can help," Ryan said from behind them. Nicke had forgotten that he was there, watching for her. "I'll help you dig."

Zeph nodded. "I'll need to get help from David anyway, in order to get these supplies moved."

"You should probably take the commander back to the city," Ryan said. "Something doesn't smell right."

Zephyros nodded, and Nicke felt a mounting frustration at being excluded from their conversation.

"What do you mean, Ryan?"

He looked to Zephyros deferentially before shrugging. "That axle is sawed right through."

Nicke and Zeph both looked at the same time, and sure enough, there was a straight cut two-thirds through the wood of the axle.

Someone had tried to kill her again. But this time, someone else had died.

"Oh earth," Nicke whispered.

"Ryan," Zephyros said, his tone deceptively quiet and calm. "Can you help Stefan and Marie bury Lily? Somewhere under the trees should have the ground soft enough."

Ryan nodded and took a pick out of the wagon, passing it to the waiting Stefan. They moved off and began to work.

"I think you'd be safer at the camp, to be honest," Zeph said to her when they were alone. "David doesn't harbour you ill-will."

"That we know of," she said with a baited breath. It felt like her circle of trust was getting smaller and smaller.

"That we know of," he confirmed with a nod. "But I think it's the better idea."

Nicke dipped her chin, then moved away from Zeph when he went to retrieve Ryan's horse. She found herself kneeling next to the slave who was slowly and carefully washing Lily's face.

"I'm very sorry, Marie," Nicke whispered. She reached out to take the woman's hand, but she flinched back. Nicke didn't take it personally.

"She was newly married, commander. Her husband is supporting in Auntu."

"Tell me what I can do, and I'll do it. I'll give money, goods, whatever he needs when he returns."

Marie looked at her sadly, a resignation in her eyes. "It's always the same."

"I'll find a way to make it better, I promise."

"I hope you can keep that promise, general. I really do."

"Nicke?" Zephyros called, loosening the second stirrup on Ryan's horse. "Do you want pillion, or I can walk but we won't get there before dark and will have to camp."

"We'll go fast. We're already late."

Zeph nodded and mounted the warhorse. He put out a hand to her and she clambered up, sitting in the saddle as he sat behind her on the horse's rump.

"Camp here tonight, if the spirits don't bother you," he said to Ryan. "I'll be back in the morning." At Ryan's nod, Zeph leant in closer to him. "And try to find a signature. No slave's life is worth this."

Nicke's awareness exploded around her as they trotted into the forest. The orders he easily gave; the way those orders were listened to.

He had positioned Laertans who had been fiercely loyal to the Rex, and turned them to his cause. He knew everyone by name; he had no consideration to rank; he gave instructions to soldiers. He'd convinced Ryan, who had been her shadow since she was a teen and would report every transgression to the king, to let Zeph not only touch her, but abscond into the forest with her. Nicke didn't know whether it was trust or fear, but either way, Zeph was acting as Ryan's commander. David's words and the sentiment behind them returned to her ears and her hands began to shake.

Zephyros, the slave turned citizen, was planning a coup.

By the time her mind had spun, the horse was travelling a comfortable canter and she found herself whispering into the wind. He heard her, all the same.

"Zeph…?"

"Mmmhmm?"

"You need to stop this."

"Stop what, rose?"

"Stop planning a coup."

"Who says I'm planning a coup?"

She laughed outwardly, the ringing filling the mountain air despite having very little mirth.

"I'm Laerta's strategic general, Zephyros, and *I* say you're planning a coup."

He slowed the horse down but didn't stop.

"You would prefer I standby and let that family destroy mine." His hands tightened on the reins and she resisted the impulse to sooth them.

"It is what is safe," she sighed.

He chuckled. "This isn't safety, Nicke. It's starvation while food is left to rot. I intend on feeding the masses."

She knew what he meant, even if his words were wanting. It was the same reason he grew frustrated when he saw a problem without a solution, or when he was humbled by inclement weather. He abhorred things he couldn't control, and sought to make a world where he didn't need to cede rule in order to have his needs and wants met.

"Lysander is as good as dead, Zeph."

He stiffened behind her and she felt the hard bulk of his arms tighten. "That's not true until he is in the ground."

The fierceness and surety of this statement convinced even her, who had given her husband up for dead the moment he'd left the city. No wonder he could convince Ryan that the sky was green or David that the sea was potable.

"I hate that you've given up on him," he whispered. "He doesn't deserve it."

"None of us deserve this, but you have to think harder, Zeph. They will execute Sophie just for being your sister, and Matthew for being her husband, and Samuel for being his brother. Any of *your* brothers that return will also get the sword, simply for being of your household. You'd condemn Lysander as easily as I have."

Hesitation, then, "I'll take your advice and pull it back, but I won't stop."

"Then you may as well drive this horse over a cliff and kill us both. It'll be easier."

His knuckles whitened as he held the reins, and she hoped she'd gotten through to him. It wasn't worth it.

Better to live a half life than no life at all.

* * *

Nicke didn't have many warm memories of Alix. One was when Alix taught her the Malptian songs in secret, as a child while she crooned to a baby Kallum. Another was her soft hands along Nicke's locks, running her fingers through it with oil slicked up her arms. Standing side-by-side, one might have questioned their parenthood: Alix had the dark hair and the black eyes, with an olive skin closer to their father's complexion; while Nicke's russet colouring matched her hazel eyes and made her hair light in comparison. Different parts of their father and mother, combined.

Nicke had been too young when she was taken, and only in hindsight had she noticed her sister begin to shrivel under the hand of her new husband. There was a gap of three or so years between when they had been taken and when the king of Laerta had deigned to marry Alix. Laerta was almost aggressive in their laws of marriage, and even her queens were bound by them. As it were, Alix had to be of-age, twenty in Laerta, as well as versed in Laertan government and politics. It took enough time that Nicke remembered her sister before Lyon had her in his fists. Kallum came quickly after their marriage, a spitting image of her, but when the king tired of her, he gave her rein to explore other options.

Dannehs was sitting, legs crossed, at Alix's feet when Nicke came into the room, using charcoal to draw a picture. It was a fine rendition of a chamomile flower, and that Nicke could discern it from a daisy or a dandelion showed his talent. If he wasn't born of this house, he could have joined the Theory quite easily.

Nicke sat on the floor at her sister's assent and pulled the boy into her lap.

"Do you like it?" he asked, voice tentative.

"It's beautiful," she confirmed. "Can I keep it?"

"Oh, I made it for Kallias," he said by way of apology. "For when he gets back."

"Go and put it in the pile you've made of them, Dannehs," Alix said. "He'll want to see them all when he returns."

The boy bounded out of the room on winged feet, leaving the sisters.

Nicke looked at the shaded windows and thought quietly of the day's calm. It was unnerving, like the centre of a storm. "How are you feeling?" Nicke asked. She knew Alix worried, and knew that her sister was not as resilient as she once was.

"Tired, just tired." Alix drew her hands over the curves of her face and rested her chin at the apex of her meeting wrists. "Were you injured in the accident?"

"No, just some scratches, but even they have healed now."

"I was sorry to hear about the slave."

"I offered them comfort but they didn't want any."

Alix nodded and smoothed her hands over the navy blanket that covered her lap. Nicke absently considered Malptia's response to Alix: whether she would have been a queen worthy of their city. Nicke was confused by many things in their situation, but the main one circled her mind.

"Why can't you read, Alix?"

Her sister looked up sharply and then turned back to her lap, now picking at the threads. "I can read."

Nicke felt sadness weave the air like an expert dancer. It curled around her mind and heart, squeezing. "Barely. I'm not saying this to be cruel, but, I mean: you were groomed to be queen."

"I don't want to talk about it."

Nicke nodded, not wanting to interrupt the peace they enjoyed. Perhaps Alix simply didn't like to read.

"I may have been groomed to be queen, but I never was going to be."

A wrinkle appeared on Nicke's brow.

Alix's face was drawn, like hope was optioned and then discarded. "Malptia don't go purely by succession. It's the most suited child that ascends, after a series of tests, and I am sure you would have surpassed me."

"Are you sure?"

Alix nodded. "I think one of the reasons they had you after so many years was because I was particularly ill-suited to the role and they held out hope." Nicke shook her head but Alix didn't acknowledge it. "Not everyone is suited to the role thrust upon them, Nicke. Some of us are moved about the board without heed to our own wants."

Nicke sighed. "And what do you want, sister?"

Alix looked up then, tears in her eyes. "I want a farm. And a husband who loves me. One who lets me sing, and dance."

Kallias. Alix's joy found from the same house as Nicke's. Kallias was older than Lysander, she knew, probably by quite a few years, and when Kallias had first taken a shine to Alix it was as a field slave. Lysander had saved him by sponsoring him, and had probably saved Alix in the process.

It was on the tip of Nicke's tongue: the memory of Lysander's joy as he beheld her that morning roiling in her now. How she could relate to Alix's plight as the men they loved moved out of reach.

"If I was queen of Malptia, I could have taken any consort I wished," Alix said, looking to the sky.

"And if you were queen, you could have assented to mine," Nicke replied.

A shadow of a smile lit Alix's face. "Yes, and I would have."

It was a rare moment of solidarity between them, and both knew it would cut itself short just as quickly as a life is held taut then snapped.

It came as a scroll, bound by Sophos's red seal.

* * *

Nicke walked to Sophia's first. Zephyros was at the war camp and couldn't be reached before he returned in his own time.

Sophie was sitting in Matthew's lap when Nicke knocked and was bid to enter. His chiton was wet with tears and her brown hair looked like a storm had rifled through it. Matthew had come home for the sowing and was returning to the field soon enough.

"Do you know?" he asked diplomatically, before Nicke took Sophie's hand.

Nicke nodded. "I was with my sister when the scroll came."

"To you?" he asked, confused. Nicke shook her head but didn't elaborate. She knelt next to Sophie and was overwhelmed by the hopelessness in the woman's eyes.

"I'm sorry Sophie. Kallias was a great man."

She whimpered through her tears. "He didn't even die for a good reason. Fever, the missive said."

"I know. It's a waste."

"This whole thing is a waste," Sophie said. "And Matt has to go back next week. And Zeph will leave soon too, when he becomes a citizen. Lysander and Drakon probably won't come home and Auntu will pay it off like they always do."

Tears were beginning to spill down Nicke's cheeks now, the truth of it drowning her.

All of them, lost.

And Kallias wasn't even lost for a good reason. For most of Laerta, the reason was essential. The reason for death on the field was either to glory or to a city's disregard. The words written in the missive Nicke had sent blew through her mind like a toxic wind: Lysander would have his glory, rather than the poor death Lyon no doubt mounted onto his wife's lover.

Nicke drew on Zeph's words. "Lysander is still alive, so is Drakon, and Zeph and Matt. They're still with us, Soph. We can't forget that."

She stood then and kissed her best friend's forehead, willing her mind clear and her grief short. In vain.

Matthew followed Nicke out and shut the door behind them.

"I'm going to tell you something," he started, "and it's only because I am going back to the fields in a week."

Nicke nodded, knowing Matthew was relatively safe in their lines. But if fever could take a Secondary like Kallias, it could take a Primary like Matthew.

"Sophie's pregnant."

"What?"

Matthew tried to suppress a grin but failed. "She's pregnant. She didn't want to tell you before she told me."

Nicke's mouth slowly closed. "That's why she had me petition for the winter sowing."

"Yes. I need you and Zephyros to look after her for me."

"We'd do it without your needing it, Matt. I'm happy for you."

The joy of it, and the sadness of it, weighed her down.

Afterwards, Nicke stopped at the Credo and went to her office, locking the door. A fire was already withering in the braziers and she stoked it with the kindling supplied. When it gave enough light, she began to write, ink on paper, to Lysander.

She wrote of what she couldn't include in a letter. Of the happiness that filled her. Of how the sickness was retreating, but how she was more tired and less clear-headed.

Of how his joy quickened and moved, even now. Even without him. Even with his name on the wind that told her of souls passed and things lost. The letter wasn't long, just enough to acknowledge it to the earth and let the ground sing its knowledge.

When Nicke was finished writing, she passed the parchment through the flames and turned it to ash.

She'd written the same thing every day since she'd suspected, and then known. But she wouldn't tell him unless he came back whole. Until then, it would be just for her.

CHAPTER TEN

Zephyros

Birdsong lifted him from his drink-induced stupor and told him the time. Morning. Spring. Flowers budding and bees moving between them like some kind of dance. He used to notice the flowers, but now, they paled.

His head hurt. His heart hurt. His will was weakened and his strength muted.

But, still, the day began even without his consent.

He left his bed a mess, like much of the rest of the house had been for a month. No visitors came except Sophie, who was too sore to clean, and Demetria, who filled him with so much anxiety at the conversation he'd yet to have with her that he declined her offers of help most days.

Kallias would be furious with him, he knew. But he wasn't here to tell him off, so why should Zeph care?

The damned brute should have chastised Zeph himself, if it was so important to him. If he died of fever, Zeph would eat his cloak. Fever; ha.

But more than that, it was one promise made and then fulfilled. Lyon had threatened Kallias to hurt the queen. Too many people were privy to the spare's likeness to his true father and Lyon felt the need to nip questions in the bud. Zeph had never truly met the king, but he felt a hatred so carefully kindled that it would burn Laerta to the ground.

'*Use the anger. Let it force your hand,*' his uncle used to say. His anger had rarely served him well, even when it was justified and flaming. The calm that came on the tails of his anger was more productive than his fury ever had been.

He'd come to Laerta furious. Now that he was integrated into this community, he saw the gaps in the society that someone of his station could weaken and exploit. Not quite a slave; not yet a citizen, but with Laertans leaning to his word and listening for his instructions, it would be easy to relieve a certain king of his carefully cultivated power.

They'd destroyed one brother with another probably not far away. Lyon would be next.

He swallowed the wrath as he would a particularly tough piece of beef. With a bit of work and a strong will, he managed it. He'd only been able to be angry in the quiet of the house after the day was done because Sophie was so distressed. Demetria had mentioned that she thought it may be the baby making it harder, and with Matthew off again, she was having a difficult time. Laerta had such a leash on the pregnant women of the city that she wasn't allowed to work, either, so she was essentially whittling her days away at home.

Waiting for the next scroll.

Zeph shook himself. Today was not a day for sadness. Today was a day for answers.

He dressed in a chiton without embroidery. One of the ones he'd elected to keep from Demetria's cull. All of Lysander's chitons fit him, but his sandals and leather slips did not. Zephyros was left with his own very buttery, very rich leather moccasins which would pinpoint him as a wealthy man as soon as he stepped into the villages. But, he wasn't a citizen yet. He'd been permitted arms as a pseudo-krypteia if a threat was to amount to the city while the army was abroad, but he was still, strictly, a slave. He only had the history of Laerta to learn, and it was illuminating in the worst way.

Once he was dressed, he walked into the city with the lilting fragrance of flowers in his nose. Breathing in, and out, was its own specific kind of joy. When he'd been taken in by the Kurdan navy, one of their most harrowing tests was a dive to the bottom of the bay to retrieve a clay circlet. This proved their might, prowess, or simply how tolerant they were for pain. Zeph was very tolerant, but he had still valued every breath since.

The town square which led into the king's residence was busy with a market day. He paused at a stall to look for some zucchini seeds, knowing Sophie could use something to tend, and was rewarded with a blinding smile from Marla, the stall holder.

"I don't have zucchini," she said easily. "I do have climbing beans." She perused her collection, the ease of conversation flowing from her. "They say that when a king is killed, climbing beans grow at the site."

"Beans?" Zephyros questioned.

"Because of the colour. Green."

"Are the kings in this scenario green?"

Her laugh tinkled. "No, silly. In the stories, their eyes are green, like the beans. They're easy enough to grow."

He gave her some bronze coinage with an old king's face on it.

"Do you need help growing it?" she asked, chin dipped and hands busy wrapping the seeds in paper.

"Are you calling me a poor gardener?"

"No, just that they aren't common seeds. I could come by and teach you. Maybe as a before-dinner activity?"

He looked at her properly. Blond hair tapered around her face, most of it held back by a braid that snaked past her neck and into the front of her peplos. Eyes the colour of turquoise and skin that would make milk seem dull, he did find her pretty. Perhaps it was simply a momentary weakness.

"They must be amazing seeds to grow in time for dinner," he replied, loosening his jaw and rubbing his hand over the stubble that had evaded his knife that morning.

Her laugh irritated him, though, and he abandoned the idea.

"Thank you for the seeds."

He turned, but felt her eyes blazing into his back.

It was a small part of him that thought it easy enough to take a merchant like Marla to his bed. Easily gained, with no chase and no difficulty. Perhaps he was thinking too much of love and what it was worth, but he felt a keen regret at the thought. When Lysander came back safe to them, then he would think about it. Moving on was just that: the tinge of black that always escaped your regard and only answered to unanswerable hope.

"Zeph!" called the blacksmith as he approached.

"Birdy, good day?"

"Good enough. What can I do for you?"

"I'm after a specific kind of necklace, if you have any silver?"

* * *

When he reached the king's residence, multiple packages in hand, he didn't bother with the compound except to slink quietly towards the kitchen. It was bordered by the same high wall that protected the house major, with the garden sprawling up the hill towards the jungle. Demetria was there, as he'd expected, but she wasn't working. She was reading.

"What's that about?" he asked, leaping down off the outer wall and landing cleanly.

"Zeph, for earth's sake!" she yelped, immediately reacting by hitting him over the head with the tome. "Don't do that. Knock on the door like a normal person."

He evaded her swat for a second time and came to rest next to a basket of off-cuts for the chickens.

"What are you reading?" he asked again.

"Recipes. Why are you here?"

"Always so suspicious, Ria."

"Only when you're involved. You've always got some scheme or another."

He sighed loudly, forlornly. "I came to ask for relationship advice."

"She's married," Demetria dismissed, turning back to her book.

He faltered, glad that her eyes weren't on his face before he recovered. "Is she? Then why did she ask me to cook her a meal?"

The maid looked up then, question cocked in her eyebrow.

"*Marla*. Who did you think I was talking about?"

She shook her head. "I don't know. But Marla sees you as a prize, nothing else."

"Do I have to be something else?"

She shrugged, eyes remaining glued to her book, like she didn't care one iota about his comments. "Do what you want, but Marla will swallow you whole if you let her."

He kept up the pretence of joviality, but inside, his nerves were ripping him apart. He sat at the table and took a bowl of carrots towards him. Eyeing Demetria, he picked one of the smaller ones and began chewing. "Maybe I'll let her."

Ria snapped her book shut and rounded on him. "Do you know Karl?"

"Yes I know Karl."

"With the red hair. More muscles than you."

"Yes—wait, no."

"Well," she continued, even though she knew Zephyros was now both the tallest and the most well-built man in the city, and was very proud of that fact. "He's got eyes on Marla. Is he your friend?"

"No."

Demetria opened her book again. "Then she's using you to

make him jealous and I'd steer clear."

"That's a better reason than *'she'll swallow you whole'*."

She shrugged again. "Maybe so. Now, why are you here, other than to eat my carrots?"

He sighed. Zeph didn't want to have this conversation. He was truly dreading it, because it was ridiculous. But, with one brother lost and the others hanging over his head, he'd made some decisions in the past month.

Sophia was right. There was no way that two people like Zephyros and Demetria could like so alike and not be related. He'd initially thought cousins, but...

She must have felt the shift in the air because she gave him her full attention. He almost wilted under it, but was suddenly sure of his path, anyway.

"Sophie... said some things a while back now."

"Is she okay?"

"Yes, well, no, but not anything you're not aware of. This was before we got news of Kallias."

He began to roll his hands in his lap and his shoulders bunched.

"Zeph, you're making me nervous."

He took a deep breath and said it quickly, hoping to the earth that she didn't ask for him to repeat it. "Are you my sister?"

She looked at him calmly. Nothing else passed over her face except the kind of serenity when pieces of a puzzle fall into place. "Yes."

He'd expected a different reaction. He said as much, then, "Why didn't you tell me?"

Demetria swallowed, quietly, then reclined back in her chair like she was preparing for the worst of it. He knew her well enough to see the fear there.

"I was four when my—our—parents died, and I remember my father. When you crested over the hill and into my front yard, a gift from Kypt but with my father's mouth, eyes, and innate strength, I hadn't known true fear in my life until that moment."

"That doesn't explain why you didn't tell me."

She looked into the house, then took his hand to lead him out of the gate. "Let's go for a walk."

They didn't speak as they weaved through the outskirt roads, coming eventually to rest at a bluff that overlooked the river. It was quiet, and he felt like he could breathe for the first time since he'd received Kallias's death notice.

"I didn't tell you because I wasn't sure," she started. "You almost gave me a heart attack when I first saw you, but how can you trust your own four-year-old thoughts?"

"I can understand that. You told me of him, before. That he was a giant."

"Like you. But every father probably looks like a giant to a little girl." She nudged a rock over the ledge and watched it fall into the water below. "How did Sophie pick it up?"

Zeph laughed suddenly. Because it was obvious, now that he knew. "We look like twins, Ria."

"We aren't twins though," she said definitively. "I remember a baby; my mother holding him."

"Chrysanthe," Zeph whispered. "Like the flower."

He waited for her to begin, he still reeling from it. Something so easy as this was thrown into his lap, without any effort on his part. Family seemed almost drawn to him, either chosen or born.

"I don't remember much. I don't remember our father's name or where we were born. I remember being thrown into a dark box and it being opened by strangers who then told me they were my cousins. That I was to be kept by them, now; that my parents were dead."

"Do you think we're Boornean?" he asked.

"I don't know. Do you know the Boornean dialect of Kyptian?"

Zeph shook his head.

"Then probably not, I'd say. I don't think we're Laertan; green eyes and red hair aren't common here. Maybe it was Kurkia. You stayed where you were born."

"Brynne never mentioned it, if we were. There was no other family around." Zeph thought quietly. Though he was of Kurkia, he was taught the very specific Laertan style of warfare and politics. Perhaps they were Laertans. "If my uncle was from here, he would have been at least trained Secondary."

"A citizen?"

"Yes, I think so. He taught me things even only the Tertiary know. Sophie thinks we should check out the slave villages, but I don't think Brynne was of slavery."

"I was only taught brews and some such. Things slaves know."

Zeph shrugged. "Even if we are Laertan, it doesn't explain why we were separated."

"Slaves get separated all the time."

He nodded his agreement. "Do you think we should check the villages?"

"It probably merits looking into. Is that why you dressed in rags?"

Zeph laughed. "Yes. I didn't know if they would speak to me dressed like a citizen."

"I can sniff around, if you'd like? Ask unpointed questions."

Zephyros nodded, then said, "Do, I mean, do you think there are any more? Siblings, I mean."

"Don't you think you have enough?" she asked sardonically.

The grief pierced his chest, striking the lightness from his heart. He looked down at his hands and whispered. "I suppose it's one for another, right?"

They discussed it until night fell.

"I'm going to be missed," she said, standing. "I think we should keep this quiet, just for now, until we can figure out a bit more about what it means."

"Can I tell Sophie? She basically already knows."

"Yes, I guess that would be okay."

"And Ria, if we declare it, then you automatically come into my household. You won't have to be a slave anymore."

She smiled at him sadly. "Maybe once Nicke is out from under Lyon's fist, I can. Until then I need to tend to her injuries when she receives them."

He watched as she retreated down the hill, away from him and into the gathering darkness. A whole new world opened up just as another closed.

Because he knew their father's name. Knew that he'd heard it as a child, when his uncle had been infuriated into unguarded speech. It was a common enough name, but Chrysanthe was not. The combination was notable. Zephyros shook himself and reached to the ground to pick at the grass. It was the colour of the deep forest. The colour of his eyes as they matched his sister's which matched the frieze that stared at him everyday at the Credo.

Green. Unusual in Laerta, except for in one place.

* * *

Zephyros threw himself into his work. The extra tutelage that he'd been roped into at the children's camp ate into his days simply because of the travel. He was quickly gaining the credentials needed for citizenship, which would mean he was shipped off to war with the others. Nicke had him not only scribe, but participate in the strategy lessons and Zeph felt the deft hand of training that he hadn't asked for. Sophie slept at his house because she was too sick to do much more than drink milk from the goat and embroider. This meant that the other women were commonly at his house, too. So there was always extra food to be had and extra work to be done. It kept his mind off Lysander and Drakon.

So when Zeph was directing the oxen with skin glistening in the sun, and the messenger walked across his fields rather than hollering, or, more commonly, leaving the letter in the box and journeying on, his gut turned to water. Foolishly forgetting a king's promise, he received the scroll with Sophos's seal.

"I'm sorry, Zephyros," Bryan said.

"Only one scroll?" he asked.

"Only one."

He nodded, slowly. Disbelieving. "Please fetch Nicke to my home."

CHAPTER ELEVEN

Nicke

Nicke was at home when the messenger found her. She remembered the light tilting, just, as though the curtains of the window paid no heed. She'd just changed her peplos to a chiton, blue to white. Her sweat stuck the fabric to her like a film. Like a barrier. One touch, and it would disintegrate.

Her hair was out, long down her back, and her fingers were sticky from the pear sauce. He knocked on the back door and she looked up to see him: the man they knew was only sent with poor news. They had no brothers or cousins at war; none of their household were accounted for by him.

But then he opened his mouth, telling her that Zephyros had asked that she meet him at the stone house on the other side of the river. The stone house that was her joy and her safety. She dropped what she'd been carrying and focused her eyes towards the sun. She already couldn't see; she'd already lost her sight as her bones creaked.

Only yesterday, Zeph had mentioned that he expected a letter today. She thought that maybe, perhaps, it was just that.

But no. He wouldn't risk requesting Nicke from this house if it was simply that. He wouldn't risk her.

She didn't remember the walk, but she remembered the quiet of the wind. It didn't badger her chiton. Didn't break the film of sweat.

She didn't remember knocking on the door. She may not have knocked. She may have barged right into the home that was, by rights, hers.

But she did remember how Zeph looked at her. She did remember his mouth moving. She did remember that no sound came out.

She remembered the floor as it met her hands. She remembered the tickle as she cried. She remembered allowing Zeph to pick her up and hug her to him. She remembered the gut. Her gut; as it left her bottomless, without any ground to fall to. She remembered the shudder in her breathing and how her bones groaned.

She remembered some of Zeph's words. Words like 'distraction'. Words like 'bravery'. Words like 'loved'. She didn't know whether these were his words, or whether they were the words in the scroll.

She remembered falling into dreams of Lysander's touch; of his hands on her face and her body. She remembered those touches turning from gentle to fire to flame. She remembered his eyes as she closed hers, and the emptiness when they cleared. Dead.

* * *

She breathed half breaths. Pinned: a chasm with no floor and a temple with no roof.

This was Hades, the land where shades marched frivolously. An in-between place where liminal time was meaningless.

She looked around her in the hope that here, at least, her chest wouldn't compress to the point of breaking. Here, even if it was only shadows and feints, she could find him. She could see more of him than his resigned, sad eyes marching away from her. She could feel more than the quickening in her gut. But she was only what she could achieve; nothing more.

Her voice didn't echo, and if his shade was here, it had retired.

* * *

He's gone.

CHAPTER TWELVE

Zephyros

The air was acerbic when he touched it. It melted his face into uncanny lines, deep, from his eyes to his hair and then through the bridge of his nose to the creases that formed his frown. Every impression pained him like a wasp sting. But instead of flitting away on the wind, it burned well into the days that followed.

Or, at least, that's the only way he knew to express it.

His brother was dead, and dead with him were the last vestiges of Zephyros's tolerance. It had begun its decline when Kallias had fallen, but it was truly gone on the day Lysander was reported downed. Although they'd known it was coming, nothing could have prepared him for the onslaught of grief that rolled off him in waves. The air was tight. Water held no joy. Food was mechanical.

More than that, the house was so quiet. As if even the ants as they marched and the flies as they sang their metallic tune were humbled by the defined show of strength of the city's king. No one below his notice; no one who would dare. And it was like this even when the wind whipped or the goats complained through the open back door: when a question was asked, no one answered; when a song was sung, no one danced. When breaths sounded in silent halls, you didn't wonder why the corridors of life were suddenly still; you asked why the breaths interrupted that silence.

Unwanted, unneeded: too loud for the mournful cry of a foundation in tears.

Things had to be quiet so the living could remember the voices of the dead, lest they be forgotten or mistaken for birdsong.

But that was no reason to lose himself. Not really. His sisters, plural, needed him, even though Demetria needed him only insofar that they'd only just found each other and were moths to each other's flame.

Nicke, though. Her world had cinched and then shuttered when she'd arrived on his doorstep. He saw it in her eyes. She didn't want this to be the reason she was here. She wanted to live and love in this house. She needed this to be the place where her husband wandered, sparing a touch for her shoulder as she hunched over a troublesome knot. But, instead, they'd had a day or two before they never saw each other again. Unimaginable.

Zeph was watching her sleep. Lysander's pillow was wet and bunched in her arms like a newborn babe. Sometimes, he heard her whimper his brother's name and wondered at how close they had come to happiness. He didn't envy her waking moments when even sleep forced her mind to the grave.

Zeph almost shushed Demetria when she began to speak, the walls already forgetting their old master's voice.

"She needs to wake," she said. It wasn't a harsh whisper, but a meaningful breath close to his ear.

"Leave her be, Ria. She needs the sleep."

"It's midday, Zeph. Alix would have covered for her overnight, but not for the rest of the day too. She has her own duties."

"You would send her away from her husband's house, now, of all times?"

"Don't take that tone with me. I don't like it, but I still have to keep her safe. We have to keep her safe."

"No. She's my household now. She's not going." His voice was quiet steel, a blade honed and ready. Demetria simply matched him, sharpened edge and all.

"Zeph…"

"I'm not discussing it. She's not going."

"Do you remember the last time we made a choice like this for her? It ended in a broken wrist."

"Yes, I remember clearly."

"She needs to go home so I can care for her."

"Care for her here!"

"I can't! I am still a slave until you are no longer one and the ephors recognise what we already know. Until then, I am a slave, and I am responsible for Nicke's health. You're being selfish."

"Me?!"

"Yes you! We have to think of everyone, both of them need protecting and the place to do that is at her home."

Zeph's chest heaved.

Both.

Demetria must have realised her mistake. She drew her hand to her mouth.

"Speak," Zeph barked.

A breath, then, "She's pregnant."

His knack slammed into him, and he shook his head to clear it.

"What?"

Demetria closed her eyes. "That's why Sophie had to marry them, because of the risk."

His will, already a wall of defiance, stood strong. It enclosed them as a unit and he knew that breaches would be treated swiftly and finally. "Then she's certainly not leaving. Even if it's a grey area, legally, that she is part of this household, *which she is*, then it is a certainty that that child is."

He stood from the chair abruptly and left the bedroom. He needed air in a world that was devoid of it. His throat was closing and his knack was screaming at him to keep her in his presence. He would raise arms against any that harmed her, and he knew, instinctively, that that day would be soon.

He found his way to his hutch of a desk, riddled with ink, paper and scraps. It was where he did most of his thinking, his planning. It was where Lysander's last letters to him were kept, and where one for Nicke was ready to be passed to her. He retrieved it first, putting it into his cloak pocket, before opening the small wooden box that held his own collection.

The scroll was here too. Both scrolls. They said different things, but Sophos was apologetic in both. His account of Kallias's sickness was unabashedly sceptical, and his tale of Lysander's sacrifice was doleful. He'd been the one to lead the spies as they tried to open Auntu like a nut. Lysander was the tool that sent the shell flying.

How he got to be in that particular situation was a question Zeph wanted answered. He was a krypteia, not a spy or a man likely to have had many of the skills needed to fulfil such a role. He knew it must have been a king's orders, and thought of the missive that Nicke had refused to sign when Lyon had choked her then left her for dead. Perhaps he'd gone ahead anyway.

A note had arrived with Lysander's scroll, but he'd not had a chance to read it yet. He pulled it out.

Brother.

Why did he start with that? Why would he use the term Zeph knew he barely deserved.

I have some bad news.

Worse than the news your words arrived with?

> *The missive came that it is time for the long wall plan. I don't have to write as to where I was assigned. I fear this will be my last letter. I haven't written this in my letter to Nicke. I don't want to burden her with it, and I hesitate to do it to you, either.*

Very considerate, brother.

> *Remember the power of your own citizenship. Remember the power you hold when the spear fits into your hand like a*

glove. Please protect my wife. Please don't let her think this is
her fault. She will blame herself; please don't let her.

And remember, Zephyros. Remember that your place in
Laerta is earnt with your blood. Do not be cowed. Do not
yield.

You're better than most of them. Tread carefully.

Still the tears wouldn't fall. Zeph couldn't see for the shame of it. Of a life so easily snuffed. Lysander had been resigned as he had walked towards his doom in a way that Zephyros would never understand. What was the point of living if not with a sword pointed at all threats?

"Zeph?"

He turned to the dining room and saw Sophie outlined by the sunshine. She was in her nightgown, as she always was these days. Her eyes were red and her face was splotched with water.

"Soph. What is it?"

"I just... I'm worried about you."

Zeph stood a bit straighter. He'd been stoic, and calm, even with his fury bubbling. But he'd made sure that his sisters were the recipients of his strength at a time when they were basically coursing through fate.

"Don't worry about me," he said, walking towards her.

"You haven't cried yet," she explained, voice soft. "It's important to cry."

"All in time."

He drew her into his arms and rested his cheek on the top of her head. His breathing slowed in time with hers, and he was sure that their heartbeats moved to the same rhythm too. He'd never realised how bereft of love his life had been before these quiet moments with people who called him family.

He returned upstairs to find Nicke awake and Demetria brushing her hair.

"Zeph..." Nicke said, tears starting. "I have to go."

He knelt down on the wooden floor. "I'm on my knees begging you to stay."

She shook her head and took a flower from the nightstand. It was small, white along the edges and red in the middle. "It'll be worse the longer I'm gone. And besides, I received a note from the War Rooms. I'm going there, not home."

"This is your home now, okay?"

She nodded tentatively, and he knew she was lying to him.

"You can take my horse. Ria, can you saddle him, please?"

She looked to Nicke for confirmation, and Nicke quietly said, "It's okay. I'll be down in a minute."

Demetria nodded and left them.

Nicke moved slowly, a ship through water. Her peplos was a deep blue that hid it well, he supposed, and he wasn't willing to look closer. Nicke pulled her cloak to her neck and it only highlighted the work she was doing to keep from falling apart. Her throat was working hard to keep the sobs abated, but then, quietly and without fuss, he saw her spine straighten and her will push all else aside. It was like watching a tree refuse to bend in the wind. When trees refused to bend, they broke.

He stood when she was before him and reached into his cloak pocket to produce the last letter. She yelped when he held it out, but he took her hand and circled it around the paper.

"I don't want it," she cried. Eyes full of tears and upturned to him in supplication, "Please. I don't want it."

"Why not?"

"Because he'll blame me in that letter. His shade will haunt me for what I've done."

"That's not true. He would never blame you."

"If he didn't, then he should. It was my fault."

"You can't believe that."

"I'm a commander of war, Zeph. Every man dead is my fault."

He couldn't argue. Didn't want to. "Please don't go," he said.

"Zeph…"

"Please just… At least let me come with you."

She shook her head, a small smile his only gift for the offer. "I won't have Lysander's death be in vain. Nor will it be ignored."

She produced a paring knife from her belt and Zephyros moved so fast that neither of them saw it. He had her small wrist encased in his large hand, staying the knife.

He knew how easy it was to feel like a knife could solve insurmountable problems. He'd felt it when his lover had first rejected him, then died. He'd felt it when he'd first appreciated the situation of his slavery. And he could see the cold calculation in Nicke's eyes as they bored into his.

"Hurting yourself won't make your pain disappear."

"I'm going to make it so he can never use me again. Trust me."

Against his judgement, and the screaming of his lungs, he did. He let her go.

Coldly, she reached to the braid newly spun in her dark hair and cut it off, close to her scalp. Both of them looked at it as it fell to the floor.

"Do they do that in Kurkia, Zephyros?"

"Yes. They do that everywhere."

She'd removed her hair in mourning. A wife, who, without her other half, had lost part of herself in grief.

"I'll be back later," she said. As she passed him, she put out a hand and squeezed his wrist. In camaraderie, in thanks, in appreciation: he didn't know. But he did know that she was walking to her death, and there was little he could do about it.

* * *

The number of pitying looks he received before he could finally sequester himself in the library made him want to burn the place to the ground. Friends and mentors looked up from a laugh, or a grin, and suddenly stopped, as if he was the source of pain for them and it wasn't appropriate to be joyous in his presence.

This was the worst of it. He could handle his sister's worry, welcomed it even, but the Laertans here didn't know him well enough to presume concern.

At least the children were honest. Those grown were too uncomfortable with death for a country built on war.

I'm sorry Zephyros.

He was the best of us.

You don't have to be here today. You can go home.

He wouldn't begrudge you taking a day off.

Zephyros didn't honestly care about much at that point in time except to be alone.

He retrieved a ladder and climbed to the tallest shelf in the library in search of the dustiest tome he could find. He had to seek out something about Laerta so weird, old, unknown and forgotten that the city would be forced to trade his knowledge for citizenship. He wasn't sure what was delaying the process when surely Laertan needed as many on the fields as possible. Perhaps if he were to provide something novel, then he could retrieve his sister from the bowels of that shit-stain-of-a-king's house, and could provide a proper petition to keep his brother's wife, and her child, under his care.

Single minded and harsh. He might get whomever it concerned to put that on his gravestone. It defined him.

The book he'd taken was navy blue and the cover-print had disappeared from handling. It was heavy, but the pages were thin at the front.

Once he brought it down, he sat in the darkest corner of the place and dragged a table in front of the door so he wasn't disturbed.

Sophie would be very proud of him, because he began to cry. With his back to the wall and the weight of the world on his shoulders, he let the tears flow quietly down his cheeks. His fury had never before turned to sadness. It was one of his weaknesses, certainly, that he wouldn't—couldn't—turn to face his misery. Instead of approaching himself frankly, he remade the barren cold into formidable heat. The sword he carried was flaming, if only so the tears running down his face dried before they could be seen.

Who was he to cry, anyway? He'd known Lysander for just over a season when he'd left and the world had turned halfway since then. He'd spent more time in Laerta without his brother than with him. Much less time than Sophie, than Nicke, than Drakon, who still hadn't sent a letter. Why was Zephyros entitled to tears when others were more deserving while being stoic? Nicke was in the War Rooms now, discussing how their strategy had killed her husband. If she could bear that, with the tragedy that was her life, what the fuck gave him the right to silence; to misery?

That was the heart of why the pity struck him cold. He didn't deserve it, and he should have been in Auntu to prevent it.

And besides, this was something that needed a little fixing. Something of Lysander remained, even if it was fragile. All he had to do was keep Nicke safe.

He dragged the book onto his lap and opened it gingerly, then set out his inks and notes. Finding something, anything, that would award him his Laertan armour.

Of course it was a book of Theory. Philosophy, one written in Boornean and of the school that was sacked when Laerta claimed their land. Hidden beneath the disappointment, Zeph was quietly surprised. From his knowledge, none of the texts had survived.

As he flipped the centre board, he huffed. It turned out that this text hadn't survived either: a box had been cut from the middle and an unembellished bundle wrapped in twine sat in its heart. He pulled it out and almost discarded it before the instinct he rarely ignored pounced on him. His knack wasn't kind in its insistence, and he discarded the book to take a knife from his belt and cut the twine.

He had no idea how old they were. The paper was the same as the type he used. Not Credo stock, but his own supply where he wrote errant thoughts and fake plans to throw off different scents should someone come sniffing. He took the book back and surveyed the surviving writing. The front credited Roppar, under the Kingship of Scoit of Boornea. Zeph wiggled his nose at the dust as he calculated: Scoit was the king who had seen his end at the hands of Laerta, but that gave no indication of how old the papers themselves were.

The bundle was correspondence, that much he could tell without delving in. It was written in faded black ink, common enough, but the seal on one set was red which was exclusively for official letters to and from the war front. His heart flickered in response: perhaps he had stumbled over something useful, something to gain him his mantle, rather than this simply being an exercise in distraction.

He looked up, again instinctively, and met each eye of the frieze that stared down at him. Laerta was partial to painting a particular type of face. He quashed the question, but knew that his attention being constantly drawn to the gaze of hundreds of Laertans as they warred was noteworthy. Not often had his actions been spontaneous and frivolous. Usually he did things on purpose, even if he did not yet know what. Like how his lie to Kypt hid his strategic mind, claiming to be a sailor and not a lieutenant, which had led him to slavery rather than death. And then how his lie about being entirely ignorant of Malptian had led him to Laerta's shores. And then how his falsity in claiming to be a house slave, not a field hand, had led him directly to his lost sister.

Nothing had guided those choices. No part of him calculated the likelihood of an easier life should he claim one thing over another. He was certainly more suited to farm work than housework, but had claimed it all the same.

So, why? And why did he have an instinct that screamed to be heard?

Zephyros turned back to the letters. His crying had abated and his already frayed nerves electrified him. First across his hunched shoulders and then down to his crossed knees, braced cold against the stone.

The first letter was from Galyn. Galyn, seventh of his name Laerta Rex.

The old king's letters were here, where they'd been hidden by an unseen hand.

My light,

I tire from being away from you. I tire of this wet countryside with its hidden crocodiles and venomous snakes. Southern Kypt is different to how I imagined, and only slightly different to how you described. I especially grow tired of the constant talks that amount to naught. If you had told me that the country of your birth wished to delay me from you til I was cold in my grave, I would believe you. The man drones on so.

Yes, yes. I know he's your brother. But surely, this particular meeting could have been a letter. I only needed to know whether he wanted me to differentiate cotton tariffs from wool. His 'yes' or 'no' would have been enough, and to be honest, we have the Theory for a reason. Sean or Kus could have dealt with this.

I hope to be home for the summer. Keep an ear out for my thundering feet as I run home to you.

Galyn.

P.S. When are you going to accept my marriage proposal?

This was a personal letter. Zeph knew almost nothing of Laerta's kings other than Lyon's bastardry and his father's corruption. This was the king that sponsored Lysos, Lysander's father, because of his fine leather work. Zeph wouldn't be here if not for him.

Zeph knew that his father's name was Galyn, but it was common enough. More than once, his uncle had muttered that Zeph was just like his father, and Demetria had said the same thing. But Brynne had never said a word about his mother, and Zeph used to think that perhaps her loss hurt him to his core and he'd never quite recovered.

Zeph had heard her on the wind when he'd needed the comfort, like a gentle touch on his skin. Chasing down the feeling of care and motherly love and failing to find it was a wound festered, and his uncle had never tried to fill the void. He was a tutor before he was a caretaker, always, and it reminded Zeph a little of the way that the boys and girls were taught at the Credo. Harsh, disciplined. But, then, those children go home to their parents. If their parents had died: at war, or childbirth, or of fever; then they were given to childless couples, but only if that couple was married. Laerta was quite strict about it. Marriage was the foundation. The start of the relationship.

And it turns out that Galyn the king had had a bit of a false start in that regard. Zeph giggled involuntarily. It was ridiculous to decline a king, but reading it, the woman he was writing to may have been royalty herself. There were noble exchanges between Laerta and her allies, even though Laerta didn't partake in noble families. Instead, Laerta sent their Senate members and received nobility in return.

The letters looked like they were in order, so Zeph picked up the next, much shorter, letter, and blew the wood shavings from it. It was folded down the centre and he touched the crease. It felt cold, as expected, but his knack purred. He hushed it, as he sometimes had to do, and it quieted.

The letter was only a few lines.

Oh Galyn, you know I need time to think on things. I had a very attractive offer, just recently, from the baker and I feel like I must consider it.

!

Written at the bottom, almost hidden from view, was simply written: *Yours*.

Reading the games of these two people, obviously in love and flirting from years behind him, threw recent events into stark relief. It seemed impossible to love someone, then marry them, and keep them. To spend each day as if you had as long a trail in front of you as you do behind. It was cruel, this fate, to doom his brother as it had.

He picked up the next letter and noted the change in paper. It was also longer, and more formal. Some parts were crossed out, reconsidered, the poetry shifted around until it rolled off the tongue.

Galyn, King of Laerta, seventh of this name, do promise you into my keeping. Your safety, your heart, your mind, your body, and your soul are under my protection.

The last four words were crossed out, and replaced with *will always be mine to protect*. Zeph secretly approved of the change. It was an oath, rather than a statement of fact.

The next section was so scratched that he couldn't figure out the words, then:

I give you the promise of my love, the warmth of me behind you, my care when you aren't well, and my sword when you are.

Zeph pushed the paper away. These were marriage vows. The words spoken when the priest retreated and the earth consented. Laerta didn't have gods, per se, but did think that the ground with its bounty would keep them accountable for their actions. Zeph didn't understand it. But, then, he didn't really have to. He'd never envisioned himself married at all, so it was a moot point.

He wondered whether Galyn had been able to marry the woman he was sending letters to, or whether something kept them apart. The fact that he offered his sword, despite it obviously being a euphemism, meant that some kind of danger may have been close by. Or perhaps that was simply part and parcel of being a king.

He drew out another letter, this one later still.

Dearest,

I know you told me not to worry, but Meghan is hearing whispers in the Credo and brought them to me. Ambitious swines like Kallum are spreading lies about your impotence with Malptia and how he could stop the incursions. Politics isn't working, and I fear for the children.

I know he's your brother, but I need you to think more about what his warmongering would mean for your family, and less about what it means for your country. Laerta will continue, but he is directly challenging the safety of your rule.

Please. Please leash him.

Love,

Theia.

Zeph felt like he was receiving repeated static shocks as the words processed through his stricken mind. He couldn't make enough sense of it. Taking one of his quills, he dipped the ink with shaking hands and drew a straight line down one of his parchment papers. It curled at the bottom and he flattened it with his dagger. He drew a notch across the line and began to space out the events he knew of, in the order in which they occurred.

First, Galyn had been king, and was killed in a hunting accident. Gored.

Then his children had been killed when a wagon, its axle

sawed in two, was travelling down a hill. No survivors.

Kallum, Galyn's younger brother and Lyon's father, became king. He agitated for his war with Malptia, which lasted enough years for him to not see the profit he'd expected, and instead turn to less scrupulous methods to gain coin. He already had at least one son, perhaps another, by that point, born young from a love match.

He'd lasted long enough to negotiate Alix's marriage to his son, but not so long to crush Malptia under an iron fist and demand tribute in the form of a war prisoner and colony status.

Malptia's queen had died in that conflict. Its consort king had survived, and was faced with the same impotence as Kallum had feared of Galyn. Malptia became a colony of Laerta, and Nicke became Laerta's greatest war weapon.

Zeph looked at the timeline and refused to put pen to paper for the part that was missing. Galyn had a wife and the heirs had a mother, after all.

Theia. An unusual name in Laerta. Bloom; yellow flowers; a summer's wind.

Zeph turned back to the frieze, and thought the impossible. It was only a thought, after all. What harm could it do?

Suddenly, a scream wrought its way through his head and split him open. Pain, horrible pain, then darkness, left him unable to breathe. He was beyond comprehension as his own self tore at him; moving him and bruising him.

He packaged the letters roughly into their string and shoved them into his satchel. Leaving the inks and pens, he ran, shoving the table away with a strength he did not know he had and ignoring every voice except for the one in his own mind's eye.

His knack, his instinct, had never done this before. It had hollered and demanded attention even while it directed him easily to its bidding, but it had never stolen his ability to breathe. It had never had the urgency of a drowning man on the cusp of taking in a lung's water.

Zephyros ran. He ran as fast as he could until he saw the echo of road-dust coating the air. In front of the cloud went a horse, pulling itself towards the river.

Towards his home.

His knack did not let up and he followed it. When he reached top speed, it urged him faster. When his lungs were spent, it pushed the air from him. Frenzied panic was what this was. The promise of blood and horror at the end of the road.

If only he'd listened before; when the blood had yet to flow and the horror could be prevented. He'd had the vision so often since he'd met her that it had become a single white cloud on an overcast day. Her blood spilling into the dirt and her life draining from her.

The trail of the cloud led to his front door. He could see it open, the darkness inside bleeding into the afternoon sun. Doom waited there, he knew, but he ran anyway.

The screaming in his head stopped when he entered the yard and he pushed into the house. Lyon, the fucking king, had his red back exposed and was kicking an unconscious Nicke on the ground like it would be his last act.

Zephyros would make it a promise.

CHAPTER THIRTEEN

Nicke

He'd chased her like a hound.

When she'd presented to the War Rooms, she'd ignored her grief, and had ploughed through the afternoon like her husband hadn't just died and she wasn't discussing the next move that would send more Laertans to their graves. She was there until the day was on the verge of twilight. She and her captains and lieutenants discussed phalanxes, gained ground, digging in, and other ways to starve the city. One man raised plaguing them, but she had dismissed it as callous and stupid. Plague didn't care which colours its victims wore; it only cared that they brought it home to their partners and children.

They'd eventually settled on the mines. Hoplites would move north and swarm the silver mines that were funding Auntu's war effort. It was simple enough and could be managed on the field without much intervention from Nicke.

But then her brother had arrived. His face was grotesque in the best of moods and, not for the first time, Nicke wondered at how Kallum was born, let alone supposedly any others.

"Nicke, go home," he'd growled through his teeth like a dog.

Ryan, her guard and the only person permitted, jogged after her when she'd been dismissed. She'd pulled him aside and begged him to let her go; to not go to the king and relay her whereabouts.

He'd known, of course. He was with her almost as much as Demetria.

"Are you still a spy for Lyon?" she'd asked desperately, walking the path from the War Rooms with him.

He stumbled on the path, his mouth working before sound could come out. "Lysander was my cousin, Nicke, on our mother's side." Like the reason was obvious. "But more, Laerta shouldn't be like this. Commanders living in fear of their king."

Nicke nodded and squeezed his wrist. "Please give me a head start."

She'd run then. Run to Lysander's: where the stone walls would protect her as sure as her own word.

Nicke had heard the horse galloping before she could get into the gate, and only just bolted the door in time for his thumping to dislodge it.

"You did not have permission, sister!" he yelled. "You belong to me!"

She searched every room and felt the floor melt away from her stomach. No one was here. Zephyros wasn't here.

That was when she'd vowed two things to herself: one, she'd take up Zeph's offer of arms training; and two, she'd listen to his instincts before she would hear her own. He would revel in it, but it was better than leaning into her pride.

She had been sure that Lyon would, for some reason, respect his own country's laws. More than that, she had been sure that those with their arrows cocked in the trees would see her running and him chasing and focus their ire.

But perhaps they weren't ready. Perhaps Laerta would only turn on a king when the successor murdered him and his heir. It was a harsh lesson that she'd first learnt from her father, then her sister, and finally from the soldiers she'd entrusted. No one was coming to save her. She would die here as sure as she breathed.

Nicke sat in the study, at Zeph's desk, and took Lysander's last letter from her pocket. It was folded like a small bird, wings aloft. He used to make these for her when they were trainees in the same stream. Stupid jokes were written on them most of the time. This one was no different.

Nicke,

 First things first. Why did the goose refuse to eat?

 Are you ready for the answer? No, you think of one first. I want to hear it back from you. You always were the superior jest writer.

 Given up?

 Because he'd swallowed too much propa-gander!

 See? It's terrible, so I await your response.

 Things are quiet here, so I have some things to say.

 Firstly, I have loved you all of my life, and I will love you beyond when I turn to dust. I love the way you smile small, like you don't want anyone to see. I love the way your hands play the lute with no instrument in front of you, almost testing the air for how it will receive your thoughts. You usually do that when you're thinking, but you did do it when we were in bed, which makes me wonder about what was on your mind before even the birds were awake.

 Secondly, I want promises from you, beyond what I was able to wrangle when I married you. I want you to remember your strength, your drive, and that no matter which room you enter, you will be the smartest in it. My star, you eclipse them all. Promise me that you will never forget it.

 Thirdly, I want you to love beyond me. I will not have you without love for what will be a long life. Promise me. Now. Say it. "I promise."

"I promise, Lysander."

Thank you, good.

Please stay close to my brothers and sister. Delay Zeph's citizenship, if you can, to keep him home.

I love you.

Lysander.

He knew, of course. Of course he knew.

The banging continued until the hinges on the door began to strain. She placed the letter, back in its shape, into the box where Zephyros kept his own. Then she turned, and waited.

CHAPTER FOURTEEN

Zephyros

If Zephyros had hesitated, even just for a moment, he may have noticed the naked surprise that Lyon exuded when he first turned to look at him. His small brown eyes were humbled by a too-wide forehead and the weakness of his chin made his mouth almost completely disappear when he opened it.

"Who the fuck are you?" Lyon snapped.

Zephyros didn't answer him. He took advantage of the king's brash display to punch him in the face and was rewarded with a satisfying crack that would comfort him for years to come.

With Lyon momentarily down, Zeph's attention shifted to Nicke: the dark hair covering her face, the way her cloak had become a darker scarlet, the lightest movement from her centre. She'd curled around her middle, arms protective, and a new fire kindled in the depths of his gut. He'd not yet paid a visit to this manifestation of his biggest weakness. His anger made him callous, he knew, but the way it now turned his regard, rather than thwarting it, was welcome in the context of this brutality in his own house.

Lyon stumbled, his face streaming with blood, but quickly recovered and attempted a swing. Zeph didn't see it in time and took a blow to the head. He may have lost his feet if he'd been a slighter man, but, as it were, Lyon was a foot shorter than him.

He was a bit sick of this, if he was totally honest. He needed to tend to Nicke, and Lyon was like a mosquito in a nursery.

"Answer me!" the king screamed, for a question Zeph had not heard. Instead he answered what his rage demanded of him.

"My name is Zephyros, and I am Lysander's brother." Then, with his muscles turning to calm fury, he took Lyon's wrist and kicked his legs out from under him. He dragged the king of the land like an unruly toddler from his house, lest he stain it any further. When he reached the border of the yard, where the well-pump was dug so as to be impossible to move, he took the time to both dislocate the king's shoulder, earning a yelp, and snap his wrist in two, earning a scream.

Binding him was like attempting to wrangle an eel with his bare hands, but eventually Lyon was tied and bound and unconscious thanks to a well placed punch to the face.

Zeph returned to the house and found Nicke breathing shallow breaths and bleeding.

"Nicke?" he whispered. "Nicke, please."

She didn't respond. He turned her to her side and tilted her chin back. It didn't improve her breathing, but it did mean she couldn't lapse into a position that would cause her throat to close.

He'd never forgive himself for this. For leaving. For not following her when he knew her doom was nigh. A smaller part of him, the part not consumed by this new and productive wrath, cautioned him that he would never be able to protect her, or anyone, completely. To do so would be to bind them as effectively as the king was bound to his water pump. Telling a woman like Nicke, who was a commander in her own right, what to do would be folly.

"Zephyros!" came a yell from the yard.

"Here, Ryan," he called back.

When Ryan shadowed the door, Zeph motioned him in. A gasp followed as he caught sight of Nicke, followed by a stream of curses.

"I need you to listen to me carefully, Ryan," Zeph said calmly.

"What the hell happened?"

"Ryan," he snapped, finally drawing his attention. "I need you to do exactly as I say. Fetch Demetria here, now. If you see Sophia on the way please send her home too. Don't tell anyone else what has happened here. Go now."

Ryan hesitated only for a second before acquiescing to Zeph's orders.

It felt like an eternity before Demetria was kneeling beside him.

"She's in a bad way," Zeph whispered. He didn't know the extent of the damage because he'd been too cowardly to look.

Ria nodded and stroked down Nicke's face. She flipped back the red cloak and a small gasp escaped her lips. "I don't know if this can be fixed, Zeph."

"You must. Please."

His sister looked at him then and he saw the truth in her face. "Please do what you can."

He moved away and could feel his bones crack in the effort.

Ryan hadn't returned, and Zeph was secretly thankful. His machinations in Laerta were concentrated on those easily swayed. The way Ryan had taken an order when he'd heard it gave Zeph hope that he wouldn't have to kill the man when all of this was through.

He found an ice-cold bucket of water in the kitchen meant for drinking and he swung it recklessly, wetting himself as much as the shit-for-brains king. Lyon started, shocked into consciousness by the action. He writhed in his bindings.

"You'll pay for this, slave," he growled.

Zeph didn't laugh at him, though the impulse coursed through him.

"The only reason you still live, king, is because that woman in there has earnt the killing blow. But, I warn you and any you send after me and mine: if you set a foot in the vicinity of any of the men or women in my life, I will end yours. Do you understand?"

Lyon barked a laugh and spat out a glob of blood. "You have no power here."

Zeph looked around him, seeing that there was no one close.

"You've failed to energise your standing troops, king. The Laertans that remain in this city are primed for your downfall. This may tip them. But," Zeph moved his hands wide, "I'm a generous usurper. I'll give you a month to get your affairs in order before the hoplites in Auntu come home for the harvest."

Lyon had stopped glaring at him. It was almost acceptance. Like he'd expected this for a long time and was relieved to finally put a face to the feeling.

"You look just like your father," he said eventually.

"That's what they tell me."

Zeph took a knife from his belt and cut the king's ropes.

"Now get the fuck off my estate."

Lyon didn't look back as he ran.

* * *

She would die and it would be his fault.

Lysander had died. So had Kallias. Drakon too, maybe.

All of them would die and he would have failed.

"Zeph? She's awake."

"Do you think she'll want to see me?"

Sophie looked at him curiously. "Why would she not?"

"Because I didn't protect her. I failed her and Lysander."

Sophie shook her head. "You can't do everything, Zephy. Sometimes the world moves even when our eyes are closed."

She took his hand and led him through to Lysander's room. It had been a day, and she was still here. He'd received a note from

David, Nicke's second, of the whispers that surrounded the city. The story told at the Temple and the Credo implied slightly different things than Zeph knew to be true, no doubt embellished by Jane and the like to make Nicke sicker than she was and Zephyros more heroic than he'd been. None of the stories had the heart of the tragedy, though.

Lyon hadn't sent his krypteia. Perhaps he was doing as Zeph said: paving the way for his own brand of rule to be moved.

Nicke was indeed awake. Diminished. Hurt. Quiet. But awake.

Zephyros stood behind Demetria as she talked Nicke through the herb regime she would be confined to. He watched her eyes glaze as it was discussed, and her own reckoning of her body came to the same untenable conclusion.

It hadn't been a choice. It was harrowing, especially as the question went unasked and unanswered in the room where the child had been created. If the world was as it should be, love created would not be able to be destroyed so easily.

"Do you want to see her?" he asked quietly, interrupting Demetria.

"She's..." Nicke replied, hope dying in her voice.

Zeph nodded. "I'll go and get her for you."

He moved before he could be subjected to her pure sadness. It already filled the room, the house, the city, all the way to where Lysander's bones were buried on a plain far from there.

They'd put the bundle on the dining table, some blankets taken from Sophie's prized fabric. Little ducks graced the hem of the blue silk. Zeph touched them lightly, wishing for anything other than this. His own life would be a poor trade to the devil if it would bring this bundle back. Lyon had been thorough, and he would die for it.

Zeph picked up Lysander's daughter and took her upstairs. He sat on the bed and waited for Nicke's word to pass her over. He waited quietly, his own tears spreading across his face.

He felt Nicke shift in the bed and kneel next to him. Her face leant on his shoulder and her hands kept her steady on his own arms.

"Can you do it please?" she whispered.

He gently uncovered the perfect features of the newborn. You couldn't mistake her for sleeping, but she still looked peaceful.

"What colour were her eyes?" Nicke asked.

"Blue, like her father. But I think most babies have blue eyes."

"I dreamt that I heard her crying and thought…"

Zeph shook his head. The air was heavy with unshed emotion. Not just sadness filled the space. There was a hopelessness: a tyranny of apathy that threatened to swallow them.

"I was worried that I would have had to bury you together," Zeph said. He looked to her, but her eyes were still on the face below them.

"Demetria says that I've turned a corner."

"Do you want to hold her?"

Nicke looked like his suggestion may just destroy her.

"You might regret it if you don't."

Eventually, she nodded and sat back at the headboard of the bed. He settled alongside her and passed her the bundle. The girl looked right in her hands, like fate had been thwarted and instead of what was meant: a child to a doomed relationship; instead a different path had been forced. Zeph wondered where the turning point had been. Which action had needed changing to take them to the end point of happiness.

Instead, here, a woman held her dead hope in her arms.

Zephyros said, gently, wondering whether she heard him at all, "I'll be just outside the door. Call when you need to."

She didn't respond before he left the room. Already the walls were forgetting the voices that had carried within. He opened the landing shutters and climbed through to find himself on the verandah roof. He slid to the thatch and leant with his back against the stone.

Sophia would be proud of him, because he hadn't stopped crying since she'd admonished him.

Demetria and Sophie joined him eventually, and Ria passed him a bag of hard alcohol to share.

"She'll be okay," Sophie assured them, shaking her head at the bag.

"I think she'll need someone with her all the time," Zeph said. "Did you call on the Theory Master?"

Sophie nodded. "Tomorrow. At the Temple. He said we could do Lysander and Kallias at the same time."

Zeph nodded.

"I think we have to ask Alix about Kallias," Demetria added. "Nicke said that she's inconsolable."

"I would be too," Sophie replied. "And to what point, in the end? No one looking at Dannehs would think the king his father."

"Just to be a bastard," Zeph said. "One of these pricks that think that because he can do something, he should."

"Words like that could get you killed, Zeph," Ria replied.

He turned to Demetria and saw the fear laid bare. But Sophie laughed lightly.

"He's encouraged worse in the Credo. You've been busy, haven't you Zephy?"

"Doing what?" Demetria said, strong and hard.

Sophie shrugged and tilted her head. "You're mentioned in the whispers. Someone who sees what needs changing in Laerta and shows no fear to do so. Someone who has gained the loyalty of slaves upwards. Earth sanctioned, almost."

"To which branch of Laerta does my influence extend, sister?" he asked her.

"David I'd say is your most ardent senior follower. He thinks the sun shines out of your arse, likely not helped by your proximity to his superior. So does Sam, for that matter, and most of my husband's family."

"What the fuck are you talking about?" Demetria said. "Zeph isn't positioning himself. That's madness."

Sophie gave him another tilting look. "If you say so."

"You're not, are you Zeph? Promise me that you're not."

"Laerta needs changing, Ria."

She shook her head violently. "You're not the man to do it."

"Why not?" Sophie said. "It's what Lysander sponsored him for, after all. His political mind as well as his harsh tactics."

"Because I only just gained you back. I don't want to lose you to a stupid play at being king."

Confusion floated across Sophie's face but it cleared quickly. "It's true then?" Both of them turned to her. "That you're related?"

"Demetria recognised me when I first arrived. I look like our father, apparently."

"Siblings?" Sophie said, a bit too happily.

Unwillingly, his mind turned to the afternoon that felt like an aeon ago. Of letters, and marriage vows, and green eyes. He hadn't yet accepted its truth, but probably would with time. What a fine coincidence that would be when it came to light.

"Please don't keep agitating, Zephyros. Please." Her words were earnest, begging.

"It's already started, Demetria. I probably couldn't stop it at this point."

Her anger was palpable. "When?"

"When the hoplites return from Auntu for harvest."

"So four weeks?"

Zeph nodded. He didn't voice it, but he suspected that was the real motivator for his brothers' deaths. Kallias, in particular, was a believer in him. He tried not to think about it much.

"Zephyros!" came a yell from below them. The sun had dipped behind the house and verandah was shaded in darkness.

"Speaking," he bellowed back.

"You've been summoned by the Senate on order of the king! We're to take you into custody until your appearance before them."

"Then you can come back then," he yelled. He turned to his sisters. "Give me a moment."

He slipped into the house and walked down the stairs, keeping to the balls of his feet. His weapons chest was already open and he moved towards it. All the blades were honed, their handles oiled, but his favourites laid on top. Movement behind him caused him to still, but only for a moment. He recognised the stepping pattern.

"Let me deal with them," he whispered into the dark.

Nicke came up next to him. He glanced into the study and saw the sacred bundle placed on his cleared desk.

"No, Zephyros. Let me sort this out. You can't barricade yourself in this house for the rest of your days, a sovereign island in the middle of Laerta. It has to go through the proper channels."

He took a kopis, the one he first received when he'd presented to the Credo with Lysander, and gestured her towards the door. "Only if you feel well enough." She nodded and he followed her out the front door.

Two krypteia in their grey cloaks and one other man who Zeph didn't know stood in his front yard. The third man started at the sight of Nicke and began to move towards her.

"General," he said as he took a step forward. Zeph growled and he hesitated. "We'd heard the worst. That you'd been killed."

Nicke shook her head. "I am here, Paul. Worse for wear, but alive. What is this about wanting to arrest Zephyros?"

The man eyed Zeph and straightened his shoulders. "He's being charged with murdering, now probably attempted murder, of you, and of brutalising the king."

Zeph hadn't had a chance to relay what had happened to her. So when she turned to him with a question in her eye, he smiled serenely and winked at her.

"That's not what happened," she said clearly. "Show me the missive."

Paul seemed reluctant to do so. "I was given clear instructions to take him to the Temple."

Zeph would have laughed if the situation wasn't so serious. He knew that the lockup was at the Credo, but doing that would settle him into his power base.

Nicke must have known it too. "Show me the order, Paul."

His determination and fear mingled in his gaze, especially as it turned on Zephyros. He was in the middle of a decision, one side towards their cause, the other away.

"I will bring him in myself," Nicke assured, sensing the shift. "When the time comes."

She turned and walked back towards the house, head high and confident.

"See you later, *Paul*," Zeph promised.

He bolted the newly repaired door behind him and caught her just as she collapsed from the effort of standing straight.

"Do you want to sit or go back to bed?" he asked.

"Take me back to the bed. I'll need all of my strength for tomorrow."

He hummed low in his throat and picked her up under her knees.

"I could have dealt with them, you know," he said. "I'm good with a sword."

She shook her head and he felt her muscles stiffen as she resisted leaning into him. It was a clinical movement that reminded him of what she'd lost so recently.

"Paul is in the Senate. If you'd killed him, you'd definitely be condemned. As it stands, I can talk my way around it."

He placed her on the bed and brought the blankets up to her chin. The night air was newly cool.

"I'll send Ria in with something to help you sleep."

"I heard you speaking earlier," she said, sheer exhaustion in her voice. "It's true? You're her brother?"

Her eyes were closed by the time he answered.

* * *

It didn't feel right to Zeph that it should be a beautifully sunny day on today, of all days. The Temple grounds were quiet except for the birds that rudely sang their song. Spring was meant to be a time for beginnings, but the endings were coming so thickly that he couldn't turn without grief striking him.

Demetria stood next to him, a bit of a way away from where the Master of Theory was marking the plaque. He wanted it perfect before Nicke got here, and demanded as much. Perhaps if he'd been a more considerate man, or more patient, then the Master would try to go a little faster.

"Do you think our parents are inscribed here somewhere?" Demetria whispered to him. "Like their names, since you think they were Laertan?"

"I'm certain they were Laertan," he replied absentmindedly. He hadn't yet discussed his intrusive thoughts with her as the rest of the world had crashed over him.

"Then they might be here. Sometimes even slaves are buried here."

He could see her eagerness to search for her mother's name, but he knew she wouldn't find it. Queens aren't buried in the Temple grounds, but on the sacred mount that shielded them to the west.

But he couldn't tell her that. Not yet. Not until he knew for sure. How would someone start a conversation like that, anyway?

"It is finished, Zephyros," came the Master's voice. The old man stood from the bronze plate as they went towards him. "As you requested."

Nicke had decided on a name for her daughter, one that would have made her the apple of her father's eye.

Lysida was inscribed with thick letters, to battle the weather, with a light touch to name her lineage below it: stating clearly and without question that she was the product of her father Lysander, son of Lysos, and her mother Nicke, daughter of Helen.

He'd paid extra for the poem from the songs. Nicke enjoyed poetry, even though gifting this verse onto her daughter's grave may mean she would never enjoy it again.

Speak, small one
All that you desire, all that
you need.
I will gift it in Hades's Hall.

"It's perfect. Thank you," Zeph said.

The Master nodded and took the plate from the worktop. "I'll have it placed..." he looked around the compound, "somewhere sunny. It's a horrible thing that's happened. We'll be ready for the rites at around midday." With that, he made to leave them.

Zeph stopped him before he could walk away. "Near Lysander's plaque, yes?" he asked, voice deceptively light.

The Master's feet shifted. "People lost at war have their own space."

"How much will it take?" Zeph continued, ignoring his words. "To put her with her father?"

"It's not how it is done. She's lucky to get a plaque at all because she wasn't born alive. It's only my immense respect for her mother that had me do it."

"How much?" Zeph asked again. He put a plaintive tone in his voice, more vulnerable. "Lysander never even knew she was pregnant, and the babe was only a month or two off birth anyway. Please."

The Master sighed, long and drawn, and nodded his head. "Okay. Lysander will have to go in the common section. See you at midday, then."

He walked away and left Demetria and Zeph staring down at the newly shined bronze.

"There's only a few hours until the zenith. You should get home to help Nicke and Sophie with Lysida. I'll collect the flowers and prepare the site."

She nodded, then reached out to squeeze his hand. It was warm, when everything else felt cold.

The space was already cordoned off. They would do Lysida first, and the reason was two-fold. It was to give the immediate family time for privacy and their own grief. Then, when Lysander's time came, each man who had known him and came to bear witness would see the bronze tablet of his declared child sitting just below his.

Then they would know the story beyond the rumours at a time when it was needed most. Zeph had been charged with a hangable offence, and he needed those in attendance to bear witness.

He cleared small debris, like twigs and leaves, creating an unobtrusive pile at the side. The wall loomed over him. Next to Lysander's plaque was a weathered one naming a Brode, child of Verity and Sam. On the other side sat a newer one, not yet truly weathered, naming an Aster, child of Harold and Caitlin. Zeph didn't recognise any names in the immediate vicinity of Lysander's space, predictably, but he hoped that his brother would be in good company.

He'd collected some things to put behind the metal. Nicke had chosen to keep Lysander's grey cloak that he had left behind when he'd marched. She'd said it still smelled like him and she had fallen asleep curled inside it every night since. So he'd gotten Lysander's favourite mug, the paring knife he'd kept at his belt when he'd needed to skin an apple, a lock of his wife's hair, and some ash from their hearth to keep him warm in the underworld. He laid all these out on the provided table, ready to be placed as the songs were sung. Lastly, he held a gold laurel in his hands and gently stroked along the edges. It was Zephyros's hope that Lysander would be able to join them, in spirit at least, as they feasted and celebrated life without him.

It was a pitiful amount to say about a man, but he had little else. Nicke wanted to keep most of it for herself, and Sophie had declared that she wanted the house to be as it was when he'd been alive.

Zeph had written a letter too, apologising for his part in this failure and how he would seek retribution. How he would ensure no other harm came to Nicke again, and how he would make sure that he had the power to do so.

He didn't have to wait long for the three women to arrive. Demetria held the bundle while Sophie held Nicke. Zeph stood and met them at the centre of the Temple grounds. He offered Nicke his arm and she took it, gently leaning on him. Sophie glanced at him quickly in thanks, and he was suddenly aware of the strain this must have been putting on her, more than was obvious.

He led Nicke to the place the Master had chosen.

"In the sun," she whispered, looking above his head.

"For most of the day. She'll get the morning light, too," he confirmed. Her grip on him tightened and he helped her kneel in front of the plaque.

Gingerly, almost reluctantly, she touched the engraved name that graced the metal.

"Do you think he would have liked it?" she asked.

"Yes," Sophia replied.

"He would have loved it," Zeph confirmed.

The Master of Theory joined them then, and Zeph helped Nicke to her feet.

He intoned the rites, the mysteries of death. It was why marriage and birth were the domain of the Trade: tangible things that had explanations and simply needed the mechanical assistance that the Trade excelled at.

But death? Unknowable, impenetrable and impossible. Firmly a Theory discipline as they tried to discern where a baby, an innocent, could find solace in the underworld.

But Zeph took heart in the fact that Lysander would be there to hold her tight.

They stood by as the Master took the bundle from Demetria. Lightly, he rubbed scented oil on her forehead and hummed a tune. Like the rites at a wedding, this was between the earth, the Master and the person buried. They couldn't hear what he murmured.

Gently, he placed her into the little open slot in the walls of the Temple and gestured Nicke forward. She went with a book of poetry about the love between a parent and a child, a small knitted dog, and a toy horse that Zeph had whittled.

When they were placed, the Master took a rod from an open fire pit and placed it onto each side of the plaque, making the metal molten. Then carefully and slowly, he applied it to the entry point of the tomb and sealed it shut.

Zeph was holding onto Nicke again and she sagged into him, tears running. He held her and tears from his own face wet her hair. But then she took a breath, and he felt her broaden herself into this new life absent her husband and daughter. The weight hadn't crushed her even as the sun beat down on her child's grave. Zeph still held her, but she stood on her own two feet, now.

The Master then turned to them with regret in his eyes.

"I'm sorry," he said, to Nicke in particular. "I couldn't stop them."

It was an odd thing to say in the circumstances, and Zeph almost dropped her in order to reach for his weapon.

Rough hands, tight with callouses and warm with the day's heat, grabbed him from behind. Nicke scrambled but was pushed into the dirt as Zeph threw off the first man. The second punched him in the head and he saw stars above them.

"Where is your right?" Nicke said harshly as Zephyros was

shoved to his knees. The first man had recovered and held his shoulders still.

"Order from the king to take him to the lockup," answered the first man. Zeph recognised his voice as a krypteia.

"Show me," Nicke said, putting her hand out expectantly.

"Nicke," Zeph murmured. She turned her molten eyes to him briefly. "Now isn't the time. Let them take me."

The second man laughed and Zephyros's anger rose. "If I wanted out of your hands, fool, I'd be gone and you'd be dead."

He stopped laughing.

"Zeph…?" Nicke said. She had regained her steel in the face of the threat, even though Zeph knew she was barely capable of it.

"Let them take me and do what you need to do this afternoon."

"This is madness, Zephyros," she replied. "They can't take you during a funeral."

He smiled knowingly at her. "That's exactly why they're taking me, rose. It won't be for long."

She glanced between the men that held him, and eventually, after an eternity of weighing her options, she nodded.

"I will see you tonight," she said, a warning more than anything.

Then he was lifted to his feet, and taken to the main building of the Temple, leaving his silent sisters and Nicke behind.

* * *

He'd only been wearing a chiton when they'd arrested him, and the cold was becoming bothersome. He sat on hard stone, bench too generous a word, the floor of hard dirt under his feet causing the curls of pain from freeze to alight on his legs. Gingerly, he curled them under himself, sitting with his arms relaxed and his head tilted back against the stone. He knew he'd end up here, even if he hadn't known when.

The wind had picked up and the metal door faced west. Zeph wondered, absentmindedly, whether the cast door was installed recently, just for him. Or for any who came after and who wouldn't last twenty minutes locked up in the company of the Credo.

Zephyros couldn't watch his brother's funeral from this vantage point, the openings all faced the wrong way, but he could hear the general murmurs of his and Lysander's friends as they spoke afterwards. He didn't know what Nicke had told them, but his absence either condemned him or spoke the story true. He hoped more would see it for what it was, and that Nicke had enough influence to stir them to his side. If they needed convincing, then he was in a trickier place than he'd anticipated. But most of the people in attendance already felt the change on the breeze, the westerly summer air coming strong.

He hoped that this wasn't his hubris being rewarded.

"Zeph, it stinks out here," came Nicke's voice when it was full dark.

"They didn't give me anywhere to relieve myself."

"Yes, well. Hold it in like a real man."

He smiled and she came into sight from the south.

"They won't let me in, but I brought this for you." She passed him a bit of cheese, some bread and a covered pot of what smelt like stew. "Your sister is furious, more than I am, I think. The stew was her."

"Which sister?" he said through a mouthful. He'd not eaten since the night before, being unable to stomach anything.

Nicke paused. "Sophie."

"I'm worried about her," he admitted. "The strain of the day can't be good for her."

"She's stronger than you know. I couldn't also carry a cloak, but I'll fetch it now. I'll be back soon."

She left and he ate the food in silence, wishing this burden had fallen on someone who hadn't already lost so much. Wishing he was at home, and they could share a meal in the attempt to close one chapter and open another.

She came back with a green cloak and passed it through the grate. It was a welcome weight across his shoulders.

"Also this," she said, passing him a letter. "Bryan delivered it this afternoon."

It was a letter from Drakon, Zeph's last brother. He tucked it into the pocket of his cloak. The only light was from the braziers on the outside of the building, so reading would be too difficult until morning.

"I'm sorry, rose," he started when she sat on the bench facing the metal door. "It never should have gone like this."

"Most nights, I have a very specific type of dream. A king, I don't know which one, stands above me and removes my head from my shoulders. I can feel the tickle of the blade against my shorn hair, and they say that I'm too much like my mother. I always wondered whether it was premonition, or simple fear. Sometimes it's Lyon, sometimes it's my father, other times it's someone I don't know. But always, it ends in my death."

"They say that when you die in dreams, you die in real life."

She shrugged. "Well, I die every night, then."

"Why are you telling me this?"

"Because I want you to appreciate that rather than Lyon beating me to death, instead you saved me."

He scoffed lightly and she pinned him in that commanding way of hers. Like he was being a particularly stubborn student.

"You don't understand, Zeph," she whispered as she leant forward. "No one saves me. No one ever has. They react; they clean the wounds and cringe at my screams, but no one has ever, ever intervened in the way you did."

"Too late for Lysida. Too late for you, almost."

"If you're going to sit and stew in self-sorrow, then I'm going to leave."

He looked at her fiercely. "I'm allowed to be upset by things."

"That you are. But perhaps wait for a time when your anger isn't the thing standing between you and death."

He huffed and took a bite of the cheese. He was good at shoving his feelings down until he forgot they existed. Like a broken cup in the back of a too-full cupboard.

"Okay. I've swallowed my sadness. Now what?"

"Now, we plan."

CHAPTER FIFTEEN

Nicke

Every single day was difficult.

Every day she waited for the sound of crying, for the snuffling of tiny nostrils new to the world, for a fist to curl gently around her finger in knowing.

Losing her daughter was, somehow, infinitely worse than losing her husband. Perhaps because she'd been mourning Lysander since he'd left on his march, and he'd effectively been dead for eight months. With the king's promises to him and his own resignation to it, how could she not? She'd seen his death so often that it felt inevitable by the end. Of course, if she was given the opportunity, she would jump at keeping him whole and safe with her, but they could only love within the bounds of their own ability. She had loved Lysander, loved him still, but he was dead. His letters were from a ghost, and she had responded as one.

She had pinned her hopes on his child. It was stupid not to put protection in place earlier, when her missed blood first drew questions from Demetria. Her friend had implored her to do something other than maintain the status quo, but Nicke hadn't listened. A word to Zeph would have had her whisked from here, she was sure now.

Not much was more important than keeping the baby safe, in hindsight. Not her position as general, not her nephews or sister, not the city of Malptia that was held as a threat if she were ever to abscond. No. She should have left when she could still ride a horse comfortably, and Zephyros would have found somewhere for her to live quietly. She was sure of that now, like she wasn't sure of much else.

Regret flowered where hope died, a never ending cycle that defined the bounds of her life.

Since Lysander's funeral, she'd only ventured out of the house after dark. There was always a chance that she could be killed on the road by men sent by the king or on behalf of him. Though, Nicke knew, the best and easiest way for Lyon to stop the thorn in his side from festering was to keep her alive. She being murdered while the current scapegoat for the act was wasting in a cell would certainly go against him. It would unravel the lies the king had been spreading.

So, instead of waiting for sunrise, she woke up an hour earlier, when the sky was slowly becoming navy instead of midnight blue, and she walked west to the sacred mountain. It wasn't far, and the path started just outside the city. She wore a grey cloak, one of Lysander's, with the hood up to obscure her.

When she reached the outlook, Nicke sighed long and hard. The mountain air felt like a frozen fire in her lungs despite the warming weather. Each draw of breath was a struggle. In and out, in and out, until it felt mechanical rather than necessary. She needed to remember how to breathe, most days. It was only recently that she could walk further than the city. Demetria had said that she hadn't lost too much blood, not more than a normal birth, and that Lyon had only landed four or five blows before Zephyros had bound him. It had saved her life, no question, but it was enough to destroy Lysida.

If she was honest, she wished that her death had come that day. It would have been easier, cleaner, for Lyon to finish off his life's work and for Laerta to be forced into war on both fronts. Auntu on one, the hoplites already stretched thin on the fields, and

Malptia on the other. Her father would have warred, no question.

All people ever did was react. If she was hurt, they tended her. If she screamed, they cringed. If she was killed, they would war in revenge. Not once had Lysander deigned to come between her and a blade. Never had Alix decided to complicate her own binds to protect her younger sister. For all of their insistence that it shouldn't happen, it did anyway. And she was left covered in blood with wounds that burnt as they healed.

It was a question of fate and deliverance. Why had her mother, the surest bow-arm in Malptia, been slaughtered when her defence melted away in the onslaught of Laertan tactics? Why had her father, weak in the worst way, permitted his children to be taken from their birthplace? Why had Lyon, who had ensured the perfect hostage, been so willing to let her die to sate some intrinsic need for power?

Nicke knew from experience that war was seventy percent strategy and thirty percent luck. So was it luck, or strategy, that ensured that Zephyros had pulled Lyon from her just as another kick may have been the one to take her from this earth?

It was difficult to conceptualise, but it would almost certainly be easier for all players if she'd simply cease. If her soul followed that of her husband and child into the underworld. Quietly: without fuss.

Her homeland would get their revenge, and Laerta would be defeated on land. Her sister would be free of the binds her husband placed on her. And Nicke could face the calm that awaited her in a way that she could control.

Sitting with the wind in her face, air in and out, she could see the homecoming it would be. An easy thing amongst a life of hardship. She'd considered her lot, refusing to be less than the best at what she put her mind to, but she was tired. Tired of the fight. Tired of the pain. Tired of...

Tired of the pain.

The pain.

Nicke gingerly touched her body where Lyon's foot had caught her and ran her fingers along it. Usually, when he inflicted an injury, it burnt for the duration of its slow healing. A gift from the earth to the kings and queens that presided over it, his gift was destructive and horrible. It meant her broken wrist still burnt months after he snapped it but it was how she knew the asp wasn't his doing: because the pain of it would still be coursing through her to this very day.

But as she touched her skin, it didn't hurt. It didn't burn. She attempted to look for the bruise, but found her skin clear.

Thoughts turning from their melancholy to a mystery that needed solving, she abandoned the peak and made her way home.

When she walked through the door, Demetria was sitting with Sophie at the dining table cutting carrots.

"Look!" Nicke said, opening the side of her peplos.

Demetria, always concerned, leapt up. "Is it bruising worse? Painful?"

Nicke shook her head. She passed the side opening across her navel, still marked with the lightning scars of bearing a child, small as they may be, to where an especially prominent bruise had surfaced three weeks ago.

"They're gone!"

Demetria studied her skin, touching it gently.

"Strange. Sophie, come and look."

Both women leant in, trying to see where Nicke had been hurt.

"I can't see any evidence of it at all," Demetria said. "They should be coloured for months yet."

"I wonder what it means," Nicke replied. "Maybe he's losing his power."

She didn't truly know how it worked. It was in the domain of the Theory. But every ruler had a power, and it was connected to their rule of the land. If Lyon's power was diminishing, then it was transferring to someone else. Nicke didn't think there was a morality element: it wasn't as if the earth had decided he was suddenly unfit to rule. Rather, an inevitable transfer of power was coming.

"Have you had breakfast?" Sophie asked. She was sitting reclined, her hair tied back and her own joy on display. Nicke didn't resent her for it, but felt the pang of wanting shoot through her.

"No."

"Yes, where were you this morning?" Demetria asked, setting out the muesli that would make their meal.

"I... went for a walk."

Demetria frowned, but quiet things required secret minds, and Nicke intended on keeping her early morning jaunts untold until the time came when she felt well enough to do otherwise.

Nicke sat down and was passed the milk. She began to eat.

"Have you seen Alice yet?" Demetria asked Sophie.

"A-huh, she's Matt's aunt so I've been seeing her when I see his mother."

"Is that often?" Ria said.

"Every week or so. They think it'll be a boy."

"How can they tell?" Nicke asked. They looked at her and she could feel the kid gloves coming on.

"They used a ring on a piece of string," Sophie replied. "If it went side to side, it's a boy. If it goes in a circle, it's a girl."

"Plus the fact that Matthew has four brothers, and his father has three, and his grandfather had at least five." Demetria smiled over her warmed milk. "That probably has as much to do with it as anything."

"Yes, well. Won't be long now until we find out."

Nicke felt agitated. It wasn't the conversation, though the ease at which Sophie spoke of the future struck her. There was something eerie about the space they were in. Like it was half in this world, and half out of it.

The talk turned to the Temple and how Sophie's students were managing, and Nicke's claustrophobia began to itch her skin. She was rarely idle, usually with sketching or weaving or war to occupy her, so sitting quietly at breakfast may be a bit too slow for her overwrought mind. That, or the small buzzing in her ears was making her want to stick her head below water until the feeling ceased.

She needed to do something. Anything.

"I'm going to go and see Zeph," she announced, interrupting them and reaching for her cloak again.

Sophie and Demetria looked between them then back at her.

"Why?" Sophie asked.

"The trial is tomorrow, and he's probably hungry."

Demetria shook her head. "Jane has been taking him food. We agreed that you would steer clear to ensure the rumours didn't cloud his chances."

"Me seeing him once isn't going to cause talk, and besides, we need to go through what will happen tomorrow."

"He'll hang and there isn't a damned thing we can do to stop it!"

"Ria!" Sophie admonished. "That's not true."

"It is true, especially if Nicke muddies the waters." She turned her angry green eyes on Nicke. "He stands a better chance if you aren't seen there."

She was right.

"Fine." Nicke deflated and sat back down.

Of course she was right. Nicke was sure that the trial had been delayed simply so Lyon could spread his rumours.

That Zephyros had beaten Nicke when he'd found out she was pregnant with Lysander's child.

That Lyon had tried to stop it, and Zeph had beaten him too.

That Nicke and Zephyros had been sharing a bed, despite her

marriage to Lysander, he sacrificing himself abroad for the city. And in a jealous rage, Zeph had turned on her.

Which turned Zephyros, doting brother, into a beacon for ire. It was tied to his early slavery, and caused a rift in the city that would be difficult to heal. Many had seen Lyon's own handiwork on Nicke's skin, but not enough to make a difference.

Nicke sat and began to unravel the thread holding her peplos to her waist.

The trial was tomorrow. And she may lose another one.

* * *

Though spring was upon them, the air had the heavy quality of a mid-summer's day. The flowers were sickly sweet in her nose, just as the plants and sky held too much colour. It was overwhelming.

She'd done as Demetria said: she'd stayed away from Zephyros. The reports from David were that he was in good spirits despite the death hanging over him, and that Jane had briefed him each day on what was being spread. To say that he was furious was an understatement, but she was quietly glad for it. His fury was productive; was the thing that would prevent his demise today. She knew it instinctively, as much as she knew that the sea was blue despite never personally having seen it.

Nicke sat quietly in the Senate beside his two sisters and waited for them to bring him in. Demetria was fiddling with a spindle as Sophie sat completely still. Nicke watched the Senate file in, the thirty or so members who may make a difference, depending on their response to the ephors' verdict.

When he rounded the corner, Nicke had to force her breath from her mouth. He'd been beaten, she could see, probably multiple times over the weeks since Lysander's funeral. Some bruises were mottled, some were shining. Others had the deep red blotches of a blood vessel still bleeding, and would probably scar.

Overall, his visage was of a swollen criminal. But his spine was straight, and his shoulders square as he faced the room full of Laertans waiting to condemn him.

Demetria dropped her spindle when he was pushed to his knees and Nicke reached out for her hand, squeezing tight.

"He won't die today," Nicke whispered, and Demetria shook her head.

"I think he may, Nicke."

They watched as two krypteia stood guard next to him and the ephors looked down. Magistrates elected from the cohort of the Senate, they kept Laerta to the law of its roots and ensured no section of government gained supremacy. The position was re-elected every five years and once a person had had a stint, they couldn't be reelected. Dynasties were prevented in that way, so the story went. Ephors being selected from the same ten or so families each time was neither here nor there.

Cali, a Master of Theory with blond hair and a biting rhetoric, watched Zephyros like a python ready to curl around a meal. Maria, seated next to her, was ruffling papers and gave him little notice. Samantha, the youngest on the bench, was watching Nicke closely, perhaps for signs of the circulated rumours. Rick, like Cali, was watching Zephyros with an intensity not to be matched. Jonny, the oldest and most wizened, was speaking quietly with Paul, the senate member who had first called for Zeph to turn himself in.

The fury she kept buried slammed into her and robbed her of breath. Perhaps it was the loss coursing through her veins, or perhaps she was simply tired of Laerta's assertion of rightness, but she was ready to go to war unarmed. Lyon wasn't in attendance, so there was no one to focus the anger at.

Samantha raised her hand for quiet, and the Senate, seated mostly behind the three women bearing witness, hushed.

"We're here to determine the true facts of what occurred in the last moon, at the estate of Zephyros, brother of Lysander. Lyon, son of Kallum, asserts that he found Nicke on the ground being beaten by Zephyros and pulled him off her, leading to Zephyros landing blows on the king. He is charged with brutalising Nicke, sister to Lyon, and the king."

A general murmuring erupted at the charge. Nicke knew some of the voices carrying through and hoped, beyond hope, that they may make the difference today.

"We know the king's story well now, but have yet to hear Zephyros's and Nicke's. Nicke, I believe you have other witnesses to call, yes?"

Nicke prayed, to no one in particular. "Yes, Samantha."

The ephor, green in her position and unabashedly eager, gestured Nicke forward and she stepped gingerly into the light. Dozens of eyes stared her down, but she'd been through worse. She stepped towards Zeph and gave him a small, encouraging glance.

Fury burnt, and try as she might, she couldn't disperse with it.

She told them what she knew. What she remembered of running through the forest, coming upon Lysander's house and barring the way, of how Lyon broke the door down. She didn't remember much after that except the gentleness of Sophie, Ria and Zeph as they cared for her through the haze of pain and grief.

Not only that. She spoke of the other injuries, catalogued across her skin, that called the king a liar. Scars from when she was a child and he'd taken a hot poker to her collar. Scars across her back of being whipped with a switch. Cuts. Scratches. Bites.

"More than that," she said quietly, putting her peplos back to rights after lifting it to show where she'd been flayed on her thigh. Her marks shamed the people elected to positions of power here, and she wished them to smart with the feeling. "Many of you saw, or heard, my screams. You were there and turned your faces. Zephyros did not. And now Lyon wants to kill him for it. Well, I say: over my dead body."

Rick, the retired Tertiary ephor, was still looking at Zeph like he was a puzzle he was yet to piece together. Samantha, for her part, looked horrified at Nicke's description. But Cali, Maria and Jonny looked as they had at the beginning, like Nicke's words had no power to move them.

Nicke gestured to Sophie to stand and relay what she'd seen. She wasn't there when it had occurred, but had heard of it from Demetria later. Sophie was a member of this Senate and a Master of Trade: her words carried undeniable weight. After she sat down, Nicke turned to the door and saw shuffling feet just outside of it.

"Ryan?" Nicke called. He peered around the doorway and she gestured him in.

He began to tell his tale, beginning with how he tried to delay the king from pursuing Nicke through the trees and ending with what he'd seen of Zephyros's gentle care.

Despite the amount he risked speaking like this, he still told the story as it had happened. He was, for all to see, one of Lyon's supporters, one that had been Nicke's shadow since she was tall enough to cast one. And here he was, speaking to her cause rather than the king's. Nicke was glad that Lyon was absent, and sent a prayer to the earth that he would remain ignorant of it.

It was then that Nicke appreciated the work Zephyros had been doing with the Laertans here, and believed him when he said that Lyon's days as king were numbered. Her bruises healing at a normal rate proved it too.

Zeph had stayed mercifully silent so far, but his eyes burnt with controlled malice.

"And then when I couldn't find Sophia, I went back to the Credo and spoke to David about what had happened," Ryan said. "He can vouch."

"David has been sent to Auntu," Cali responded. "On urgent business."

Ryan deflated. Nicke tilted her head, having only spoken to

David the day before. He hadn't mentioned the trip.

"It is irrelevant. Does Lyon have any other witnesses to vouch for his version of events?" Nicke asked.

The ephors shifted in their seats.

"So... no," Nicke deadpanned. "So I suppose the question is, whether you believe a general, a Master of Trade, and a guard; or the king?"

Maria quirked her head. "Give us some time to convene."

They left through the back door and Nicke felt a weight lifted. How could they decide on Lyon's version with her own overwhelming evidence to the alternative?

She looked down at Zeph, still kneeling with his back straight. She didn't reach out, or speak to him, but just stood alongside until the ephors came back into the room ten minutes later.

"Zephyros," Jonny started. "We have agreed that it is unlikely that you were the one to cause Nicke's injuries. Especially since the word of your compatriots spoke so highly of you and the love you held for your brother. However, we have also agreed that it is likely that you did also snap the king's wrist and cause him to bleed."

Zeph's breath caught but Nicke relaxed. The capital crime had been dismissed. If Zeph had acted in her husband's stead to protect her, then he was permitted to draw blood as a member of her household, even from a king. It was a manifestation of Laerta's trust in marriage and partnerships.

"This leads to the question of whether Nicke was Lysander's wife, or your wife, when the incident occurred," Jonny continued. "Either would excuse your treatment of her abuser."

"Could I have killed him?" Zeph piped up and Nicke rolled her eyes.

"Ahh, under Laertan law, yes, you could have killed him," Maria said.

Zeph's eyes turned almost gleeful, but Nicke was bereft of how he could use it to his advantage. It would need her to be bait, and she'd be damned if she was going to be forced into Lyon's company.

"Sophia," Nicke called again, the first part of the day won and the second just beginning. Sophie stood and took some time to rearrange her peplos, it mauve and the rich colour that denoted her status. When it was done, she detailed how she married Nicke, the rites she'd undertaken, and swore on her craft that she had undertaken them honestly.

Samantha, the Trade Master, looked at her carefully. "Now Sophia, you know that kin can not marry kin. It causes conflict."

Sophie looked defiant. "It was my gift to my brother before he left for Auntu. And I refused to allow King Lyon to disrupt it, knowing the marks he left on Nicke. If we had called on a different Master, he would have prevented it. This was a way to protect her when her husband went north to fight."

"The fact of the matter still remains," Samantha said. "It's against our ways for kin to marry kin. I'm afraid that means no marriage occurred, and Zephyros did not act in defence of a member of his household."

Nicke stood quiet; still: thinking. There was a single argument she'd yet to make, primarily because it aired the part of her that she would have preferred to keep quiet. Laerta's rites were based on the old ways.

"Rick," she started, addressing the Tertiary representative. "How did you marry your wife?"

He looked startled, like he'd forgotten where he was. But then his eyebrows bunched in thought. "We lived together; had a common-law marriage."

"What did that entail?" Nicke asked.

He went a bit pink around the ears, and she didn't envy the feeling. "I, ah, she came and lived in my house and I, ah, made her my wife."

"You took her to your bed to make her your wife?" Nicke clarified.

Rick just nodded a few times.

"And in Laerta, that can make a wife?"

"Those laws are outdated," Cali interjected. "Rites are what happens now."

"Feels like an arbitrary distinction," Marie mused. "They do similar in Kypt. Then it simply becomes a question of the couple's choice."

"But Kypt has a lower opinion of marriage than Laerta."

While the bench bickered amongst themselves, Zeph leant over towards Nicke.

"What's the punishment for me if they decide he wasn't your husband?" he whispered.

"Death," she replied absently.

He looked at her sidelong. "You jest."

"They may settle for taking one of your ears."

"Huh. I'm quite partial to my ears."

"Then shut up, and let me concentrate."

"...question of the child. Whether it indicates the intimacy of the relationship."

"Hmm, but she may not have been Lysander's."

"Please," Nicke beseeched when she'd heard enough. "I have loved Lysander since I was a girl. Lyon wouldn't let me near him, let alone to wed him, in a direct affront to Laerta's supremacy of marriage. So our only chance was to marry in secret, with only the approval of our close family. Lysander's brother protected me when I needed it most. Please don't condemn him for that."

Jonny shrugged. "Then what do you suggest? If you were Lysander's wife, it turns the king from someone managing his own household to a murderer." He shook his head. "We can not decide this yet. We need time to convene, speak to some Theory and Trade Masters."

"He needs to be locked up. He'll kill her next," Zeph seethed from his knees. She could have hit him. He was getting a reprieve, and was throwing it away in anger.

"We can't imprison the king until we find a solution, it's unconscionable. No. We will make haste with it, but can't decide yet."

With that, the ephors exited the room. Talk erupted around them, including shouts of derision and anger at the delay. Some in the Senate wanted to see a man hang, and had been denied the theatre.

Zeph was unbound and rose slowly to his feet.

"Can we go home now, please?" he mumbled.

Nicke nodded. Demetria came up next to her and rested her forehead against Zephyros's chest. He put an arm gently around her, and Nicke could see the physical strain he was under. Pain and exhaustion mixed.

"Let's get you home."

* * *

The next afternoon, Demetria made soup from the last of the pumpkin vine. It was salted to an exacting taste, and the bread partnered with it was heavenly. Nicke ate her fill in silence, listening to Sophie prattle about Matt, the baby, how excited she was for Drakon to come home. Zeph talked about his most recent letter from his last brother with what could have been excitement, but all Nicke could think about was how tired he looked.

When Sophie was in the orchard collecting fruit and Demetria was inside sewing, Nicke offered him a slice of almond bread and sat down next to him on the bench that overlooked the river.

"He would have been proud of you yesterday," he said, taking a bite. "For the way you spoke."

"He would have been proud of you for how you kept your mouth shut."

Zeph laughed airily, falsely. A weight had settled on him.

"You're allowed to be sad now, Zeph. You can leave your anger behind if you want."

She leant over and laid her cheek on the tip of his shoulder, his navy cloak soft against her skin. A sigh escaped him and he tilted his head to the sky.

"Just for a time," he confirmed. "There's still work to do."

"I know what you're doing, and I want you to know that you don't have the support for it. Not yet."

He leant away from her, and she straightened her neck. He studied her features, trying to see the truth she told. She searched his eyes in kind. The colour was muted in the shade of the verandah, the mottled green of a marsh rather than the vibrancy of a forest.

"I have to try," he eventually said.

She shook her head. "Please. Please listen."

"You sound like my sister."

"Which sounds like sense."

"You expect me to pause in these machinations after seeing exactly how he injured you? After your testimony yesterday?"

She bit her tongue. She didn't want to argue. "I just don't want you to die," she said honestly.

The wind picked up and whipped her hair against her face. She'd tidied the initial rough cut she'd delivered to it, but it remained unruly. Stragglers moved into her vision and she was getting frustrated with it.

"You don't think I'll succeed?" he asked.

That wasn't it. She thought him a good chance, actually, provided the hoplites did return from Auntu in time to take up arms against their king. If the rumours had reached them of his apparent indiscretions with her, though, it made the chance riskier. Lysander was popular, and the interactions the Laertans had had with Zephyros were limited to before they'd marched. He was still a slave. But, then, there were many slaves sponsored in Auntu, and Zeph was a favourite of the servants here. How he'd managed Lily when she'd been killed by the cart spoke to that.

"Do you know why I assigned you to the war camps?" she asked.

"I thought David assigned me."

She shook her head. "It was his idea, but the choice of man was mine. The children of sponsored slaves were being systematically killed in the camps; children of Laertans currently in Auntu. Karl came down with more bodies than anyone else, and you were sent to fix it. If David was sent to Auntu to prevent his testimony yesterday, I think it was a very poor tactical manoeuvre on Lyon's part. He will tell those marching of what you've done for their children."

He frowned at her. "Then why don't you think it will work?"

"Because I think the timing is wrong. There are moving parts not under your control."

"He'll kill you next time, rose. I can't let that happen."

She turned to look at the river again. Her spine was straight and her face expressionless when she said, "Please just wait. Wait for a sign, or an omen that you can't ignore. But just, wait."

"Wait for you to die?" He rubbed his knees with his palms and flicked his thumb against them. "Any time you leave this house could be the opportunity he takes. You don't want me to die?" he asked harshly. "Then why can't I say that I don't want you to meet your demise?"

Nicke didn't consider her own life in the balance. The things she wished to live for had since been buried. Zeph reacted to her silence by leaning away from her. His eyes were furious, but his mouth looked bereft of the ability to emote.

It was betrayal, she realised. He felt betrayed by her lack of will to survive.

"Zeph—"

"No," he seethed. "Rose, how can you possibly think us able to live without you? It is childish of you to not consider us, like you're an island in the centre of the sea."

Nicke wanted to laugh. The impulse was ill-considered and she fought not to give in to it.

He was so *different* to what she was used to.

"Okay," she said in response to his outburst. "I accept that you want me to live. Now you must accept that your coup is missing the support it needs."

He looked like he was going to argue further when his eyes went to the middle distance behind her. She turned and saw a cloud of dust kicking up against the wind.

"Drakon," Zeph murmured. He turned to her and pointed his finger. "This conversation isn't over."

"Earth forbid you don't get to have your say, Zeph."

He thinned his mouth before he launched from the bench and began running to the road. Nicke didn't follow, but instead went to the orchard in search of Sophie. If Drakon had made it home, then Matthew was probably looking for her.

When Nicke found her, she was mopping up her tears before hefting a small basket of lemons into her arms. Nicke took the basket and shared the news. Sophie lit up and almost ran back to the house, leaving Nicke alone in the orchard.

She touched a leaf of one of the trees, fingering along its veins. It was beautiful in the mottled light and Nicke dipped her chin as she dropped her hand. Steeling her spine for inevitability, she began to walk back.

Nicke felt the first crack form in her armour when she saw Sophie engulfed in her husband's arms at the front door. She shored it up, mortar drying, before she was able to welcome Matthew home and touch him gently on the shoulder. Then, she moved into the house and saw Zeph still beating Drakon on the back.

"Look what the cat dragged in!" Zeph said happily, pointing to his brother.

"Drakon," Nicke said, smile on her face. She tried to show true joy, but the sight of her best friend finding peace in her partner's arms had tempered her. She reached for Drakon anyway, giving him a hug around his middle. He stiffened, but recovered quickly.

"I don't think you've ever touched me, Nicke," he said happily.

"Benefits of a new household," Zeph interjected. "See, watch this." He planted the palm of his hand on top of her head, shuffling her hair like a pet dog. She growled at him and moved out from his reach.

Drakon laughed, but didn't attempt it himself. His joy was short as he gazed at her, however, and she knew what was coming. The requisite acknowledgement of things occurred in absence.

"I'm sorry you lost the baby," he said quietly. "If we'd have known..."

She shook her head. Time for that had passed.

Every single day was difficult.

Drakon seemed to understand and reached out to place a hand on her shoulder. "You're family now, Nicke. No harm will come to you."

She didn't believe him.

Drakon expressed an annoyance at what he called 'feminine influence' throughout the house: the result of the women having the run of it while Zeph was in his cell. He touched the inside of the brazier, playacting at it being dust, and smoothed it through his fingers.

"We'll set it to rights, make no mistake," he laughed. "But now, I'd like to wash and eat and rest."

When he'd departed to his own house, and Matthew and Sophie had made their way home, it was suddenly quiet. Demetria was humming in the corner, a Laertan song.

Zeph bit into an apple and suggested that he and Nicke should take Drakon to Lysander's stone. Nicke didn't feel like attending, but relented at Zeph's insistence. Something about letting grief to the air.

Drakon's house was on the way, so they dropped in to suggest it to him.

"What about Kallias's?" he asked almost absentmindedly once they were on their way.

"In a different section. There wasn't enough room where Lysander was originally placed. Alix and Dannehs chose the spot."

"We did the rites for them on the field, too. Did you know that Auntu took a fifth column from the wall charge? More Laertans we won't get back."

Nicke paused mid step, but kept pace.

"I also heard rumours of other things, Zeph," he continued.

Zeph spared Nicke a glance before answering. "They're on pause at the moment, until I can better predict which people will be where and when."

Drakon nodded. "I think that's smart. And if the ephors let you stay in our household anyway, what's the difference, truly?" he said to Nicke.

Zeph scoffed. "The difference is slave children dying and them being safe and well. No. I won't abandon the plans completely, but I will wait on the advice of my general."

Nicke rolled her eyes again.

They entered the Temple to find it crowded. Many mourners were here: some from the march, some come to cry over the plaques of the dead or missing.

Nicke let Zephyros lead the way as she moved back to speak to Drakon.

"Tell me about the fifth column. How many?"

"Around two hundred. They're as good as dead, Nicke."

She shook her head. "Auntu has kept prisoners of war for years before. Until they're sure we won't pay for them."

Drakon shrugged. "Sophos will know more."

Nicke nodded and they approached Lysander's plaque, Lysida's directly below his.

Drakon laughed in a mirthless way. "He would have liked the name. For his father, too."

Zephyros dragged an unused bench over and the three sat under the cool of the shade. View of them was blocked by the building, but Nicke still didn't feel comfortable touching in public.

"Did you get my letter about the cart?" Zeph asked quietly. "Sawed in two."

Drakon nodded. "Yes. Ryan, you said, was helping you with it? Why do you trust him?"

Zeph looked deferentially at Nicke. "Because I trust him," she said. "He spoke for Zeph at the Senate, too. That takes bravery."

Drakon hummed low in his throat.

"What is it?" Zeph asked.

"I just don't know why someone would target you, other than Lyon. It's almost certainly him, so why investigate it?"

Nicke felt perplexed. "Because his magic prevents healing. I've healed both from the asp and the cart, so it can't have been him."

"But you can walk," Zeph whispered. "If his power reduces your healing time, how is it possible that you can walk only a few weeks after him beating you?"

"His power has been reducing," she explained. "The earth must be withdrawing it in preparation for a new king."

He gaped at her. "What do you mean?"

"I mean that the kings and queens of this world are gifted power, and Lyon's is reducing. You didn't know this?"

Zeph shook his head. "So Alix?"

"My sister has the ability to prevent her cycle." He looked confused, and Nicke clarified. "She can stop children."

Zeph's mouth opened further. "In everyone, or just herself?"

"Just herself; she's not a witch."

"Oh, right, of course," he said sardonically. "Only a witch can do that."

"Could this conversation happen sometime else?" Drakon asked. "Have you two been bickering the whole time we've been in Auntu?"

They answered 'no' at the same time and Drakon tilted his head.

"Who do you think is responsible for the cart other than Lyon?" Drakon asked. "What motive?"

"I don't know," Nicke replied. "But I am a general. Any spy for Laerta's enemies would have motive to bring me down."

Drakon hummed in his throat, giving the question rise. "Makes it harder for me to track, that's for sure."

"Yes, well. No one will hurt her on our watch, will they brother?" Zeph said.

Drakon's face turned wolfish. "Not if I can help it."

CHAPTER SIXTEEN

Zephyros

Zeph couldn't concentrate. He'd tasked himself with reading about the Third Boornean Incursion in which Laerta finally claimed the land. It happened around the same time that the book which had held the letters between the king and the queen—decidedly *not* his parents—had been written.

It was a study in marsh tactics: channelling and forcing to an advantage. He couldn't see how Boornea had lost. The country was swamp, with inhospitable coasts and sheer mountains to their northern borders. King Robar of Laerta had simply... driven a small band into the rugged country and conquered it. It wasn't a war, hence the name, but like a slice of delectable cheese on a silver platter that Robar had seen, wanted, and taken.

There were tactics, certainly, and it mainly came in the form of the type of soldier the king took with him. That it was Robar himself that led the brigands probably spoke to the loyalty of them, which always improves chances of success. No archers, but crossbowmen to more easily hide the weapon. No spears, but short swords only. Their armour was leather and worn constantly under their clothes. Zeph didn't envy that aspect. The chafing would have been immense.

They had tracked along the coastal roads, going town to town, claiming to be sailors day tripping for supplies until they reached

Boornea's main city centre. They'd waited until Maios, the festival of the flowers, when the king of Boornea usually put in an appearance to participate in the sacred rites. But he never made it. Robar broke into the king's house and murdered him in his bed, along with his wife and daughter, while his men took the palace and surrounding essential infrastructure. Boornea didn't have a chance to mount a response.

There was no account of how the Boorneans reacted to this, except to plead for mercy from simply their fear of Laerta's prowess. Or at least that was how it appeared to Zephyros. Apparently his new home had a reputation for slaughtering citizens as a way to subdue them. Those that were not killed became slaves, and many graced Laerta today. Boornea now provided heavy taxes to Laerta and was one of the sources for their servant stock.

Zeph read this with the naked eye of scepticism. No city folded like that. It was ridiculous. Nothing spoke to that more than the Boornean Rebellion, only five or so years ago. He'd still been a sailor in Kurkia's navy, in the inbetween space of progression: no longer green; not yet experienced. He'd heard about the way the Boorneans had rebelled and been crushed for it.

His own opinion of the sequence of events was that it was this success of Laerta that convinced Kypt to try and claw back their old colony of Kurkia. Laerta was their main ally, and the forces of Kypt and Laerta combined gave them the expertise on both land and sea.

He also thought that Kypt had eyes elsewhere. Auntu, Kypt's direct eastern neighbour, had lain dormant for much of King Robar's reign. It was one of the reasons he had found it so easy to hold onto Boornea. Galyn, his son, had not been a warmonger. Between the Boornean Incursion and the Laerta-Malptian War, some twenty-six years, Laerta had not engaged in much warfare at all. Instead, they'd invested in their Theory and Trade schools, improved the social mobility of slaves and servants, and created enviable infrastructure.

The histories written of Laerta confirmed it. Simply their existence was testament to the city's swerve into the arts. Many of the tomes written were in verse: beautiful, haunting, but at times charming. Zeph could see why Laerta was a nation proud of its heritage.

But what was obvious from more recent accounts, was a Laerta in strife prior to five years ago. Lyon liked war as much as grandfather Robar, and aside from their swift and effective reaction to the Boornean Rebellion, which was arguably within the last five years, Laerta had been a bit of a limp fish. Their hold on Malptia was tenuous at best, and Zeph had suspicions as to what kept it held. Boornea had been agitating and, to use totally honest language, rioting for years. Kypt had demanded much but received little.

He knew what had changed. Zephyros appreciated why Laerta saw Nicke for the gift she was and held tight to her leash so she could be their answer in conflict. He'd met few people with such promise, let alone a political hostage to keep an old man abroad from raising arms.

Unwillingly, his mind went to the price of such talent. Brutality; akin to horror. When she'd shown the Senate her injuries, he could have bent the metal holding his wrists simply by the heat of his fury. He'd been furious when he'd first arrived and seen the bandage about her wrist, and he'd be furious until Lyon was dead.

But he wouldn't stop there. There was a good reason to read accounts such as Boornea's loss to Robar. One man and multiple supporters, acting to rid a city of its king.

Zeph wasn't a warmonger. He was a liberator, a rescuer of the weak. He also wasn't a stupid man. He saw his own reflection distorted back in his mind's eye, and how those two were the same thing in the end. One hand took, while the other gifted.

This was why fate had brought him here unfalteringly.

And he would not be cowed.

"What are you reading that has you looking so intense?" Nicke chimed from across the room, breaking his downward spiral. "I thought you were going to set the book on fire."

"Boornea."

"Which one?"

"The second last one."

"Oh." She sat back, looking disappointed.

"What?" he asked.

"Well, I was here for the last one. I could answer your questions."

"I know you were here for the last one. It's the only reason Laerta won."

She shook her head. "That's not true."

"Whose idea was it to strip the city of writing material?"

She hesitated. "Mine."

"And who thought it best to burn down Casper Wood and smoke them out?"

"Me."

"And who was it that sent javelins instead of bowmen, simply because it was the rainy season and arrows would be blown by the prevailing winds?"

"Yes, but you're forgetting that it was Sophos that decided to mobilise Malptia."

Zeph cocked an eyebrow at her.

"But I concede your point."

He turned back to the page, but could feel her gaze still on him. Like a brand of regard that he couldn't ignore. Not for the first time did he think on this ability of hers to cow people to her will. He would ignore it, though. He would leaf through the book like he was concentrating and show her that she was now at home, his home, and she could give the resilient commander routine a rest.

He wasn't going to expect much from her, other than company, and she needn't be on her guard to—

"I know you're not really reading."

He looked up absentmindedly. "Sorry, what was that?"

"You're a terrible liar, Zeph."

"I *was* reading. I was finding out how the phalanx is useless in a marsh, and that's why soldiers have to be trained in smaller groupings too. More agile."

"If you say so."

"That's true though, isn't it?"

She thought for a moment. "Yes, and no. Any formation can be a liability. Best to avoid the marsh altogether. If you haven't been able to select your perch for battle, refuse to be drawn in. But for that to work you need to have an iron flank."

He snapped the book shut, frustrated. She reared back and he watched, part fascinated, part horrified, as she retreated from the conversation and became impossibly smaller. Her eyes looked to the door, an exit, and flicked back at his fisted hands. He relaxed his fingers and put them under him as he sat in the chair.

She was scared. He'd seen the same reaction in slaves.

"I'm sorry," he said first. "I just... I want to talk about something else. I know you draw, but you've never shown me."

She was still distrustful, he could see. It was late afternoon and the sun was disappearing onto the other side of the house. There was no one here but them.

"No."

He nodded, rolling his shoulders. "Can you tell me about it, at least?"

"I... I draw nature."

He waited, leaning forward. She still looked shaken but it was moulding into something else. Maybe embarrassment, or shame.

She sighed and stood. "Let me go and find some."

She flitted past him and up the stairs, looking healthier every day. He knew it would be many moons before he could reliably make her smile, but each time the sun rose, so did his hope.

He stood, quickly and unobtrusively, sneaking across to the desk and retrieving the small package wrapped in paper. Inside was a leaf shaped amulet, slid along a silver chain that would compliment her skin. He put it on the table and waited.

He was watching the light of the day disappear when she dropped a bundle of scrolls in his lap. He let out a small *'oof'* from the weight of it.

"Thank goodness I didn't throw the Boornean tome at you," she said.

He wrinkled his nose mockingly, then opened the first scroll.

A riot of colour met him. Detailed, in black line and iridescent tones, with scratched notes on form, habitat, habits, was the drawing of a scarab beetle. Around the size of his hand, the illustration was as if angled from the ground, with a black, spiked leg pointing towards him. Greens began where the wings were nestled, fading gently to a jewelled blue and eventually a stark black around the bottom edge. Two small black pits that could be eyes stared out, with their corresponding antenna standing to attention.

A thin black line pointed to each feature, naming them in turn.

"This is amazing, Nicke," he whispered. "How... how do you do this?"

"With my hands, usually."

He laughed, a deep rolling sound. "And here I was thinking that I'd underestimated your talents too much already."

He got a glimpse of a smile, and he would hold onto it.

"Let me light the braziers," she said.

He didn't really pay attention, so mesmerised was he by the next drawing. This one was of the river, just beyond the bend, where the bluff stood sentinel over the cascades. It was where he and Demetria had first discussed their newfound connection.

Where he went to try and hear his mother's voice. Where he went to cry.

The drawing suddenly brightened and he looked up to see that Nicke had dragged over one of the braziers to sit above him. She then stood behind his chair and the sweet tones of vanilla met him.

"I like this one," he said. "It feels unfair to call it talent when you obviously put so much work into it."

"Yes, well. Providing a bit of beauty to cancel out the bloodshed may prove my saving grace."

She moved away before he could reply, and began lighting the other braziers.

"Can I watch you draw?" he asked. "Now?"

She hesitated. "Why on earth would you want to do that?"

He shrugged. "Is it so strange to want to see a Master at work?"

"Don't let the Trade hear you say that."

She walked away again, this time heading to his desk for parchment.

"My pencils are at the king's residence—"

Not home, he noted.

"—but do you have any charcoal? I can use that."

He stood and his world tilted a little. Shaking his head, he made his way around to his desk and opened the bottom drawer. "In here, but it's rough."

"I'll only shade with it, mainly."

He passed it to her and she took it over to the dining table. When she reached it, she pushed herself into Lysander's chair and placed the materials in front of her. He sat down opposite her.

"Now, I will only show you this on one condition," she said.

He shook his head. "I'm not going to learn war codes, rose."

"Then I am afraid that we are at an impasse."

He stared at her, just as she stared at him. He knew she had far greater experience in this particular type of intimidation, but he had a few aces up his sleeve.

He began to whistle, which he knew drove her up the wall. It was a shrill tune, one he'd learnt as a boy and had annoyed his uncle just as much.

"Stop it," she said, suppressing a laugh. "Stop it," she said again, gaining control of her face in order to look stern.

He took the paper from her and scrawled: *start drawing and I'll stop*, then passed it back, while the tune built a crescendo of annoyance.

She scrunched up the paper and threw it back at him, hitting him in the mouth and granting her a small reprieve. He simply began again.

But he was getting a little breathless, and finding it difficult to keep the tune in its highs and lows.

Still, she didn't give in. Stubborn like no one else.

If he was honest, that may have been the reason he loved her.

But that was a thought for another day. Another time.

He coughed suddenly, bringing his whistling to a close. "That doesn't count!" he said, pointing at her.

"It does, Zeph, it does."

She picked up the charcoal, her grip delicate and fine, then she dropped it. It tilted out of her hands like it was caught on a swell.

She tried again.

"Zeph..." she whispered. He heard it from far away. One of the calls on the wind that so often caught him in a bad moment. A warning.

His knack rolled him clean off his chair, pushing him to the floor. He shook his head to clear it, but found the action wanting. He needed to soothe it, but didn't have the ability.

He tried to stand but only made it to his knees.

"Nicke?" he called when he saw her slumped over the table. "Rose?"

She may have been breathing, he couldn't tell. But her hands were loose next to her serene face. Eye closed, as if in sleep, and mouth slack.

Perhaps this was for the best. Perhaps this way, she could be free from the fear, misery, and apathy that had been plaguing her since she'd given her husband up for dead. Since Lysida.

Zeph would go to his grave regretting his every action that day.

"Nicke?" he managed to whisper again, until the effort became too much.

He slumped down to the floor, back against the carpet so lovingly woven by his sister.

His sisters would be furious about this. At how he and Nicke had basically given up. What was the point of being safe and well if it was at the edge of a knife?

His vision cleared a little and he was able to roll onto his side.

No. *No*, this was not how this happened. His instinct overwhelmed him and pointed, very directly, up to the brazier currently smoking like an old man. It wasn't only the smoking, but the smell: it was earthy; almost tart against his tongue.

His knack growled at him and he growled back.

Move.

He made it to a crouch and crawled his way across to Nicke. Taking her dropped hand, he dragged her onto the floor, her peplos askew. Praying for her to forgive him, he pulled her alongside him towards the freshness of the air outside, trying his best not to breathe the poison too far into his system.

When she'd finally cleared the front door, then the verandah, and had slumped onto the grass, he didn't wait before joining her there. Lying side by side, the stars twinkling into existence above them, as the poisoned air they'd been breathing burnt, then dispersed from the open door.

He was glad it was close to summer, because otherwise he may have been cold.

His hand snaked across the grass and grasped hers in an

attempt to keep him here and centred.

But it was no use, and the darkness claimed him.

* * *

Zeph sat quietly, contemplatively, as he watched his brother pace across his living room floor. His agitation showed in his shoulders and he had a growth along his chin that betrayed his distraction with the events of a week ago.

Zeph himself was angry, but probably for a different reason.

The rest of the march was delayed in Auntu. He wouldn't get his revenge and seize the city until after the ephors had decided about Lyon's crimes. They couldn't depose the king because there wasn't anyone waiting in the wings.

There was, but Zephyros didn't yet have proof of it.

Oh, he was also angry that someone had been able to invade their home and plant a fast acting toxin that would burn when the braziers were lit, but he could be angry at two things.

"We can hardly guard the house at all times," Drakon threw out, like he had multiple times before. "What if Sophie had been here. We'd have another dead baby on our hands."

The comment stung like nothing else, and Zeph felt his hackles rising. "I got us out, Drakon. And Nicke might not have been the target this time." His brother turned to him, and Zeph shrugged. "Lyon might be getting desperate. He knows I'll kill him the next opportunity I get. And besides, it's still a mystery as to why Nicke was targeted in the first place."

He saw a shade of black cross Drakon's face. His eyes glittered, just a little, as something surfaced then was quashed in Drakon's mind. Zeph's knack rose, tilting its head in question. Zeph knew better than to ignore it, but he had also just received his brother back, and didn't want to argue.

Nicke walked in and both of their heads turned to her.

"Where were you?" Drakon asked harshly. Zephyros knew he was agitated, but he also knew that Nicke didn't deserve such ire. Her headaches were only getting worse, and she was simply returning from where she disappeared to every morning: the mountain to the west.

"I went for a walk," she replied, reservedly. "Did something happen?"

"Nothing happened," Zeph replied. He leant back in his chair, chin pointed at the ceiling and neck exposed. "Drakon's just taking out his anger on everyone else."

"I," Drakon said dangerously, "am trying to figure out who continues to put our dear Nicke's life in danger. More than you're doing! If anything, you're making it worse!"

Zeph closed his eyes and took deep breaths. Six months ago, he may have hit Drakon for less, but time and loss had put things into perspective.

"That's not fair, Drakon," Nicke said. "Zeph's been the one to save me each time, if you do remember."

"Don't," Zephyros whispered. "Don't argue. Please. I can't stand it."

Drakon huffed. "Then do something other than invite death into our midst."

He heard his brother leave the house. His eyes were still closed in a silent prayer for strength and power. Helplessness had overwhelmed him.

"He doesn't mean it, Zephyros," she muttered, close by. "He's lost as much as any of us."

Zeph nodded, but kept his eyes closed. The air was warming as the sun rose in the air and he could hear the distinctive whistling of his sister, the taller one, as she ventured towards the house. She basically lived here now: Alix had apparently 'offered' her to Nicke as a gift. But there was little chance of Demetria staying with the queen after the events of the last two or so months.

"Zephy," she called from the door. He opened his eyes and saw her haloed in the freshness of a new morning. Her hair was tight against her scalp and she held a basket full of bread rolls in her hands.

Zeph smiled, but it faltered when she ventured closer. She had dark circles under her eyes and a gauntness that only came from a lack of nutrition. Rather than pin his sister with questions, Zeph stood as she chatted with Nicke and fetched her some oats swamped in goat's milk and drizzled in honey. He put it down on the table and pointed at it.

"Eat," he murmured.

Demetria shook her head. "I already ate."

"It wasn't a suggestion, Ria."

She shared a look with Nicke, and the latter shrugged before taking her leave and venturing upstairs.

"What's up your arse," Demetria said as she sat behind the bowl.

"You aren't eating," he replied, producing his own bowl. "And it's worrying me."

Demetria picked up the spoon and considered it. "I'm eating enough. It's been a stressful few moons."

Zeph reached out and took her hand. "I'm sorry, Ria."

"For what?"

"For the coup; for the fires. For almost dying multiple times when I could probably have helped it. I hadn't considered the toll it was taking on you."

Her jaw worked hard to contain her tears, but they sprang out like a leak.

"I couldn't wake you," she whispered. "You or Nicke. You wouldn't respond."

He knew, of course. He'd woken the following afternoon with a splitting headache.

"It's a horrible feeling, Zephy. When you feel powerless to help someone."

He nodded, but didn't interrupt.

"And what will you do when Lyon is returned to his kingship and he finally succeeds in having you killed?"

"He won't."

Her tone turned frustrated. "What makes you think that? He certainly could, and there wouldn't be anything to do to stop it."

"Nicke says he's losing his power. The land is rejecting him. He won't be king for long."

It was something they'd spoken about after they'd awoken. Nicke didn't know if the smoke was Lyon's doing because his effect had weakened anyway. This time it could have been him.

But Zeph didn't think so. Setting a toxic herb into a brazier and then waiting for it to be lit was a sneaky method. And if Lyon was one thing, it wasn't sneaky. He was brash; open. He wanted to mark Nicke's skin to show the world how she could be leashed by him.

He was bereft of other candidates. Something told him that this was against Laerta, not Nicke herself. She made sure they were never beaten on land, and there was something so impersonal about planting a poison to be ingested later.

They ate their porridge in peace, listening only to songs of the birds.

By mid morning, Demetria was reading a book with her feet on Zeph's lap as he mended a chiton. It was one of the nicer ones that Lysander left behind. He'd asked Nicke and she'd said it was okay for Zeph to wear it, but he was a little broader in the chest than Lysander and it needed to gain a few inches at the centre. He was mid tying-off when the messenger came.

"Zephyros?"

"Bryan, good morning."

"Good morning. Morning, Demetria."

"Morning," she hummed.

"What do you have for me?" Zeph asked, standing and earning a grumble from his sister.

"A message from the ephors. They've come to a decision. They would like yours and Nicke's attendance at the Senate this afternoon."

He nodded and took the note that outlined the summons.

After Bryan had left, Zeph ventured up the stairs to let Nicke know.

He knocked gently on Lysander's door, but, having not heard a response, he poked his head into the sacred space. It was gloomy inside because of the drawn shutters and he found her sleeping curled in the bed. As usual, she was nestled in Lysander's grey cloak from when he was still a krypteia. Zeph doubted that it retained its smell, but whatever comfort it could bring her would be welcomed by him.

He looked down at the summons, and saw it was slated for midday, and that was only an hour or so away. The note read as if it was a suggestion that they attend, or could be construed as such. So, with only a small fear of her wrath should he be put to death without her there to stand between him and the blade, he closed the door and left her where she was.

* * *

Lyon was obviously back on his bullshit. Zephyros was suddenly glad that he'd left Nicke at home where she wouldn't be subjected to his vitriol.

"I'm the king," he said, time and time again, like it was a secret that was just bursting out of him. Zeph could only reign in his own rolling eyes for the third go of it.

"Yes," Maria, an ephor that Zeph had come to know in his musings at the Credo since the trial. She was recently returned from Kypt, and was stalwartly loyal to Sophos. Zeph found it interesting that Jonn seemingly afforded no loyalty at all. "So when a king, who should be held to a higher standard than the rest, beats a member of his household hard enough that she loses a baby, shouldn't he be brought to heel?"

"I'm not a dog to be brought anywhere by the likes of you," Lyon said. "She is of my household to do with as I wish."

"Was," Zeph said lightly. He couldn't help but provoke the situation; one of his many flaws. Lyon turned to him, murder in his gaze. "Was of your household."

"That's it, is it?" Lyon replied. "She plays a whore to both brothers, does she? Easy enough to manipulate them then."

Zeph was suddenly thrilled that he hadn't woken her for this. He continued to look bored with the proceedings, and then kept his eyes locked on the bench.

"This is stupid," Lyon announced. "If she didn't marry Lysander, then I could beat her as I wished. And it means that Zephyros loses a limb for brutalising me because he didn't do it in defence of his own kin. That's the bottom line of it."

"With all due respect, King," Rick said. "We have already heard all of this. No. The reason we summoned you today was to tell you that we are going to seek the advice of the Oracle in this. Each of the parties can nominate someone to go to her in their stead, or attend themselves."

"I will go," Zeph said immediately. "I will go for my brother, his wife and his child."

Rick nodded as if he had expected this.

"I will send my son, Kallum," Lyon said.

Zeph's knack shook him and he knew that something dangerous was afoot. He hadn't seen Kallum much at all since Lysander had died. Nicke had stopped teaching them, so he had stopped scribing the lessons. As she grew stronger, she may go back and he would toddle along behind her, inks in hand.

"Maria, Cali, and I will go," said Rick. "Dismissed."

CHAPTER SEVENTEEN

Nicke

It was quiet, almost serene when Zeph came home. The afternoon had gotten away from her and she found herself simply watching the sun as it set. Warmth suffused her bones and it could have been mistaken for contentment.

The shame of it burnt. Barely more than a moon had passed, but she found herself being able to complete tasks without needing to bar the way to her intrusive thoughts. Things like the Senate were different, she knew: when something needed undivided attention, her mind was primed to provide it. She could cloud her thoughts with the necessity of other things. But when her hands were idle, or when they weren't but the chore took almost no thought from her, her mind decided to stray into the darkness.

But this afternoon, she'd been able to follow the garden path of her thoughts and channel them into a place where she didn't begin gasping for breath. Part of it was talking. Alice, a matriarch of the Theory who had lost every child she'd ever borne was probably her saving grace. They could draw, mix pigments, paint, and talk.

Nicke had to have faith that speaking about it would work in her favour, rather than the simple action of voicing the demons enabling them to find her.

Her dreams still terrified her, but she didn't think they would ever ease.

She put her hands in Lysander's cloak, it sheltering her from the harsh spring winds. They always picked up this time of year, like a merchant demanding payment in advance. Summer was usually more beautiful if the spring storms were unabating. A balance; nature's match.

The cloud of dust that heralded Zephyros's arrival dispersed quickly in such a breeze. He walked his horse around the back of the house and she tried not to notice the strain to his shoulders. He'd had an agile physique when he'd first arrived, but now it was honed into what Laerta favoured: a downward stroke rather than a bow's draw. The image of the Credo's frieze.

She was sure that he was an accurate shot, and, though Laerta did produce some archers, this city did not value such skill. Cowardly; too cunning.

He walked onto the verandah and took the seat adjacent to hers. They were comfortable wicker chairs with plush woven cushions that drew him in. A small table sat between them and he reached out to the pitcher of water sitting in its centre.

"Don't be mad, rose" he started, before taking a great gulp.

She didn't react. "I'm not your wife, Zeph. I don't have the right to be mad at you."

Once he'd finished drinking, he carefully placed the jug next to his chair as if the sideboard it belonged on was about to be part of a violent display. She was content. She wasn't going to react in anger right now.

"I think you may be anyway." She glanced at him and saw him defiant. He was already ready to defend his actions, whatever they may be. "I'm going to Boornea."

She looked at him sharply then, pledge to not react in anger forgotten. "Why?"

"The ephors have requested the Oracle's opinion. I am going as your representative."

"Why on this green earth would you agree to that?"

He hesitated, then she saw his spine steel. He wasn't going to be convinced, no matter why he'd decided one way or the other. She suddenly felt tired.

"I volunteered."

He was right. She was mad. Furious, even. When she found underlings reticent to adhere to her rule as the law it was in the Credo and the War Rooms, she often found a dispassionate part of herself that could see into their souls and cut them loose. Her head would tilt and her eyes would sharpen until they mumbled their apologies and did what she said anyway. It had occurred more when she was younger, greener, and her opponents thought they knew better.

She didn't react this way to Zeph, the wayward slave that had been more than that since he'd first arrived here. Instead, she reacted probably exactly as he'd feared.

"What the hell were you thinking!" she yelled. She almost launched from the chair to box his ears for his idiocy.

"I was thinking of you," he replied calmly, like they were having a conversation over tea. He met her eyes then sent them to the ground. "Lysida should be here with us, not in her crypt. And Lysander deserved better than this country gave him. This is one way to fulfil my debt to him."

"You're a damned fool!"

"Then I'll be the fool, rose. It is done."

She stood then and she saw the flash of fear travel across his face. Still wrapped in her dead husband's cloak, she went into the house to retrieve her shoes and put a stop to this madness.

He followed her in, predictably. "What are you doing?"

"Stopping you from getting yourself killed." Her voice turned disbelieving. "The Oracle. Do you hear yourself sometimes when you speak?"

"Better than anyone else. You can't stop it, Nicke."

"Watch me."

He stood in the doorway, as if there weren't more exits to the house.

"Let me explain, then."

She looked up at him, his height surpassing every person in this city and probably across the continent, and she saw a determination she'd often herself felt.

"It is a simple jaunt," he said lightly. "Kallum is attending for his father, and three ephors are going."

"Which ones?" she interrupted.

"Cali, Maria and Rick."

"Cali will have orders from Lyon to poke a knife through your ribs."

"Oh, no doubt. Lucky for me that I've proven very unkillable."

"Kallum, too. He'll have something to prove."

"He is a mere child. I think I can manage him, too."

"So you've got it all figured out, haven't you."

He lengthened his gaze, tilting his chin up and a teasing smile lit his mouth. "Yes, I think so."

"And here? What happens when you, the only thing standing between me and the knife, and Demetria and the noose, take a country trip for a fortnight?"

A shadow crossed his face.

"Oh, rose, you may say many things to me, but to underestimate my determination to keep you and my sisters safe should never be one of them. I haven't yet laid plans, seeing as I only just returned from the Senate with these tidings, but never doubt that I will."

She realised something trite about him then. Something that painted him a little differently.

He was furious. And rather than yelling, or throwing furniture, or threatening his demons, he became unerringly articulate. For some reason the notion of this made her laugh. She broke out into giggles even as he stared her down. He wasn't intimidating, and this made her giggles turn into outright laughter.

"Why are you laughing at me?"

"Because you're ridiculous, Zeph."

The line between his eyebrows became more pronounced.

She shrugged. "I just noticed that you use big words when you're mad."

His expression stayed determined, and he looked at her like this was neither the time, nor the place, for her vapid observations. It was one of her strengths, noticing things like this in her lieutenants and captains. She needed to know when they were angry.

Zeph, however, was neither her lieutenant nor her captain.

He was her best friend, she realised. A simple camaraderie borne of his refusal to concede and the simple way he eased her every nerve.

"I'm going," he said. There was no pretence in his words. "Trust me to bring home a solution to this."

She did. She did trust him and the idea enthralled her. How such an easy thing as his company had brought her to the point of faith. It had taken her years to think similarly of anyone else, but how could she not? His conviction was tempered only by his fury, a deep well that lay within him and would burst to the surface as a geyser did a lake. He was trustworthy, and she felt worthy by comparison.

"I trust you," she replied. "But if you come back dead, I'll never forgive you."

His mouth quirked in his arrogance, bordering on hubris. That alone made her fearful. "I was hoping to convince you to spend the duration in the children's camps," he said.

She didn't need to voice the question for him to answer it.

"It is your domain. You decide who stays and goes; we can plant those loyal to you there as a barrier between you and the king. Drakon could be summoned there, too, and there will be enough people to ensure that whoever currently has your name written in blood won't be able to get a foothold."

She blinked slowly. It was a good plan. "And your sisters? If Lyon decides revenge is best spent on those you love?"

There, again: the shadow that turned his eyes from spring growth to old-world forest. "Demetria can go as your maid. Sophie…"

"She's too close to her time to travel, Zeph."

"Matthew will be staying for a bit. And she's in the Senate, a Master. There would be grander consequences for the king should he target one of the Temple's own."

"She'll have to stay out of sight. Maybe go to Alice's if the woman will take her."

His face morphed into something close to triumphant.

"I'm still angry about this," she reminded him.

"And I'm sure you'll be angry about this until I take my dying breath."

"Not in the next two weeks," she warned.

"Not in the next two weeks," he assured.

The clip of a trot made his serene face turn back into that of a man armed and dangerous. She took a step back into the house, not knowing the visitor but wanting to retreat just in case. He ventured into the yard to greet the caller and she missed most of their quiet conversation. He wasn't yelling, yet, which gave her hope that this was friend, not foe.

"Nicke," Zephyros said, leading them into the house. Behind him stood her sister, clad in a grey cloak that washed out her usually golden complexion. Her skin was sallow, and her hair hung limply in its intricate pins.

"Alix?" Nicke croaked.

Alix eyed Nicke from bottom to top in the assessing way she always did.

"Zeph, can you give us a moment?" Nicke asked.

"Wait," Alix said as he made to leave. She turned to him and Nicke's respect for Zeph increased four-fold when he bowed his head deferentially. "You're going to Boornea with Kallum?"

"Yes, queen."

She audibly swallowed. "I need a favour, even though I know that I don't deserve it."

His eyes flickered to Nicke and she saw how true he found those words. He'd never thought kindly of the people who stood by when she was injured, petrified, or brutalised.

"I need you to protect my son," Alix said into heavy silence. "He's young and inexperienced. I need him safeguarded on the road."

"Will he not be sent with guards?"

She shook her head. "It will make the party too large and move too slowly. That's what the king told me."

"And in return?" he said.

She took a deep breath. "I will ensure the king is waylaid while you are out of the city. I know that's your worry, and I'll do my best to alleviate it."

"How do you propose to do that?" Nicke asked

Alix's mouth turned down further, and she straightened her spine. "I'm his wife. How do you think I'm going to do it?"

"No, Alix," Nicke said. "Don't sacrifice yourself for this."

"We all sacrifice something. Mine is less than yours." She turned back to Zeph. "Will you do it?"

He hesitated only a moment. "Yes, I will do it. But I expect your queen's witness should your husband murder either of my sisters, or Nicke, while I am away."

Nicke breathed out slowly, quietly, but the damage had been done. A small light shone in Alix's eyes and Nicke, who knew of her training in the court of their homeland and how it had prepared her for a life looking for threats, knew that her sister had already connected the various dots.

"Huh," Alix said. "And here I thought, with all the time she was spending here, that you were lovers." Zeph looked confused and glanced at Nicke for clarity. Alix provided it. "Demetria. She's your sister."

If Zeph had been a lesser man, the blood may have drained out of his face. Instead he straightened his shoulders and brought a menacing presence to the room that even Nicke wanted to shy from.

"Yes," he replied.

"A gift from Boornea and a gift from Kypt, united in Laerta," Alix said lightly. "What are the chances?"

"I will do as you've asked," Zeph confirmed. "I have errands to attend to. You may stay for a meal if Nicke wishes you to, but otherwise, I want you gone from my house by the time I return." He bowed, slowly, a challenge, then left through the front door.

Alix turned back to Nicke and Nicke nodded her head. Of course. Of course she wanted her to stay. She hadn't seen her in too many weeks, and they were full of heartache and horror.

Before she did anything else, Nicke embraced her.

"I'm sorry," Alix whispered. "I'm sorry about everything."

"It's okay."

"It's not, but I appreciate the sentiment."

Nicke directed her to a chair and she sat in what could only be described as a hollow way. Her shoulders hunched and the cloak dwarfed her.

"I'm sorry about Kallias."

Alix nodded. "Fever they said."

Nicke shook her head. "He was too robust for fever. And Sophos's scroll to Zephyros was sceptical, too."

"We're all sceptical. For all the good it does us." Alix turned to Nicke and assessed her again. "I'm glad you're no longer at the mercy of his every whim. When he broke your wrist, I thought he would pull back because it prevented you from doing work. But then…"

Nicke hesitated. Her sister was the only link to a past well behind them.

"I called her Lysida," Nicke said. "For her father."

"Yes, I think he would have liked it."

Anger licked Nicke's gut but she swallowed it. It wasn't Alix's right to say. She'd known Lysander only in passing, a glancing shot in the streets of the city. Though, she may have an inkling of him from his brother.

"How's Dannehs?" Nicke asked.

Alix sighed. "Melancholic. But he didn't know Kallias was his father, simply a man who took an interest in him. He'll probably only make the connection when he's older and I fear it will end with Lyon's head on a pike."

"I don't know if Dannehs is tending to violence in such a way."

"No, perhaps you're right. Plenty of time to learn, then."

Alix took the meal of bread and roast meat from Nicke with eager hands. "He misses you, of course. Both boys do."

"Do they know what happened?"

Alix shook her head slowly. "They heard some rumours I suspect. Kallum asked when you were going to return for their strategy sessions."

"Not any time soon. I won't even attend the War Rooms after they let your husband chase me down."

Nicke could feel her sister's restraint. Well groomed and wasted in a country like Laerta.

"What do you think will happen, pet?" Alix said quietly. "Do you think the ephors will come back with a new king? Someone plucked out of the countryside? Lyon's brother is dead, he has no cousins, and Kallum is too young to be king."

Nicke swallowed roughly. "So you would choose to let him be free because it's convenient?"

Alix shrugged. "We all do what we can to keep our children safe."

The comment smarted. Yes, she could think of just the things Alix would have done in her stead to protect her child. Failure was a piece of iron, once scalding, now frozen in a barren ground simply waiting for the witless to pick it up. Whether that iron was a sword, forged and sharp, or a simple hole-ridden cooking pot from which regret could flow, the metal still burnt when it was touched.

"What did you say?" she whispered. Quiet. Like she was a general and the woman in front of her was a mark.

Alix sighed. "Keeping Lyon as king will ensure that Kallum can follow him. I have to protect my son."

"You think this will protect him? That the brutality his father is teaching him won't be the end of him, instead?"

"It's all I can do," Alix said, determined. "My son will come back to his father the king and the usurper whose house you call abode will not."

Nicke already knew that Zeph was slated for death. That part didn't surprise her. It was the callousness, the drive so new in her sister who didn't have the heart to face the world beyond her chamber most days. The gossamer blinds of the windows that echoed Malptia were only sheer under a bright light, and Alix was too dull to see.

The fury burning under her skin felt like it glowed. Cleansing and right, her eyes turned black in the ensuing tremble of her voice.

"He's stronger than the forces working against him," Nicke seethed.

"Even so," Alix replied with a lift of her shoulder. "He will not be king."

It was the first time Nicke had conceptualised Zephyros's machinations as majesty. He was aiming for Laerta Rex, striving as high as he could get in a city such as theirs. If he died in the attempt, would the earth grant him the sustaining greenery at his resting place, as the stories told?

"Get out of my house," Nicke said, voice strong and sure.

Alix looked at her then, and if her back could have straightened further, it would have. "He's in love with you, you know," her sister said. "I guess some rumours are close to truth."

"Out."

Alix stood and paused a moment to sniff the air. "Fury doesn't become you, sister, but that's why the tests would have chosen you for queen. It isn't by birth order, as you well know: the sister-gods instead invoke a trial of wits and strength. You would have survived it, but, then, you'd have your twin for competition."

The feeling was akin to drowning.

"I'll let you ruminate on that for the next time you decide to throw me, a queen, out of your shack."

Nicke watched her go as the sun set behind her.

* * *

It wasn't true.

She would have remembered.

She would have known.

How did her parents keep it secret? How did Alix?

An heir lived in Malptia. In secret, ready to assume the throne likely with airs of destroying Laerta for what they had taken.

He sat in his usual seat, pushing his oats around. "You're quiet."

She trusted him. But this could destroy nations. Or rebuild them.

"Just thinking about some things Alix said."

Demetria joined them and sat next to Zeph, across the table from Nicke. She began to fuss over her brother: pouring him more milk, passing him the honey. It reminded Nicke of a mother hen. Which, Nicke supposed, she was in a way. She'd been ensuring Nicke's person basically her whole life. Only when Nicke had given in to the onslaught of kindness and decided that trust was more valuable than hurt did Demetria turn from maid and possible spy into something akin to a sister. She couldn't pinpoint exactly when it had occurred, but the past year felt brief in hindsight.

"What did she say?" Demetria asked.

Nicke's face dove into her hands and she rubbed her eyes. "Lots of things."

Ria harrumphed, but didn't press. Nicke secretly thanked her for it.

"Are you both ready to travel?" Zeph asked. "Ryan will escort you to the camp before I leave the city, in case something goes wrong." He had to attend the Senate and wait for the ephors to be ready before they could leave. He could abandon the trip if something went awry.

Nicke hadn't slept a wink, but nodded all the same.

"I have a few things left that I need to dry before I pack them," Demetria said. "Won't be long."

"By the middle of the day?" When she nodded, Zeph said, "Okay."

She and Demetria said their goodbyes to Zeph in a similar way. Hugs around the centre and assurances of safety while absent. Alix's words about Nicke's apparent sister weren't the only ones swirling as she watched him ride away. Like the happiness, which showered her in shame whenever she remembered to mourn her husband and daughter, this caused her throat to close in guilt.

Nicke intended to use the morning they had in the city to run some errands. The wind was low when she set out with Demetria. Ryan watched from a respectable distance, and Nicke quietly wondered whether it was loyalty to his cousin or coin that kept him by her side. She was no longer under the Rex's specific type of protection, but Ryan still guarded her.

"Where are we going?" Demetria asked.

"The market," Nicke replied.

"Why?"

"I want to know about which herbs can kill a person when burnt."

Demetria stopped dead and Nicke left her behind. She only had a small window of time.

"And how do you expect to find that out?" Ria whispered when she'd caught up.

"By asking the apothecary."

"You, general of the army with a known animosity towards the king, are going to go into a merchant and ask how to kill a man with herbs."

Nicke slowed. "Well, when you put it that way."

"It's madness."

"Yes, but how else will we find out?"

Demetria spied around them again, found her mark and gestured him over.

"Ryan, we're going to Chinto. Are you willing to accompany us?"

He looked nervous, unsure. "Zephyros told me—"

"My brother says lots of things," Ria dismissed. "We're going either way. Do you think he'll be angrier that you went with us, or left us on our own."

Nicke baulked a little at her candour and how she openly named that Ryan was following Zephyros's orders.

Ryan agreed, and walked a little closer if still out of hearing distance.

"Are you going to tell me what Alix said?"

"Which part?"

"The part that has you so bothered."

"She just mentioned some things I didn't know about Malptia." Nicke hesitated, deciding suddenly to keep her newfound sister to herself. Ria looked at her sidelong. She wasn't convinced that that was all Nicke was pondering. "She also said that your brother is in love with me." When Ria stayed silent, biting her lip and glancing away, Nicke threw up her hands. "Does everyone know?"

"I don't think Zeph does, to be honest. He's too loyal to Lysander to do anything about it, anyway." She paused, then, "Do you...?"

Nicke shook her head. "He's my best friend, but I don't love him; not like that."

"He's got a big capacity for love, so I don't think a bit of heartbreak would hurt him too badly. He'd recover, take it on the chin like everything else."

"I hope you're right."

They walked to the slave village in silence and only spoke when Ria suggested that Nicke pocket the silver chain around her neck. "You want these slaves to speak to you, and not because they're intimidated." Nicke did as she said and followed her into the market.

"Good morning," Demetria said to one of the women washing at the well. "Where can we find a herbalist?"

The woman pointed and turned back to her chores. Her consideration of Nicke was glancing at best.

The herbalist was in a small alcove connected to a small house. Mudbrick, with almost rotted shutters and a bowing wooden door, they never would have found it without direction. A small sign identified the place as home to knowledge and wisdom both. Nicke wondered which she needed in that moment. The knowledge of the herbs; the wisdom to use the knowledge.

"Hello?" Demetria called out, rapping on the window frame.

They didn't wait long before a woman of extended years appeared. Her hair was onyx and the lines on her face were deep and curling. When she smiled, Nicke felt the air stop.

"Good morning to you both," the woman said, then she looked behind their shoulders. "Do you know that a man with brown hair and a good spear arm follows you?" Nicke looked behind them, but couldn't see Ryan.

"Ahh," the woman said, "he's your guard. Right then. Six gold coins and I'll tell you your futures."

Ria laughed but Nicke stayed silent. "We don't want our futures," Ria said. "How much for herbal knowledge?"

The woman worked her tongue around her mouth. "Four golds."

Ria glanced at Nicke and she produced the coins. The old woman could smell a mark, and had identified the two women with thick fabric on their backs as such.

"We were recently made aware of a herb that, when burnt, produced a toxic smoke. We were wondering if you knew of it," Nicke said.

"A few things can do that. None you'll like."

"Try me," Nicke said.

"It is said that one grows on the cliffs of Kurkia. Bound by white thread and picked on the spring equinox, it leaves the taste of soft love on your tongue even as you die. Another is borne in Kypt, along a seashore. It blooms yellow, then bleeds red but only when picked by a young sister betrayed. The third, and the one I'm guessing is your herb, is only found on the fields of Auntu. It requires a steady hand as the flower-milk is as deadly as the smoke made from its dried leaves. It is a quieter poison, less obtrusive. If you hadn't remembered the smoke, it never would have been seen."

The woman turned to Demetria, her eyes ablaze with knowing. It was stars and their shine in her irises, and Nicke recoiled from the comprehension in her gaze.

"What's your name, girl?"

"Demetria."

"No, that's not it."

Demetria glanced at Nicke and the woman followed the movement. "K—Khloe. But no one calls me that."

Khloe? A line appeared between Nicke's brow.

"Of?"

"Boornea."

"No, before Boornea. Where did you escape from?"

"My brother thinks we hail from Laerta."

Nicke looked at Demetria sharply. Zeph hadn't mentioned his suspicions, but, then, when would he have had the time? His education was Laertan, no doubt about it, but if he and Demetria were Laertan, then it would ask and answer questions both.

The old woman smiled. It showed a mouth of perfect white teeth, rare at her age. "Yes. Laerta you are; its own blood spilt on a moonlit night." She leant in closer and Demetria mimicked the action. "It's the eyes, you see. Our king, Laerta's own blood, has your eyes."

"The king has brown eyes," Demetria said, voice quivering.

The woman shook her head. "Not my king. My king is the one the earth has been calling to. You, too, have felt it. The way the birds fly east on the heels of the spring winds. Hailing from the west, he will bring Laerta to her knees, and we will thank him."

"Ze—" Demetria started before Nicke hushed her.

The woman turned her stare on Nicke, and fear dug deep into her gut.

"Malptia's Rose," she sang. "You bring him more danger than you know. He will hesitate to his fate because of the hold you have on him."

"I'm not stopping him."

"Nor are you cutting him loose. He strives for you, when he should be striving for his country. You know this. You will feel it, soon enough."

Nicke nodded, hating it, absorbing the feeling of losing something she'd not ever gained. Zephyros was angling his chances to fell Lyon, and she had asked for him to wait because of her own fear reflected.

But that wasn't what Nicke had come here to ask.

"Who set the herbs?" Nicke said outright. If the woman was a prophet, then best get their money's worth.

A wolfish grin. "It isn't truly you they want to kill. They have a festering wound that they expect your death to fill."

"Who?"

"The herb is found in Auntu. Who else?"

Who else indeed. Not Matthew, who, though returned from the field, had not had access to the house to tamper with the fires. Not Lyon, whose methods were garish and performative.

His knowing grin when he'd assured Zeph, only days ago, that Nicke's life was safe with him flashed in her mind. The way he'd touched the ash of the brazier and commented about the wrongness of femininity in the house. How the methods were quiet, small, and untraceable.

It was a difficult thing to condemn a man based on a seer's words, and Nicke felt bereft of a way to convince Zephyros that his brother was the one that was trying to kill her.

"We have to tell Zeph what we've learnt here," Nicke said desperately to Ria.

The old woman grabbed at Nicke and held her forearm in a vice-like grip. "Your role is to die. It's the only way."

"And what do you think will happen when he returns to me in the wall?"

"Oh, he will rage, but that will be used as the final push. Without it, it will be years and countless lives before Galyn becomes our king."

"You want my sacrifice?" Nicke said bitterly. "It's not on offer."

"Then you doom us."

"So be it."

The woman let her go and retreated back into her hovel. Nicke was breathing hard, fast. She ran from the village and only stopped when the small houses were far behind them.

The revelation of her assassin paled in the face of the woman's comments about Zeph. She called him king; said that he was Laerta's blood. It may simply be a slave's recognition of the uprising brewing in the undercurrents of the city, but Nicke didn't think so. The frieze had green eyes, and so did he.

Nicke's knowledge of the kings before Lyon were sketchy at best, but she knew of the heirs killed and their mother murdered.

"What was your mother's name, Demetria?" she asked, taking breath after breath without achieving air.

"Chrysanthe," Ria said.

Nicke slowly closed her eyes, then opened them. Her head tilted back in resignation, in regret. Galyn was a common name; but Chrysanthe was not.

How did fate navigate them here? How did a slave with only a passing regard for them become rooted into Laertan soil? He came and could have been sent to a mine, a farm, a position far from here to break his back and spirit under the wandering hand of a cruel master. But, instead, he came to their house and pushed his way into Laerta's crumbling weaknesses to assert his rightful place. To right a generational wrong; not just Lyon's violence against Nicke but Kallum Rex's violence against the previous king.

Zeph wasn't planning a coup; he was targeting his own usurper.

"It's an unusual name in Laerta," Nicke said.

Demetria nodded. "I know. I looked for her at the Temple stones but couldn't find her."

"You won't find her there. She's buried on the western side of the sacred hill."

Demetria looked at her like she was new and malformed.

"Chrysanthe is a royal Kyptian name," Nicke clarified.

"But Zeph thinks we're Laertan," Demetria tried desperately.

"You don't understand, Ria. Chrysanthe is the name given to the first-born girl, every generation of Kyptian royalty stretching back hundreds of years. Your mother was Kypt's Princess Princi."

"Then... what the old woman said. Zeph..."

Nicke nodded. "You and Zeph are Lyon's dead cousins. Your father was killed by a boar and Lyon's father failed to have you killed when he was regent. You're the heirs to Laerta."

Demetria picked up her pace, but Nicke slowed. She needed to think.

"We need to catch him before he leaves," Demetria said.

"No," Nicke said. "We let him go. Either he comes back king, or we tell him when he arrives."

"But Nicke—"

"No. The Oracle will identify him. It's her role to identify him."

Blinding clarity assaulted her. How he had dismissed her questions about his knowledge of their sacred stories. His small enquiries about the frieze and all it beheld under a royal green gaze. How he had so willingly gone to the one place that could speak the truth of his story, with the exact people who needed to bear witness. "He knows," Nicke said. "That's why he volunteered, the bastard. He already intends to come back a king."

Demetria's scoff was half a sob. Betrayal and panic swirled in the eyes that matched her brother. "How could he know and not mention it?"

Nicke shrugged. "Do we really know him at all?"

She stretched back her shoulders and threw on a mantle she'd hoped lost. The poise and position of general was ill fitting, but she would fill it out as she politicked for him while he was gone. To ensure a smooth transition. To sure up the power base. To have him come home to a welcoming city, in need of a king, and the military might to overthrow a bad one. The hoplites in Auntu may not be back, but there may still be work for her to do.

But to do that, she had to avoid her prophesied death at the hands of Zephyros's brother.

CHAPTER EIGHTEEN

Zephyros

Most of the travel to the Oracle would be on horseback, his gelding surefooted and comfortable with the pace. The beast snapped if another rider got too close, gnashing his teeth in a truly fearsome display that was simply that: a display. It suited Zephyros well. He needed to order his thoughts, practise his surprised face when the Oracle named him king, and give the right amount of heed to the ephors that currently only spoke amongst themselves.

The Oracle was finicky, apparently. She, being prepubescent and abused for it, would grant each person only one answer. Should the question be wanting, the answer could be gibberish. Riddles, all, and the questioner's own punishment for partaking in her personal horror. But, Laerta was pious even without gods to guide them, and the Oracle was as close to a god as Laerta allowed themselves. Zeph only knew this because his uncle had told him. Things, apparently, an heir should be across.

They stopped at a creek half a day from the city to fill up their water-skins and give the horses a break. It hadn't been a hard ride, but Zeph cooed at his animal, unable to bring himself to verbalise the name Lysander had preferred for him. Not out of respect for his brother, nor out of a sense of shifted loyalty as the horse came easily to Zephyros's hands when he'd died. No. It was because the name got stuck in his throat for how stupid it was. Lysander had explained that he was a child just home from the Credo's camps when his own father had presented the beast and declared him his. Apparently, when Lysander, a boy of thirteen, had attempted to draw the new horse into the lean-to that sat beside their house, he'd thrown his head, broken his lead, reared and, apparently, shrieked in fear.

Why, one might ask?

Well, apparently a cat had been sleeping very soundly in the shed and the horse had deathly feared the feline to the point of almost killing his new master.

So Lysander had named him Mouse.

A war horse. A horse with a lineage as long as Zeph's supposed origins, even though he had been gelded to better suit Lysos's intention of being a horse for a child.

And Lysander had fucking called him *Mouse*.

Zeph couldn't bring himself to say it.

He gave the gelding some of the apples he'd stashed in his pack, lending him soothing words as the day cooled with the disappearance of the afternoon sun. They'd not set off until late morning, a good hour after Zeph had said his goodbyes to his sister and Nicke. He'd not seen Drakon or Sophie, the former doing his own thing and the latter sequestered in her husband's family's fortress of a farm. They'd taken to her like bees to sugar water, and he knew she'd be safe there. Matthew had received a small reprieve because of Sophie's imminent birth, and because he was under Sophos, and not Jonn. Zeph hadn't expected him to be available for Demetria and Nicke's protection, his focus falling solely on his wife, but Zeph had given plenty of coin to Samuel, his brother. Coin bought loyalty like nothing else, but he suspected that many of the people he'd approached would have done it anyway. They knew Nicke, had heard her screams. Many of them had also been drawn into Zeph's plans well before this particular trip.

He glanced to the copse of trees to the south of the glade where their horses watered, and spied Kallum struggling with some ties. Zeph had made a promise to the queen and had received some in return, but now that he was in the midst of such an obligation he found himself shying from it. Kallum had shown his ire in every way possible. In the strategy sessions, he'd been openly hostile despite his aunt's admonishment, and here, under the regard of the ephors, he may be an impossible nut to crack.

But Zeph was determined to crack him. He was sixteen, and Zeph had been sixteen once. He'd crawled from the intense hold of his uncle's expectations and had breathed the feel of freedom so deeply that he'd never returned. To relieve the shackles and then place them back? Impossible. It was the vision on the cave wall made real; the fog keeping the ship docked cleared.

Even though the hands of terror did not fall upon Kallum's own flesh, it could have manifested in other ways; in worse ways. The fear can fester and grow, pus in a fiery wound. Zephyros couldn't help but think that Kallum's opinion of him was not his own, but rather another's simply reflected and refracted.

Zeph's plan was simple. Keep the boy, almost a man, safe as per his mother's request. Then fill his empty cup with so much trust, surety, and faith that he would turn the knife he no doubt held. Loyalty was funny, especially in children. When they left the eaves of their parents' control, and were given a small gift of kindness in a measured way, they would puddle like a block of ice left in the sun. It wasn't meant to be manipulative, though. Zeph simply saw a child tightly controlled, and sought to see the boy without the binds.

He ventured over and offered Kallum's horse an apple. The mare, at least, far away inspection had implied a mare, turned her head dutifully towards the fruit and took one sniff before devouring it. Zeph held fast, forcing the beast to take a bite rather than giving up the whole fruit.

"Do you want to give her the rest?" he asked Kallum. He offered the half-eaten apple and smiled.

Kallum gruffly shook his head. "He doesn't take kindly to slave food."

Zephyros's eyes squinted in confusion, firstly at Kallum, then at the horse he was sure was a mare.

"Do you know much about horses?" he asked casually. Gently, he ran his hand down her flank and she, over-familiar, sniffed at his pockets. He gladly gave her the rest of the apple in supplication. Unobtrusively, he looked under her belly, and was proven right.

Kallum didn't reply to his question, but he may not have heard it.

"She's a beauty," Zeph said, standing straight.

"*He*," Kallum corrected, on the rude side of direct.

Zeph shrugged, leaving him alone. "If you say so."

They made it to a small village on the southern side of the Jehagi Mountains the following day. The hills separated the rural population of Laerta from the outlaws of the country's outer territory. This was where slaves often ran, the hard life in the highest peaks more valuable for the freedom it bought. Zeph tried again, already ingratiating himself with Kallum's horse. The mare meandered over to him when Zeph was caring for his own horse and checked his pack for goodies.

"Nothing more for you in there," Zeph murmured, patting her gently on the nose.

Rick, the Tertiary ephor with grey speckled through his hair, brought his own mount to the same tree and tied it there. "There's a Master of Trade here that I thought we could ask for shelter or food," he said.

Zeph dipped his chin, blinking in confusion.

"If that's acceptable to you?" Rick continued. He shifted his weight from one foot to the other until Zeph responded with a shrug.

"This village is small, poor," Zeph replied. "I didn't see many animal pens or crops as we entered. I don't know about taking from the mouths of those who seem barely able to feed themselves."

Rick surveyed him, then nodded. "Right you are."

"I will hunt something," Zeph continued as he took his bow from his gelding's back. "Would it be possible to get a fire going while I'm at it?"

Rick nodded and withdrew.

Zeph played the conversation back as he first strung his bow, then made into the trees. Perhaps Nicke had spoken favourably about him, his strategy, and Rick was professionally interested in the new blood he could bring to the Tertiary.

Or perhaps Rick was simply sick of Cali and Maria for company.

Zeph returned to the camp mostly set up. The village's Master was also seated around the fire, his wiry hair and gaunt appearance proving Zephyros right. This Master likely performed marriages and funerals both, despite the Theory's turf being encroached by the practice. The people here required it, and having both Masters would be surplus to their needs.

Kallum was seated apart and Zephyros produced a knife from his belt and passed it to the boy. Kallum eyed it but didn't take it.

"Do you want to learn how to clean the goat?" Zeph asked, gesturing to the kid he'd felled. It would be enough for two or three days before the sun got to it.

Kallum surveyed him, and Zeph shrugged. "I can just show you now, and you can have a go when you feel comfortable."

"Demetria showed me how to clean a chicken once," he replied.

Zeph smiled. The knowledge couldn't hurt, since the queen already knew the connection. "She's my sister, you know?"

Kallum's face opened. "Really? How?"

Zephyros stepped away from complete truth. How could he tell this boy that his grandfather had murdered Zeph's own father, casting both he and his sister out into the world? Instead, Zeph spoke a lie that burnt his tongue. "Slavery means you get bought and sold. We were very lucky to find each other in Laerta."

The prince's mouth closed and then he his eyes suddenly went wide. "That's why mum gave her to Nicke. Because she's technically your household. I suppose you do look alike, but I miss her."

"You could see her, if you wanted. My home is open to you as Nicke's family."

A cloud passed over Kallum's face and Zeph then knew he'd pushed too far; too fast. He turned to the goat and began to skin it.

When they were eating, Rick sat beside Zephyros and complimented him on the choice of meal. Zeph returned his thanks to Rick for placing the meat over the coals.

"My wife detests cooking," he offered. "She's Kyptian and since she moved to Laerta, she'd been of the opinion that such a thing is beneath her." Zeph chuckled, and Rick asked, "And what does it mean? The name?"

"Zephyros was the Kurdan God of Spring and the west winds that lead into summer," he explained. It was an old god, one that few in Kurkia or abroad knew of. Kypt had done their work well in suppressing the Pantheon.

"You're Kurdan, yes?"

Zephyros took some time to rearrange his maroon cloak to more effectively keep the warmth in. "Yes. I came to Laerta via Kypt."

"One of the war gifts. Yes, I remember."

Zeph looked at him sharply. Rick shrugged. "Sophos told me of you."

Zeph hadn't supposed he'd been noticed at all, let alone enough to be spoken of between Laertan leaders. He'd kept to himself as everyone had encouraged him to, and had watched his brothers be killed, like everyone had foretold.

"What did he say?" Zeph ventured.

Rick looked at him sidelong, lingering on his eyes. "That you were wasted in Secondary. I knew why you were placed there, of course, we all did. But wasted, all the same."

"Tertiary is your stream?"

Rick nodded. "I taught Nicke and Lysander when they were younger. Nicke defeated every puzzle I threw at her, surpassing us all. But we taught her, kept her at the Credo as long as we could, and encouraged her to turn to teaching so she was excused for staying there."

The spark of a flame began in Zeph's chest, licking his heart and infusing his vision with warmth. It felt like war: the drive to maim and kill to protect his home from those that would do it harm. It wasn't honed or calculated like a precise strike; instead it was frenzied like a fire made in a droughted field.

Zeph would one day light a match and watch as every single person that had done his home wrong burnt. It didn't matter that Rick or Sophos or Alix or Lysander had tried their best when their best still almost got her killed. Part was self-immolation, his own guilt smarting; and part was misdirected to the helpers rather than the perpetrator. The frenzy ate at him all the same.

His gaze may have seared the flesh of anyone he regarded, so he kept his eyes low.

"I would welcome you to Tertiary, Zephyros, when we return, if you wanted it. Sophos is getting old, and I doubt Nicke will return to her station. We need fresh blood."

"Kurdan blood? The same blood you ensured ran into the sea?"

Rick smiled tightly. "Your blood is Laertan. You know this; don't shy from it now."

Yes, his blood was Laertan. Yes, he knew why the mountains here sang to him and called him home.

Zeph fell asleep, his borrowed leather armour chafing his skin, but the melody of the stars lulling him into dreams.

* * *

It was uncanny. His neck was sluggish to respond to his command for movement. Like it was bound, or tired. His eyes opened to a close darkness. A blanket thrown over his head, or a small box blocking out the light. He didn't feel the need to struggle, though, because curious giggling was coming from the other side.

"Where's Khloe?" the question rang out. It was a bell on a merchant's door, or the curious feeling of mirth tied to knowing.

The darkness snapped to bright, and Zeph's eyes shied away from it.

"Here I am!" came the reply. He laughed, joyously, like nothing could or would ever be wrong.

She was seated in front of him, short legs crossed and a blue chiton on her slight frame. Dazzling green eyes pulled him towards her and she giggled like a song. Her hair was long, brought under control by tight binds, the light of the hearth fire glinting to make it red.

He attempted to speak, but found tension tightening along his lips and drawing a line between his cheeks.

The darkness descended again, and he was devastated. The sight of her was all he could ever want to see again, and lost so suddenly.

"Where's Khloe?" came the voice again.

Zeph's devastation quickly turned to tears. He'd been given everything he wanted in that small moment, only for it to be ripped away.

The blanket disappeared and her eyes no longer shone. They were worried, clenched in the way children do when they fear both the wrath of their younger siblings and the wrath of their parents.

"Leave off, Khloe," said a deep voice from behind him. "He may be tired."

Zeph was lifted from the ground, his limbs losing tension as large hands tucked him to a larger body at the hip. The smell was almost as good as his sister's smile had been. Warm. The exact place he wanted to be.

"Do you know where your mother is?" the voice asked.

"No, papa."

Their father hummed.

Zeph tried to look at him. Tried to get a glimpse of the face he'd so often wondered about. Whether it was as Demetria said, and he was Zeph's twin, or whether the sight of him had aged like a ruined castle. His chin may be different, his cheekbones not the same.

But Zeph couldn't see him, and would probably die wondering.

He was gently placed, furs under his baby head, and a soft woven blanket about his middle. A Laertan lullaby, so often sung in his own house, crooned out of his father. He reached out, a single fist requesting help to hold onto the world.

"Gal..." his father whispered. "Don't be afraid."

Zeph worried his forehead.

"It will be hard, my boy, but that is why it is important. Difficulty means things are worth doing."

Zeph tried to speak again, tried to strain his mouth open, but it was no use.

"Look to Malptia, when the time comes. She will guide you."

His father disappeared in a haze of smoke, like he'd walked behind a campfire. And Zeph was left with only bitter notions of comfort and home.

* * *

He snapped awake, taking in lungfuls of air like he'd been close to the grave and only just escaped.

His father. The man who had no face and only a thick baritone to identify him. Calloused hands to sooth him in sleep and an urgency to warn him in life. Zeph hadn't remembered his voice and hadn't heard it on the breeze when he'd gone looking, but he knew it all the same. It was the answer to an unasked question and it rattled him that the spirit of his dead father deigned to warn him from the underworld.

Difficulty was the point, of course. Nothing worth doing was easy. Was this not the mantra he'd repeated since he'd taken up his city's blue cloak and declared himself a sailor? Did it not permeate his every decision, his every vice, the very way he managed himself and his affairs?

If overthrowing a king was easy, he wouldn't have bothered.

The difficulty was the point.

He didn't know the true fate of his father and would probably never know. A man speared looked an awful lot like a gore wound, and the dots connected through his mother's brief but telling letter of warning said it was Lyon's father who had committed the deed.

Zeph had not truly considered that much of what he'd yearned for as a sullen and isolated child had occurred since he'd ventured into Laerta. Not only could he add a blooded sister to his side, someone he already knew he could rely on without question, but he also had cousins. It was still dark, but he sought Kallum in the gloom. His cousin's son. Kin.

More than he wanted.

More than he needed.

But, still. Kin.

His vow to the queen that he would care for her son suddenly took a different hue, and he welcomed the lack of obligation to the task. It was a given, truly, to task himself with caring for a cousin. Zeph didn't know how the ephors would react to what may seem like inevitable civil war, and if their solution would be to kill Kallum before he could retaliate in his father's stead. Zeph would be ready to protect him.

The east was beginning its trek from midnight to morning, and Zeph rose. Today would be a day for crossing these blasted mountains and beginning the arduous task of learning to breathe half breaths in the stench of the deltas. Zeph didn't favour such conditions.

Once they were off and riding, the morning already half gone by certain travel companions not used to travelling, he dropped his gelding back to sit a comfortable distance to the side of the boy. He had a few days before they reached Boornea city, and from there a day's travel by boat to the outer islands, so Zeph thought it best to impose himself.

"What do you think of this country?" he asked, gesturing to the mountains around them.

He thought Kallum would simply ignore him, an annoying bug forcing itself into his space, but he responded with a sigh.

"The Jehagi Mountains are the highest peaks this side of Auntu," he said dispassionately. "When Laerta first claimed Boornea, King Robar sent men into them to flush out the bandits and outlaws. Only four parties came back, and of them only five people were uninjured. Since, each king of Laerta has attempted to tame them with little success." He paused and looked behind them, towards the plains of Laerta's food basket. "So I suppose I think them rugged, unattainable, and annoying."

"You think the mountains are annoying?" Zeph said with a laugh. "Mountains don't speak, or think."

"Yes, well. Each king has tasked himself with conquering the unconquerable. I suppose my skin is next." There was resignation in his tone, a reluctance Zephyros had only glimpsed so far.

"How do you propose to scale them?"

Zeph felt the air shift and Kallum shift with it. He tightened his shoulders and the whites of his knuckles showed.

"I don't know," he said eventually. It was a difficult admission. "I didn't come here for tests, slave. Especially from you."

Zeph worried his brow. "I wanted your opinion on a part of the world that is new to me, Kallum. That's all." He tried again, his framing of the question wanting. "Do you think they're beautiful?"

"They're mountains. They simply present difficulty."

Kallum went to turn away, but Zeph stopped him. "You can be yourself here, Kallum. I'm not here to test you."

He scoffed. "My aunt's pet and my father's rival, and you think I can be myself here?" He shook his head, then his mouth spoke his truth. "Everything is a test, in the end."

He rode away and Zeph felt the small opening close up like a bothered clam. It was a habit of his. He came on strong, letting his own ease manifest. But when others were uneasy, well, it often turned into something else.

They rode into the afternoon, stopping briefly to water and rest the horses, and Zeph tried again. This time it was among the ephors as they sat next to the creek.

"Kallum, can I tell you the story of how I first left my uncle's house?" Zeph asked.

"No, thank you."

Zeph started anyway. "I was fifteen, and an idiot. An absolute numbskull, but I considered myself both learned and ready to be out from my uncle's wing. So, rather than stay and be robbed at knife point, which happened twice, or spat on by donkeys and men both, which happened more times than I have fingers, I decided to move from our small village to Kurkia's city. I thought I was smart, and I thought I was ready. My uncle was ready to prove me wrong, though. He sent men after me to bring me to heel, and their methods were, though not as rough as his, on the..." he searched for a word, "rowdy side."

"Why are you telling me this?" Kallum drawled.

"We're getting to that, prince," Zeph assured him. "Now, these men, as I've said, were not the gentle sort. So when they eventually caught me and returned me to my uncle, with a black eye, three broken fingers and only half a scalp of hair, my uncle didn't only kill them for their trouble, he murdered the entirety of their troop."

The ephors sat silently and Kallum's mouth was wide. Zeph focused his own intentions: to speak to the fearful part of Kallum. His voice turned quiet, thoughtful.

"You'd think that he would have maybe presented their heads to me in apology for my treatment, but no. Instead, he broke my lower leg so I couldn't run again. He'd been shamed by my making off, the truth of the freedom I craved plain for all to see. And if my uncle was anything, it was proud. Pride drove him and pride sustained him. Pride is the devil in men who think they know better, and seek to ensure you realise it." Zeph picked up a stick and poked the mud, causing a river of water to trace around his foot. He leant in to Kallum, the next words for him alone. "That is why I will never be the one to test you. Because you could run: you could decide that this life you've been gifted by the earth is wanting, just like you would of any gift that caused your eyes to water and your nose to bleed. And I wouldn't break your leg to stop it happening. I'd probably advise against it, especially in the light of what you've told me of these mountains, but I wouldn't stop you. I never will. I swear on my life that you can be who you want to be, here."

Zeph stood, and took his leave of them. He glanced back at Kallum as he disappeared through the trees, and saw the child slack jawed and brimming with tears.

Following the story, Kallum didn't shy from Zeph's questions, or his comments. Zephyros was even able to get a laugh or two out of him, when the timing was right.

When they came within two days of Boornea's city, Zeph decided to push into the void he'd created in the boy and finally, *finally*, improve the boy's sparring technique. It had been atrocious when he'd attacked Zephyros on the road, and he doubted much had improved since then.

"Kallum, is it true that you favour your left hand?" Zeph

asked.

Kallum rolled his eyes. "You have seen me both write and spar. You know I do."

"And it wasn't coaxed out of you? In Kurkia, I favoured my left and my uncle forced me to learn both to surprise opponents."

"No," Kallum said. "I can't do anything with my right. No one tried to get me to, either."

"What was your uncle's name, Zephyros?" Rick interjected, in what could be a conversational tone. Zeph was sure he'd been bursting to ask more since he'd heard his tale.

"His name was Brynne, ephor. He unfortunately died when I was fifteen." Zeph turned back to Kallum. "Would you like me to teach you how to compensate for it?"

"What?" the boy said, surprised.

"You don't need to favour your right to close the gap in your technique. There are some small tricks you can use."

"I'm a fine fighter," Kallum said proudly, jutting his chin. He looked like his father, a little, in this light.

Zeph heard a small laugh from Maria behind them. "You may be a fine fighter, prince, but Zephyros is probably better. Let him teach you what he knows."

Zeph wished her quiet. It was hard enough to get Kallum to open to him, let alone learn from him. But the boy's technique was fatal and he'd made a promise to his mother.

Kallum struggled under the ephors' gaze until Zeph drew his attention by passing him a spear. Zephyros gently corrected his grip. "It's no comment on you, I promise you. And this is not a test, I promise that, too. But these mountains are dangerous and I would like you to be able to protect yourself."

"Why did no one mention it?" he whispered back. "The flaws."

Zeph shrugged. "Perhaps they never thought you'd be in a position to need correction."

"My father doesn't have such flaws."

"Your father prefers to beat women senseless and I was able to bind him without a sweat. I guarantee that his flaws are more than yours."

Zeph straightened and gestured to the glade. Kallum followed him cautiously, and Rick and Maria watched with rapt expressions. Technically, Zeph was one of Maria's men, and Rick wanted to poach him to the Tertiary. Perhaps something would ride on this bout of teaching.

"Take the spear and stand like this," Zeph said. Kallum did as he was told. Zeph watched him move and wondered whether anyone had been game to actually teach him properly. An heir's training was separate, so much so that Kallum had not attended the children's camps where much of the finer techniques of the spar were taught.

"You're holding it straight," Zeph said gently. "Try and turn it a little so it follows the arc of your arm. It will then not be something to be mastered, but a part of you."

Kallum did as he said, and Zeph launched a small, light bout against him. Kallum was able to deflect, but without much strength behind it.

"Roll your shoulder forward three times to loosen it, then we will try again."

Again, Kallum followed his instructions, and when Zeph came for him again, his deflection was surer. That's when Zephyros knew this was as much a confidence problem as it was his technique.

They practised for the duration of the lunch, and each time they stopped afterwards until they made it to Boornea city.

*　*　*

They had left the mountains with their cool air far behind, and had trudged through swamp for the duration of the time since. Kallum was slow to open his thoughts, but on the morning that they first spied the golden city nestled between two separate river deltas, Kallum was ready to spar without prompting from Zephyros. He'd improved, but it would take time.

"You're keen," Zeph said, a little irritably.

"I thought..." Kallum said, baulking at his tone.

"No, no," Zephyros dismissed. "You thought right. My nights have just been filled with bad dreams. Plus, I'm just naturally grumpy."

Kallum smiled a little at the joke and readied his own kopis. He wasn't tall enough for the spear to be effective, Zeph had decided, so they'd moved on to the short sword.

They talked as they sparred. Easy words among difficult training often opened up the soul.

"Did your uncle teach you all this?" Kallum asked.

"No. Some was him, the early technique, the foundation, was him. But much of it was honed when I arrived in Laerta. My brothers were merciless, to be honest."

"Why?"

Zeph looked at him and knew a shadow had come over his face. "Because we thought that if I proved myself good enough, Laerta would let me join them on the march. I couldn't go." And now two brothers were dead. "It didn't work, of course. My theory studies kept me in Laerta. And good thing too, in the end. If I wasn't in Laerta when Lyon came for Nicke, she'd be dead."

The words burst from Kallum like a water-skin heated. "We didn't know! We didn't know before. We were told that it was genuine punishment. That she deserved it and she was plotting against him. We didn't *know*."

Zeph put up his hands in supplication, almost a begging action for calm. But Kallum continued, a lifetime's fear receiving a small outreach without the means to stop the flow.

"Dannehs and I were kept away from the other kids and only knew her at home and in the Credo where he rarely ventured near her. It was only when he snapped her wrist that we knew. He tried..." A sob, breaking the flow. "He tried to tell me that she needed to die to prove Malptia broken once and for all, and that if..." Another gasping breath in. "If she didn't die by his hand eventually that it would be Dannehs or mum who would suffer because he needed me as heir and he needed Malptia to *lose*. And then he told me that the only way to make a king is force. That love and anything like it doesn't come into it and I, Zephyros I *can't*. I don't want to hurt my aunt or my brother. And he gave me this." He produced a small knife from his belt, the one he used to peel oranges on their journey north. "And he told me that if you came back then he'd kill my brother."

Zeph watched, helplessly, as the child in front of him offloaded many years' worth of pent up thoughts.

"And Nicke will never forgive me for the loss of her husband and child. Never. And I miss her so much and she's one of the only people who has ever cared about us but I didn't do enough to help her when she needed it."

"Hang on, stop right there," Zeph interrupted. Kallum had lost his kopis to the dirt during his speech and held his face in his hands. His dark hair made a mop over the top of his fingers. "Nicke would never blame you for it, ever."

"Then Lysander does. His shade haunts me."

"My brother knew the value of control and how difficult such a thing was to break. If he didn't, then he wouldn't have loved Nicke so well. Something else haunts you, and it isn't him."

Zephyros had been this, before he'd escaped to the navy. The slow, viscous drowning of parenting that went beyond strict, beyond control, to lay you down so as to walk on your very heart. Kallum's wracking sobs had come from his own mouth. Zeph had escaped the threats, for the most part, just as Kallum had escaped the physical scars.

Things manifest in different ways.

Zeph sat down next to Kallum and drew him into a hug. He clung onto Zeph's chiton like a drowning child, begging for a rock onto which he could alight from the fear. Zeph let him, gently rocking him, affirmations in his ears, until he quieted. Then, Zeph put his hand out for the knife that had been marked for his death, and Kallum gave it to him. Easily, and without fuss, Zeph drew the knife against his clavicle laterally, a small well of blood amounting. He then wiped the flat of the knife along it and whipped it through the air, drying it. He passed it back to Kallum.

"Proof that you tried." Kallum laughed in the uncontrolled way teenagers do, and Zeph fought a smile. "And you'll be relieved to hear that I'm quite hard to kill anyway. People have been trying for years."

"I honestly don't know why he thought I would be successful. You sleep fully armoured."

"Yes. Once we are finished with the Oracle, I'm going to find a fort of a room, with a lock, and sleep soundly just in my skivvies."

"You knew, didn't you?" Kallum asked, defeated.

"Yes, I knew. Cali, too, has orders for my death."

Kallum's eyes went dark, a jolt of surprise passing through him. "An ephor? But they're meant to be impartial."

"No one is ever truly impartial, Kal."

"Only my aunt and my mother call me Kal," Kallum said slowly.

"May I?" Zeph asked.

"I suppose. Length-ways, through Nicke, I suppose we're kin."

Yes. They were.

Zeph stood and offered his hand to Kallum. When the boy rose, Zeph brushed some dirt off his shoulder and they began to walk back to the small camp. Today, they would board the vessel that would take them to the Oracle.

"Have you met the Oracle?" Zeph asked.

To his surprise, Kallum nodded. "Heirs are presented at birth.

My parents made the trip then, and I went when Dannehs was presented, too."

"Spares too?"

Kallum dipped his chin. "Now that I'm older, I wonder about it. But then, it was just a big adventure. I think my father was keen to claim him."

Zeph didn't pry, but it felt strange to go from a mere slave in Kallum's eyes to someone akin to a confidant. He was telling Zeph family business, which could get him into strife were he to venture this information anywhere else.

"Do you know much of the folktales of Boornea?" Zephyros asked. When Kallum shook his head, he started the tale of the Oracle's founding. Before recorded history, of which Boornea's was longer than Laerta's, there was always a mist that appeared when the moon was dark and the dogs quiet. One day, it gathered around the outer islands, obscuring them from the shore. Then, a bright light split the sky in two, so bright that the blind are said to have seen it and so sudden that it caused shrieks of fright to ring out across Boornea. The men of the mountains, the tribes of the swamp, and the citizens of the city all beheld the sight. Then, as suddenly as it came, it stopped. Three brave women ventured out in a boat to those islands, and when they drew close, they heard the whimpering of a small child. The islands were known to be uninhabited, with fishers only staying in rough weather, but here was this girl. Her bright blond hair matched the light they'd seen, and her crying evoked the way the hounds had screamed. One woman tried to draw her into the boat, but she refused to go. Another tried to light a fire to warm her, but she doused it in water.

Then she told each woman the day and manner of their deaths, and the women fled. Though they had been brave, they were not foolish. On their return to the mainland, four men decided that they were both brave and foolish, and ventured to the island to declare the girl the Oracle. And so it has been. Four men are given the task of managing the myths surrounding her, and the girl gives her riddles to those willing to part with enough coin.

The same girl that descended from the sky, apparently. Not at all likely that they simply replaced her every few years, dyed her hair, and that a graveyard as big as a field sat just behind the temple that held her. No, couldn't possibly be.

Kal was quiet after Zeph had finished the story. The telling had taken them into the main part of the city, and they sat together and waited for the ephors to be finished with the archon of Boornea.

Eventually, Kallum whispered: "Do you really think they kill those girls when they get too old?"

"Why don't you ask her when you see her?"

"Because I have to ask whether my father is the rightful king."

Zeph had his own question, but didn't know if he'd have a chance to ask it. "Yes, I'm sure. Otherwise she would be hundreds of years old."

"But why?"

Zeph shrugged. "Men in power do what they like. That's why Laerta has ephors, in an attempt to balance the power. If they worked as they should, then Nicke and Lysander should have been able to petition them before it turned truly dangerous, don't you think?"

Kal nodded. "They could have married and she would have moved to his household."

"That's right. But instead, they weren't able to. Your father stopped them."

Kallum looked at him sidelong. "I don't know if he meant what happened or if it just got out of control."

"Something else to ask the Oracle."

Zeph left him where he was and walked to the outer wall of the port. It was quiet, a storm brewing on the horizon that had little to do with the weather. From here, the salt air in his lungs and the wind whipping his newly Laertan hair, he could almost imagine himself in his city of Kurkia. The island was only a little beyond the outer islands of Boornea, to the west. He'd be able to see the peaks from the Oracle's island, mist permitting. Easily, he'd be able to pay passage back.

After the years of the war away from the village where he'd grown up, and the time in Kypt and then Laerta, he'd not been back in almost ten years. The thought of the birds chirping him awake, or the rustle of the amber trees that were unique to that part of the world, made his heart swell in anticipation.

But he'd not come to Boornea to run away, and an old part of him screamed at it. Yelled, hollered, for him to leave the yoke of Laerta and all that was expected of him there. But he was no longer a slave, not really. And he had a different job to do in this place so like his homeland.

He missed them. Earth, he missed them. He could only hope that they were still well, alive at the least, and that he'd done enough to keep them safe while he was gone. Every night he looked to the stars for guidance, for a sign that they were okay. But the only messages that came to him in the dark was a refrain repeated.

Look to Malptia. She will guide you.

Nicke. Of course it was Nicke. But her health was only one part of the whole. If any of them were to fall, it might destroy him.

That might be the point.

His knack had quieted as they'd moved further from Laerta, and his reliance on it had become obvious. He could no longer trust his own intuition to provide clues as to liars or danger and it gave him disquiet. If it was tied to the land, then that would make sense. But he'd had instincts in Kypt, and on the navy ship before that. Not as loud, certainly, but it had existed. Now, it was just, quiet.

So quiet.

"We're ready, Zephyros," Rick said as he walked towards him. "Are you?"

"You know, don't you?" Zeph asked him. He was tired of lying about it.

Rick looked at him pensively. Zeph was no longer a puzzle, no longer a riddle to be worked out. "I was a general for your father. Yes, I know who you are. You look just like him."

"There seem to be many people who have lots of knowledge without much ability to use it," Zeph said drily.

"I have some more, if you want it."

Zeph desperately, desperately did. But he hesitated until his yearning had subsided and he could make some decisions with clarity. Rick took pity on him.

"It isn't anything bad. It's just some things you should know, that might fill some gaps." He gestured to a small alcove, but Zeph stayed out in the sun. They sat on one of the benches, away from Kallum as he sat in thought and the other yet-to-appear ephors.

"Firstly, your name is Galyn, but I suppose you already knew that. Your sister is Khloe, your mother is Chrysanthe, and your father is also Galyn."

"Did they suffer when they died?" he asked, already knowing the rest. It was foremost in his mind.

Rick's hesitation said enough on the matter. "I don't know about Galyn, but Chrysanthe... They wanted you dead, not her, and when you disappeared I think they took it out on her." He ran a hand through his hair and Zeph's own fists balled in what could only be anger. "That brings me to another thing: Brynne, if it is the Brynne I think it is, was not your uncle. He's your cousin. He disappeared from the children's camps, where he was finishing the Tertiary training, when he was seventeen and wasn't heard from again. He's Lyon's younger brother. And it appears that he took on your heir's training himself."

"He was a brutal bastard," Zeph said dispassionately.

"That doesn't surprise me. Kallum Rex was brutal, too. His wife died having Brynne and it destroyed him."

"Why are you telling me this?" Zeph asked.

"Because I owe your father more than my life, and righting this wrong is key to it."

"Obligation speaks louder than purpose."

Rick sighed. "Right you are, Zephyros. I hope the Oracle can light our way in more than one matter."

* * *

They were welcomed into the stifling heat of the temple, a king's ransom in gold passing from their hands into the priests', to sit in a semi circle around what could only be described as a stage. Zeph sat opposite Kallum with Rick on his side, Maria at the head, and Cali on her other side. The room was quiet, dark, and hummed with anticipation of the Oracle.

Slowly, it dawned on Zeph that his life could end here, today. Cali or Maria could take their surprise out on him in a fit of anger. Or the Oracle could call to him as a barrier to the current king's chances, causing his own head to roll.

He had little time to dwell on it before a young girl was led to the space before them. She was prepubescent, not more than eleven years old, with white blond hair and shining blue eyes. Her skin was waxy, translucent, and the flesh of her delicate hands folded together almost in supplication. Standing, she may have only come up to his elbow. The priests who had so willingly taken their coin dragged her into the centre of the room for the performance that they'd paid for. Zeph had to remind himself that this was sacred; this was the key to it all. How he kept his sisters and Nicke safe.

But the cost suddenly seemed too great if it caused a single discomfort to the child in front of him.

"Speak your question," a priest said, addressing Cali. She'd likely been given the task of outlining recent events and relaying them, so the answers provided to the ephors could solve their little problem.

Cali didn't stand, but the Oracle moved towards her in what

seemed like curiosity.

"We come to ask whether our king should be deposed or kept. He beat his common-law sister, causing her to lose her child, but she had only conceived the child against his will as the head of his household. We request guidance."

It was easily said, and curtailed the anger Laerta held for their current king.

"You've already lost," the Oracle sang. Her voice was like a bird in a winter storm. "The king will be a king no longer once this trip is done. He will shift, and change, and become something different. You've already lost."

"So we depose him?" Rick asked, almost eager.

The Oracle shook her head. "There will be no need. You've already lost."

"What have we lost?" Maria said, the final question afforded to the ephors as a bloc.

The Oracle continued to shake her head, frenzied. "Everything. Your city will lose its way, the ties holding it to the earth departing west. Anchorless, and without heed to law or good, he will ravage the countryside. Blood, red as the eclipsed moon, will fall and feed the decay of the soil. No. You have lost everything by coming here."

Her eyes turned and he felt her gaze.

"It wasn't your fault, Galyn."

He didn't want to ask a question in case it was the wrong one.

"What did you say?" Maria whispered.

"Zephyros," Rick said, staring as if into the sun. "Ask her who your father is."

The Oracle tilted her head. "Why would he ask what he already knows? He knows who his father is; who his mother is. Whose voice calls to him when the yellow flowers rustle in the breeze. So why would he ask?"

"To prove it beyond doubt," Rick called. "We can still salvage this situation, Zephyros."

"Salvage it how?" Cali thundered. "What aren't you telling us?"

Rick's eyes shone. Tears, maybe. Perhaps hope.

The Oracle approached Zeph, her soul older than her body's years. He could see the depths of the underworld; see the reflection of his own fear.

"It will be hard, Galyn, but that is why it is important. Difficulty means things are worth doing."

"Galyn, Laerta Rex," Rick said resoundingly, like the Oracle's words were only a formality.

A small sigh escaped Kallum. Maria simply stared. Cali jumped to her feet and began gesticulating, but Zeph didn't hear a word.

"Ask your question," the Oracle prompted gently. "And I will try and speak plain."

"Would..." he started, glancing briefly toward the ephors' argument. Kal just kept his eyes wide, wondering how they had gotten here. "Would they have been proud of me?" Zeph whispered.

The Oracle smiled. "They watch you from their sacred peak, sometimes arguing, sometimes wishing that they were here to guide you. When you feel your kingship gift growing and the impulse under your skin to take action, that is your mother's knife held to your purpose. And when you feel the western wind on your neck, and the instincts you hold and hone for understanding people and protecting them, that is your father's way. One is aggressive, one protective. But both are proud of the man you are, and the things you will do."

"But you said it will end in blood."

"Not your blood. Laerta's blood will remain unspilt. But it will be difficult. Choices made, people left behind. But she will guide you."

"Am I to be king?"

"Ahh," she admonished. "You've already asked your question. And I am proud of you for your choice. It was a good one. But, a further warning. Leave this room now, take your cousin with you, for to delay your return will end in her blood spilt."

"Whose?"

"You've already had a question."

"Then answer his in my stead," Kallum said, suddenly right next to them. "Answer the question."

The Oracle looked up at him, and nodded sagely.

"The one you call aunt will die if you do not return now. I fear this asking has already taken too long."

Zeph looked at Kallum and an understanding passed between them.

Zephyros wouldn't survive losing Nicke, and then Laerta wouldn't survive him.

They left the chamber, yelling behind them, to speed south on the word of a ten-year-old girl.

CHAPTER NINETEEN

Nicke

The air was pregnant; tension wove through the camp. Everyone was on tenterhooks, waiting and wondering when the next sword would fall and how it was that they had come to be here.

Nicke had always known that a king's blade would be her end. She'd thought, perhaps, the lack of dreaming of it since Lysida had died was a sign that it was no longer to be her fate.

The last two weeks told of that folly. He would kill her in the end, just as he had a hundred loyal hoplites in his search for her and Demetria. Dead. So easily dead.

They had been hiding in the caves since the second incursion, but it had gone wrong. It had all gone wrong.

"Commander?"

Like that would save her.

"Yes?" she called back.

"There's word from the northern scouts. He's back."

Swallowing was difficult, but she forced her throat to work in worry, in hope, in the way that told of labour yet to be attempted.

It had all gone wrong. Zephyros returning while she still breathed was a miracle that couldn't be understated; prophet be damned.

"Thank you, Jane. Can you bring him here when he arrives?"

"Yes, general. The heir is reportedly with him, but no one else."

She silently thanked the earth.

The caves were only three hundred or so paces into the forest surrounding the children's camp. Nicke had chosen the location to keep an eye on the numbers of slave children being killed, and to save the remaining ones from an anonymous death on the mountain. The caves were an added bonus.

She didn't think Zeph had organised the Laertans of Auntu. She didn't think that his acts incited them to the point of Lyon having to put them down. No. Instead, the king simply killed the sponsored slaves; the ones who had worked with Zephyros and knew Lysander and Kallias and who were sick of the way Laerta treated their people. The pieces would have held together if Zeph had have been here to wield them, or if Rick or Maria had been able to defend the ephors they'd left behind.

Lyon was no longer a king in the Laertan sense of the word. He'd become something else. An emperor; a tsar: absolute power without the mediating courts. Anyone that had shown even leniency to Zephyros or to her was dead.

Sophie was still alive, only by virtue of being Matthew's loyal family. Even if she wasn't safe, she would give birth any day now.

He'd been gone less than two weeks, and everything had fallen apart.

Then suddenly he was in front of her, the tallest man she'd yet seen. He made a sight. His beard, a whole fortnight's growth, was sprinkled with bright red flecks to be the same auburn of his hair. He was armoured in leather, with a dark blue chiton over the top and a maroon cloak on his back. The dust from the road almost obscured him, everything but his eyes. They were bright sparks on a dark night. He was all she'd wanted to see for several dark days and the sob that escaped her couldn't touch the relief she felt.

"Rose..." he said, hesitant and suspicious. But she couldn't fathom telling him of all that had happened while he was away. So, instead, she walked to him and leant against his chest and cried. His calloused hands drew around her trembling shoulders and she almost collapsed in sheer gratitude. That she didn't have to bear the losses by herself anymore. That she could lean on him for ideas or direction when she couldn't solve things by herself.

"I'm sorry, Zeph," she whispered.

"Why?" he said, gravel in his voice. "What's happened?"

"Lots of things."

"Then we should speak." He pushed her away and looked at her with a gentleness that hid his certain fury. "But first I need you to tell your nephew that you forgive him."

"Kallum?"

Zeph nodded. "He's under the, hopefully mistaken, impression that you hold him responsible for Lysander's and Lysida's deaths." Nicke started, her mouth open, but Zeph raised a hand to pause her. "Nicke, I spent a mere two weeks with him, showed him love that held no obligation, no test or scrutiny, and he opened up like a dam under flood. He's terrified of losing you. I think before anything else, you need to speak to him."

She took a breath. "Of course I don't blame him. How could I?"

He nodded. "I know, but you know how children can be. Someone says something to them, and they hold onto it."

"You think the idea was planted?"

"Oh, I know it was planted." He turned to the mouth of the cave, and called: "Kallum?"

The boy looked withdrawn and many years older than when he'd left. Like the world had descended, and, at the same time, had left him weightless.

She drew him close and felt his tears wet along her shoulder.

"I'm sorry," he cried.

"There's nothing to be sorry for, Kal. Nothing at all."

"But I didn't act."

She kissed the top of his head before murmuring to him. "I want to make a few things clear, Kal. You will never be responsible for the acts of your father. They are his alone, not yours." She pushed him away and searched his eyes for his agreement. He nodded imperceptibly. "I would never expect you to endanger yourself for almost any reason, you're too precious to me for that. And lastly, there will be nothing, nothing at all, that would stand between you and me. *Nothing*. Do you understand?"

"Yes," he whispered.

Her eyes sought Zeph as she held the teenager, and what she saw in his gaze frightened her more than much else. She let Kallum go.

"Kal," Zeph said. "I need you to take my horse and go straight home. Make sure your brother and mother are there, too, and stay inside. Lock the door to your mother's rooms, if you can."

"Why?" Kallum asked.

"Because that is where you will be safest."

"You're going to challenge him, aren't you?"

A glance towards her was all the warning she got.

"Yes, I am."

Her chest bottomed out. He wasn't ready.

The last two weeks had unreadied him further. They would be lucky to escape this with their lives.

"Go now," Zeph said.

Kallum hesitated only a moment before leaving the cave. She heard the gelding galloping away and took three deep breaths before she was able to speak.

"Zeph, you can not do this."

The burning in his eyes already said how little use this would be; that he had decided, was decided.

"You know too, don't you?" he whispered. The cave seemed to distend then contract as she stared at him. The entrance left him mostly in darkness except for the rippled reflection of the sun on water. It gave him an unearthly quality. Like she was speaking to a god, and not a man who sought to become king.

"Yes." The word was simple, but untethered.

She had always been political. One had to be in order to survive this life. Her politics had never been turned from his favour before. She had positioned his training thus, and they would reap his death as the reward.

He kept very still and she was reminded of an animal curling around an injury.

She took a breath. "A prophet in Chinto told me and Demetria."

He didn't acknowledge that she had spoken for a time.

If she was honest, she knew before then. He had always had an air of royalty. His eyes matched the frieze. He'd been taught Laertan techniques since childhood and beyond that, the people here accepted him almost instinctively. Like it was their right.

"I found letters," he said. "That's where I was when you were attacked. I was at the Credo's library and I found letters between the king and queen. Chrysanthe. Demetria remembered her name, and I knew my father's. But Galyn is a name common enough."

Nicke nodded. "Yes, when Demetria spoke your mother's name, that confirmed it."

"Rick, he told me of it. Of my uncle's actual relationship with me. He was Lyon's brother. I don't know what led him to take me across the sea, but it makes sense in hindsight. Rick knew before the Oracle even spoke. Apparently family resemblance is a curse. I wonder if that's why I was warned away from Lyon."

"Who warned you away?"

"Sophos. And when Lyon finally laid eyes on me, it was when I was breaking his wrist. He told me I looked like my father."

"Lyon would have been close to twenty when your father was killed. He would have remembered him."

"He's my cousin, turns out." Zeph huffed a laugh, shaking his head. "I suppose I have to grow used to killing kin. It is a family trait, after all."

Nicke couldn't help it. She stepped towards him and put a

hand on his arm. This small moment, before they had to flee lest they be killed, was all he would allow himself.

"You didn't keep it from me, did you?" he whispered.

She shook her head. "No. I would have told you. But that's why you went to the Oracle; for confirmation."

"I didn't ask the question. I couldn't. What would you ask if you had a portal to the knowledge of the underworld?" He scoffed. "I know what you would ask. I couldn't ask about my parentage. I only wanted to know if they were proud of me. How weak is that?"

She didn't acknowledge his bait. "Are they?"

He shuddered, swallowing a sob. "According to a tortured child, yes."

"I'm sorry, Zeph. None of this is easy."

He turned to her, eyes both red from tears and dark with thought. The air was turning; freezing like the first calls of autumn. She couldn't delay any further. Lives, more than just theirs, were at risk.

"Where is my sister?" he asked, already knowing.

"Lyon..." She took a gulp of air. Since Demetria had disappeared, she'd needed his clear head even though this would do anything but clear it. "Lyon has her. But we don't know where. We've had so many losses, Zephyros. Lyon has lost his mind. He killed the ephors that were left; we had to hide the children; I don't know who is still alive in the city."

He took it all in with a tight mouth. The shadow that plagued him eclipsed his face and he became something other than what he was. The man who always had a joke at hand, and who refused to wallow in pity, was gone. He was replaced by single-minded purpose with the face of Laerta. She was glad that she was already touching him because otherwise she may have recoiled.

"Zeph?" she said when his blank face had become too much. "Zephyros?" He was still looking without seeing.

What would she have done in the same situation? If Alix had

been taken, held missing, a hostage to a man hell bent on destroying her? Nicke didn't need to imagine. Not really. Every time Lyon approached Alix, she was in danger. But part of Nicke accepted that she was helpless in such a scenario. She could neither wield a blade nor inflict enough damage to protect her sister from the man she'd been forced to marry.

Zeph, though, could drive a knife through Lyon as easily as look at him.

"Zephyros," she repeated, stronger this time. She couldn't let him kill himself in search for misplaced identity. They needed to get what was important to them; who was important; and leave. "Zephyros!"

He didn't look at her. He would be useless in a war, if this was how he froze when odds were stacked. She let the hand that lay on his forearm drop down his skin and squeeze his hand. "Zeph, please." He tilted his head then, and regarded her. She recognised him, finally. "We will find her, and then we must leave. Lyon is too powerful."

"The ephors declared me king."

Fear seeded. "Samantha and Jonny are dead. Sophos may be too. Jonn was in Auntu collecting the remaining Laertans. He," she choked on the words, "he..."

"Rose, I must do this for everyone's betterment. It goes beyond your safety, now, but the safety of the slaves and the safety of the populous. He'll simply extend his reach if we do not stop him now."

"Please," she whispered. "Please listen. You can't win this."

"I already have the support. My people are scattered throughout this country."

"Two weeks ago, they were, but everything has changed. Lyon —"

"Lyon will die."

"No!" she yelped. "Please, *please listen*. He isn't only holding your sister as a hostage. He's killed all of them, Zephyros. All of them. The men, the women, some of the children; their mothers when they came. We couldn't protect them against such an onslaught."

He breathed deep. A steadying action. One that anchored him to the ground of his birthplace. "Nicke, what you are doing is giving me *more* reason to kill him."

Her fear suddenly turned like a dial. "Don't be stupid. You can not defeat him now. He holds all the power." He looked down his long nose at her and it infuriated her. "Who is the expert here, Zephyros? You? With your minimal training and small wins? The day is lost. Retreat."

"The day has not yet been decided. I decide whether to retreat or not."

"Says who? You said I was your commander. Then I say, we retreat."

He bent down a little, eye to eye with her. A fury built in her own heart. She knew these techniques from the War Rooms, the Barracks, the Credo when people attempted to know more than her and consistently came up short. That he, a man who knew her talents and had decided to ignore them, was engaging in these theatrics incensed her.

"You may be my commander, rose. But I am king." Hubris rolled off him; soon rewarded.

"You're king when you win. Right now you're simply a man with an overstated heritage."

He laughed, the noise grating. "You think you have the sum of it. And how did you come to this conclusion? Did the various people tell you of the movements I'd made, the plays I'd wrought, the positioning on the field I'd guaranteed. They don't even know the sum. Any of them could be the betrayer that had their sights on you, so no, they don't know everything."

Her breath caught. In everything that had happened, she'd

forgotten about the risk of his brother. Another blow, probably. He misunderstood her reaction to his words.

"Do not tell me that I cannot win. I can, and will, but not before I retrieve my sister from that madman."

He stalked away from her and left her in the darkness of the cave.

Before she could tell him that Lyon had had four hundred Laertans killed as they'd marched from Auntu.

Before she could tell him that one of his brothers was the one responsible for the asp, the cart, the smoke.

Before she could tell him of the loss of Laerta's sacred institutions that would have guaranteed him the crown.

He was king, after all, but not in all the ways that mattered. Coups required people, and all of Zephyros's had been killed while he'd journeyed north.

She knew what she had to do, but first they had to find Demetria. She was the key to his sanity.

* * *

She caught up with him when he was already with Jane and Samuel. Jane's arm was still in a sling and Samuel's eye had turned black since she'd seen him last. They both bowed their heads at her when she approached.

"Commander," Jane said. She didn't wait for her acknowledgement before turning back to Zeph.

"It was a week ago. We took Nicke and Ria to the caves early, after the second attack from the krypteia. Since then, we've kept fighters near them but not obviously."

"When exactly was she taken?" Zeph demanded.

"Day four or so after you left," Jane continued. "We've been looking for her ever since, I promise you."

"Do you know what he could have done to her in that time?"

Zeph all but yelled. His hands balled into fists and then relaxed.

"She's alive, Zephyros," Nicke said. He turned to her, still furious. "He won't kill his only way out of this."

"Is that why the searching has been lax? You think he couldn't do worse than kill her?"

Her own anger flared. To suggest that she didn't know the effect of the wounds he inflicted was offensive. She quickly quashed the unhelpful feeling.

"We don't have the people to access the city," Jane said. "We've had to send spies and most don't return."

Samuel had remained quiet. He was here at great risk, not only to himself, but the narrative his family had kept strong in the past two weeks. Their farmhouse was a fortress, unable to be accessed without the express permission of Samuel's mother. She was royalty herself, and was protected by an army of her own making. She'd refused to let her family out, the story went, so if Samuel was viewed here, the tale would fall apart.

Sophie was in with them, protected.

Zeph spoke quietly in her ear, a close conversation she feared would rankle the loyalty of Samuel and Jane because of the proposed secrecy of it.

"Where would she be, rose? Tell me that you have ideas."

Nicke swallowed. "Yes. She's either at the house, the Credo, or the War Rooms."

He nodded. "I suppose I'm due in the city anyway."

Jane leant in to listen so Nicke whispered her reply. It wasn't that she didn't trust her; it was that she trusted Zeph more, and Zeph was whispering.

"You'll be killed."

Zeph shrugged, his trademark arrogance rolling from him in waves. It relaxed her, inexplicably. The shade that had covered him since he'd arrived had lifted. Perhaps it was being back on Laertan soil; perhaps it was direction. He needed a path to follow to not lose his mind completely, and that road led to the city.

"I'll check the house," she murmured. "I need to make sure Alix is all right, anyway. And the boys."

He leaned in further. His breath was warm on her cheek. "Absolutely not happening."

"You're not king yet."

"Do I have to bind you to keep you here?"

"You could try."

"Jane?" Zeph called, eyes still meeting hers. "Make sure our illustrious general stays put while I go and find my sister."

She smirked at him, her mood lifting to match his. It was manic, but unstoppable. They continued to stare at each other while Samuel and Jane watched on. "Jane, who did you directly report to?"

"David, commander. Before."

"And in lieu of David, who do you then report to?"

Jane hesitated. "I would say he would likely report to you first, general."

"Traitor," Zeph whispered.

"That makes Jane *my* woman, Zephyros. Sorry to disappoint."

She turned from him and walked towards the barn they'd erected for the horses. She entered the building with the tension crackling within her. A mare she'd since taken a liking to lifted her head and she offered her hand while one of the older children saddled her.

"You have to promise me three things," she heard from behind her. She didn't turn, or respond. "One, you will go straight to the house and no where else. Two, even if she isn't there, you will stay there until I fetch you. And third, if she *is* there, you wait for me to join you before you engage with him. Do you understand?"

"You overestimate my ability to do as you say."

"I think it's more an underestimation of you, actually."

She turned then, and saw him framed by the door. "Please," he pleaded. "Please be safe. I can't lose you both."

She nodded, and he cupped his hands to assist her onto the mare.

"I'll get Mouse, too."

He cringed at the name, as he always did, and it convinced her that this persona he'd adopted was simply a film to get done what he needed to do.

"Stay safe. Good decisions, now, rose."

She simply regarded him for a second, drinking in his face, then kicked the horse into a canter out of the barn and into the brightness of the afternoon.

CHAPTER TWENTY

Zephyros

He watched her go, the sun twisting through her hair and making it glow, with her red cloak dominant behind her.

Zephyros wasn't a praying man, but he begged the gods for her safety in that moment. Begged and pleaded like a small child at their father's knee.

He turned and walked with Samuel to the main tent, where the maps were pegged and the chests kept. Jane was already inside, and she bowed when Zeph entered.

"None of that yet," Zeph said, walking towards the table. He hated this tent. Hated how cramped it made him feel.

"Okay, Zeph. Just practising."

He smirked. "Tell me what we're up against."

"I think she may be at the Credo," Jane said. "We've been unable to get in to check, but lots of servants have been going in and out, implying Lyon might be there."

"For eleven days she's been at his mercy," Sam said. "Any reason we should expect her to be alive?"

"The commander's right. He wouldn't kill her."

Zeph's hands went to his face. "I'll go when we're done here." Finding his fingers in his hair, he pulled at the too-long strands, making some fall from the leather tie behind his cowlick. They found their way into his eyes and he dropped his hands. "I have to try."

"We have been watching, but I must admit that Nicke was our priority," Jane said. "I'm sorry, Zephyros. We worried that if we went after Ria he would use our movement as a signal that she wasn't properly guarded and try to find her."

"How long were they in the cave?"

Samuel and Jane shared a glance. Neither of them wanted to provide him with the real danger they'd been in.

"Since the second day," Sam said. "They've been picking at us like rats. They were able to get Nicke onto a horse before we defeated them the second time."

He leashed his anger at the ineffectiveness of his band before it could surface.

"So you moved the two of them to the caves? Whose idea was that?"

"Ria's," Sam said.

"And when was she taken?"

"Two days after we moved them there," he replied. "It happened when Nicke was here. We were trying to make sense of the march's movements from Auntu when one of the Secondary's teenagers told us what had occurred. Every man we left there to defend her ended up dead."

"Gods, why were they able to defeat them? I left you with well trained Laertans, hoplites you'd honed yourselves."

They exchanged a glance again and Zephyros took a breath.

"We've lost a hundred alone, here, since you left," Sam said. "Many were killed in a purge of the city before they even made it here. Apparently the Barracks is full of corpses with no one left to bury them. He took his anger out on Laertans loyal to him. Ryan only just got out. If Matthew hadn't already moved to mum's house, he would have been killed too. Bryan, Lydia, Timon, all dead. Rion survived, but only because he played dead, and he'd been devoutly Lyon's since he was a brat. The king's gone mad."

He took another breath.

You've already lost.

"It's worse than that," Jane continued. "They were marching back for harvest, as you planned. I don't know how much work David or your brothers did while they were there, but the grapevine was full of hope. As the march entered Laerta, Jonn had his hoplites turn their swords on the loyal, killing them in their sleep. They're all dead. David too."

He will shift, and change, and become something different.

Zeph tried to take another breath, but couldn't. It was like air had evaporated.

"What of my brother?"

Sam shook his head. "No one's heard anything from Drakon since you left."

He could be one of the dead. In the Barracks, on the fields between here and the city. At home, where Lyon had spread his malice.

"How many dead?"

"Four hundred," Jane replied. "A good portion of Laerta's army. Direct orders from Lyon."

"They say that kings go mad when the land rejects them and they lose their magic," Zephyros said. "He brutalised Nicke beyond recognition and she healed in a normal amount of time. The earth has abandoned him."

"So he kills his army? That's ridiculous."

"No, he murders mine." His neck cracked when he moved it, so tense was his stance. The wind had picked up outside and he could feel the atmospheric change that spoke of stormy weather on the way. All the better to cover his tracks.

"I think the commander is right, Zeph," Jane said. "I don't know if we can do this. I'll follow you to the grave, but I think this might be folly."

Zeph turned to Sam. "Can you return to your mother's today?"

"No, but even if I could, we have so few on the ground."

Looking between the two people in front of him, in their competence and their ability, he had to hold onto hope that not all was lost.

"Perhaps if I cut the snake at the head, the rest will fall into place."

Jane looked at him sceptically. "Or perhaps he was a hydra all along."

"Rick, Cali and Maria were behind me. Sam, you need to scout for them and keep them out of the city. They'll be murdered on their return." Sam nodded, and, with a quick glance to Jane, he bowed and left the room.

"I need you to disperse everyone else. Get them away from Laerta, into the hills. If I don't succeed in the city, then at least you have a head start on running."

"Zeph—"

He held up a hand. "No. Lyon needs removing, but I won't risk loyal Laertans now that we've lost so much. I need to get my sister out and then I'll go after Lyon."

"You don't understand, Zeph. In Chinto, you're already their king. Here, too, the children know you and love you. It will take more than Lyon's brutality to stop the dream these people have created." Jane paused, her mind working. With a decision made behind her eyes, she said, "And besides, we know you're the true king. You aren't simply a common man sick of the hard rule of a dictator, you're a son returned."

"How do you know that?"

Jane shrugged. "Sophos told me, but others had heard whispers. All it takes is whispers. It's like a tower of cards coming down in a breeze. If Lyon was a better king, it would be more difficult for mere words to lose him loyalty."

"Sophos?"

"Oh, yes. Sophos was a student when your father was king.

Apparently he was a memorable man; imposing, much like you."
Jane laughed, then her mirth turned contemplative. "It's easy to see
you as king, Zeph. But it is you that we're loyal to, not your line.
These people died protecting those that you love, and they will
continue to, even if you fail now. You've started something that
won't stop today."

Zeph was surprised by the speech. It was easier to be an
anonymous slave, borne of poverty and a drive towards a better
country for the people around him. It was harder to admit that his
royal blood had nothing to do with it. He wasn't chosen to avenge
his father and mother's murder. He was simply here, and saw
injustice like the sun.

He nodded, anyway. Acknowledgement was the baseline of
what he owed Jane. "Any tips for the movement of people around
the Credo?"

Jane shook her head. "You know how it is. One way in, one
way out. Built that way on purpose."

Zeph nodded. "Then I better get going."

Jane walked him to the barn. Zeph mounted a horse and rode
away from the camp without a glance back.

He cantered up the path, nodding to friends as he passed,
wondering how far ahead she was. Seeing her whole was like a
balm after weeks of worry. Demetria was a spike. She'd trusted
him to keep her well, and instead he'd volunteered for a journey
that might have killed her. Receiving the sacred acceptance of his
sister had healed him more than time ever could. That his uncle, or
his cousin, as it turned out, was not the sum of his kin was such a
bare-faced relief. And the gaining of his other cousins in the form of
Nicke's nephews, even if one was more his own nephew through
Kallias, made him desperate to preserve this life he'd created in
Laerta. Who would he be without Lysander's home, hearth, and
family? How could he be genuine, authentic, without hesitation, if
what made him so was so cruelly stripped? But, he supposed, he'd
be dead, so wouldn't care anyway.

The crown wasn't worth this, but that wasn't why he was doing it. Even if Nicke didn't own his entire heart, he would need to guarantee her safety. He owed it to his brother, her husband, to guarantee her. The shame of his affection burnt through him when he could no longer keep it to heel. At times like this, when he had so much running through his mind, he could barely keep track of what was permitted and what was forbidden. His telling her what to do was certainly on the forbidden list. The way she'd looked through him as she'd ridden away may have been permitted, but his instinct to reach for her was not.

He couldn't think of it now. It would drive him mad.

The woods were quiet, even if Zeph could feel the eyes he knew were planted there. Scouts, soldiers, the occasional archer he'd trained himself for exactly this situation. More than simply his sister was relying on him, and he needed to be more than he was. He needed all of himself to make this a success. He still had hope, even if everyone else had given up. Laerta would survive Lyon.

He dismounted before the forest opened up. His knack, brought back to life by his feet firmly placed in Laerta, whispered to him. It wasn't the force of strength that had sent him home when Nicke was beaten and Lysida killed, but neither was it ignorable. It only said a single word.

Run.

And he would ignore it, to his own peril, he knew. The sweat gathered on his brow with the exertion of ignoring it. He wouldn't run without his sister. Once she was safe, he'd consider it.

He took off his dark blue chiton and replaced it with a white one after he'd circled the forest to be close to the Credo. Its high walls dwarfed him as he stared at them. Once, he'd run amok here to distract enough guards and krypteia so Lysander could have a quiet moment with Nicke, and he'd feigned ignorance before being dragged to the Temple where Sophie had claimed him as new and stupid.

He would miss her if he died. She was a cool breeze on a harsh day. The only lightness in the room, usually, until she was the only sadness. Her gentle care gave him permission to be sad, and he'd miss it. She had important work to do, and would probably be smart enough to disavow him. He hoped her mother-in-law's influence would be enough to keep her alive and whole.

And that didn't even take into account Drakon.

Another brother likely dead.

Run!

The Credo wasn't crawling with people, but a stench met him as he surveyed the high walls. Far too high to climb, at least five men tall. Zeph was blessed with height, but it would not be enough. He sat in the forest near the entrance with his eyes open and his ears piqued. In the half hour he watched, only two men had left the compound and neither were armed. He felt the warnings of his captains to be sorely overstated, but he didn't fancy having too much blood on his hands today. He waited until the sun had moved a few degrees to the west, into the eyes of of anyone watching from the entrance, and walked from the forest. He got as far as a few paces into the compound before someone called to him.

"Stop there!"

He ignored it and kept walking. He relied on Laerta's reluctance to use any kind of ranged weapon, folly on their part, to at least enter the building. He could fight his way out of most tussles, but his instincts told him that the Credo held less danger than he was expecting.

He took his spear from his back. Two armed men stood before him, one with a kopis raised and the other with his own spear. He didn't know them, which said that they were probably recently of Auntu. Some of his rebel army's blood had probably stained these blades at some point.

"Zephyros, you can't come in."

"Why not? I am returned from the Oracle with news in advance. I thought to find Nicke or Sophos here so I could tell them first."

"And why would you not go to the king?" the one with the spear said.

"Yes, but I am unlikely to be given an audience on my own. Are either of the generals here?"

"Sophos is here. Nicke is missing," the one with the kopis said. Spear grunted at him to quiet.

"And the king?" Zeph asked.

"At—"

"None of your business!"

Not here then. Demetria wouldn't be either.

"My apologies. Can I please speak to Sophos."

"Yes, he is in his office," Spear said.

Spear's eyes were intelligent. He had a plan forming that would cause Zeph to fall foul. Probably a trap. This was the Credo, after all. High walls, cells: with no help should he become stuck here. He would have to be quick to avoid it.

Zeph nodded. He replaced his spear and walked past them. His ears kept track of their mumbles as he walked away, his gait confident and not at all anticipating the scheme. It would probably be easier for him to leave now, the bodies of the two men behind him and the next likely location of the king his purpose, but he genuinely had questions for Sophos.

The general who had been Lysander's mentor. The one who was strong enough to send fighters to their death abroad but not strong enough to prevent the injuries wrought under his very eyes.

Yes, Zeph wanted answers. Whether he had the time was another matter, but Sophos was unlikely to survive the current upheaval.

He met no one else as he walked to the strategy rooms.

Sophos was in his office, where Zeph had first met him. He looked older than when Zeph had last seen him. The death must have been weighing on him.

"Sir," Zeph said. He stood tall in the door, a look of apathy on his face. Sophos started when he spoke and almost jumped from his chair.

"Zephyros, what the hell are you doing here?!"

"I came to check if this was where my sister was being held by my cousin, but that plan changed when the place was deserted. So, instead, I came to see you."

"You can't be here! It's too easy to trap you!"

Run!

"I'm well aware of my limitations, sir. But I doubt many of us will survive the current king, and I have questions."

Sophos stood and reached for the scruff of his neck. Zeph dodged him, eyes sharp in warning.

"We didn't work so hard to keep you alive for you to toss it away!"

"Then tell me quickly and I'll be on my way."

His face turned purple, his blond hair on end.

"You were the one Brynne was sending letters to, weren't you?" Zeph remarked.

Sophos slumped into his chair, defeated. His hands ran over his skin causing scratches. "Theia was my fault. I was the one who convinced her that he wouldn't kill her when he found out."

"Kallum Rex?" Zeph leant against the table, his arms crossed.

Sophos nodded. "He'd always coveted his brother's wife. He'd married young and had lost his own wife when Brynne was born. I was sure it was one of the reasons he wanted Galyn out of the way. So he could marry your mother."

Zeph couldn't breathe. The air had left him and he felt cold to the bone.

"So he murdered your father. When she rejected him, he

turned his sights on you and Khloe. Khloe was successfully shipped off to Boornea, but you were more difficult because Kallum thought the Kyptian way the right one, where only boys should inherit, so he ignored your sister. Kallum was meant to be your regent. We fooled him. Theia left east with a slave boy, and Brynne left west with you. She was going to circle around, but even that plan relied on her being a distraction. I didn't think Kallum would kill her for it. I thought he'd be happy with you out of the way."

"Who gave you the right?" Zeph said quietly.

Sophos looked at him, eyes sad and knowing. "Your father trusted me, and I failed him. You too."

"Demetria is my sister. She'd been a slave for Lyon without knowing why or how."

"Demetria?" the old man asked, confused.

"You didn't know?"

"I knew we'd recalled her. But only because she was of age in Boornea. I didn't know what happened to her when she got here." His hands dismissed the notion of Zeph's sister, almost like he was beyond his capacity to care.

"You didn't check?" Zephyros barked.

"She wasn't my priority. The heir was."

After three temper-leashing breaths, Zeph said, "Well, she's been in Lyon's clutches since I went to the Oracle. Perhaps you should have kept better tabs."

Horror crossed Sophos's face. "Nicke...?"

"Is currently preparing to leave, if her talk was any indication."

Sophos nodded. "You should go to her father. He will protect you. From there you can organise to take back your city."

Zeph shook his head. He was tired, so very tired of the schemes and the politics and the knowledge of mentors and friends that could have changed the course of the day. Instead, they'd kept quiet and saved their own skin from a mad-king's blade. Zephyros didn't want anything to do with a city that was throwing him, and the people he loved, to the wolves.

"Once my sister and Nicke are safe, I'm not coming back."

"You would leave us to him," Sophos replied levelly.

Zeph tilted his head. "Last I checked, I didn't owe this city anything."

"Your mother would be disappointed in that reaction."

RUN!

"Yes, well. If she had known when to run, she might have survived."

"Your parents did the best they could."

"I have letters that disprove that. I didn't know them, and can't speak for their character, but I do know that Chrysanthe warned my father of exactly the kind of threat that felled him. He obviously did nothing, causing the destruction of Laerta you see today." Zeph shook his head. "You don't wait and see when the people you love are in danger. You act to protect them."

"Like how you're throwing yours and Nicke's life away to find your sister when she's probably already dead."

"Don't mistake me, old man. This is not the inevitability of harm, but the hope of life. There is a middle ground you can take if you have the courage." Zeph stood, his height eclipsing and his arms still crossed. "Did you know when you first met me?"

"No. It took until the second day, when I saw your spear work. It has a signature."

"I'm sorry to disappoint you."

He shook his head. "I'm the one who has failed you. If I live through this, then I swear to you that I will open the city gates when you return."

"I won't be returning."

Sophos smiled in the indulgent way parents do. "We'll see."

Zeph accepted the disagreement, but didn't engage. "Where is the king?"

"The War Rooms."

Zeph didn't wait. He'd waited long enough.

CHAPTER TWENTY-ONE

Nicke

Kallum had followed Zeph's instructions. All the doors to the house were locked tight. Windows that had shutters were closed, those that didn't had the curtains drawn. There were no guards here, though. It was quiet.

Nicke walked to the courtyard that sat outside her room and approached the window. The wind was blowing harshly, whipping her hair about her face, and it was the feeling she'd craved when she had been reduced to her small quarters in a king's house. Of course, in the weeks since Lysander's death notice, she'd been in a king's house unwittingly. A different king: a different stroke of the blade.

Perhaps that was why the dream had left her. The threat was no longer hanging while she slept.

Taking a small knife from her belt, she cut a line along the windowsill that she'd used to gauge the weather, and ripped it upwards. The fabric tearing sounded like a cannon in the quiet, but she continued until she knew she could fit through the frame. Slipping into her room, it surprised her by being untouched. There was nothing here that couldn't be replaced other than her mother's rug, but she could hardly haul that away. Hopefully it would be here when, *if*, they came back.

She didn't know where they would go, but knew Zeph would

have an idea. He was full of ideas.

She didn't pray to the earth for his safety. The emergence of his knack, the premonitions that had been growing since he'd arrived, spoke to how the earth was receiving him into its care.

Nicke listened closely at the door for footsteps, or calling, or anything else to indicate that Lyon or Demetria were here. That Kallum could lock up the house, and Mouse was currently tied to the post outside, spoke to how the king was likely absent.

Opening the door, she peeked outside but found it silent. On quiet feet, she walked to Alix's apartments and knocked.

"Kallum? Alix? It's me."

She didn't finish before the door swung open and Alix embraced her. It was such a shock that Nicke almost pushed her away.

"I've been so worried, Nicke!" she yelped. "Where have you been!"

Alix pulled her into the room and locked the door behind her. It was full of dirty dishes and unwashed clothing: the results of two weeks of terrifying actions on behalf of the king.

Dannehs sat in the corner, his eyes down and sad, and Kallum stood near the window looking through the shutters.

"I've been at the children's camps," Nicke said. "Is Demetria here?"

Alix shook her head. "No one is here but us. I've only heard snippets of conversation and what Kallum has told us. Is it true?"

"Is what true?"

"Is Zephyros the king?"

Nicke shook her head. "He was named king by the Oracle, but that relied on Lyon not decimating Laerta's laws. Now he's simply undertaking damage control."

"He said he was going to challenge him," Kal said. "He needs to challenge him."

"He doesn't have the manpower to challenge him. Lyon

murdered most of them in the barracks and as they moved from Auntu's fields. Laerta will not have an army after this. Zeph will be killed as soon as Lyon becomes aware of him. He can't challenge him."

"Rick and Maria are fighters," Kallum pushed. "Surely when they return they can declare him king?"

"Kallum, do you know the upheaval that comes with a split country? Even if Rick and Maria, and Cali for that matter, decide Zeph is king, he needs people to implement his rule. It doesn't switch on the turn of a dime. That's not how this works. And besides, Zeph won't risk his sister."

"Ria?" Kallum gasped.

Nicke nodded, surprised that he knew. "Lyon has her somewhere and will kill her if Zeph even whispers his intentions."

"But Zephyros warned Lyon of the coup. Told him to make ready," Alix said.

Nicke's eyes sharpened. "What?!"

She glanced at her sons. "He told him that he had a month to get his affairs in order before Zephyros came for him. That was six weeks ago. That's why Lyon has gone mad."

Hubris. It was hubris for all that he was and all he would be. His arrogance had often infuriated her, and no more so than now. To tell a king like Lyon his plans of aggression before they were guaranteed and in motion was idiotic. And it might have cost his sister her life.

"He has to challenge him," Kallum repeated. "He has to become king."

"Why?" Alix said. "Why are you so adamant about it?"

Kallum's face became hooded and Nicke knew the answer. It spoke in his lessons, his techniques, his stubborn refusal to be even adequate in an heir's training.

"Because if Zeph is king, then that means I don't have to be."

"Of course you'll be king, don't be stupid," Alix said. "It's what you were bred for."

"I don't want it," Kal whispered.

"Sometimes we are forced into the things we don't want." Alix turned to Nicke as if seeking help, and she was suddenly aware of the change this had wrought over her sister. It may have been a small shift, but it was a shift all the same.

"How did Lyon know Demetria was Zephyros's sister?" Nicke asked quietly.

Alix's eyebrows furrowed in challenge. "I have to protect my sons."

"Did he threaten them?"

Her eyes flicked to Dannehs, then back again. Despite the position it put Zephyros in, Nicke appreciated her sister's choice. If she hadn't have swapped the information, to essentially sacrifice a grown woman for a child of eight, Nicke would have been disappointed. Nicke walked towards Dannehs and knelt in front of him. He was absentmindedly playing with a boar on wheels and Nicke brought him gently into her arms. He sobbed and squeezed her like his life depended on it, and she couldn't let go. Kallum came next, his long, gangly arms surrounding them both as they rocked on the floor.

"Do you know where Lyon is?" Nicke asked over the tops of their heads.

"Yes," Alix replied.

"Tell me."

"No. You'll simply tell *him*."

"If you think Zephyros is not already on his way to Lyon as we speak, you underestimate him."

"I've underestimated him in the past. Why stop now?" Alix curled her legs underneath her, hiding her ankles under her skirt. She suddenly looked old; tired. "You have to go, though," she said. "You can't stay in Laerta. You'll die."

"Was it true?" Nicke asked, face turning in the continued

embrace. "Do we have another sister?"

Alix nodded. "If I've done everything else, I've not lied to you. Not about that. You're the younger twin. The world knew mother was pregnant, so they had to produce a child, but only one. The lack of whispers since then shows the secret is kept."

Galloping met her ears and she released Dannehs. She had already decided, in a way, to take her husband's nephew with her. He would be safer as anything other than Laertan until Lyon's control either wrought Laerta undone, or was washed away by a weary populous. Kallum was already up and away, checking through the shutters for danger.

"It's Zeph," he whispered. "What's he doing here?"

"He came for her of course," Alix said, dropping her face into her hands. "He'll always come for her."

"Alix," Nicke said. "Let me take Dannehs with us."

"No."

"Zeph is his uncle, and I—"

"The answer is no."

"NICKE!" came a call from outside.

"Please. We can keep him safe. If you've already bargained for his safety with Lyon, chances are it's going to happen again."

"I don't want to go," Dannehs whispered.

"NICKE!" the shout came again. She wanted to hush him.

"You should let him go," Kallum said to his mother, beyond his years. "I need to stay because he won't hurt me. But he already said that if Zeph came back alive from the Oracle he would kill Dannehs in revenge."

Nicke's breath caught. It was new information.

"Nicke!" Zeph's voice suddenly sounded desperate, and she left the apartment door open as she hurried to him. Run was too strong a word, her own instincts to be as quiet in this house as possible eclipsing her need to calm his voice.

She climbed out of her window and was able to see him

through the vined trellis, soft and bright with new growth.

"Nicke!" he called again. He was still mounted, the horse fretting beneath him.

She ran to him then, and he turned his sword towards her before dropping it completely on the ground. She picked it up as he dismounted, the honed blade pressed between them as he crushed her to his chest.

"I'm okay," she said.

"He's at the War Rooms."

"Then why are you here?"

"Because I needed a clear head before I went there."

She gently pushed him off.

"I went to Sophos. He knew the whole time. He'd been corresponding with my uncle my whole childhood."

"Sophos?"

"Yes. He's at the Credo. I... Nicke, I don't think we can do this. Sam and Jane told me of the losses. They're too great."

She took a breath, exhaled, and took another before she answered. "Then you run."

"No, *we* run. I'm not leaving here without you. Sophos believes your father will take us in."

Nicke thought quickly. Yes, with Laerta's army decimated by Lyon's rage, Malptia would be in a better position to accept them. That would mean war for Malptia, though. And her father would accept Dannehs without question, too.

"Yes, he will," she confirmed.

A horn sounded in the distance, a call to arms that made her blood chill. It came from the direction of the Credo.

"Stay here while I go and see what that is." He tried to move away but she refused to let him go. Touch seemed essential for some reason. Something so long denied refused to be released. "I have to check."

"What do you want me to do?"

"Stay here until I get back."

"No, I can be useful. I'm a strategist, Zeph. That's my job."

"But you don't know weapons and you'll be at risk."

"I have to do something!"

"No. It's probably a trap, anyway, and I'd like you as far from there as possible."

"So you sit me out."

He huffed, frustrated. "I'm not *sitting you out*. I'm keeping you alive."

She swallowed, a lifetime of doing so. He saw the action and his face softened.

"Rose, I—"

"No, you're right. I won't get involved."

He visibly relaxed and she let him go. He mounted his horse and turned it without a look, galloping out of the yard, disappearing into a cloud of dust, perhaps for the last time.

The horn was used by krypteia as a rally, but Zeph knew that. It was what they were rallying towards, what they had deemed threat enough to gather the Rex's forces currently dotted throughout the city, that iced her blood. Zeph may think himself strong enough, smart enough, quick enough, but even he could fail surrounded by a hundred krypteia bent to his downfall.

Nicke was unwilling to leave herself out of this fight. He was only here because of her; because her husband had made Zeph take an oath on his death, and she wouldn't abandon him to sit pretty at her sister's house.

"Aunt?" Kallum said from behind her. "Even if he doesn't make it back, you need to go with Dannehs."

The many facets of her goals circled around her mind, strangling her thoughts. She needed to find Demetria, who was at the War Rooms. She needed to save Dannehs, who was a child slated for death. She needed to keep herself safe, if only to keep Zephyros sane.

But this all culminated into a single-minded folly.

She would go to the War Rooms and find Demetria, taking the chance that the krypteia only called to arms by a direct order by Lyon and he would then not be by her side.

"Can you please get Dannehs ready to travel?" Nicke asked as she pulled Mouse's reins from the post that held him.

"Zeph said—"

"Zephyros says lots of things." She mounted the horse, the saddle already adjusted for her. "But he's not king. When you can, please meet us in the forest to the west, south of the oak tree you broke your arm in as a boy. Be ready."

She turned Mouse, red cloak on her back and hood over her hair, to the path behind the house that held the War Rooms.

* * *

The cloak allowed her to pass unaccosted through the trees. She heard rustling above her, but whether it was beast or man was difficult to discern. The krypteia should have been called away, but the snakes ignored the horns for the most part.

The War Rooms unfolded in front of her, the compound as it had been when Lyon had last chased her from it. She'd not been back since, unable to stomach sacrificing herself for a country that had ignored her highest pleas. The place had been a refuge before that moment; a haven where she could speak clearly. Another part of herself destroyed on the whims of a king.

Quietly, she moved towards the central room and heard the distinct scraping of a knife on stone. Slow, steady, the sharpening of the blade matched her steps as she wished herself stronger and more eager to do what had to be done. She had a small knife, not enough, but perhaps it could be the difference in delaying him as the events in the city played themselves out. She wanted to give Zeph enough time to spring the krypteia's trap, survive, and make it here.

Only after the scraping stopped, her foot catching a stone and sending it flying into the gravel pathway with enough noise to alert Lyon to her presence, did she reflect on Zephyros's words as they'd left the children's camp.

I can't lose you both.

She didn't think he would, but the danger spiked in her blood. There was a faint line between bravery and foolishness.

Nicke walked to the open doorway of the room, surveying its semi-darkness and the tables and chairs in their usual places. A scrape drew her attention to the back of the room. Lyon sat on the floor, propped against the wall with his red cloak laying over him in ordered folds. Demetria lay in a puddle of blood next to him, the edges dried into a dark maroon.

"Sister," Lyon crooned, looking only at the knife. "I'm surprised to see you here."

Nicke stood still at the door, gulping down air. Demetria's face was haloed in red as it leeched into her hair. There were wounds crisscrossed over her flesh. A gaping slice ran along her forearm. A penetrating stab marked her upper thigh. A flay passed over her face. She lay still, and Nicke couldn't tell if she was breathing or whether she'd already left this world for one without pain.

"These are my rooms, Lyon. I belong here."

"You belong only where I say so. As it has been since you were barely a girl. I won't accept any less."

"Is that why I've been in Lysander's house, against your will, for weeks now?"

"An unfortunate side note, but easily rectified."

Nicke sighed. "It's over, Lyon. Your reign is at an end. The ephors have proclaimed it."

He laughed, slow and steady, the scraping of the stone faltering only a moment.

"The living ephors will be dead soon enough. I wasn't born to be the cousin to a king, just as you weren't a born queen. We each have our role to play."

"When did you know Zephyros was the missing heir?"

Lyon looked at her then, and she saw tears streaming down his face. In exertion, in pain, or in fear, she didn't know.

"When he took you from me. That animal bound me to take what was mine. Now, I'll return the favour."

Her eyes flicked to Demetria as the stone was pushed to the side and a knife brought to the maid's throat.

"Don't," Nicke said, pleading. It was all she had. Frozen, watching the horror unfold, she was useless. Useless when the odds were stacked.

"The throne is mine, and Kallum's after me. My own generals turned against me, my men forced to kill what should have been loyal soldiers. I am Laerta, and instead I had to spill Laertan blood on Laertan soil for a slave's ambition."

The tensing in his muscles revealed his next move. Nicke launched forward in reply but was held back by the whisper of an arrow through her free hair. It struck Lyon's shoulder and his knife clattered to the ground with a yelp from him. Another twang sounded and it pierced through his dominant hand, locking it to the stone wall behind him. Then he screamed like she'd never heard before: a wounded animal without hope of reprieve. Equal measures furious and disbelieving, he was pinned in place by an expert aim.

"Time to go," Zeph said from behind her. "The krypteia are a minute behind me."

She took a breath before running to Demetria and dragging her away from Lyon's grip. Her injuries were worse up close, with skin missing in many places and the bruises only just turning green from their original purple. He'd been brutalising her since he'd taken her, and Nicke almost couldn't move for the sob that escaped her. Rage was something new. It blinded, caught her by surprise by how little she could see outside this single purpose.

Unable to help it, she grabbed at her small knife and sliced across the king's face, earning a howl from him as blood poured from his eye. It was a shame: she'd been aiming for his neck.

Demetria was moved from her grip and she turned the knife, only to find Zephyros lifting his sister into his arms.

"We have to go."

"Kill him first!" Nicke screamed.

"Nicke, we don't have time. Please."

The naked fear in his voice forced her to move her feet, even against her own will.

Lyon still screamed behind them as they left the War Rooms. The sounds of what could be a hundred men crashing through the jungle towards their injured king rang through her bones.

Mouse reared as he smelt the blood, but Nicke steadied him. "Up," Zeph said, giving her one cupped hand. She did as he said, and grunted as Zeph deposited Demetria on her lap. He ran beside her as they moved through the forest, shouts behind them now just entering the War Room compound.

"What happened?" she called, straining to keep her grip on Demetria.

"Jane and Sam are dead. The krypteia herded the Laertans that were in the forest to one spot and the call was the signal to start killing them."

Something she would have to process later as they came out of the woods near the king's residence. "Did anyone survive?" she asked.

"Yes. The children were further out than could be herded." He shook his head, tone tight. "I don't know."

They remained unaccosted with their hoods up and the populace themselves running scared throughout the polis. Unnoticed; the same as everyone else in trying to escape the bloodshed. Passing beyond the city limits and into familiar woods, the pathways that criss-crossed Lysander's estate were easy for their stead to follow. Mouse took them directly to the farmhouse.

When they made it to the estate, he stopped the horse in the yard and took Demetria from her lap. He laid her down gently under the olive trees.

"I'll tend to her wounds so she'll survive the journey west. You have five minutes to collect anything you want to keep, then we're leaving."

Nicke started in the bedroom where she'd only had one night with Lysander before they'd succumbed to Laerta's brand of loyalty. Everything here was precious. Everything valuable. But she could only take a pocket's worth of items.

The letters were the obvious choice, so she took them, along with the necklace Zeph had given her before he'd left for the Oracle. She swapped out her own red cloak for her husband's grey, leaving the symbol of the Rex behind her as she ventured downstairs. The desk was strewn with clutter and she searched through it to put the box that had Zeph's precious items into her satchel, along with some of her drawings and a small book of Laertan poetry.

"Why the fuck won't you just *die*," said a resigned voice from behind her. She turned to behold Drakon's figure set against the dining table. He was dishevelled, unkempt and bearded like a man who had been living rough for weeks. He was sitting hunched in Lysander's chair. She must have walked right past him to make it up the stairs.

"Apparently I'm hard to kill," she said quietly.

"Yes, but die you must."

"Why, Drakon? Why must I?"

"Because you're their answer. You make sure Laerta stays strong, powerful on the field, and they will be rendered useless by your death."

She shook her head. "Laerta is already useless. I'm leaving and don't intend on coming back." Nicke began to step sideways, slowly, towards the window that looked over the orchard. "Did

Lysander know that you were the one to slip the asp into my bed? Did Kallias?"

"Of course not, but they weren't treated like a slave as I was. This country valued their efforts and erased mine. Zeph is the only reason Laerta stopped killing slave children at the camps."

"That's not true," Nicke said.

Drakon shrugged. "With you out of the way, Laerta would have lost Auntu and be forced to lick their wounds here, where the slaves would have been safe."

"Nicke? We have to go!" Zeph called from outside.

She stepped to the right, closer to the window, and Drakon produced a knife. She moved closer again, and he stood.

"I should have just sliced you when I had the chance, and not worried about whether my brothers would abandon me for it."

"Zephyros will kill you if you hurt me," she said, loudly and sure.

Drakon tipped his chin down. "Zeph is as good as dead, anyway. We all are. But you seem to survive, somehow. Always on the right side of an accident."

She stepped again and Drakon moved around the table in the same way.

For the second time that afternoon, Zeph's weapon appeared before he did. A blade succinctly held to his brother's throat made Nicke's breath seize.

"Really? All this time?" Zeph said, frustrated and tired. "What the fuck, Drakon?"

Drakon didn't blink. He just stared, eyes burning, as Nicke made her way slowly around the table.

"Even when we trusted you to find out who was threatening her, you were calculating her death. Even when Lysander loved her." Once Nicke was behind Zeph, he between her and Drakon, Zeph let go of his brother. "You're the last brother I have left. Please don't make me do it."

Nicke was well aware that they were wasting time. They would have been easily tracked through the woods.

"It's the only way to guarantee Laerta falls," Drakon muttered.

"We're leaving anyway! We probably won't be back. What difference does it make?"

"It made a difference before Auntu. Before Lyon went mad."

"You would have taken one of Lysander's main joys for your own twisted ideas of what Laerta should be. People will always suffer under oppressive systems, Drakon. It isn't one person propping them up just as one pole doesn't hold a roof. Killing your brother's wife wouldn't have given you the result you wanted."

"But then the slaves could rise up, and there would be no generals to protect the system!"

"Nicke was being killed by that system!" Zeph shouted. "She was a cog! Not a gear!" He took two deep breaths, chest causing his shoulders to rise and fall. Drakon's eyes flicked to her, and the promise on his face must have made Zephyros's decision for him. He took his small blade and, without ceremony, pushed it into his brother's neck. Drakon's eyes went wide before he dropped to the ground. Zeph turned to her, eyes glazed, and threw the knife into the wood of the floor, embedding it there. His face was contorted, trying to suppress everything that had occurred in order to address the danger they were still in. His eyes raised after a few seconds and she saw the world reflected.

It wasn't enough to leave. Part of him would not survive this day, and whether it was an essential part was hard to say. She hoped he would come back to her, eventually, but now, he was simply a husk that moved them to safety.

"Time to go," he said gruffly.

A horn in the distance silenced him and he didn't hesitate to take her hand and race out of the house. She mounted as he lifted Demetria, and the still unconscious woman was deposited in front of her. Zeph ran as Mouse trotted, Nicke unsure how he found the strength to continue.

When they came upon the oaks where Nicke had told Kallum to meet them, she slowed much to Zeph's frustration.

"We need to wait," she said harshly. "I'm not leaving without him."

He swallowed his anger and instead channelled it into stalking the trees around them, scouting for danger. Nicke waited, listening. The birds didn't know what had occurred this day because they sung their twilight songs as if blood wouldn't be what fed their worms tonight.

Two horses approaching constricted her nerves. The galloping pace would outrun them, if they were able to move off immediately, and Nicke knew that Kallum would probably be on foot. Zeph had abandoned his bow at the War Rooms, and his loud footfalls met the galloping to a head.

It could all end, here, in this grove. She supposed it could happen in a less beautiful place, or even in the dark, rather than under a vast sky of newly twinkling stars. Life was rarely what she imagined it to be. She could barely remember Malptia, and had no experience in it other than what her sister had preserved. But she would have liked to have died seeing it again.

Shouts erupted, and Nicke readied herself to move off. Something kept her silent, and still, like a rabbit hunted. But when Zeph emerged, his face grim but his eyes bright, she looked behind him to find Dannehs seated on a horse in front of Ryan.

"Kallum?" Nicke asked.

"He's gone back home. We agreed it was safer." Zeph gestured at Ryan for Dannehs, and the child was passed down.

Nicke watched her guard, seeing him truly for the first time. He had been a spy for Lyon, and that may have saved his life these last two weeks. What he was doing here now was treason, the magnitude of which could murder him still. Ryan dismounted and bowed low to Zeph; something new.

"Take the horse, king, you won't make it without it."

"You know of the losses sustained this day?" Zeph said. When Ryan nodded, Zeph put his hand on his shoulder. "Don't risk yourself, Ryan. If you are questioned, provide answers to keep yourself alive. Tell the others the same." Zeph glanced back at her then leaned in further. "I owe you more than my life. Please stay safe."

"Yes, king," Ryan said.

Zeph approached to take Demetria from her lap and Nicke jumped down, launching herself at Ryan. He stumbled back as she squeezed him and couldn't bring himself, from years of controlled training, to engage in the hug.

"Thank you, Ryan."

He just nodded, and she released him.

"Go now," Zeph said from behind her, and Ryan nodded and took off into the trees.

Nicke mounted Mouse again, and Dannehs mounted in front of her. He hadn't said a word throughout the exchange, fear lacing through him.

"Where are we going?" he croaked once Zeph was mounted with Demetria.

"Malptia," Zeph replied. "Your grandfather awaits us."

Nicke took a final look behind her, to the city that she had come to know as home. She wished she hadn't, because the setting sun framed it in a halo of red. Blood on the ground answered in the sky.

Then it disappeared behind a ridge and she dutifully led the way out of Laerta and into the western mountains. Riding towards her birthplace, which would hopefully be their salvation.

A life for a life, a sorrow for a sorrow: matched in dignity and need, they ventured forth until the trees swallowed them whole.

ABOUT THE AUTHOR

Based in Sydney, Australia, Maddy is a school librarian and has qualifications in social sciences and law.

She taught herself to read as a preschooler, and began writing when she was a young girl, starting with a short story of how dragons were thought extinct because they simply only answered to the tenor of children's voices (and who listened to children, anyway?).

Maddy writes primarily low fantasy, but with works across genres. Her debut novel, From the West Comes the Wind, is an exploration of the way hope answers darkness and how we all can strive for light.

Scan to go to mehosking.com

SCAN ME

WHERE TO FIND OUT MORE

Mailing list — mehosking.com/stay-in-the-loop

Website — mehosking.com

Facebook — facebook.com/mehosking

BOOKS BY THE AUTHOR

Earth and Gods Series

From the West Comes the Wind, Book One

Through the Mountains Stirs the Breeze, Book Two (**OUT LATE 2022**)

To the East Roars the Tempest, Book Three (**OUT 2023**)

Companion to the Earth and Gods Series

A Dagger for the Sun King (**OUT 2022**)